Ever the Wayward Sky

Gray Door Ltd.

Contents:

Chapter One:
The War is over; But There's no End in Sight

A light haze lay over the North Carolina ground. Sergeant James Taft stepped out of an officer's tent.

"Yes Sir, I will, first thing this afternoon." He replied while moving from the entrance.

As soon as he was completely outside, he became aware of something unusual. The low sound of cheering began to erupt on the far side of the camp. Sergeant Taft turned towards the strange sounds just as his lieutenant stepped out from the tent behind him.

Both men were around the same height and build; five feet ten inches, more or less. However, Sergeant Taft had short dark hair that wasn't curly and unruly as the lieutenants was. And, James also wore a mustache and goatee, which was popular among the Union cavalrymen.

"What's going on, Sergeant?" The lieutenant moved up beside James, and both watched as a spontaneous celebration appeared to be overtaking the entire camp.

"I don't know, Sir. But it seems to be moving this way." As Sergeant Taft said this, soldiers walked at a rapid pace closer to the two men. They yelled and shouted along the way. One man came swiftly towards them, waving his hat and cheering loudly.

"What's going on soldier?" The lieutenant asked when the man came closer.

"Lee surrendered, Sir. He surrendered to General Grant." Then the man jogged away, shouting and jumping as he went.

The lieutenant looked at Sergeant Taft, who looked back at him. They both seemed to be in disbelief. Then, as more and more soldiers came running through the camp shouting, both men began to smile. They turned and shook hands; congratulating each other for surviving.

James Taft had seldom thought or believed the war would end. After more than four years of fighting, he had a difficult time accepting this reality. As the next few weeks went by, however, the twenty-three-year-old sergeant began to accept that he had indeed survived the war.

Eventually, his unit, the 9th Pennsylvania cavalry began to muster out in Kentucky.

"What are you going to do now, Sergeant?" A young private asked James as they left the headquarters building. Sergeant Taft examined his discharge papers. He seemed to be a bit confused and disoriented.

"I'm not sure, private."

"You're not sure? Ain't you going home, Sergeant?"

"I suppose I will. What are you going to do?"

The private laughed. "Oh, I got so many things I'm going to do! The first thing is, I'm going to marry my sweetheart, Dolly. Oh, she is a beauty! You got a sweetheart, Sergeant?"

James glanced at the young man.

"No, I don't suppose that I do, Private."

The young man laughed again. "You should get you a sweetheart."

The man stayed with James as they turned in gear and finished other various tasks to complete their discharge. He spoke with almost no restraint. James didn't care though as his mind was absent of anything to talk about.

He felt lost as he said goodbye to his horse. He felt naked as he turned in his revolver and rifle. The saber he'd bought with his money, he gladly packed it with his other meager belongings.

James couldn't seem to break away from the numbness that had taken over him. During his trip home to Pennsylvania, he again became lost in thought. He remembered those he knew that had died in battle. He considered the men he had killed in combat. They wouldn't be going home, ever. They still lay on the battlefield in the cold earth. The war was over. Why couldn't he be glad like so many others? Why did he feel that he shouldn't be leaving the army and yet at the same time, feel that he could not endure any more of the savage brutality he had gone through for four and a half years?

His hometown presented a celebratory atmosphere as James stepped off the train. Banners were hung all around, welcoming the victorious soldier's home.

"James, James Taft! Welcome, home James! My, my, I barely recognized you. You were, what, eighteen when you enlisted? You've grown into quite the man, and hero for that matter."

2

"Thank you, Mr. Carleton." James shook the man's outstretched hand as a small band struck up the Battle Cry of Freedom. A few of the town women handed out baked items, and one of them poured a cup of black coffee for him.

He looked over the small train station as he sipped the coffee. It hadn't changed much over the years. Yet everything seemed different now.

An elderly lady approached him.

"Your mama is going to be so happy to see you, James! She came down here several times hoping you would arrive with some of the other boys that were coming home. But you've all been coming home a few at a time now after the main group returned."

James smiled at the woman; she had aged considerably in appearance since he last saw her.

"Yes Mrs. Johnson, the cavalry had some extended duties to perform. It took a bit longer for us to muster out."

"Well, no matter. I know she'll be very happy to see you. We're all so proud of you boys."

Mrs. Johnson then took her small handkerchief and put it close to her eye. "It's just a shame we lost so many good young men to that," she acted as if she wanted to say something else, but then continued, "that, terrible war."

James tried to sound compassionate. "Yes Mrs. Johnson, I agree."

"Well James, you tell your mother and the rest of your family hello for me. And we're just so glad to have you back."

Mrs. Johnson then went to speak with another soldier that had also returned on the train.

James moved out of the station and began walking through the Pennsylvania town that he'd grown up in. Memories rushed back to him as he passed buildings and landmarks. Some of the memories brought emotional feelings of his father, who had died when James was only fourteen.

"James? It surely is, young James Taft!" An older man in an old suit came up quickly to him with an excited expression on his face.

"Hello, Dr. Weston," James said with not nearly as much excitement as he shook the extended doctors' hand.

"James, it is so good to have you back. I'm sorry you didn't get the big parade and all. We had a big to do when our boys from the regiment returned. I wish you could have come home to that."

"It's alright Doc. Mr. Carleton and some of the ladies met us at the station."

"Well, that's good, James. We've tried to have someone at the station as you boys continue to come in."

"I believe we'll be some of the last, Doc," James replied.

The doctor looked down and shook his head a little. "It seems we've lost so many." Then he glanced back up to James. "Do you need a ride out to your place? I can have the horses hooked up to my carriage."

James smiled. "Thank you, Doc, but I would like to walk. I could use a good long stroll."

"Alright James, I understand."

As he moved on out of town and towards his boyhood home, a dark feeling came over him. He gazed over at the "swimming hole" that he and his brother John had swum many times in. Now the laughter he remembered seemed so far away. His heart felt as if it could no longer recover such a joyful time. The death he had seen and dealt with now anchored him to a place neither high nor low. He simply existed.

He continued towards the family home and memories fluttered through his mind. Races with his brother and friends; some of whom now lay buried in the earth of a distant battlefield. Still, James couldn't shake off the darkness to receive the warm thoughts he desired. Maybe, the sight of his home and his mother would stir the embers of joy that he hoped were still in his heart, somewhere.

Slowly the two-story house came into view. As James moved closer, he became frightened. He slowed down and felt a sense of dread. How could a man who had been in more battles than he could recall be terrified of returning home?

James stopped. He stood at a distance from the house. As his heart beat faster, his mind struggled for an answer. Slowly, the problem began to unravel as he searched his very soul. The questions revealed their ugly presence in his thoughts.

Would they see the terrible things? Would his mother sense the blood and death on him? Would his nephew and niece feel the heat of the hell he had passed through, time and time again? Surely, they would know. He started walking again but felt the weight of these concerns with every step he took. Sweat dripped along the side of his head as these thoughts entrenched themselves into his fears.

4

With the reluctance, he had felt before racing into a battle, James forced himself to continue moving forward. The aging house came into view as did his niece who was outside. She had grown much since the last time he had seen her. The years had changed her dramatically from the four-year-old girl he remembered. She had her back to him and was kneeled over, picking wildflowers.

James stood outside the small wooden fence that was in obvious need of repairs. He watched his niece in silence as she hummed and picked the flowers one by one. He felt himself trembling in anticipation of her noticing him. Would she scream in fear? Would she see the things he had been through and cry from sadness?

He wanted to do something to let her know that he was behind her, but he felt too frightened to do anything. Then, as she turned, she noticed him standing outside the fence. She stared at him for several seconds with a slightly startled expression. James smiled a little smile at her.

"Uncle James?" She took several small steps towards him as she asked this.

"Hello, Grace." He said to her, relieved that she couldn't see the wariness inside him.

Grace cautiously walked over to the fence. She then extended her handful of flowers to him. James took the flowers and softly said. "Thank you."

"We've been waiting for you Uncle James." As she said this, James' mother stepped out to the front porch and immediately put her hand to her mouth and began to weep.

"James...!" She moved quickly down the porch towards him. His brother now came out and then his wife, with their son behind her. All of them began to say his name and rush to hug him.

Later, he sat in the main room. Everyone sat around him as if he was about to tell a grand tale. His sister-in-law brought him a drink.

"We've been hoping you would show up any day now James." His brother John said and then continued.

"Ma waited at the train station again and again when the regiment began to arrive, but no one could tell us anything about the 9th. We finally stopped going to the station. No one seemed to know anything about the cavalry."

James took a drink and sat the glass on a table beside him.

"Well, we had some extra duties to take care of. We watched over some of the larger reb units as they surrendered. I didn't know how long it would be or I would have written and let everyone know."

His mother appeared to glow from joy.

"No matter, James, we're just so happy to have you back, son."

"Yeah, James, we'll get this place back into shape in no time with you back!" His brother John added.

James smiled a little. He felt strangely out of place sitting peacefully with his family.

"Yeah, we'll do that John." He picked up his drink, more from being nervous than needing it.

As he took a sip, his mind searched for the reason he felt so uncomfortable. He didn't want to talk about farming. He didn't want to think about getting the place back into shape. He felt depressed even considering these things.

Then, with no warning, his nephew Johnny unexpectedly asked a question.

"Did you kill a bunch of Reb's Uncle James?"

John immediately reprimanded his son as everyone looked around in shock.

"Johnny, don't ask such a thing!"

"Why Pa, I want to know?"

A strange sensation swept over James, and he had to get up. He then replied with obvious discomfort, "That's alright, John... I think I'll get some air for a few minutes."

He left the room as the others tried to explain to young Johnny why he shouldn't ask such questions. James stepped out onto the porch and sat down on the steps, in the dark.

His heart beat rapidly. He realized something terrible now. Only when Johnny asked him that question did he feel alive again. What was wrong with him? He ran his fingers through his hair.

John stepped out on the porch behind him. He sat down beside his younger brother.

"I'm sorry James. He's just... so young."

"No, it's alright. I just needed some air. I'm not used to being inside. We slept under the stars as much as we did anywhere else."

John glanced over at his brother. He took a deep breath of the moist night air.

6

"I wanted to join up, but with Pa gone and two young children."

"No... John. You did the right thing. You're the real soldier for taking care of Ma and this place. I'm sorry that I ran off and left you like I did. I had visions of being some hero, I suppose."

The two men sat quietly for a few minutes and stared out over the dark fields in front of them. Then John said with a softened voice.

"Sounds like your unit had it pretty rough. Up against Forrest and Morgan, seems the 9th took on some of the toughest."

"Yeah, I guess we got our share of it," James replied.

"Well, at least you didn't leave anything out there on the battlefield." John then slapped James on the leg. He stood up and walked back into the house. James then said in a small voice, to himself.

"I'm not so sure of that."

As the days passed, James felt himself sinking further into depression. He tried to work on the family farm but couldn't focus on the tasks. Darkness slowly began to swallow him from the inside out.

"Well, we finally pulled that old stump out of the South field." John attempted to sound encouraging at the dinner table.

"That's wonderful. That old tree always irritated your Pa. I'm glad we took care of it, and it is gone." His mother glanced over at James after saying this.

Her son sat staring blankly at his plate of food. He heard nothing they had said.

His mother turned and looked across the table at John, who then glanced over at his wife, Velma. All three now watched James as he held his fork over his food and appeared to be far away.

The two children took notice of what was occurring and began watching their Uncle also.

Realizing the children were watching, Velma stood up and took a pitcher of water over to James.

"Would you like some more water, James?"

He almost shook as he came out of the apparent trance.

"Oh, no Velma, thank you."

Johnny laughed a little, and this caused Grace to giggle as well.

"You children eat now. No playing."

"Yes, Grandma," both children replied, almost in unison.

James looked around the table with a lost expression on his face.

"I think it'll rain tonight," John said in an attempt to bring supper back on track. "What do you think James?"

"Yes, it might."

He knew something wasn't right. He realized now that he'd been somewhere else. He didn't know what to do about it, though. He glanced around at his family. He loved them dearly, but he didn't belong here. He wasn't sure where he belonged, but he knew now that it wasn't here.

Later, as James lay down to sleep, the rain began. The soft pattering of raindrops outside his window caused a soothing effect, and he drifted into sleep. Then the thunder came, and as James slipped farther into slumber, he found himself on a faraway battlefield again. As the sounds of the storm erupted outside, the cannons roared on the battlefield of James' dream.

"I heard them was Morgan's boys over there, Sergeant."

A young private nervously spoke to Sergeant Taft, who was riding back and forth in front of the men. James reined his horse in to answer the young cavalryman.

"Don't matter who they are, Private! That cavalry unit is protecting the Reb's flank, and we'll run them off the battlefield, or die trying!"

When James said this, the private appeared to calm down. But he was still obviously frightened. All the soldiers appeared concerned. The horses moved underneath them nervously; sensing death to be close at hand. Smoke from the guns drifted through the unit's ranks as James scanned the faces of his men.

He then moved closer to the young private. James thought he might be able to say something to calm the young man, but as he came near, the soldier began to speak.

"I sure got the feeling that I'm going to be one of those that die trying, Sergeant. You ever get that feeling?"

James reined in his mount again, trying to calm it. The horse quivered under him in an apprehensive excitement for the battle at hand. Then, James lied to the young private. He always lied in these situations. "Almost every day, Private."

After James had said this, the man calmed some more. He smiled a little. James smiled slightly as well, and then he thought of several other men that had told him the same sort of thing over the years. They all died on the battlefield after telling him this. The cracking of rifle and cannon fire became intense. He positioned his horse to the front of the unit, ready for battle.

Their lieutenant rode swiftly up from the back of the unit.

"Alright boys, it's time, let's give'em hell."

The lieutenant then pulled his saber out and nodded to their bugler, who immediately sounded the charge. Sergeant Taft spurred his horse just as the lieutenant charged forward.

"Let's go 9th," James yelled out, and his heart began to pound inside his chest.

The ground began to tremble as the horses burst into a gallop.

James looked across the field at the enemy just as bullets began to sing around him.

He became hot as the blood rushed to his head. Then, as always, he slowly became numb as the specter of death approached.

He put the reins in his mouth and lowered his head as if facing a fierce wind. He could now see the enemy's faces clearly.

As the gap closed, he pulled his saber out with his left hand and his revolver out with his right.

The famed "Rebel yell" could be heard from the opposing forces, sending chills down his back.

Now everything began to happen at lightning speed. The two cavalry units collided with the ferocity of a train wreck. As he moved into the Confederates' ranks, he swung his razor-sharp saber and took a Rebels' head almost entirely off from the shoulders. He then turned to his left and fired his pistol into the chest of another, removing the man from his horse in the process.

The sound of bullets flying by him mixed with bodies being struck and cries of pain, all mingled with anger, leather, and metal striking metal.

Another rebel rode up to his right. He was young, and James could see the fear in his eyes. He fired his pistol, but James anticipated it just in time to move. The bullet whizzed by so close that he felt the heat. He maneuvered his saber as the young soldier attempted to cock his pistol again. He lunged the blade forward and felt the steel sink into the mans' body. He watched briefly as the soldier realized James had just ended his life.

He pulled the blade from the man and turned to his left as another soldier was about to fire his rifle at him. James quickly aimed and instinctively fired his cocked pistol. The soldier leaned back as the bullet hit him, firing the gun into the air before falling from his horse.

The enemy was all around him now. He shot another Rebel from his horse. Another one rode toward him as if to avenge his comrade. James shot him also as he tried to swing his saber.

He wanted to get out of the enclosed fighting. He maneuvered his mount to the right, then ran another rebel through the back with his saber. He struggled to pull the blade free as the soldier fell backward onto it.

A bullet cut through the side of his coat making contact with his flesh. He remained on top of his horse. He spotted the enemy that fired the shot. He aimed his revolver and shot as the soldier tried to shoot again. James' shot almost removed the soldier's head.

He pressed his right arm against the wounded side as the pain came. Angered, he spurred his horse forward. He swung his blade and the contact nearly took a passing rebel's arm off.

Another rebel rode toward him at a furious pace, seeming ready to take James down with his saber. James lifted his pistol and shot him from his horse. Then he immediately ran his blade into the side of another rebel that had moved close to him.

James sensed another enemy soldier taking aim; the shot intended for the young private he had spoken with before the start of the battle. James lifted his pistol and pulled the trigger. The clicking of an empty revolver was all he heard. As the young private turned, he would see the bullet from the enemy that would kill him. James yelled out.

"Noooo...!!"

He cocked the pistol again as the rebel fired. The young private jerked back as the bullet slammed into his chest. James again pulled the trigger; again, and again, the clicking of an empty pistol.

"James?"

The Rebel then turned towards him, and everything slowed down. James raised his saber as the hot blood flowed to his head and caused a flash of anger inside him.

"James, are you alright?"

The battlefield began to fade. James slowly saw his room by the light of a lamp that his mother held. He found himself sitting on the edge of his bed. His left arm raised as if he were pointing a

10

pistol, while his right arm elevated halfway and pointed from his body in a manner suggesting a saber was ready to be used.

He blinked several times and looked to his mother, who stood in the doorway with a lamp. She appeared very concerned. Then, John stepped up behind her. As James lowered his arms, Grace and Johnny stepped to the door to see what the commotion was. At last, Velma stepped to the door behind John.

"I guess I was dreaming. I'm sorry if I disturbed anyone."

"Come on children; Uncle James just had a dream." His mother attempted to usher the children away from the doorway. John seemed to want to say something but couldn't find the words. Velma turned and went back towards their bedroom. Finally, John spoke in a nervous tone.

"Well, good night James. I'll uh... I'll see you at breakfast." he then waved slightly and left for his bedroom.

James sat in silence on the edge of the bed. His heart continued to race long after everyone had settled back into their beds. He told himself that he hated the battlefield. The smell of smoke and blood still permeated his nostrils, even though it was only a dream. And yet here he sat, on the edge of the bed, in darkness and silence, reliving the vivid dream over and over in his mind. He wanted to be there again, and this frightened him more than any battle ever did.

As the morning light slowly peeked over the horizon, James' mother stepped out onto the porch where her son sat in a weathered chair. He gazed out to the horizon and only glanced away as his mother sat down across from him.

Several minutes had passed before either spoke. His mother began, softly, but seeming to struggle for her words.

"I wish... well, I just wish your father were here, James. He would be so much better with something like this."

James glanced at her and smiled a little. He then turned back to watch the morning sun creeping up. After a few seconds, he spoke with a slow but resolved tone.

"I never really thought about what I would do after the war, Ma. Because I never believed, I would live through it." He paused and his mother looked down a little as if his words pained her some. He then continued with the same tone.

"I can't stay here. This... staying in one place, it's doing something to me. I'm not for certain what, but it's not good, I know that."

11

His mother continued to gaze down at the porch, appearing to almost cry. After several seconds, she straightened and again spoke softly.

"You shouldn't run from your problems, Son."

He turned to his mother and examined her face. He loved her so much and wanted to make her understand that he had no desire to leave. He tried desperately to find the words. She looked back to her son with a hope that he might be able to stay. But as she gazed into his eyes, James realized what he needed to say.

"I'm not running from them, Ma. I've got to charge them, at full gallop. It's the only thing I know how to do now. I've got to meet them out there... somewhere, and overcome them, or die trying. I don't know what the outcome will be, but I know now what happens if I stay here."

A tear ran down his mother's face as she realized his words were true, and she would once again be losing her son. She put her head down and wiped the tear away. She nodded a little as another tear dropped to her lap.

Later that morning, John approached his brother, who had walked to the creek. James sat on a large rock, the same one the two had used as young boys to jump into the water.

"It's been a long time since you and I went swimming here." John then sat down beside his brother.

James turned and glanced at him. He then looked back to the creek and tossed a small stone in, as if he'd been waiting for a reason to throw it into the water.

"Yeah, feels like a different lifetime. I've been thinking about those days; before..." James acted reluctant to even say the word.

"Before the war..." John said, with the tone of a big brother. He wanted to confront the problem and resolve it.

James sensed this but knew the problem was not as simple as removing a tree stump.

"Yeah, before the war," he replied without looking up.

Again, the silence prevailed and the soft flowing creek, along with a few birds was the only sounds heard. Finally, John felt the need to say something.

"Ma says you're going to leave?"

James reached down and picked up another small stone, then replied.

12

"I can't stay here any longer, John. The war did something to me. I don't know what, exactly, but I know I've got to move. If I don't, I'll get sick."

John looked over at his brother and tried to find an answer. He could think of nothing to change his brother's mind. With no solution in sight, he decided to do what he could to be a friend.

"Where are you planning on going to?"

James glanced at John and felt glad his brother was trying to understand. He tossed the small stone into the creek.

"West, there's a lot of room to move around out that way. I saved most of my pay from the Army, so I should have enough to get me by for a while. I'll give Ma some money before I leave. I know it won't be the same as having an extra hand around, but maybe it'll help some."

John could only nod in agreement. He knew his brother would stay if he were able to. He patted James' leg and stood up.

"Will you be coming to dinner?"

"Yeah, I'll be back later, before dinner."

John nodded and began walking back towards the house. James again stared at the creek, as if it might answer some of the questions in his mind.

As the sun crept up towards noon, James left the small waterway and went back to the house. He decided he would leave as soon as he could get a good horse and the proper equipment together for an extended trip out West.

Over the next several days he purchased a good mount and all the necessary gear, including two brand new Colt Army revolvers and a Henry rifle.

The departure day came, and he said his good-byes, then moved down the road, away from the house where he had grown to be a young man.

Upon reaching the creek, he turned the horse around and looked back at his home in the distance. He didn't want to leave it. But in his heart, James knew he had to. Something inside him would not rest. The battle within had to run its course, somewhere and somehow. Staying here would only worsen the situation and disrupt the family he loved. With this thought in mind, he turned his horse and moved down the road, towards the struggle he knew he must face. Out there, in the West, somewhere, an unseen enemy awaited him.

Chapter Two: Independence

As James rode, he felt good to be moving again. Somehow, the swaying of the horse felt like home. As time went by, he found himself in a haze that helped ease his mind.

It was no longer necessary to think about anything other than the ride and where to stop and sleep. James examined the landscape and forgot the eyes of men he'd shot during the war. He considered a method for traversing a creek rather than the flash of hot blood, which ran through his veins as he charged onto a battlefield.

He knew this was the best place for him to be. James didn't know how to resolve the battle within himself, but he knew this would be a place he could live until a solution came.

As he passed through the small towns, he examined the people, the women, and children. He wondered if he would ever have a wife and children. Then he would get through the town and stop thinking of such things. He could again clear his mind and focus on the ride.

Soon, battle-scarred lands passed by and mass graves littered the trails; evidence of the war that was still fresh in his mind. Too slowly for James, these haunting scenes became fewer and fewer as he moved farther into the western regions.

Along the way, James replaced his Northern farmer clothing with the buckskins, leathers, and apparel of a western woodsman. Soon he began to gain distance from those memories of the soldier inside, which beckoned him to another challenge on the fields of death.

This man fought to avoid the bear or the snake that threatened to spook his horse. He concerned himself with these matters and tried to purge his thoughts of the warrior he had been.

James wandered into Independence Missouri in the fall of 1865. The rough frontier city welcomed the lone rider with many loud sounds, and a gun shot several blocks away. He pulled his buckskin coat a little tighter as the crisp autumn wind found its way into the open folds of leather.

He found a suitable stable for his horse and then carried his Spartan belongings down the street to a boarding house.

The warmth and smell of a wood stove swirled around him as he stepped into the doorway of a large two-story house. A man that looked to be in his forties sat talking with a pretty woman that was obviously half his age. They both looked at James suspiciously as he stood directly in the doorway.

"Can I help you?" The young woman stood up and moved towards him.

"I was wondering if you have a room to rent." James sat his saddlebags, rifle, and other various items down after asking this.

The young woman eyed James and just as she was about to reply, the man stood up and asked in a tone of contempt.

"Where are you from Mister? You don't sound like you're from around here."

James glanced over at the man, who continued to walk slowly towards the lobby area where James stood.

He then turned back to the young woman.

"I'll pay in silver coin."

When James said this, the woman immediately became more attentive.

"Yes, well, we do have a room, if you have the rent in silver." She stepped closer to him and smiled after saying this.

"I asked you a question, Mister. You need to show some manners. Or is it that you're a Yankee and don't have any manners?"

The man expressed obvious frustration that the woman had told James she had a room.

"Frank, please. He has the rent in silver coin. I don't care where he's from."

Now Frank turned to the woman.

"Mary, that's why we got so many of the Yankees coming down here. He doesn't care about anyone around here. He just flashes some silver coin and gets what he wants."

James said nothing but fished a silver dollar from his pocket. He held it up for Mary to see.

"Right this way Mr.?"

"James Taft."

"Yes Mr. Taft, your room is upstairs. It'll be cash in advance, though."

"That's fine." James picked his gear up and glanced over at Frank, then began following the young woman up the stairs.

Frank sneered at him but said nothing else.

After paying the rent and getting settled in James went to the bath house and got a much-needed cleaning. That night he slept soundly, as he'd not slept in an actual bed for some time.

The following morning, he came down to breakfast and found a table with several other boarders, including Frank who didn't appear very glad to see him.

"Good morning Mr. Taft. I'm Millie. You rented a room yesterday from Mary, my daughter. I was out on midwife services."

James nodded to the woman that entered with a platter of biscuits. She was an attractive woman, in her forties perhaps. James could see where Mary had obtained her beauty from.

"Pleased to meet you Ms," He then sat down at the table.

Mary came into the room and glanced over at James with an eye of interest. She served everyone eggs to go with the biscuits. He noticed she gave him an extra egg. Frank also saw this from across the table, and again his face twisted slightly with anger.

James ate his food and excused himself from the table. He then went to the stables to check on his horse. The weather was cold, and a brisk breeze nipped at his face as he walked through the city.

Eventually, James found himself in a saloon, drinking a beer and staring at the wall.

A dance hall girl came up and sat down at the table with him. She was pretty and appeared to be around twenty years old. She didn't say anything at first but merely sat, starring at James. He glanced back at her, and she smiled at him. The saloon was almost empty, and neither one said anything for several minutes.

Finally, she spoke with a strong, but sweet Southern accent.

"You ain't a farmer... and you ain't no cowboy. You look like a soldier, 'cept you still got all yer arms and legs. What is it exactly that you do, Mister?"

James took another drink of his beer and didn't reply right away. He sat his glass on the table and continued to look at the young woman. She never turned away from him, and he tried to think of an appropriate answer.

Then James answered her, and as he spoke, he found himself getting further and further into a deep hole.

"Well, I don't like to talk about it. But I work for the government."

16

The young woman continued to stare at him but seemed a bit impressed.

"Really, and jest what is it you do fer the government?"

James took another drink and gave her a bashful expression.

"I really.... don't like to talk about it, Miss."

Now the young woman became even more intrigued.

"Why don't you like talking bout it? It can't be that bad."

She moved even closer. James turned his beer up and finished it. He sat the glass on the table.

"Well, you see..." He then stopped, acted nervously and as if he needed another drink, but the glass was empty.

"Here, I'll get you another beer."

He handed her a coin, and she took the glass and darted away. Soon she returned and sat the beer back on the table in front of him.

Then, she moved very close to James and put her arm on the table, propping her head up on her hand. She starred expectantly at him as he took another drink.

"Uhm... well, you see, I'm a, well, I'm a government-certified 'tongue' inspector."

The woman sat back a little and looked at James as if he were crazy.

"You ain't no such thing!"

James looked down at his glass and expressed embarrassment. "You see, that's why I don't like talking about it. I always get that reaction." James took another drink and turned away as if hurt by her words.

He was beginning to enjoy himself now and perhaps due to this, never considered how far he would go with it.

The young woman sat back up and closed the space between them even more.

"So, jest what sort of 'tongue' inspecting is it you do then, Mister?"

"Oh, cattle tongues mostly, but I do some horse tongue inspecting as well, from time to time."

"Why would anyone need ta inspect cow tongues?"

James glanced down at his beer and became solemn.

"It's a new type of science. A lot can be determined from the tongue. People are just now beginning to realize how much can be discovered simply by examining a tongue."

Now the young woman inched closer to James and leaned towards him.

"Like what? How can ya tell anything from lookin at a tongue?"

"Well, let me see your tongue, and I'll show you."

The woman appeared apprehensive about this.

"It won't hurt, I promise you. I just want to look at it."

After James had said this, several more men walked into the saloon. The piano player stood up, walked over and sat down behind the keyboard. He then began playing a chunky sounding rhythm.

"Well, alright, if it fer sure ain't gonna hurt."

She leaned over to James and stuck out her tongue.

"Hmm, yes, fascinating," James examined the woman's tongue with interest.

"Wha....wha ouu seee...."

She tried to look at James and speak while keeping her tongue out.

"Yes, I see you were born, hmm yes, you was born somewhere South of here."

The young woman pulled her tongue back in quickly.

"Yeah, I was! That's amazin.... How'd you see that from jus lookin at my tongue?"

James had a little difficulty not laughing as the woman again leaned over to him and put her tongue out for him.

"Wat else duo see?"

Slightly, James smiled as he had now become very amused with the charade. He leaned over closer to the young dance hall girl and examined her tongue again.

As he studied her tongue, he could smell her perfume, and then, he happened to glance down. There before him was the young woman's exposed cleavage. He quickly looked up, but immediately his eyes were irresistibly drawn back down to the beautiful sight.

"Yes, well, um, I see that..."

He had by now become very distracted as she leaned even closer towards him with both arms on the table. This created a situation that pressed her breasts together and allowed the top of her dress to open up enough for him to gain a great view of her ample female attributes.

"Wat, wat, do uoo see?"

18

"I, um see that." He struggled for something and began to feel flush as he could not pull his eyes away from her chest.

"I see that uhm... your mother, she was very beautiful."

The woman tried to smile with her tongue out but gazing upwards.

"Yeaa,sthee wazz! Thathas inkredable!"

"And, I see that, um." James again stumbled as he began to feel warm from the sight of the young woman's chest and the two beers.

The dance hall girl then glanced down, as James struggled for something else to say. She became aware that he was, very closely, examining her chest. She pulled her tongue back into her mouth.

"Uhm hmm, and what else iz it ya see?" Her eye lids lowered a little as she asked this.

"Well, I see that uhm your father..." James glanced up and realizing he'd been caught, froze.

The young woman stared at him for several long seconds but never moved. Then, she finally spoke.

"Yer fer certain an inspector, Mister, but I'm thinkin yer no tongue inspector." She then leaned back as James remained frozen with a blank expression on his face.

For a bit longer the young woman watched James, while she reclined in the chair. Then a sly smile erupted onto her face.

"I like you... even if you are a Yankee; which I'm thinkin you are. Yer a rascal! It waz real clever the way you got yerself a sight of me like that."

James sat back and smiled. Although "getting a sight of her" wasn't his initial intention, he didn't make an effort to explain this since she appeared to admire him for it.

Now the young woman smiled even brighter and sat back up in her chair.

"My name is Nancy." She held out her hand.

"James Taft." He leaned forward and shook her hand, then picked his beer back up.

Perhaps due to the close inspection of Nancy's cleavage, James now examined the rest of her a little better. She had light brown hair, and it was put up in ribbons, as most dance hall girl's hair was. She wore a knee length dress that was colorful and expressed the general risqué nature of a young lady in her profession. She didn't have the look of a prostitute as some dance hall girls; she still appeared fresh and somewhat unblemished for her early twenty-something age.

She stared at him now, and he watched her as the piano continued to bang out chunky saloon rhythms.

"So where are you from Nancy, other than the South?"

"Huntsville, Alabama. If you'd been payin more attention to my tongue, instead of other things you was lookin at, you mighta known that, Jimmy." Nancy then winked at him.

James winced a little.

"I prefer to be called James."

Nancy leaned up close to him. He could smell her again. He liked that.

"Well, if'n ya ever want to be gettin another sight of me, you'll be makin a ception' ta that rule... Jimmy." She then sat back in her chair and waited for his response with a sultry smile.

He considered this as he gazed into her blue eyes. After another drink from his glass, he replied.

"I suppose under those conditions. I can make one exception."

She again smiled brightly at him. She was very beautiful. He smiled back.

He began to feel nervous, though, as many different thoughts started to run through his mind. He'd never considered becoming attracted to a woman in a saloon. He'd only stopped in for a drink. Now he found himself feeling quite interested in Nancy.

"I suppose I should go now." He turned up his beer and sat the glass on the table. He stood up as she continued to half recline in the hard-wooden chair.

"Yeah, you better go Jimmy. I ain't never liked a Yankee the way I'm liken you. You better go now. You be sure ta come an visit me though, ya hear?"

James turned and glanced down at Nancy. She turned away from him as if also trying to fight an attraction inside herself.

"Yeah, I'll come back sometime. Thank you, Nancy."

She turned to him and smiled, but then frowned immediately after that. Then, she turned away from him again as he left the saloon.

When James entered the boarding house, he found Mary directly inside, cleaning a table. He noticed she was dressed very well for doing house cleaning.

"Mr. Taft, how was your morning?"

"It was very good, thank you." He began to walk up the stairs.

"Would you like to come into the parlor and warm up?"

James realized she must have put the nice dress on for him. He didn't want to be entertained by her right now, but also didn't want to disappoint her.

"Yes, alright, I suppose that would be nice."

Mary nodded slightly and walked with him into the parlor.

Sitting across from each other, Mary smiled at James, and he smiled back. He had already become uneasy by the recent attraction to Nancy. He felt reluctant to have his heart pricked by another beautiful young woman.

"You know, so many of our fine young men died in the war, Mr. Taft. I find it refreshing to speak with a gentleman such as you. May I call you James, Mr. Taft?"

"That would be nice, and I prefer James."

Mary smiled delicately, and James couldn't help but sense the contrast between her and Nancy.

"Would you like something to drink, James?"

"Well, a glass of water would be fine."

Mary stood up and walked by. Her dress brushed against him as she passed. He sat in the warm room, feeling uneasy.

Soon Mary returned with a glass of water. James thanked her and took a drink as she sat again .

She turned to the fireplace as if giving him an opportunity to look her over. He did look her over, and she was a fine specimen of a woman. She had darker brown hair than Nancy, and yet it was softer in appearance. Her face was perfectly symmetrical, and she would certainly turn any young man's head on the streets of Independence.

Seeming to sense his attention was on her, she brushed her hand along her neck as if removing a bothersome strand of hair. Then, when she had given James enough time to absorb her feminine qualities, she turned to him.

"The weather has certainly turned cooler hasn't it, James?"

He found himself desiring the atmosphere of the saloon now. Though any man would envy him at this moment, James felt as if he would burst at any time, should he sit here much longer. The chunky piano rhythms and the unpredictable nature of Nancy called out to him as he struggled to find small talk.

"Yes, it surely has turned cool on us." He grimaced now as the fire crackled in front of him.

"Is it too warm for you James?"

Her voice was soft and sweet, as honey dripping slowly from a dauber. It floated into his ears and melted as a subtle mist. And yet, he found it difficult to sit and endure this pristine atmosphere. Why was this? A beautiful and refined woman sat before him. She had taken the time to dress and prepare her delicate hair, just to entertain him. Now she wanted his conversation, and he could only think of leaving as quickly as possible, or to run to the rough and ill-reputed amenities of the saloon.

"No, I'm fine, thank you."

"You remind me of a soldier, James. Was you in the war perhaps?"

Now he could almost endure no more. He didn't want to speak of the war. The constant speaking of such things tortured his mind. He knew well she wanted to be impressed. She wanted him to tell of gallantry and her, in turn, would flatter him for his brave deeds. He felt a strange feeling of despair as he realized his thoughts were so far from what most considered normal. He ran his hand along the side of his head as he tried to find a response.

Just as Mary began to react to the lengthy pause, Frank walked into the boarding house and then straight into the parlor. When he saw James, he immediately expressed disappointment.

Though James wasn't glad to see Frank, he was relieved by the interruption. It didn't last long, however, as Frank sat down and immediately showed an interest in James.

"Mr. Taft, just what is your purpose for being in Independence?"

"Frank, please!" Mary said.

James glanced at the two.

"Mary, you should be more careful. We know nothing of this man."

"You're not my Pa, Frank. I'll be asking you to leave my business to me."

James stood up.

"If you'll excuse me, I need to go... check on my horse."

"You didn't answer my question, Mr. Taft!"

James glanced at Frank as he stepped away from the sofa and moved towards the door.

"Frank, would you just hold your tongue." Mary objected again.

James now replied to Frank with a stern voice.

"I'll also be asking you to leave my business to me, Mister."

This immediately infuriated Frank.

"You damn Yankee! You come back in here and say that to my face!"

"Frank, you.... Ahh." Mary stood up, rushed out of the room and past James; apparently upset.

James stared at Frank and considered taking him up on his offer. His blood became hot. He felt the same rush that always came before a battle. He liked the feeling and almost moved back into the room.

Frank starred at James with fire in his eyes. He moved his right hand slightly. James realized a weapon was probably in his coat pocket. He examined the space between them and felt he had time to take him down before Frank would be able to reach the weapon.

James paused. He realized this was the very thing he'd wanted to get away from; why he left his home. He realized that he wanted to take Frank down and destroy him. The rush of blood felt good, and this frightened him.

James turned and walked towards the stairs. He had already checked his horse and just wanted to get away from the situation.

"You better leave while you can, boy... I know you're just a yellow-bellied coward."

James ignored Frank's insults and continued to his room.

He lay on his bed, attempting to calm down. He stared at the ceiling. Everything was out of place in his mind. He finally kicked his boots off and slept.

The next few days James arose early and left the boarding house before breakfast. He would check on his horse and then eat somewhere in town.

By this time, people were moving into Independence and all around the outside of town in preparation to travel the Oregon Trail.

One morning James took his horse out for a ride and came across a mass of wagons and tents outside of town. He studied the congregation of people from afar. He had been avoiding Mary and Frank, but now he wanted to be around people. A few hours later he found himself walking into the saloon.

"Jimmy!" Nancy immediately moved towards James and pushed away another dance hall girl that was approaching him. She took his arm and led him over to a table.

"Why haven't ya come ta visit me, Jimmy?"

She sat him down in a chair and immediately sat down in his lap. He could smell her perfume and feel her warmth. She gazed into his eyes, and he felt frightened and excited at the same time.

"I've been busy; I'm sorry Nancy."

"Ya been too busy fer me, Jimmy?"

He could tell now that she was a little tipsy.

"Ya gonna buy me a drink, Darlin?"

"Sure, and I'll take a beer." He reached into his pocket and pulled out a silver dollar. She took the coin and went to the bar. Soon she returned with two beers.

She sat his beer down and then she sat down across the table from him. Again, the piano player began banging out the chunky rhythms as several more men came into the smoke-filled saloon.

She took a large drink of her beer and then looked at James.

He felt fascinated with Nancy. He'd never seen a woman drinking beer before, or for that matter, he'd seldom seen a woman drink.

"So, where've ya been, Jimmy? I don't like too many Yankee's, but I kinda like you. Why ain't ya come ta see me?"

She was beautiful and yet dangerous to James. He felt even more attracted to her, and this was a gamble at the very least.

"I've missed you too, Nancy."

She stared at him with a contemptuous smile that he was becoming very fond of.

"I didn't say I missed ya! I jest asked why ya haven't come ta see me." She took another drink of her beer.

James leaned back in his chair and watched her. He smiled slightly as she wiped her mouth with her hand and realized he was looking at her. She smiled seductively, then leaned forward. She positioned herself so that her dress opened slightly on the top, once again giving him a "sight of her."

"I have missed ya, though, Jimmy. But don't ya go thinking too much about that."

He looked her over with a grateful expression on his face. Nancy stared at him as well. They both wanted to find something to hold onto. Finally, James replied.

"I don't think too much about anything anymore. But I have been thinking about you. I think you distract me from things. Things I don't want to think about."

Nancy thought about this as her mouth twisted ever so slowly. Her eyes glistened from the beers.

"That's why I like ya so much... you damn Yankee. You gots a troubled heart. I knew it was something like that. I ain't ever liked a Yankee, but you got a troubled heart, jest like me."

James grimaced a bit when Nancy said this. He realized this half-drunk woman spoke the truth. Perhaps this was why he found her so attractive. Mary was the picture of what any sane man should want in a woman. Yet, he wanted to be here with this provocative woman that most would consider being tainted. The piano player changed the tune now, but it still had the same chunky, banging rhythm as the previous one. They stared at each other as the music created a festive atmosphere. Both searched for something in the other's eyes.

"You're right Nancy. But what can we do about it?"

She stood up, moved over and sat back down in his lap. She put her arms around his neck. She looked into his eyes and said, "You gots to find a place where the thing that troubles yer heart is the thing that's most useful to ever one around. Then they'll love ya fer that awful thing inside yer self. That's why I'm here, Jimmy. I ain't got no place else I can be. My heart's troubled by a man. Now I find men like you and give' em some comfort. It doesn't fix me, but it makes me feel better fer a while."

She then hugged James, and her breasts pressed against his face. She smelled of perfume and beer. He did feel better, and yet he also felt as if he were falling. She spoke the truth and answered a question that burned inside him. But now he realized he had no place to go. Where could a man go and find something useful in the thing that troubled his heart?

He put his arms around her, and for a brief instant, his unsettled soul was peaceful.

As the days passed by, James continued to avoid Mary and Frank. He would ride around Independence but nearly always ended up in Nancy's company by the afternoon.

25

She would be half drunk, but somehow never became too drunk to entertain him and the other customers. She would dance on the stage and smile as the men yelled out to her and the other dancers.

James would buy her drinks, and he would find himself almost drunk by the time the saloon would close. Then, he would stagger to the boarding house and sleep until almost noon the next day.

He would then get cleaned up and again go for a ride in the early afternoon. As he rode around Independence, he became more and more aware of the gathering multitude of people and wagons. He sat on his horse as the cold wind nipped at his face. Watching from a hill, James began to wonder about this "Oregon Trail." The thought intrigued him momentarily, but then he rode back into town and found himself once again at the saloon and in the company of Nancy.

The winter days began to blur by in a routine of riding around the Missouri town until late afternoon and then eagerly entering the smoky saloon, to Nancy's sweet Southern greeting.

"Jimmy, come over here to me, ya damn Yankee!"

James moved over to the colorfully dressed saloon girl.

"Give us a couple of beers, Sam."

James put his arm around her. She felt warm, and he could smell her fragrance as she moved close to him.

The bartender sat two beers on the counter. The piano player moved from a table to the piano and began playing a catchy rhythm that James had become familiar with.

The two went to their usual table and sat down. She quickly downed half the beer and then gazed into his eyes. This had become their routine. He came early in the day so he could have her all to himself for a while.

"You mus really like me, Jimmy. I like you, but I'm thinkin you like me more."

James gazed into her eyes for a few seconds and then took a drink of his beer. After setting the glass back on the table, he replied.

"You make me forget. I like to forget."

She put her elbow on the table and then lowered her head and placed her chin on her hand. She looked at James, and her eyes belayed a young girl that still resided somewhere deep inside the troubled young woman.

"Forgettin don't make it go away. I know bout that cause I try ever day ta forget. Forgettin only makes ya feel better for a lil while."

The chunky piano tune seemed to dance inside his head as he examined her and considered what she had said.

He wanted her so badly. He wanted to take her away and somehow make them both forget. He'd never asked her exactly what it was she wanted to forget. She never asked him either. They both seemed to be tainted and unfit to exist anywhere that was considered 'civilized.'

James took another drink of his beer as several men came into the saloon. Smoke from Sam's cigar floated around his nostrils. The bartender put his cigar in a tray and poured the two men a drink.

Nancy laid her arm on the table and then rested her head on it as if she was tired of trying to forget.

She seemed to be the only person in the world that understood how he felt. He stared at her as the saloon atmosphere invaded the innermost crevices of his mind. She looked back at him and gazed into his eyes. He could see her pain.

She raised her head, seeming to sense James had penetrated her thoughts.

He realized now that he probably loved her. He didn't want to love her, but he did. She turned away from him as if she was thinking the same thing.

That night he stumbled out of the saloon as the doors closed for the day.

The days and nights blurred together now, as day after day he found himself in the comforting company of Nancy and the saloon. She also clung to James as the misery they both felt somehow became less of a burden while with each other.

Independence had gradually become more and more crowded as spring closed in and winter lost its grip on the land.

As he had done almost every day for months now, James woke up feeling the effects of the beer from the previous night. He cleaned up some and walked out of the boarding house. As he passed Mary, she turned away from him. She'd heard the stories of his time spent at the saloon and no longer had any interest in him.

He got something to eat in town and then went to the stables to retrieve his horse.

As he finished putting the saddle on, someone behind him spoke.

"Hello, Mister!"

James turned to the man.

"You look like a fella that can ride and shoot. You want a job. We need some extra men."

James eyed him with suspicion. Inside, he only wanted to stay at the saloon where he could drown his thoughts with Nancy and beer. He only wanted to hold her on his lap and smell her fragrance, mixed with cigar smoke, while the piano player banged out a tune. He wanted to watch her dance on the stage and forget about everything.

But perhaps he realized this would need to end sometime. His money wouldn't last much longer, and deep inside he knew this.

"What sort of job are you talking about?"

"We need some extra men to help us escort a wagon train up to Oregon territory. You just need to help protect the wagons and such. The pay is good if you got the experience. You got a gun?"

James looked the man over again before replying. The man seemed to be half business and half trapper. He had a buckskin coat and a city style; short brimmed felt hat. His pants were rough cloth, but his shirt appeared clean, white and more of a Sunday meeting style.

"I've got two Colt Army revolvers and a Henry rifle."

Now the man perked up.

"Well, you're just the man we need. You got military training?"

For some reason, James continued the conversation with this man. He had no desire of leaving Nancy. But now this job offer had somehow loosened her hold on him.

"Four and a half years with the US Cavalry."

Now the man became very excited.

"Listen Mr.?"

"James Taft."

"Mr. Taft. We'll pay you a dollar a day. Your meals will be covered by the wagon train. All you need to do is help us protect the wagons. Typically, I require the hired men to do additional duties. But considering your experience, all you need to do is keep an eye out for trouble Mr. Taft. I assure you of that. I need a man with your training and I'll treat you right if you sign on with me."

James made no expression. Then he replied casually.

"I'll consider it, Mr.?"

"Harvey, George Harvey. And you can find me on the West side of town. Just ask around some of the wagons camped out on the West side of town and they'll help you find me. We'll be leaving in a week, Mr. Taft. I hope you decide to join us. Oregon is the land of promise right now. You would love it. By the time you got to Oregon, you would have enough money to set up a nice little homestead."

James nodded, "I'll contact you if I decide to take you up on your offer Mr. Harvey." He then led his horse towards the doors.

He rode out of town and to the wagons and tents gathered. He sensed an excitement from these explorers, all ready for departure to Oregon territory.

As James sat on his horse gazing out over the mass of people, an idea came to him. He could take Nancy out West. They could build a new life in Oregon territory; a life far away from the memories. The thought excited him more than anything had in a long time. Surely, she would like the idea. This could change everything for both of them.

After returning his horse to the stable James anxiously made his way to the saloon.

"Jimmy!"

Though he didn't like the name "Jimmy," he had come to love hearing it from the flamboyant Southern beauty.

Sam automatically placed two beers on the counter soon after James entered the saloon. Nancy moved quickly up to him and took her beer with one hand and his arm with her other.

The saloon was already busy as more and more people entered Independence in preparation for their move to Oregon territory.

Since their normal table was occupied, the two moved to a table towards the corner of the room. He sat down, and Nancy almost jumped into his lap. She nuzzled up to him, and her chest pressed into his face. Everything went away, and for a few moments, he thought of nothing but the smell of Nancy and the warmth of her close body.

The piano player continued to force a chunky rhythm from the instrument with his usual banging style on the black and white keys.

"Buy me a whiskey, Jimmy!" Nancy was in a rowdy mood now. James pulled a silver dollar from his pocket and handed it to her. She stood up from his lap and went to the counter. Shortly she returned with two shot glasses of whiskey.

"Here's you one Jimmy."

She sat down and gazed into the amber liquid with a slight smile.

James tried to think of the best way to ask Nancy about Oregon. He decided to say it straight out.

"Nancy, I'm thinking about going to Oregon territory. I would like for you to come with me."

When James said this, Nancy immediately lost her smile. She turned slowly away as she still held the whiskey in her hand. James watched her closely now as this wasn't the reaction he'd expected.

She turned back to him with a frightened expression. After glancing down at her drink again, she suddenly turned it up, downed it, and then sat the empty shot glass on the table. Her face expressed the strong jolt from the taste.

Seeming to gain some courage from the whiskey Nancy looked at him and replied.

"Ya don't want a woman like me, Jimmy. I ain't no good fer no man."

She glanced down at the empty shot glass and expressed shame.

Now James wanted her even more. The fact that she felt she wasn't good enough for him made him desire her that much more. He moved closer to her.

"I don't care about anything Nancy. I want you with me. We can start new in Oregon territory. We can get a piece of land and not have to worry about anything anymore."

Now a tear rolled down her cheek. She shook her head as if his words were hard for her to hear.

"No Jimmy, nooo, I can't."

He put his hand on her arm as the smoke, and the banging piano accentuated the strange feelings both were dealing with at this instant.

"Why can't you Nancy? Why not? Just go with me; we can forget together. We'll just think about us and nothing else."

Now her eyes were full of tears as she looked into his. She grabbed his shot of whiskey and downed it. She ran the back of her hand across her mouth and sniffed from crying.

30

"I jus can't Jimmy. You don't understand."

She stood up and walked away from the table quickly. James stood up, but then sat back down. Now he felt like drinking. He began to drink whiskey. He watched Nancy dance on stage later that night. She wasn't happy. He wasn't either.

Around midnight the saloon sat almost empty. Again, Nancy sat down across from James at their usual table. Both showed signs of drinking far too much, mixed with sadness from deep inside.

As Sam cleaned the tables and the Piano player closed up his keyboard, James spoke in a tone of disappointment.

"Why don't you want to go with me, Nancy? What's holding you here, this?" He moved his hand to indicate the saloon.

"No, Jimmy... It ain't this." She whined and then laid her weary head on her arm. Both were exhausted from the night of burdened hearts.

"What then? What's keeping you here?"

She raised her head and looked at James. Her hair was a mess, and she was apparently worn out and half drunk. She was still beautiful. She was beautiful and troubled just like him. He wanted so much for them to leave and try to make a life where they could both forget. Finally, she replied to his question.

"It ain't that I can't leave here Jimmy. I jus can't leave with a..." She paused and looked away. "I jus can't leave with a... Yankee."

Now James became angry, and for a brief second, he didn't care for her. But then she turned to him and continued.

"My brother Martin, he was killed by a Yankee at Chickamauga. I know it weren't you that done it Jimmy, but I can't get that from my heart. I can't be with you all the time, do you understand?"

Chickamauga... suddenly, memories of that bloody mess came flooding back. How many rebels did he kill at Chickamauga, seven, eight, twelve? No, it must have been more, much more. He unloaded his revolver and rifle, again and again, every day of that battle. He seldom missed by that stage of the war. He suddenly realized, he indeed may have killed her brother.

Now James turned away from her. Why did she say Chickamauga? Why couldn't it have been Gettysburg, Antietam, or any other battle that he had nothing to do with? He would have had a chance. Now he knew there was no hope. Neither could live with these thoughts every day and, neither had the ability to persuade the other one to overcome them.

"I'm sorry Jimmy." She began to cry now and the day's events weighed on both of them.

James put his hand on her arm.

"It's alright Nancy, I understand."

"I want ta go with ya, Jimmy. I really do. But, I jus can't get over that Jimmy. I told ya, I don't like many Yankees. I like you a whole lot, though, and if things were different, I would love ya. And, maybe I do love ya... But I jus can't get around that Jimmy." She wept now and wiped her eyes again and again.

"No, you don't have to be sorry Nancy. I understand." He continued to stare out at the floor. Another saloon girl that had fallen asleep with her head on a table stood up as Sam roused her. She staggered towards her room upstairs.

"I've got to go." James picked himself up and walked in a daze past Sam, who was still sweeping the floor.

As he went out the doors, he heard Nancy.

"I'm sorry Jimmy. I'm sorry."

When he awoke the next day, James felt awful. He lay in bed and stared at the ceiling. The fragile hopes he had the previous day had crumbled and now felt like wounds that tormented his heart, along with the repercussions of the whiskey.

A breakfast helped some, as did the coffee. He checked on his horse and went back to his room. He wanted to see Nancy, but now knew he would also see faces of the men he'd killed at Chickamauga.

Several days passed by in a haze of loneliness and despair. He finally realized that he must do something. He had to get away and not think about Nancy or the past. Somehow, he must look forward, even though he could see nothing ahead that would help him.

He packed his meager belongings and told Mary he was leaving.

"Thank you, Mr. Taft. I wish you well."

She turned away after saying this, seeming to be ashamed of ever being attracted to him.

James went to fetch his horse. Then, as he rode past the saloon, he found himself stopping. He jumped down, hitched his mount and went in.

Nancy sat at their usual table. She turned to James. This time there was no lively greeting.

"Hello, Jimmy." She meekly said as he sat down across from her.

"Nancy."

Seeming to sense the occasion, Sam brought two beers and sat them on the table.

"Thank you, Sam," Nancy said casually, as James handed the bartender a silver coin.

James gazed into her eyes and, she also searched his. They wanted to find something to give them hope. Nothing transpired, and after a few seconds they both picked up their beer and took a drink to ease the tension.

"So, yer goin ta Oregon territory then?"

He didn't answer right away. He thought about what she said and how she said it. He wanted to remember her sweet, Southern drawl. He knew at this instant he would most likely never see her again. He took another drink of his beer and sat the glass down.

"Yes, I'm going to Oregon territory."

She lowered her head, and he could see tears struggling to escape her eyes. She buffered up and wiped one eye quickly as if she didn't want him to know.

She turned away now and stared towards the stage. Again, she wiped her eyes, though he could only see the side of her face. She turned back to him and smiled slightly.

"You'll do good in Oregon Territory. I'm thinkin they're iz a way for ya ta forget. Maybe if ya go out there, you can find a place where they need what troubles ya. If ya can find that Jimmy, maybe ya can forget." She turned slightly, again avoiding his eyes.

He glanced down to his beer on the table. She now took the opportunity to look at him closely. He realized she might also want to remember him.

What kind of hell was this? He wondered how he could feel any worse as her eyes drifted over him. The war was over. Now it was tearing her away from him. He could have loved her and together they may have been able to change the path they now seemed destined to walk. He felt angry but had no place to direct the anger inside. After she'd examined him a moment she turned back to her beer.

"I hope you're right Nancy. I hope we can both forget someday. But, I'll never forget you."

When he said this, she seemed to come apart. She put her hand to her mouth and began to cry. Then she turned to James and almost shouted.

"Get out of here, you... damn Yankee! Go ta Oregon, and hurry up." She wept openly now. The piano player stopped playing.

James squinted as the words flew past him. He slowly picked up his beer and downed the remainder of it. Nancy held her face in her hands as she continued to cry.

As he stood up, the chair screeched across the floor like a scream in the silent room.

He turned and walked towards the door.

"Jimmy!" Nancy called out, and as he turned around, she landed in his arms. She pushed her face and lips to his. Her tears dampened his cheeks as she kissed him passionately. He put his arms around her.

Nancy pulled away from him.

"Go! Go on ta Oregon. I can't love you... I can never love you. You better jest leave." She then turned and quickly ran up the stairs to her room.

James watched her until she had slammed the door behind her.

A few seconds later the piano player again started banging out the familiar, chunky tunes. James stood staring at the upstairs room as the few patrons in the saloon returned to their activities.

He wanted desperately to stay and change her mind. Her kiss lingered on his lips, and her tears brought coolness to his cheek as they gently dried.

There was no hope though. He knew that... even if he could change her, it wouldn't change him. He had no idea how many rebels he'd killed at Chickamauga. He knew it was many. He couldn't love her the way she should be loved, knowing that he may have killed her brother in that battle.

He turned and walked out the door as his heart weighed inside him. Indeed, what sort of hell was this? He got on his horse and rode out towards the wagon camp. He needed to work or do something to forget. And now there was even more that he wanted to forget.

34

Chapter Three: Bittersweet Trail

The weather was still cold as he rode into the sprawling campsite. Smoke from campfires swirled about as the women cooked the midday meals.

"Can you tell me where I can find George Harvey?" James asked a woman who busily labored over a small campfire, while a young girl of around two years old clung to her dress.

"Mr. Harvey? You can find him over yonder on the other side of the camp." The woman pointed to the West.

"Thank you, Madam."

James continued West past a multitude of wagons of all shapes and sizes; most appeared to be in good condition and adequate for the trip. A few he wondered about as they looked questionable.

Finally, he came upon a gathering of men and could see George standing on the back part of a wagon; he seemed to be giving a speech to some of the men of the wagon train.

James stopped and listened to George from a distance. He couldn't catch all the words, but the talk sounded to be one of encouragement before the long and challenging journey.

Eventually, the speech was over, and George climbed down from the wagon as the men disbursed to their camp sites. James climbed down from his horse and taking the reins close to the bridle walked towards George.

He stood talking with several men as James approached. As soon as he noticed James, he quickly ended the conversations to speak with him.

"Mr. Taft, it's so good to see you! I'm hoping you're here to accept the job."

James shook his hand as he said this. He then replied with what had become his usual monotone voice.

"Yes Sir, I'm here for the job. There's nothing around here for me."

"That's great Mr. Taft. You'll love Oregon territory. You can start new and forget all about this part of the country."

When George said this, James felt a bit better. It was something at least. Perhaps he could forget, once he was far enough away.

"Come with me, James, it is James, right? Do you mind if I call you James?"

"No Sir."

"Alright, and you can call me George if you like."

"Thank you... George."

The two walked past more wagons and people that were busy with last minute preparations. They soon arrived at George's wagon.

"Sit down James. I'm sorry I can't offer you better accommodations."

James sat down on a stool close to the smoldering embers of a morning campfire. George took a small rag and picked up the coffee pot that hung over the fire from a tripod.

"Would you like a cup of coffee?"

"No thanks."

After pouring himself a cup, George sat on a small stool that was close to James.

"Alright, here's the deal. I was hoping you would show up. I'd almost given up on you. What I need is a trail boss. What rank did you hold in the Army?"

"Staff Sergeant," James replied.

"Good, good. If you're interested, I can give the position to you. But I only have the point position still available. It's the more dangerous spot as you need to move ahead with the guide. You'll have several men under you though and can use them as you see fit. It's a dollar a day, but as the trail boss, your meals will be provided daily by several of the families. Also, there will be young men from the wagon train that will tend to your horse at the end of the day."

George took a sip of his coffee and studied James as he did so. Then he spoke again as James volunteered no response.

"Will that be satisfactory?"

He thought of George's offer for a few seconds and then nodded his head and replied. "Yes, that will be satisfactory. I prefer the forward position."

George examined him as James sat emotionless, staring into the smoldering fire.

"Good, I'm basing this on your word of owning your guns and knowing how to use them. I expect you to protect the wagon train and spot any dangers before the wagons get into trouble. If that's understood and acceptable, we'll have a deal."

James now understood that George had some reservations due to his soft-spoken behavior. He looked at George and tried to express reassurance.

"Don't worry Mr. Harvey. If I take responsibility on, I will hold to it. I'll protect the wagons, and I have the experience with my guns to do the job."

Now George appeared to relax.

"Alright, welcome to our company, and we'll be leaving the day after tomorrow, early in the morning."

He shook James' hand and stood up. "I'll show you around a little and introduce you to the families that will be supplying your meals."

They walked around the camp and George introduced him to several families as well two young men that would be taking care of his horse at the end of each day. Then they came to a large wagon.

"This is the Tyler family's wagon. They'll be providing your breakfast. We offer a break on the package price to these families if they provide our men with a meal every day. The Tyler's were next in line to get this offer, but were growing concerned there would be no hired hand to provide a meal for. I'm sure they will be happy that you hired on at the last hour."

As George finished saying this, they rounded the wagon and walked straight in front of a young woman in a long dress. She looked up and into James' eyes. This was an accident, as they both became surprised by the chance encounter. Both turned away, but then glanced back into each other's eyes as if needing one more look.

"Hello, Amanda. Is your father or mother around?"

The young woman lowered her head shyly and replied.

"No Sir, Mr. Harvey. Pa's in town, and Ma is across the camp talking with Mrs. Johnson." She then glanced back at James.

She was a stunning young woman of maybe nineteen or twenty years old. It was unusual for a woman such as this not to be married. James wondered where her husband was as he noticed how attractive she was.

Amanda had long hair that was a light brown color. She had it in a bun, but James could tell from the size of the bun that it must flow down to her midsection.

Mr. Harvey continued.

"Well, this is James Taft. He's recently hired on as the forward trail boss. He's a young man with a lot of valuable experience. I wanted to introduce him to you and your folks as he'll be needing breakfast from you every morning. You can let your folks know about this, Amanda. I suspect they'll be happy as they will get the reduction in price after all."

James glanced at her left hand and saw no wedding ring. He now assumed that she wasn't married.

Amanda smiled slightly about Mr. Harvey's statement, belaying she was also happy about it. James felt as he did when talking with Mary. This young woman didn't know of James' past. He was certainly attracted to her, but she should have better than him. She should have a man that was reliable and would stay in one place.

"I'm happy to meet you, Mr. Taft."

She held her hand out, and James shook it gently. Her hand felt warm and dainty, just as he imagined it would.

"Pleased to meet you, Miss."

Mr. Harvey continued.

"You'll get your morning meals with this family. There will be a light meal that you will need to eat while moving. Then you'll get your evening meal with the Jacob's family. I'll take you to meet them. They're also a wonderful family."

George began to walk away, and James followed behind.

"Goodbye, Amanda," George said as he glanced back and waved.

"Goodbye Sir and, James, she said"

He noticed Amanda smiled slightly as she spoke his name.

That night James made his bed on the ground. He felt as if he were back home. When he arose in the morning, his body ached from the hard earth. The sounds and smells of camp aroused his memories of the Army. He felt excited and an eagerness stirred inside him that he'd not sensed for a long time.

James pulled the Army revolvers from his saddlebags. The heavy iron felt good. He felt a desire to shoot them and longed for the recoil in his hands. As he strapped the leather holsters on, the leather crackled. He again tried to push the feelings down, but somehow, he had missed the feeling of a gun strapped to him. He wanted his saber also and wanted to ride onto the battlefield; to feel the hot blood rushing through his veins as death raced all around him in a grim duel that few would survive.

He again felt ashamed for such thoughts. How could any man long for such a horrid thing? He moved to the family that would provide his breakfast. He moved towards her. She would be there, and Nancy would grow farther away now.

"Good morning, James." Amanda greeted him. She then looked at his two revolvers. She appeared unhappy that he wore them, but quickly moved to prepare him a plate.

"Good morning, Miss Tyler."

Her father and mother then approached him.

"Mr. Taft, Amanda said you would be joining us for breakfast. We're so glad of that. My name is Walter, and this is my wife, Edith."

Walter extended his hand and James shook it.

"I'm pleased to meet you." He said this without much enthusiasm but tried to smile.

"Please have a seat, Mr. Taft." Edith said, "We'll have breakfast shortly," she then went to help Amanda.

Soon Edith brought him a plate of food. He began to eat but immediately noticed the Tyler's bowing their heads to pray. He quickly wiped his mouth and lowered his head as Walter asked for a blessing on the food.

Afterward, James ate his meal and glanced up from time to time at Amanda. She ate her breakfast with a delicate hand and James couldn't help but admire her again.

"So, Mr. Taft, I see you carry two pistols, and you wear them in a military manner as if you've got experience. Would you happen to have served in our recent and unfortunate war against the Rebels?"

James knew Walter asked this in a way that he could give the proper answer. If he had fought for the South, he could suggest that he'd not fought in the war or indicate he would rather have his meal with another family. He suspected Walter knew from his Northern accent that he likely fought for the Union.

He didn't want to answer the question. He wanted to get away from the war. But he realized it would certainly come up again now that he wore his revolvers.

"Four and a half years with the 9th Pennsylvania Cavalry, Sir."

Walter was packing his pipe, but when James said this, he immediately looked at him with shock.

"Good Lord! And you still have all of your limbs! God must have surely been merciful to you."

Amanda also gave James an extra look as her father said this.

"Yes Sir, he surely was."

This answer appeared to appease Walter, and he went back to filling his pipe with tobacco.

"The 9th Pennsylvania Cavalry…you must have seen plenty of fighting then. And thank God you fought on the right side of things. Heaven help those rebs. They caused so much despair, and for what I ask you, to buy and sell men and women as if they were cattle? They'll have to live with their mistake, but we all suffered from it as well."

Walter now lit his pipe and pulled several draws of smoke from it. He glanced over to James.

"Yes, Sir."

The man again nodded, as if he was pleased with James' response. After he had pulled a couple more draws from the pipe, he glanced back as if checking where Amanda was. Then, when he saw that she was out of earshot, he spoke.

"Amanda's fiancée was killed at Gettysburg. He was an excellent young man and full of spirit, such a shame. Amanda is only now getting over it. I believe getting away from the places that held memories have helped her." Walter then pulled another draw from the pipe and stared at the ground as if recalling the young man that was to be his son-in-law.

James watched Walter for a few seconds. He quickly considered the countless young men he had killed and saw die on the battlefields. An expression of pain must have developed on his face as Walter looked up and noticed James.

"I'm sorry Mr. Taft. I'm sure the war is the last thing you wish to speak of."

James recovered. "It's alright Sir. We had so many fine young men die in that war. I'm sorry to hear about Amanda's fiancée. I'm sure he fought bravely."

Again, Walter smiled a little, indicating James' answer pleased him.

"Yes, I'm sure he did, Mr. Taft. Well, I suppose it's time to get this day started." He then stood up, and James also stood. Walter went one direction, and James walked to George's wagon.

As he came closer to the wagon, James noticed six men congregated around him. When several of the men noticed James approaching, George turned to greet him.

"Oh, well here he is now men. This will be your trail boss. James Taft, these men will be your trail hands."

George pointed his hand to the men, but James only noticed one of them. This man also stared starkly at James with disdain. George introduced them one by one and then he got to the man James stared at.

"And this is Frank Reid. He has a lot of experience in cattle and worked for the railroad a few years. He has scouted and helped protect workers back in the east."

Immediately after George said this, Frank spoke up.

"We're supposed to take orders from this pup? It looks like he's still wet behind the ears."

George looked at Frank with frustration. James never turned from Frank and never attempted to reply. He had managed to avoid Frank in the boarding house, but now there would be no way to do so.

"Frank, I expect you to do as I ask. I'm paying your wages, and I feel this man can lead you, so it's my decision to make. If you don't like it, you can leave. I still have time to find another hand, but I'll not be replacing Mr. Taft as my trail boss."

An expression of anger came over Frank's face. He then replied.

"I've seen your "trail boss" down at the saloon most ever day, George. He likes ta drink and spends his money on saloon girls."

When Frank said, this George turned to James briefly as if he might deny it. James continued to watch Frank however and said nothing. George turned back to Frank.

"Did you not hear what I just said, Frank? I make the decisions around here, and if you don't like my decisions, you're welcome to leave." Georges' voice indicated he was running out of patience.

Now Frank said nothing else but continued to watch James. After George had finished introducing the men, he sent them on tasks to prepare for the departure West.

"That Frank Reid is an arrogant jackass. I would run him off, but I need someone that can handle a gun. If I ran men off for being a jackass, I wouldn't have many left."

James nodded but didn't reply. He considered the situation as George pulled a bottle from under some folded clothes.

"Whiskey," George lifted the bottle to James.

"No thanks, I never drink while I'm working."

George glanced at James as if he questioned his response.

"That means you won't be drinking till we get to Oregon territory."

"Yes Sir, that's what it means."

George smiled at James response. James sensed he might have been testing him with the whiskey. It didn't matter either way, though. James had drowned his sorrows in alcohol and Nancy's charms long enough. He needed to get back into a work routine. The saloon life would surely kill him one way or the other if he remained in it.

"Well, I'm glad to hear that. It seems Frank is just irritated about taking orders from someone younger than him. As long as you do good work, I'll stand behind you."

"Yes, Sir," James replied.

George went over the plans with James. He would be in the forward position and scout out any trouble as the wagon train moved west. James would also coordinate the other men on his team to protect and maneuver the westbound pioneers.

After James had understood all that George expected of him, he went to check on his horse. He wanted to go back into Independence, to see Nancy. He struggled with the desire. He had already purchased everything he needed, or he may have used that as an excuse to do so. Finally, he considered that he would likely have a beer if he went to see her. He'd told George he wouldn't drink while working. With this in mind, he forced her from his thoughts.

Early the next morning James sat around a small campfire at the Tyler's wagon. Excitement and tension filled the air as everyone prepared to leave. Months of hardship and adventure lay ahead. All anticipated a great new life in Oregon territory.

James finished his light meal and went to his horse with his Henry rifle in hand. The people moved about with a sense of urgency in the pre-light morning. He quickly saddled his mount and slid the rifle into the holster on the saddle. As he climbed onto his horse, the leather crackled. He felt good, and suddenly with this new purpose, his burdens lifted some.

He moved towards the front of the long wagon train that had begun to form along the rugged road.

"Good morning Mr. Taft! Are you ready to go to Oregon territory?" George asked him as he rode up beside the wagon.

"Yes Sir, I'm ready."

"Good, good, we must stay on schedule."

"I understand Sir." James then spurred his horse to continue moving towards the front of the wagon train.

After hours of slow movement and a massive effort to get the train into a formation, a long line of wagons finally began to move in unison.

James moved back and forth in a constant effort to keep some organization as well as checking for any threats ahead. Another scout accompanied him and also kept the train on the proper trail. He was an older man that had traveled the trail many times over the years.

James observed the rugged frontier man from a distance. His name was Hiram, and he wore a tan buckskin jacket as many of the frontier men did. His hair was long and unruly. He seldom spoke more than a few words at a time to James.

As the long hard days began to go by, the wagon train developed a routine.

James began making his bed closer to the Tyler family since he would eat his morning meal with them. Amanda spoke to James about the same amount that he did to her, which was not much. Yet they examined each other with a keen interest day after day.

Frank Ried became increasingly resistant to James' orders. But after three weeks into the journey, James felt Frank had at least reached a place in which he would do as James told him, whether he liked it or not.

What James wasn't aware of, however, was that Frank more often than not had some of the younger hands do what James had told him to do. It became a game for Frank; to find ways to avoid doing what James had ordered him to do, or to push those tasks onto other, younger hands.

"That Frank Reid is no good." Hiram suddenly said to James as they sat waiting for the wagon train to catch up.

James studied Hiram a few seconds.

"I won't disagree with that. But I've got to work with what I've got. He's calmed down some it seems." James looked back at the wagons after saying this. The leather on his saddle crackled slightly as he moved back to wait for Hiram's response.

The sun beat down on them now as they moved across the flat lands. A constant breeze helped cool the travelers, but for Hiram, it constantly blew his long hair around. He turned his horse a little so the breeze would brush the unruly hair out of his face.

"You need to watch him, James. He's trying to stir up trouble for you."

James again glanced at Hiram's rugged face.

"I'll do that Hiram, thanks."

The scout nodded and turned his horse then galloped ahead as the wagons grew closer. James felt the situation with Frank must be worse than he thought if Hiram bothered to talk about it.

The flat lands eased travel for the wagon train, and though some areas were difficult, the group knew well the more strenuous terrain still lay ahead.

As they moved across this area, James and Amanda continued to gravitate towards each other. James resisted, but it seemed almost inevitable as the days passed. Her parents also encouraged her, much to the frustration of James.

He wanted to grow close to her. She was beautiful, and as she would fill his coffee cup in the morning, he would catch a faint smell of her. She smelled like an incredible field of flowers, and he wanted dearly to go there and lay in comfort and rest.

Amanda also seemed to resist the attraction, and James knew it was because she remained faithful to the love of her fallen fiancée. As the days passed and every morning that James ate breakfast with them, she clung to this lost love less and less.

"Would you like another egg, James? I can cook you another if you would like." Amanda smiled slightly and shyly as she said this.

"No thank you, Miss Tyler."

Now she appeared distraught.

"Why do you continue to call me 'Miss Tyler,' James? You've been eating breakfast with us for almost two months, and you still call me Miss Tyler half the time." After saying this, she took his dish with an extra bit of aggravation.

"Beg your pardon, Amanda."

44

Her father then spoke up.

"And you should, James! You're almost considered family now; you shouldn't be calling Amanda, 'Miss Tyler' anymore." Walter took a couple of quick draws from his pipe as he lit it up. He tossed the small branch back into the campfire and glanced back at James as if interested in his reaction.

"Yes, Sir, thank you for you and your family's hospitality." He then glanced over to Amanda. She looked him in the eye as she did some cleanup work. She smiled to indicate she wasn't mad at him. James smiled back a bit, but this also brought the feeling that Amanda was growing fond of a man she knew so little about. How could he tell her all the terrible things that resided inside? He excused himself and went to saddle his horse.

Over the next few days, James searched for a solution. He wanted to care for Amanda just as any normal man would. And yet he felt he would be dangerous to her. He didn't know how to calm his own troubled heart. How could he manage a love with someone like Amanda? She was wholesome and pure; beautiful and fresh. He felt as if he had always walked straight from the battlefield. He sensed the blood from hundreds of fallen opponents all over him. He had the constant urge to feel the weight of the revolvers in his hands. He longed to race towards death in a struggle for survival, where nothing was for certain. How could he tell her these things? And if he could tell her, how could she possibly understand?

The next morning as he was leaving the Tyler's campsite; he passed between two wagons, he met Amanda head on, going the other way. They came close together and almost touched. He looked into her eyes and her into his. They stopped as if needing to search into the soul of the other for another second. Then she pulled from his gaze and tried to deflect the nature of the situation.

"I'm ahh, sorry James, excuse me."

"Excuse me, Amanda."

She smiled. He felt his heart grow fonder of her and the struggle became more difficult.

As he rode that day, he seemed to only think of this beautiful woman. The thoughts created torment and joy inside him at the same time. Perhaps he could leave the past behind with a lady such as this.

Hiram rode up to James, causing the tender thoughts to take flight.

"You see that?" He pointed down to the ground.

James glanced down at the Buffalo dung that littered the area.

"Yeah, signs of Buffalo. We've seen that all month."

"Yes, but it's fresher now. There are herds close by. They're moving, and we can't be caught off guard. If a herd comes through, you'll need to get the wagons circled quickly. Have the horses inside... and pray." After saying this Hiram spurred his horse and moved back to the forward scouting position.

James moved back towards the wagon train. Frank and a younger hand rode slowly at the front of the wagons. James moved up to them and then turned his horse to ride beside them.

"Tell all the wagons to be prepared to circle. There are buffalo herds near. If a herd comes through, we'll need to get the horses inside the circle of wagons as quickly as possible."

Frank looked at James for a few seconds and then replied with a tone of sarcasm.

"Oh, yes sir, I'll do that right away...Boss."

James nodded and then rode back up to his point position.

After riding a while and not turning to notify the wagons, the young man asked Frank.

"Ain't ya going ta tell the wagons what the boss said?"

Frank chuckled.

"That damn Yankee don't know nothin. If a Buffalo herd is anywhere close, we would feel the ground trembling. I'll tell the wagons when I sense a herd close by. There's no need to get ever one worked up for nothin."

The young man smiled a little as if he thought Frank was wise and maybe even clever by not doing what his boss told him to do.

That evening the wagon train circled, with the horses placed inside.

As he usually did, James slept in his clothes and with his rifle and revolvers close by. The smell of the campfires slowly dying out was a comfort to him. He felt as if he was in the Army, yet he didn't have to go out and kill on the battlefield. But in his mind and soul, the struggle never ended. He slowly faded to sleep.

The ground rumbled. On a cold morning, James glanced to his left and then right as the he rode at gallop speed onto the battlefield. The sight of his comrades on both sides greeted him. The horses snorted, and flashes of their breath shot from nervous nostrils into streams of mist. They knew well death lay ahead as man and beast hurled themselves towards each other in a violent dance on the unfortunate field, where many would soon lay broken and dying.

James lowered his head as the bullets began to sing by. He placed the reins in his mouth and pulled his pistol out with his right hand as the mass of rebel cavalry charged towards them. The terrifying rebel yell rang out from the enemy just as he reached over to pull his saber out with his left hand. The ground trembled under him as a bugle rang out somewhere and men began to yell on both sides of the battlefield.

To his left, James noticed his corporal; he started to yell out. "Let's give them rebs bloody hel...." He was removed from his horse by a rebel bullet before he could finish.

James turned back to the line of enemy cavalrymen approaching rapidly. He braced himself again as if facing a strong wind. He raised his revolver.

"James!"

He aimed straight at a rebel cavalryman riding towards him.

"James, James, wake up!"

He pulled the hammer back on his revolver.

"James!!!"

He opened his eyes to see his revolver pointed straight at Amanda. She stood over him with a frightened look on her face. Oddly, the ground still trembled under him. He tried to wake up and understand what was happening.

"It's Buffalo James! What do we do?"

He grabbed his rifle and jumped up. Amanda seemed to move into his arms as if it were a natural reaction. He held one arm around her as chaos began to take over the circled wagons. Dust, snorts, and grunts of the massive beasts permeated everywhere around them. The horses reared up and moved about nervously. Then one of the large animals slammed into a wagon to their right, causing women to scream and men to yell out. Amanda tightened her grip around James' waist.

In the dim light of a few oil lanterns, he moved to a point at which two wagons intersected. He pushed Amanda to the back of him. She held her arms around his waist and placed her head on his back.

James pulled his Henry rifle up and aimed into the advancing buffalo. He fired two rounds in rapid succession. A giant buffalo slid down in front of him. Now the others moved around this dead one. He then pulled Amanda around and had her stay by the wagon wheel that lay on the other side of the dead beast.

He climbed to the seat of the closest wagon as more buffalo crashed into another side of the circled wagons, causing more screams of pain and terror. Now gunshots could be heard as other men attempted to move the herd around the wagons.

Several men jumped up on the seats of wagons with torches in their hands. From this light, James took careful aim. He fired one shot and then another. Each shot went straight to the head of a buffalo. Each buffalo that fell created a barrier to help protect the wagon train. Now several of the other men realized what James was doing and aimed their rifles to do the same thing. Slowly between the gunfire and the bodies of the buffalo blocking their advance, the chaos began to subside.

Until long after the dawn broke, the clean-up continued. Several dead were buried, and repairs were made. The wagon train finally moved for a few hours and then set up camp again, still stunned by the previous night's carnage.

As the campfires glowed, Amanda came to James and sat down beside him. He looked at her, but neither said anything. Finally, James felt he must speak.

"I'm not very good at explaining things, Amanda. But, I'm very sorry that I pointed a gun at you."

She seemed saddened at the memory and spoke softly.

"The war," She asked.

He was impressed that she understood this. He had thought that no one could understand it unless they'd been there. He nodded to confirm her question. Speaking to her made him feel better, so he ventured to continue.

"I don't know that I'm safe to be around for very long. I can't seem to get away from it. I think something happened inside me. I dream of the battles, and it's as if I miss them. I don't know what kind of man I am, that I would miss such a terrible thing."

He suddenly felt relieved as he had never told this to anyone. He looked at Amanda. She had compassion in her eyes.

"I think you're a good man, James. I don't know why you miss the battles. But I don't believe that it's the bad things you miss. Maybe you just miss being with your soldier friends."

When she said this and then smiled, James realized he was beginning to love this woman. She put her arm through his. He smiled and felt that Amanda may truly be able to help him heal.

As the days passed by, James began to grow closer to Amanda. After breakfast in the mornings, he would ride up behind the Tyler's wagon for a few moments. Amanda would be in the back and would sit where she could see him. They would look into each other's eyes for a brief period. Then he would smile, and this would cause her to smile. After that, James would ride on to the front of the wagon train. The rest of the day he would remember her smile.

The terrain became rough, and the wagons began to move with an urgency after stopping at Ft. Bridger. The weather would be changing, and they had to get through the rugged passes before the snow came.

"We can't slow down James. This is a crucial point of the journey." George sat his coffee cup down and picked his plate up in the predawn morning. He quickly ate the last of his food and after wiping his mouth with the back of his sleeve stood up.

"I understand, Sir. We'll keep everything moving."

"Good, good. You've done excellent work. We're on schedule, but we can't lose any time now."

They moved through the wagons to get the train started. The tension could be felt as the air grew cooler and progress slowed in the rougher terrain.

James found a small flower as he was about to get onto his horse. He picked it, and a few moments later he rode up close to the Tyler's wagon. Amanda sat at the back as if hoping to see him again. He handed the small flower to her. She smiled and put it to her nose, smelled it and smiled again with joy.

As the wagons slowly crept through the hills, James carefully watched for danger. Hiram scouted ahead and would periodically meet with James to relay the path and the situation of the trail ahead.

"This part of the pass is not very stable. Keep an eye out for slide areas. When you get to the ravine, there's a notch in a tree. Take the side with the notch."

"Alright, we'll do that." After James had said this, Hiram led his horse back towards the point of the trail. James watched him as he moved around a bend. He then rode back to the wagons. As they crept along the steep hill area, he methodically checked the path they would move along.

That evening, James sat at the Tyler's campsite. He had begun to stop by every day and visit. Amanda's parents now treated him as part of the family and Amanda showed her affection towards him openly by serving him something to drink and sitting by him while they spoke with her parents. The entire wagon train began to treat the two as a couple, and though James still had reservations, he had begun to hope for a normal life again.

"We're making good time, aren't we James?" Walter pulled a puff of smoke from his pipe after saying this.

"Yes Sir, we're making fair time. We should make it through the pass before the snow comes."

Amanda appeared to have finished her work around the campsite. She came to James and laid a cloth on the ground beside his feet. She then gracefully sat down, slightly at an angle where she could turn and look up to James, but also where she could see her father.

James glanced over to Walter, and he smiled as if giving James his blessing. James gazed down at Amanda's light brown hair. She then turned to him as if aware he admired her. She smiled, and his heart fluttered with joy inside his chest. The small fire crackled, and Walter pulled another draw of smoke from his pipe and blew it out gently.

They sat quietly as the fire slowly died down. Before James went to his bed site, Amanda held his hand behind the wagon, and they tried to look into each other's eyes. The darkness prevented this, so Amanda pulled him close to her in an embrace. He could feel her breasts pressed against his chest. The heat of their bodies mingled together. He could not resist kissing her now. He leaned down and in the darkness, she lifted her face to accept the kiss as she also felt it needed to occur at this instant. It was a long and passionate kiss. Finally, she released him and pulled gently away. Their hands and fingertips were the last things to part as she disappeared into the night around the Tyler's wagon.

50

In the twilight and slowly dying light of the campfires, James made his way to his bed spot. As he lay on the hard ground, he relived the kiss again and again. He was excited and yet he remained concerned. His joy eventually overruled his apprehension and James slowly fell asleep under the stars.

The next morning after his breakfast with the Tyler's, James searched the area his horse had been tied to. Finally, he spotted what he had hoped to find. A small blue flower peeked from around a large rock. He moved over and picked the flower, being gentle in an effort not to damage it.

As the wagons slowly began to move out, James carefully maneuvered his horse around to the Tyler's wagon. The terrain was hilly and often unstable. As James approached the back of the wagon, Amanda moved to where she could see him better. She smiled, and he returned a smile. Her mother glanced out at James and also smiled, as if also in agreement of James courting her daughter.

"What, another flower for me? You're so wonderful." She reached out and took the tiny flower. Then she gently put it close to her nose as if it were large enough to smell fragrant.

"A beautiful flower, for a beautiful woman," James said with a bit of discomfort. He had little experience in this form of courtship. Amanda seemed not to notice his lack of practice in complimenting a woman and again flashed another smile to him. He then moved his horse forward to take the lead position.

The wagons crept along through a rugged area as the day moved forward. The sun warmed the cool morning air and slowly ushered in the afternoon. James moved carefully on the increasingly arduous pass. Further behind him, he could hear the noises of the wagon train.

Hiram could be seen ahead and gazing down the hillside as he also moved his horse cautiously along the narrow roadway. After James glanced at him, his horse unexpectedly slipped as loose rocks gave way. James grabbed the saddle horn and held on as the horse struggled to regain its footing. The rocks slid down the steep ledge and created a small rock slide, just as his horse regained its balance and climbed back towards the safe ground.

James' heart beat swiftly in his chest as the near fall caused his blood to rush. He wiped the sweat from his brow. Hiram could be seen waving at James from farther ahead. James again glanced down the steep hill as the last few rocks finally came to a halt far below.

He turned towards the wagon train and moved his horse around the tight trail. In front of the slow-moving wagons, he spotted Frank Reid and another young trail hand by the name of Joe Jepson. James let out a quick, sharp whistle to get their attention. After noticing James, the two began making their way towards him. James then moved back around the ridge to make sure Hiram was still there. He spotted Hiram waiting for him and turned his horse to await Frank and Joe.

Soon the two came riding up to him. Frank, as usual, appeared unhappy at having been called over by James.

"Frank go back and tell everyone I want them out of their wagons. They need to lead their horses through this area, and everyone also needs to walk close to the hill-side of the trail."

After James had said this, Frank grunted but made no other verbal reply.

James stared at Frank a few seconds; his horse moved nervously underneath him. Joe glanced at Frank and then back to James.

"What are you waiting for Frank? Get back to the wagons and tell them what I said. I want everyone out of their wagons as soon as possible. Do you understand?"

Frank sneered a little but replied under his breath, "Yeah, I understand...Boss."

"Good, I need to go talk with Hiram. Do it right away."

James then turned his horse and rode carefully towards Hiram.

Frank watched James but made no effort to do as he said. Joe watched him as he pulled a plug of tobacco from his pocket and bit off a chew. As he worked it in his mouth, to get it softened up, Joe finally asked him the question that had been on his mind.

"Ain't ya gonna do as he says?"

Frank glanced over at the young man. He turned his head and spat. Then he answered Joe casually as if he was in no hurry.

"I'm sick and tired of that Yankee telling me what to do. He's still wet behind the ears, and he's trying to tell me what's safe and what's not. There ain't nothin ta worry about. He's just bossy. I'll tell ever one to get out of their wagons when I get good and ready to."

Joe didn't think this to be a very good idea, but Frank was older than him. And besides that, James had told Frank to tell the wagon train. He nodded his head and said nothing. Frank turned his horse and moved slowly back to the wagons with Joe following behind.

Meanwhile, James approached Hiram.

"Up yonder, around that next ridge, it's very dangerous. We'll need to hold up and spend the rest of the day building the trail back up. We may be working on this section of the trail for the next day or two in fact." Hiram's horse moved about and jostled him around a bit after he said this. James gazed ahead as if imagining the narrow and dangerous trail.

"I agree. I almost went down the side back there. This entire area is unstable. I sent Frank back to have everyone get out of the wagons right away and walk."

Hiram nodded, "Good, that's the safe thing. If you tell George, I'll go on up and try to spot any more dangerous areas. Hopefully, this is the worst one." Hiram then moved carefully ahead, and James turned his horse back towards the wagons.

As he moved cautiously around a bend, James could see the lead wagons. Immediately he noticed a man and his wife on the seat of the wagon, rather than leading it on foot as he'd told Frank to have them do. A flash of anger moved through his body. He spurred his horse lightly. He carefully made his way towards the wagon train to have everyone disembark and continue on foot.

Suddenly, a scream rang out from farther around the bend. Then a crashing sound and more screams came. James searched ahead of him as the terrifying sounds continued. Then he saw it; the wagon, horses and all came into view as they tumbled down the hillside. His heart felt as if it were being ripped from his chest. Deep inside, he somehow knew the first scream had come from Amanda.

The air around him became thick as he hurried his horse alongside the now stopped wagon train. The dust floated up from the area below where the wagon had crashed down. Women stood looking down at the wreck; they wept and held their children close to them. Men were already making their way down the side of the hill. James jumped from his horse and began almost to fall down the rugged terrain as he struggled to get to the wagon. The air was still charged, and dust infiltrated his nostrils. His body became hot, and he began to sweat as he arrived at the mangled wreckage. He could now see that it was, in fact, the Tyler's wagon.

As James came to the back of the wagon, a wrenching pain overtook his body. Amanda lay halfway out of the mangled wagon. Blood seeped from her body and added irregular splotches of dark color to her tattered dress. Her hair had come out from the carefully placed bun and now lay tangled around her head and face.

"No, no... Amanda!" James began to weep as he knelt down and gently moved her over into his arms. She was still alive, but he knew enough of death to know it wouldn't be for long.

"James, I... Jam... please, kiss me." She tried to raise her hand to his face. Her eyes were becoming dull as death began to take her.

A tear dropped onto her hair. He gently wiped it and moved her hair back a little. He could hear nothing now. There was no one and nothing else around him, only he and this dying woman, which he had come to love.

James gently moved his head down and pressed his lips to hers. They were warm and soft. He realized exactly what he was losing at this instant. He would not have another kiss such as this. It was her dying gift to him. He wanted to place it in his heart and keep it safe. Her final breath she gave to James in that kiss, and she then fell limp and was gone. He held her for a few moments as he tried to understand the sudden tragic loss.

As he slowly regained awareness of the activity around him, James began to feel rage building inside. His blood began to rush through his veins, hot and full of wrath. He gently lay Amanda down. He didn't want her pure soul exposed to this darkness. It was a familiar feeling, even though he'd not felt it for some time. It was the feeling he often had before charging onto a battlefield. It was the awareness that he was about to kill a man. He stood up and turned around. He searched for the man that his wrath was building for.

Higher up, on the trail of the wreckage, he spotted Frank. He was standing, watching the activity below, as men were busy moving around the wreckage, pulling the bodies of Amanda's parents from the battered wagon.

Frank saw James looking at him. Even from this distance, Frank expressed fear. He knew this was very much his fault. He appeared nervous and moved back away from the trail.

54

James began the climb back up to the wagons. As several more men moved down to the Tyler's wagon, James climbed steadily up towards the battlefield. He knew the powder in his pistol was dry. He prepared his weapons every day as any soldier would. He knew what was coming. The events began to unfold in his mind as he made it up to the wagon train.

Sweat trickled down the side of his head. He didn't bother to remove it. He proceeded in the direction Frank had moved. He passed by the women who still stood dazed and weeping. He moved swiftly by the halted wagons; the horse and oxen. He spotted Frank ahead, he was moving away from James but glanced back as if he wanted to delay the confrontation he knew was coming. James continued towards him.

Frank came to a wide area of the trail. He looked around as James came closer. Perhaps he was searching for something to help him.

"Frank!" James yelled out to keep Frank in this area. This would be a good battleground. It was open, and there were no wagons close by. Frank stopped and looked back.

"What? Why are you follerin me, Yankee?" Frank then backed up closer to a tree. He nervously touched the handle of his revolver and kept his eyes on James.

James didn't reply for several seconds. Everything was playing out in his mind now. This would be a quick battle. Frank was arrogant. He thought this way because he was older than James. This ill-conceived notion was why he felt himself better at everything.

But Frank had likely never shot a man in the face and then watched him fall dead from his horse. Frank had probably never run a young man through with a saber and struggled to remove the cold steel from his body, as the dead man clung to the blade that had ended his life. Frank would be slow and inexperienced. Frank most likely didn't know how to move and fire at the same time to throw another man's aim off. But Frank did get angry easily. And Frank did think he was better than James. Yes, this would be short battle.

"I told you to have everyone get out of their wagons. The Tyler's are dead because you didn't do as I told you to."

People began to move around the two men, being careful to stay at a distance. It was apparent to everyone that this could turn deadly as James moved closer and found the ground he was comfortable with. He then stood facing Frank. The distance was right, and everything was set. He knew what he would do. He thought of Amanda dying in his arms. This was the only thing that mattered now; to somehow give her justice.

"You're lyin Yankee! You said no such thing! You always had it in fer me, and now you're tryin ta blame this on me ta save yer own skin."

Frank moved to the side a little more. James stayed in his spot but moved his body to keep Frank where he faced him directly.

"What kind of man won't take responsibility for his actions?" As James asked this, everything began to slow down. It was as if he were charging onto the open battlefield. In his mind, he could see what was about to happen. He also knew how to make it happen. His thoughts worked efficiently as he went over every move. Frank glanced around at the people watching. His eyes were nervous but still arrogant.

"Why are you asking me such a thing? You're a liar! You said no such thing ta me. You're a damn liar, ya hear me?"

James waited a few seconds. He then said the words he knew would bring the fight. He said them slow and loud, so Frank had no misunderstanding.

"I think a man that won't take responsibility for his own actions is nothing but a, Yellow...Bellied...Coward!"

Everything became silent in James' mind. All he could hear was his breath. Frank's face grimaced. Anger came swiftly to his twisted features. James waited for him to make his move. Slowly, it seemed, Frank, reached for his pistol.

James could feel his heartbeat. Frank took hold of his pistol. Now James moved his hand. As if it were a part of his body, James had the pistol coming out of its holster and cocked as he took aim. Frank cocked his revolver; James stepped aside just as Frank pulled the trigger. Frank couldn't adjust his aim in time. His shot missed.

James fired and his aim was true. The bullet slammed into Frank's gut. He grunted, stepped back and doubled over from the impact. The familiar smell of gunpowder entered James' nostrils. It was bittersweet to his senses. It took him back to the battlefields and yet caused him to cringe from the death it was associated with.

A woman screamed. Several children began to cry. Everything came back to James' senses now. Frank held his gut where the bullet

56

had torn into his flesh. He staggered another step back and then dropped down on the ground in a sitting position. His face became contorted as the pain began to penetrate his mind and body.

"You....damn you bastard; you gut shot me!" Frank coughed and cringed after he said this. A woman pulled her children away from the death scene. Their cries became fainter. James slowly walked up to Frank.

Now Frank tried to lift his revolver to shoot James. He struggled with the pistol and the pain as James approached. James held his gun on Frank but continued towards the dying man.

"I'll kill yo,...Ahghhh, I'll kill...you.....damn Yankee!" Frank tried again to lift the revolver while holding his guts in with the other hand. James stepped up beside him and put his foot on Frank's wrist. Frank let go of the revolver and James pushed it away with his foot. He stared down at Frank. He didn't feel sorry for him. He'd seen this a thousand times. Frank glanced up at James. His eyes were filled with hate and pain.

Now, several men and George came walking up close. James glanced at them with his revolver still held in a ready position. Most of them had horror in their eyes as they looked down at Frank. It was obvious to James that they'd never seen a man killed this way. George must have seen such a thing before as he didn't appear to be as startled by the sight.

"This damn bastard gut shot me, George!" He coughed and grimaced again from the pain. "What are you gonna do about it, George? The damn Yankee, he killed me!"

George looked at James. "What's happened, James?"

"I told Frank to have everyone get out of their wagons and walk. If he'd done it when I told him to do it, the Tyler's would still be alive."

"He's a damn liar. He never said such a thing, George. Aghhh! You....aghh! You better do somthin George!" Frank now began to writhe from the pain in his belly.

Joe Jepson approached the group in a meek manner. He came close to George and spoke in a low and humble tone.

"Sir, I heard Mr. Taft tell Frank ta do as he said an have the folks get outta the wagons. I'm wishin I'd done it myself now. I heard him tell Frank ta do it and Frank didn't do it."

"Shut yer mouth, Joe..." Frank became angry and coughed again with pain and anger.

Joe replied with a defiant voice. "No Frank, I won't shut my mouth! The Tyler's wouldn't be dead now if'n you done as Mr. Taft said ta do!"

George took a deep breath. Another man from the wagon train approached.

"I saw Frank draw his gun first, George. He shot first too. I don't know how he missed James, but Frank drew his gun and shot first."

Aghhh, damn you! Damn all of you ta hell!" Frank coughed again and now seemed to be crying from the pain.

George turned to James. "Did you intend to gut shoot him?"

James looked at George. "Yeah, I hit where I aimed. I wanted him to live long enough for us to bury the Tyler's."

"Aghh, you...damn...you!" Frank spoke with renewed anger as he now knew James inflicted the shot intentionally.

George grimaced a little at this information. He seemed to consider the situation. Finally, he turned to the other men.

"It seems apparent to me that Mr. Taft instructed Mr. Reid to have the folks get out of their wagons and walk. Mr. Reid didn't do as his boss told him to do and the result has been three people dying."

George glanced around at the men as if to be sure he had all of their attention. He then continued. "Mr. Taft confronted Mr. Reid about this, and Mr. Reid pulled his gun on Mr. Taft. At that time, Mr. Taft felt compelled to protect himself and shot Mr. Reid. Is this what we have here? If it is, then we can commence with the sorrowful task of burying our dead, and move on."

Frank grunted. He squirmed around in pain and seemed to want to say something, but instead held his gut and grimaced at George's assessment.

The other men looked at each other and then began nodding their heads and commenting that this was, in fact, the situation. After this, James finally put the revolver back into its holster.

"George, ya can't... aghh,... You gots ta do somethin, ya can't let that Yankee get away with this... aouuugh. George, he gut shot me, George!"

George and James glanced down at Frank. George then glanced at James and seemed to be searching for remorse in his eyes for shooting Frank in the gut; thus, assuring him of a slow and painful death. He found no remorse in James' eyes. James had no emotion at all in his eyes. He was in the same place he'd been many times after a battle. He was numb to anything. George glanced back down to Frank.

"You've put yourself in the grave, Frank. I don't agree with the way Mr. Taft shot you, but knowin how he felt about Amanda, I can't say that I blame him for it. We'll commence burying the Tyler family. We'll bury you before we leave."

George turned and walked towards the wreckage. James stared at Frank for a few seconds, perhaps searching inside himself for some pity on the dying man. He found none and also turned and walked away to help with the burials.

After the Tyler's had been buried, James sat at the foot of Amanda's grave. He didn't want to leave her. He wanted to protect her from the elements. He felt as if the remainder of his tattered soul had been buried with this young woman. Several men patted him on the shoulder as they moved back to the wagon train.

George was the last to pass by him. He stopped. "I'm so sorry, James. They didn't deserve this. I guess I should have never hired that damn Frank Reid. I always knew he was trouble."

James said nothing. He continued to stare at Amanda's grave. He knew he would need to leave her, but he couldn't think about it right now. George patted his back and left towards the wagons. The breeze caressed James' face. He wished Amanda could feel it in her beautiful hair. For almost an hour, James sat at the foot of her grave. He finally stood up and began to move towards the wagons.

When he came to the wagon train, he could see several men throwing the last shovels of dirt onto Frank's grave. It seems he had indeed lived long enough for them to bury the Tyler's. All the others stood by their wagons. The trail had been repaired, and everyone appeared to be waiting and watching James while he said goodbye to Amanda. He looked at some of them, and they all had the same sadness in their eyes that he felt in his heart. He went to his horse, and George yelled out, "Alright, let's move out!"

Now everything became darker, and James felt nothing. As he rode and worked, his mind was a blank slate. He returned to the days of a soldier and simply did his duty day after day. He never envisioned the end of the trail or what he would do next week or next month. There was no future now, and the past was too dark and painful to venture into. He began to live by the minute; by the hour, but never ahead or behind the present. It was the only safe place for him now. But it would come at a price. He was aware of this gradual cost, but it no longer mattered. Nothing mattered now, and even existence became more of a habit than anything else.

Almost without realizing it, James and the wagon train finally pulled into Oregon City. George re-counted the pay for James and then looked into his face. He searched for the man inside, but James appeared far away. As he put his pay into a cloth bag, George tried to think of something to help the troubled young man.

"That's a substantial amount of money, James. You can do a lot with that amount of money. Oregon is full of opportunities right now. With a grubstake like that and your youth, there's no telling what you could accomplish." George again searched James' emotionless face.

Slowly and almost as if it tired him to do so, James spoke. "I suppose that's the truth of the matter, Mr. Harvey. I won't deny the opportunity to be here. But I don't see it, and I don't feel it. To a man like me, there seems to be little opportunity anywhere."

George felt his face fall a little as the sadness of James words rang true. How can a man get past so many things and see a future? How do you ride with death as your trail partner for so long and then find a way to change it to one of life and happiness? George nodded as he had nothing left to help James.

"So, what're ya gonna do now?"

James gazed down at the ground as several wagons passed behind him and George. After a few seconds of thought, he replied, "I don't know. Someone once told me that I needed to find a place where the thing that troubles me is the thing that's needed most." He paused. "I don't know if such a place exists. And if it does, I don't know where to start looking for it. But other than that, I got no plans."

George took a deep breath and felt a need to say something. There seemed to be nothing he could say that would be helpful, though. He patted James on the shoulder.

"I wish you luck James. I hope you find the place you're searching for."

James tried to smile but couldn't bring one up. He nodded and left.

Chapter Four: How to Disappear

Oregon City bustled with people and activity. James wanted to get away from the crowd. He rented a small room on the Northern edge of the city just as the snow began to fall. It was next door to a saloon, and he could hear the piano through the walls. The banging rhythms made him feel better. It reminded him of Nancy. He lay in the cold room staring at the ceiling. Finally, he fell asleep.

The winter days began to run together as James slowly fell into the same cycle he'd endured in Independence. He ate when he had to. He sat in the saloon and drank as the saloon girls swished about in their colorful skirts. The piano player banged out the chunky rhythms he'd become accustomed to. The day would end with James numb to everything. He would stagger next door as the establishment closed. He would sleep and awaken the next day feeling so bad he thought he would die. And yet, by the time the saloon opened back up, he would quickly be at a table with a beer or drink in hand.

Occasionally a saloon girl would make an effort to comfort him. Eventually, one decided she liked him, regardless of his overbearing gloominess.

"You sure are looking sad. I see you in here every day; you look so sad." The saloon girl stared at James as she said this. She sat across the table from him as his head slumped down.

He lifted his eyes enough to glance at the woman of twenty-five or twenty-six. Then as his vision cleared some, he got a better look. No, she was maybe twenty-two or twenty-three. But she'd had a hard life, he could tell. She'd likely been in the saloons for five years, or more, and they'd not been kind to her.

She appeared weary as she attempted to smile and then continued.

"Surely things can't be so bad as to look like you look ever day. You must have some money, though, because you're in here ever day and drinkin such as you're doin now. If I had some money, I sure wouldn't be looking so sad.

"What's your name, Mister?"

James continued to examine the young woman's face for several more seconds before answering her. Her hair had been put up early in the day, but now, close to midnight, it had been battered by the day's events and most likely numerous men attempting to handle the young maiden. Finally, as she stared blankly into his eyes, James tried a reply with slurred speech.

"Have you ever seen a man shot?"

She looked a bit startled by his question. But then she replied. "Yes, I've seen a man shot before. Is that what's bothering you? You saw a man shot?"

James took another drink. He didn't want to answer the woman. But he didn't want her to leave either.

"I've seen more men shot than I can count. I've shot more men than I can count; fathers, brothers, and sons, all dead. I shot 'em down and then looked 'em in the eyes as they died."

The young woman appeared frightened, but a little excited at the same time. She looked around nervously.

"You ain't wanted, are you, Mister?"

James continued to stare at her with glazed eyes, but gave no reply. The woman then seemed to realize he meant the war.

"Were you in the war? Is that why you look so sad?"

Again, James said nothing. The beer and long hours in the saloon had him wore down as much as she also appeared to be. The piano player attempted to play a lively tune, but from the sound of it, he was also exhausted.

The saloon girl moved closer to James now. She had compassion in her eyes.

"If you was a soldier then you was just doin your duty." She smiled, and he spotted several crooked teeth. This may have helped lead her to this life and this worn out saloon. She wasn't perfect. He wasn't perfect. They were both imperfect and only fit for this miserable existence, in a world of alcohol and imperfection.

"What's your name soldier?" She seemed more attracted to him now that she knew he had killed men.

"James."

"My name is Cora." She then moved even closer to James, indicating she felt as if she knew him better simply from the swapping of first names. She put her chin in her hand and stared wearily into James' eyes.

62

"James, hmm... I like it. Could I call you Jimmy, for short?"
"No!"

Even the name hurt his insides now. This woman was too much like Nancy. He took another drink as she sat back in her chair, seeming almost as if James had insulted her. He cared little. He did watch her, though. In an odd way, she took his mind off other things. The piano player finally gave up in his effort to entertain the few remaining patrons.

As the saloon became quiet, Cora leaned back to the rough table. James now examined her cleavage as her dress opened enough for him to get a view. Cora smiled as if this were a compliment.

"Alright... James, it seems there are things that could still make you happy, though." She then pressed her free arm against the side of her breast, and this opened up her dress even more. James glanced at the dress and then back into her eyes.

"Yeah, maybe, but sooner or later we would pay for that happiness."

Cora's mouth twisted a little. She revealed in this instant that she had experienced what he spoke of. It was the same thing he felt when he thought of Nancy. Perhaps Nancy was going through the same thing somewhere; love and the absence of love; a burdened heart and the desire to ease that burden, if only for a few short minutes. James took the last drink and sat the glass on the table in front of him.

Cora slowly relaxed her arm, and her dress closed some. "You don't give a girl much to work with, James. I'm just tryin to make you feel better."

"I know you are, Cora. And you have. It's just that..." He stopped and tried to find the right words. "Well, you remind me of someone back in Missouri. I had to leave there, and I guess I'll be leaving here as well... But you did make me feel better."

Cora smiled, and James even smiled, a little. She then stood up.

"I'll see you tomorrow then, James? I know you'll be here. I think you got too much heartache to go anywhere else." She smiled another weary smile and walked away as the saloon became almost empty.

James stood up, and half walked, half staggered out the door and onto his small cold room. He lay in his bed and recalled her smile. Then he told himself he wouldn't make another mistake. His heart was already torn apart. He fell asleep with a ragged blanket pulled up over him.

The cold days continued to blur together as the beer, and chunky piano rhythms numbed him more and more. His head lay on his arm, and the table as Cora again sat down beside him.

"Buy me another beer, James. I'll give you a kiss if you do." Cora pushed on his shoulder. Then she leaned on top of him and nuzzled his ear a little. She'd become much more affectionate lately as she realized James wouldn't take advantage of her.

Without moving his head, he reached into his pocket and pulled out a silver coin. He then slowly handed it to her as several rough men walked past and then sat down at the table next to his.

"You want another one, James?" Cora struggled up, using James' back to help her stand. James nodded his head indicating he did.

He was already past the point of clear vision. He didn't want another beer, but there was nothing else. The banging piano tune finally stopped. His head spun as he tried to think of anything to pull him from this existence. He knew well it would kill him if he didn't find a way out.

"He hasn't been seen for two years. I asked about him at that trading post, the one at the mouth of the river; you know that 'Blue River somthin or other... ever one just call's it Frenchie's. Anyways, Frenchie hadn't seen him for two seasons and figures he's dead or wandered on up North somewhere."

James perked up as the two men next to him talked about their lost friend. Somehow, the thought of heading into the wilderness, never to be seen again, interested him.

"Anyone check his place? He had a cabin up on the South side of the hill, by the river fork. I saw it when he was building it, but I ain't been up that ways since three or four seasons ago." The man then took a quick drink of his beer and wiped his mouth with his coat sleeve.

"Naww, I ain't been up there fer some time either. The trappin is better on the Northwestern side of the hills. He should'a moved closer to the coast least way's, I don't know why he ever picked that neck of the woods ta begin with."

Both men nodded and seemed to consider this as Cora walked up with two beers and sat down. She noticed James had sat up more and was listening to the two men.

Cora leaned close to James. She seemed to like getting closer to him every chance she could. "Do you know them, men?" She spoke with a whisper and then took a drink of her beer.

James looked at her with slightly glossed over eyes. "I don't know 'em, but I'm interested in what they're talking about." He then took a drink from his glass and slowly turned his head so he could hear the men better.

"Well, maybe he went on up towards the coast and found better trapping grounds."

The other man thought for a few seconds. "Yeah, I suppose, but I spect he's dead, though. If'n he wern't dead he would of sold some hides to Frenchie by now."

His companion nodded in agreement. The saloon was now almost empty. The two men spoke some more about trapping and after finishing another drink left. James sat quietly considering the things they spoke of.

"What are you thinking about, James?" Cora now moved close enough that he could smell the beer on her breath. He looked at her face as if searching for something.

"I'm thinking about what it would be like to disappear." He then finished the last drink in his glass and sat it on the table with a thud.

"Disappearing, what are you talking about?" She appeared concerned, or maybe the beer had increased her emotional state, he couldn't tell which it was. He studied the dance hall girl again. In his heart, he longed for companionship. But Nancy always stood at watch in the corner, and Amanda's last kiss remained forever on his lips. His tattered heart could hold no more emotion.

James looked down at his empty glass as the saloon's bartender began to sweep around the tables.

"I can't stay here, Cora. I'll be leaving as soon as the weather permits."

Cora stared at him. "But I don't want you to leave James..." She almost shed a tear, seeming completely unconcerned about the cleaning efforts of the bartender besides her.

James didn't respond to this. Instead, he stood up. "Good night Cora." He then left the saloon and walked back to his cold room.

Before sleeping, James wrote down the information he'd heard from the men. He glanced over the directions they'd described; his map now to go and disappear. It was his new goal. He put the paper in a safe place and lay down. Finally, he slept all night and awoke with a purpose.

As winter gave way to spring, James spent less and less time at the saloon. He moved with a renewed energy. He gathered information about trapping and fur trading. He found equipment and drew maps from other trapper's memory, regarding the area he sought.

Cora became more distant as she realized she couldn't keep him with her. The day he left Oregon City, James went to tell her bye. He found her at the table they most often sat together. The saloon had few patrons, and the piano player seemed to be trying a new tune, which sounded more classical than something heard in a place such as this.

"I'll be leaving now."

She glanced up at him. "You be careful then. Come back and see me, James."

James nodded, turned and left. He felt strangely distant and unconnected to anyone or anything at this moment. It seemed he should have kissed her, or something. But the thought of being close to anyone bothered him. He continued and pushed the thought out of his mind.

66

Chapter Five: The Bear Truth

As he rode, and Oregon City moved farther away, James felt as if he was waking from a nightmare. He wanted to disappear like the trapper he'd heard about in the saloon. This thought occupied his mind more and more the farther into the wild he moved. It was best he thought; to disappear. He wouldn't hurt anyone, anymore. He would be alone, and everyone else would be safe from him. He wouldn't need to shoot men such as Frank Reid.

He traveled north unimpeded until reaching the Columbia River. Along the river, he moved northwest as he followed the vague description from the two men in the saloon.

A week after leaving Oregon City, James came to a fork in the river and a small trading village nestled in the dense woods. Smoke floated gently from the trading post's crude rock chimney. The smell of meat in the air indicated the fire was most likely for smoking meats, rather than warmth.

As he rode into the village, several Native American women sat outside a small cabin, cooking something in a large pot. They glanced up at James and then went back to stirring the contents.

A dog barked incessantly from somewhere behind one of the frontier cabins. James moved up to the front of the trading post and dismounted.

After securing his horse, he walked into the log building and was greeted by a smoky interior. The smell of meats being wood smoked and spices met his sense of smell. Once his eyes had adjusted to the dim light, he could see a variety of hunting and trap supplies sitting about the building.

A man moved around behind the counter and appeared to be tending a smoke box built onto the back of the store. He glanced out a back door and then seemed to notice the customer. He greeted James with a strong French accent.

"Hello, Monsieur. How may I help you?"

The man was not very large, perhaps five and a half feet tall. He had dark hair, almost black. A scruffy beard and mustache, and was dressed in a mix of frontier style trousers along with a well-worn gentleman's coat, over a shirt and suspenders.

"Are you 'Frenchie'?"

The small man appeared slightly irritated.

"Well, I suppose so. That is what some people call me, but my name is Garan."

James paid little attention as his concern was to confirm being at the right trading post. He pulled out a list of supplies he would require.

"I'll need as many of these things as you can supply me with."

Frenchie eyed James with suspicion.

"Just so you know, I don't give credit, Monsieur," he then glanced down nervously at the revolver attached to James' waist.

"Will you do some trading for a horse and tack?"

When James asked this, Frenchie perked up.

"Well, perhaps I can. Is it a fresh horse? I have no use for a broken-down animal."

"He's fresh and healthy."

Now Frenchie seemed to have trouble standing still. He rubbed his chin nervously as his eyes filled with interest.

"He, so it's a male? Yes, let's take a look at this horse you speak of." Frenchie then moved with purpose from behind the counter.

James followed him out the door. Frenchie's eyes widened as he looked upon the horse tied to a small post. He ran his hand along the neck and couldn't conceal the excitement he felt at possibly trading for such a valuable animal.

"So, what is it you want for this horse, just the items on that list?"

"The items on the list and twenty dollars... silver."

This statement from James appeared to frighten the merchant a little. He grimaced a bit and again seemed nervous.

"Well, uhm, I'll need to take a look at that list."

James again pulled the list from his pocket and handed it to the man.

Frenchie unfolded the paper and glanced over the items as he again rubbed the whiskers on his chin.

"I don't know if I have all of these things. And twenty silver dollars is a lot of money," his French accent seemed to grow stronger while discussing money.

James followed him back into the trading post. After much searching for the listed items and haggling over prices, the eventual

68

deal amounted to most of the items James needed and twelve silver dollars.

Packing all the gear onto a frame, he rigged the supplies so they would fit securely on his back. Before leaving the small trading village, he stopped and petted his horse on the neck for the last time.

He vaguely recalled several animals that he had rather naively named while in the Army. He'd become very fond of these horses. Then the memories of them being shot out from under him on the battlefield came rushing back. He stopped naming his horses after a few painful losses.

James hiked out of the village as the evening began to set. The noisy dog again barked from somewhere unseen. Dampness filled the air as he made his way alongside the river. He traveled northwest while completely engulfed by wilderness.

On the sixth day, he came to another large fork in the river, just as the men stated in the saloon at Oregon City. He moved southwest up a sloping hill. As he came to the top, a level area presented itself and nestled close to the hill; on the far side was a small cabin. James crossed the flat area and approached the cabin cautiously. He noticed a canoe, which was upside down beside the little dwelling.

The door was open. James sat his pack on the ground and then pulled the revolver from its holster as he advanced to the door and cautiously peeked inside.

Crude furniture was strewn about, and it appeared the small building had been open through one winter, at least. He stepped inside and examined the dimly lit interior.

A small fireplace of rock and clay sat on the right side. A makeshift bed sat on the other end of the cabin. A table and chair along with various cookery items lay scattered on the floor in disarray. It appeared a fight had occurred, or possibly, the owner had an accident while away and was not able to return. Perhaps other trappers had found the abandoned cabin and rummaged through it, taking items they wanted or needed. Either way, he wondered about the owner's whereabouts. As he backed out, James closed the door.

He decided to make camp on the level area and wait a while before assuming possession of the structure. He also didn't like the idea of being inside the cabin while still unsure of what had happened to the original owner.

Soon a fire gave slight comfort and allowed him to heat some food. He slept under the stars that night and rose early the next morning to begin his work. He moved back along the river setting traps, and after this, he started building a lean-to.

As the days moved slowly by, James watched the empty cabin. Day after day, for a month he did nothing other than watch vacant dwelling. Slowly he started to move into it. He packed the items inside and placed them in a corner, just in case the owner returned. He then patched and mended the dwelling in preparation for the cold winter months.

Although the trapping was likely not as good here as other places, James eventually had enough pelts to merit a trip back to the trading post. He found a safe place to hide his valuables. Then he loaded the canoe and made his way along the river towards the trading post.

"Well, I see you have managed to remain alive, Monsieur." Frenchie then smiled as James moved closer to the counter. Several other trappers were sorting through recently purchased goods as they prepared to pack them up and head back to the wilderness. The small village was much more active now than when he had first arrived.

"Yes, I've managed to stay alive." James then sat a large bundle of pelts on the floor.

"I won't be paying as much for those summer pelts. I just wish for you to know this right now, Monsieur."

James said nothing; he merely nodded and began to untie the furs.

After negotiations, James purchased some needed goods and began the trip back to his campsite. He felt numb. His time alone had not healed him. As he sat at his small fire by the river, he considered his situation. He seemed to be not dead, but not alive either. The next morning, he rose early and continued to his isolated home.

Several weeks after his trip to the trading village, James moved into the cabin completely. He felt satisfied the original owner would not return, and if he should, James had established that he'd waited outside for a long duration before moving in. His campsite and lean-to would at least indicate he had not overtaken the cabin immediately upon finding it.

As the summer moved closer to fall, James continued to become withdrawn. He thought of nothing but what he would do that day. Time and his senses blurred together, and though he wasn't sad, he also wasn't happy. His beard grew full and the reflection he noticed in the water from time to time, appeared to be someone he didn't know.

Summer gradually turned to fall, and James prepared for winter. He worked in solitude and thought of nothing other than his current tasks. The weather continued to grow colder as he sought out and established favorable trapping locations for winter.

With firewood cut and stocks laid up, James awoke one morning to find a blanket of snow all around. Time had become almost non-existent, but now it nearly stopped.

With traps set, he made his rounds to check them. He cleaned the pelts and prepared them for transport and sale. Often, he found himself staring into the fireplace. His mind occasionally ventured back to a battlefield or a woman from his past. The winter days lingered, and he lost all track of the month it happened to be, or if a new year had even come around.

Slowly, the cold hand of winter began to lose its grip. The snow began melting away and warmer days ushered in spring. James also felt something inside himself. He had been alone for many months, and he felt lonely, very lonely.

As he stood in the front of the cabin on a sunlit evening, he examined a tiny flower. Snow was still all around on the ground. He stared down at the flower and wondered what he should do. There seemed to be no solution for him. He bent down and picked the tiny blossom, then held it to his eyes. It was beautiful. And yet he felt unfit to understand beauty. The sun drifted over the ridge and the flower no longer glittered in the sunlight. He went back to the cabin.

Two days later James sat at the small table, facing the crude door of the cabin. He pulled meat from a cooked rabbit and ate it, bit by bit. Unexpectedly, he heard growling outside.

James stopped eating. Staring at the entryway, he slowly wiped his hands on a piece of cloth. The shadow of a large animal became visible through thin cracks, in and around the door. More growling was heard as the beast sniffed the air. James watched as he now realized a enormous bear, most likely a male Grizzly was outside the cabin door.

As he listened to the bear and watched the movements outside the doorway, he began to understand what had happened to the previous owner of the cabin. He slowly reached into his coat and pulled the two revolvers from their holsters. As he sat the pistols on the table, James recalled the furniture scattered about and the mess the cabin was when he first arrived.

The huge beast began to push on the door in a testing manner. Again, and again, it growled and sniffed the fragrance of the cooked rabbit. This animal must have recently awoken from hibernation and was ravenous now. It must have broken in, killed and then drug the previous owner away at some point in the past. James' heart began to race, and he felt his blood grow hot as the grizzly pushed on the door with increased resolve. The door would break open at any second, but still, James didn't pick up the pistols.

Now, just before a life and death battle with this massive creature, James began to think with more clarity than he had for a long time. His mind became sharper as each second ticked by and the bear pushed harder on the flimsy door. James wanted this fight; he had yearned for something such as this. He even wanted to give the bear a chance to kill him. It was like a dream, and he was playing each move out in his mind, just before the struggle occurred. The bear would break through the door and charge him. He would have only a split second to take up the pistols on the table and fight back.

Then, it happened, just as he'd thought. The huge bear broke through the door. He charged, only slowed by the effort needed to get through the doorway. In that brief pause, James grabbed the pistols. He only had time to fire two rounds before falling to the side in order to escape the massive beast. The bear was hit, but the two shots merely wounded him.

James crawled quickly and fired another round at the side of the bear as it turned. Again, the lead penetrated the body of the bear, but this was a huge animal, and it was now mad and wounded.

James scrambled for some form of safety as the bear attacked him. He rolled, and the impact of its claws landed on the floor only inches from his body. He fired two more rounds into the bear's body while struggling to get away. The beast turned up in pain, its hind legs pushed against James' lower body. James yelled out in agony. The chaos in the small building blinded both man and beast to anything beyond this life and death battle.

Working to free his legs and find a place to hide, James crawled behind the overturned table. He held tightly to his two pistols, realizing they would be his only hope. The bear now pushed on the table with James behind it. He lifted the two pistols to fire, but the table moved against the wall, and this pressed James tightly, causing him pain and difficulty breathing. He almost lost the revolvers as the bear moved into a position over the table to bite James' face. He could smell the bear's breath and knew this was the instant of death for either him or the animal.

With a tremendous effort, James turned both pistols to aim as best he could. He could only see the gun in his left hand as the right one lay in his hand on the floor behind the table. He aimed them both towards the bears head to put an immediate end to the animal's life. They were cocked and ready. If he missed, it would be death for him. With his eyesight blurring and the bear able attack, he fired both pistols.

One shot hit the bear's neck, while the pistol in his left hand was aimed true and the bullet penetrated the skull of the grizzly. It fell instantly, and the weight again caused pain for James. He pushed and struggled, finally freeing himself. Then, his entire body began to shake. It was a familiar thing, as he often shook and trembled after a battle.

For what seemed a long time he sat staring at the dead bear. He eventually stopped shaking, but still held the pistols in his hands as his mind continued in a mild state of shock. And then... he felt all alone again.

A strange sensation took hold of him. It was the realization of those few moments of the battle being the only time he wasn't lonely. Then, he killed this animal, the thing that had eased his loneliness; it became overwhelming.

James began to weep. He cried like a person who was losing his mind. He knew there was no one to see him in this state. He knelt down to the dead bear and cried for it and himself. What was he doing here? How had his life come to this? Even when he traveled far from everything, he longed for battle and then hated the death that it cost.

He cried long and hard as the sun began to set. He mourned the death of this magnificent beast, which only wanted something to eat. It was as if he was mourning his own death. He sensed that he might be losing his mind, but it didn't matter to him now. As night took over and darkness accompanied his misery, James pulled a blanket over himself and fell asleep from sheer exhaustion.

The air was cold, and he dreamt of war. Many nights he had slept on the cold hard ground after a fierce battle. The sun was creeping over the tree tops as he awoke the following morning. He sat up, and his body protested in pain. The fight with the bear had created soreness in every muscle, but he had no broken bones and felt glad about this.

As he again sat staring at the dead bear, which took up most of the room in the small cabin, he realized he couldn't continue in this lonely and desperate situation. He would go mad eventually. He must find another way to live. Though how or where that existence might be, he didn't know.

James spent the day packing. The following morning, he loaded his pelts and gear into the canoe. Returning to look over the place one last time, James felt some relief that he would be departing from the desolate life it represented. He then went back to the river and began the long trip to the trading village.

Chapter Six: Warmth of a Dying Fire

Several days after leaving the cabin, James wearily arrived at the now, very busy trading village. A few scruffy dogs barked, and trappers on horses moved to and fro along the muddy paths. Natives and white people all interacted busily with their affairs. He walked past the small, crude cabins and on to the trading post at the end of the muddy lane.

Frenchie stood outside the building, negotiating with trappers. Several young men were moving pelts and appeared to be working for the French businessman. James walked up as a small group of Native Americans approached from another path.

Quite unexpectedly, James noticed a beautiful native woman in her late teens, or possibly even twenty years old. This vision brought the realization that it had been a long time since he'd seen a beautiful lady. He watched her as the group moved closer to the trading post. Then, she noticed he was looking at her, so he turned away, slightly embarrassed.

Soon it was his turn to negotiate with Frenchie. A price was agreed upon, and the young men took the pelts that James had accumulated over the winter. Frenchie paid him, and James now looked around for the young native woman. She wasn't with the others she'd arrived with so he made his way into the trading post.

As he came inside and moved out of the doorway, James spotted the woman. She stood admiring strands of colored beads hanging from a wooden hook on the wall. He moved about as if searching for something, but was maneuvering to get a better view of this alluring woman. He was somehow captivated by her, and though he realized this, he told himself that he just wanted to get a better look at her.

She handled the beads with a fond admiration, and when he could see her face, he realized her eyes were bright and excited merely by the sight and feel of the colorful necklaces. From an obscure corner of the building, he continued to observe her.

A native man that appeared to be the father walked up to the woman. He spoke with her and she expressed disappointment. James felt that the man must have told her she couldn't buy the beads. She examined them with desire once more before turning away.

The young woman then gazed around the store, and James instantly knew in his heart that she was searching for him. He felt a jolt of excitement inside his chest, and it startled him. He'd not felt anything like this for so long that he remained transfixed by her from the darkened corner.

She then walked outside with the man he thought to be her father. After several other native men had paid for their items, James knew there was something he must do.

Quickly moving over to the beads, he pulled three strands from the wall. He went to the counter where a native woman, clothed in a mix of white and indigenous fashions stood. James suspected this to be Frenchie's wife. He paid for the beads and then went outside where he spotted the small group of natives leaving on the same trail they had arrived on.

James' heart beat rapidly in his chest as he approached the little band of natives. Before any of them realized a white man was among them, he'd walked up behind the young woman and tapped her on the shoulder. She turned and became a little startled as she looked at him. The others were also surprised and rapidly spoke amongst themselves.

James held the beads up to the young woman and made a gesture indicating he wanted her to have them. The talking subsided, and she smiled slightly, then turned to the man that James thought was her father. James also looked at the man and then said in a calm voice, "I would like for her to have these."

For a few seconds, nothing happened other than glances back and forth. Then the young woman asked her father something in their language. The man turned to James and asked in English.

"This is a gift? We don't wish to buy this."

"Yes, these are a gift, from me to her. I want to give them to her. Please allow her to take them as a gift."

The young woman watched her father and then briefly looked into James' eyes. He could see she was very concerned about her father's decision.

Finally, her father spoke.

"She may have them." He then nodded to her as if telling her she was allowed to take them.

Now the young woman's eyes lit up as she slowly reached up to take the beads. James smiled, and she smiled as he gave them to her. He then turned and slowly walked back towards the trading post.

Before he reached the small store, the woman's father came up behind him and tapped his arm. James turned and saw the man along with another older man.

"My daughter... she wishes to thank you for the gift."

James smiled slightly and replied, "She's very welcome."

The man continued as if a little uneasy.

"She and, we, would like for you to eat a meal with us if you wish."

James glanced back at the young woman; she clasped the beads in her hands, and she watched James in anticipation.

"I would be honored."

Her father appeared to understand this reply and smiled.

"We are camped along this trail. Please come after the sun reaches mid sky. We will have the meal prepared."

James nodded and then noticed the young woman smile as if she had hoped for some confirmation that he would have a meal with them.

At the trading post, James felt as if life was creeping back into his soul. He sold the canoe and purchased items and necessities to clean up with before finding a separate branch of the river to wash up. He trimmed his bushy beard and pulled a clean shirt and buckskin pants from his pack; ever watching the sun as it slowly rose higher.

He packed everything onto a rack that he could carry on his back and made his way down the path. James moved with a new sense of purpose as the sun crossed the mid-day sky.

Soon he came to a small encampment on the right. There he spotted the young native woman by a campfire. She stopped and looked at James as if she had been watching for him. They smiled slightly to each other and then she went back to work preparing the meal.

He moved cautiously into the camp, and the woman's father came out of a crude, tent type of structure to greet him.

"We are glad you have come. Everything is almost ready. Please sit and talk with me before we eat."

The man smiled just a little and James also smiled as he replied, "I'm very honored by the invitation. Thank you."

The two sat crossed legged around a fire as the young woman, and several other older women finished details for the meal.

James tried to be discreet, but he couldn't help watching the girl move about the campsite. He noticed she wore the beads and glanced at him, as if also unable to not do so every few moments.

Her father studied James and his daughter. He finally spoke as the women began bringing dishes of food to the men.

"My name is Konukoni; I am Chief of the Aqukolo. What you see here is all that remains of our once many and proud tribe."

James gazed around the camp and thought there was maybe thirty-five people altogether. He was a little saddened by this revelation. He turned to Chief Konukoni.

"My name is James Taft. I'm alone. I have no home or tribe. I'm very happy to meet you and share this meal with you and your people."

The chief nodded, and they ate in silence. The young woman sat on the opposite side of the men. She ate with the other women, and as she did so, she continued to watch James. Then, when the meal was over, Chief Konukoni again spoke.

"My father sent me to one of the white man's 'missionary church' when I was a young man. He said the white man would soon be many and the tribe should have someone that can speak the language. So, I learned the white man language from these men and then came back to my people.

"In that time, we were many, and we had land to hunt and fish. I married, and we had children. My daughter, Sachisomi, is the last of this family." He pointed to the young woman James had given the beads to."

James now realized that even though Sachisomi was very beautiful, she also had a sadness about her. He then looked around the campsite. All of the people had this expression of sorrow. It appeared to be the same as he felt. This fragment of a once proud tribe was in some odd way the same as him. The chief continued, and everything became clearer as he spoke to James.

"We were warriors. We would let no other tribes insult or push us. We went to war with a neighboring tribe. Many killed. Then the tribe we were at war with made an alliance with another tribe. Their agreement was to kill all of the Aqukolo and divide our land between them.

"On a cold morning, the two tribes attacked us. It was a surprise, and many of our people lost their lives. My father was the chief at that time, and he sent me and some remnants away. Our enemies pursued us for many days and nights; more died.

"Finally, those who followed us gave up. We have never stopped moving from that time. We have no home and no land. I worry that our time as a people is coming to an end."

He turned to James as the night overtook the day. With the flickering campfire reflecting his tired and weather worn face, the chief told James, "you may stay here tonight if you wish, James Taft. We are alike in that we have no home. We offer you a place to rest, it's all we can do."

James felt as if he had known this man for years. He wasted no time answering him. "Thank you, sir. I accept your kind offer."

The following morning James woke up to a chill in the air and light haze floating across the campsite. Sachisomi was putting wood on a campfire that had almost died out overnight. She stirred it a little and then looked over to James. When she saw he was awake and watching her, she smiled. Then her hand reached up to the strands of beads that were hanging down and held them close to her chest in a protective manner as she peered back into the fire she was attempting to revive.

As the day went by, James found it difficult to leave. None of the tribe acted as if he should go. Sachisomi brought him food and water.

He began to notice there were few young men in the tribe. The ones that were around his age were with a woman and already married. There were far greater older people than young.

When evening came they again had a group meal, and afterward, the women left the campfire, and the tribe leaders gathered around James.

"Our Shaman, Tonkiwatu, says you are a warrior, James Taft." Sachisomi's father pointed to a timeworn man that sat beside him.

The other men watched James carefully as if trying to read his facial expressions rather than understanding the white man's language. He looked around at all of them. Then he replied, "Yes, I was a horse soldier during a war between the white men. We fought each other for several years. I killed many. I still carry these battles inside me, and it seems I'll never escape them."

Chief Konukoni then translated this to the other men. They nodded and spoke with each other in a quiet and respectful tone. Then Tonkiwatu turned to the Chief and spoke for several minutes, almost in a whisper. After this, the Chief starred at James almost as if shocked. He finally spoke again.

"Tonkiwatu had a dream of you last night, James Taft. You crawled from a valley on your hands and knees. Along the way, you fought bison, bear, and men. Then, when you were very far from here, you climbed a mountain and looked down. Many people below struggled for life, and you saw the skies open during that time."

James was surprised by the Chief's vision as he had in fact recently fought a bear. Then he recalled the buffalo that had overrun the wagon camp on the way to Oregon. He looked at the old medicine man that appeared to be almost blind. Then he asked the chief.

"What does the dream mean?"

Konukoni said nothing for several seconds. Then he spoke slowly.

"It is the dream of a Chief. We don't know for certain what it means. In such a dream, the sky only opens for one who is destined to be a Chief. I think it is fate that brought you here, James Taft, would you stay with us a while? We will be moving tomorrow, but I would like for you to come with us if you have no place you wish to return to."

He paused for a few seconds and then added.

"I believe, Sachisomi would also like for you to stay."

For the first time in a long time, James felt he was where he needed to be. He thought for a few seconds and then spoke the decision he had already made right after the Chief asked him.

"I would like that very much."

Chief Konukoni smiled, very slightly, and then translated this to the others. They also smiled and spoke as if pleased about this turn of events.

The next day everyone began to pack up. Before noon the entire group was on the move. They continued for a week to travel west, alongside the river. The movement was slow and arduous. After walking all day, the tribe would stop to camp.

There was little talk during the evening meals, but James and Sachisomi communicated by gazing into each other's eyes from across the campfire. They would smile at each other as she would bring him his food and water. He knew he was falling in love with her, but also sensed this love was saving his life.

It had not been that long since he'd faced the lonely nights in the mountains. It had not been long since he'd faced a lonely death from the jaws of a bear. Somehow, he knew in his heart she was saving his life with the smiles and offerings of her love to him. He wouldn't turn this love away. He would embrace it and live.

After around ten days of travel, the group stopped to replenish their stores. The women fished, and the men hunted. James shot a large deer, and the tribe feasted. At this meal, Chief Konukoni again spoke to James.

"Sachisomi's mother and younger brother were swept away during a treacherous river crossing. She was young, but still, has nightmares about it. We never found their bodies."

James watched this honorable man speak of the sad experience as if it were only one of many such losses. His face expressed nothing in the flickering firelight.

"I think this tribe may not be for much longer. We have lost so many and cannot regain a hold of life. I just wish for Sachisomi to have some happiness in this life, even if it's only a small amount. She deserves this, James Taft. We have had much sadness. I wish so much for something good in my daughter's life."

He turned to James and smiled, though again, ever so slightly that it was almost unnoticeable.

Turning, and staring into the campfire James replied, "I wish for the same thing. I've begun to feel that her happiness would also mean mine."

The following morning the group was moving again, always to the West. James became aware that there was little discussion amongst the tribe unless something needed to be said. As the days went by it became known that everyone expected he and Sachisomi to become a couple. On a rainy day when there was little opportunity to move, James spoke with her father.

"Sir, I wish to marry Sachisomi. I realize it's soon, but I want you to know my intentions."

Chief Konukoni thought of what James had said. Then after a few seconds of silence, he spoke.

"I have known of your intentions for some time now. But to tell me of this is an honorable thing. My daughter also wishes for this. She has said of her love for you. I have only hoped she would marry an honorable man and a warrior, as her father was and my fathers were."

He stared into the fire that struggled to remain lit under the light rain. He then went on.

"You must be adopted into the tribe before you can marry Sachisomi. I will talk with the elders. Perhaps, when we camp for the winter this may be done."

The next morning Sachisomi brought James his morning meal. She smiled and knelt down in front of him. Then she gently took his hand and placed it palm first on her chest, just above her heart. She said something that James understood as meaning she was happy. Then she put his hand on her warm cheek for a second. After this, she stood up and left quickly. He felt as if she had just pulled him from a cold grave. He was frightened about loving her but knew this was where he needed to be; she was who he needed in his life.

The tribe continued to move alongside a river. Chief Konukoni told James they were going to the ocean. He explained that the Shaman Tonkiwatu had been to the ocean as a very young man and told the elders this is where they would find a place to call their own. As they moved, James and Sachisomi longed for the day they could wed.

Time passed slowly. Some days the group could only travel two miles, and other days they would travel five, ten, or more if the terrain allowed it. As winter came closer, they began to search for a satisfactory place to camp through the cold months. James was thrilled the day Chief Konukoni called him over to ask for his opinion.

"What do you think of this place, James? We are close to the river but not too close. The game appears abundant and the small hill there will shield us from the harshness of the North winds."

James studied the area. It was a beautiful little pocket field that suited the prospect of a winter camp well.

"Yes, I think that will be good; plenty of room, but not out in the open. I like this place."

Chief Konukoni smiled more than James had ever seen him do so before. He then nodded and replied, "Good."

Chapter Seven: Journey of Redemption

The tribe went to work building huts and cabins for winter quarters. James built a small log cabin in preparation for him and his bride to be. It was decided that the Shaman, Tonkiwatu would adopt James. By doing so, the gained tribe status would help make him more acceptable in the marriage of Sachisomi.

Though the tribe seemed to realize they were on the verge of dying as a people, there was still the situation that as Chief Konukoni's son-in-law, James would become chief should anything happen to Konukoni.

They also knew the tribe would need every possible advantage in recovering as a people; James was a warrior and was also considered a man of honor. At this point in the tribe's existence, any man with these qualifications as well as being adopted into the Aqukolo tribe was considered a good thing.

After several weeks of hard work preparing for the winter, the day came for the official adoption ceremony. James would endure the difficult tasks of becoming an apprentice Shaman. James' official training as a Shaman would be "when possible," and would be expected to learn from Tonkiwatu during any occasion that he could.

A small ceremonial hut was prepared for the rituals that James would endure to become an apprentice Shaman or 'medicine man' as James called it. While this occurred, the rather simple process of Tonkiwatu adopting James took place. In front of the tribe and dressed as an Aqukolo warrior, James was accepted into the tribe. As part of the adoption, Tonkiwatu was allowed to give James an Aqukolo name.

"What is the name you've chosen for our new brother." The chief asked the Shaman, as the ceremony progressed on a chilly, cloudy day. The old Aqukolo man considered this for a few seconds.

"Kalakone," he replied.

Chief Konukoni appeared slightly surprised. He turned to James.

"Your Aqukolo name will be Kalakone; a warrior's name. It roughly translates as 'The Eagle.' The name carries with it much respect, and in this case, I believe hope."

James understood the meaning of this. He knew well the tribe still endeavored to recover and return to a thriving people. Marrying Sachisomi carried responsibilities and he was ready for them.

"I understand, Chief. I'll not let you or these people down. I will be an honorable member of your family and this tribe."

Konukoni smiled his usual barely visible smile. He then translated James' words to the others, and they all spoke softly amongst themselves with gladness in their conversations.

The following morning James began the much more rigorous rituals involved with becoming a Shaman apprentice. His soon to be father-in-law spoke with him as women danced slowly around them. They tapped two sticks together while chanting in rhythm. The misty dawn evoked an awareness that James' life was about to change.

"This will be tough James. I know you've had many struggles in your life, but this, however, will be one within you, as well as outside you. To be a Shaman, you must become aware of those things inside and all around you. If you falter, it will mean failure."

James nodded in confirmation. As he did so, Sachisomi danced slowly in front of him, chanting and tapping her two sticks together. She glanced into his eyes, and he could see her concern. He tried to express confidence, and yet the unknown worried him.

The hut had smoke floating inside as James almost crawled through the small entryway. As he sat down and Tonkiwatu sat down across from him, the sounds of the women were heard, but were less audible as they continued dancing and chanting outside the hut. Konukoni came in and also got comfortable.

James was instructed to close his eyes. Tonkiwatu began to moan, or hum, James wasn't sure which it was.

For a half hour, they sat in the hot, humid hut. Smoke came from burning a type of dried plant. James became light headed and felt relaxed as Tonkiwatu continued to hum.

Then Tonkiwatu stopped humming. James opened his eyes.

"Eat these and drink this." Chief Konukoni said as he handed James what appeared to be dried mushrooms and a cup with some liquid in it.

James ate the mushrooms, and the taste was horrible. He tried to wash them down with the drink, but it was as bad as the mushrooms. He coughed but managed to refrain from vomiting it all back out.

84

"You will see things and hear things. You must reveal these to us."

As Konukoni said this, James began to feel strange. The room seemed to spin, and his vision became blurred. The chanting of the women sounded beautiful and frightening at the same time.

James found himself floating into a different world. As he saw this world, he spoke the sights and expressed the sounds to Chief Konukoni who then translated them to Tonkiwatu. But James barely noticed as his mind was scarcely able to focus on the real world.

"I'm standing on a mountain top. Below I see my mother and my father. Now I see my brother, his wife and my nephew and niece. A black bird flies from the sky and takes them away. Ahh, I'm trying to catch the bird, I jump from the mountain and fall to the ground. I'm dead... wait, no I'm not dead, but my body is broken. I can't walk."

James felt as if he were severely injured. His body ached, and his breathing became laborious. Konukoni said, "Go on. What else do you see?"

"Now, I see a general with many medals on his uniform. He's asking me why I'm on the ground. I tell him my body is broke. He says, 'It's not your body that's broken, it's your heart.' He tells me to stand. I don't think I can, but I try. I'm standing. I can walk."

James felt himself fading out. How much time passed he didn't know. Tonkiwatu handed him more mushrooms and more drink. He took them, and this time they went down his throat easily. He was sweating. He no longer could hear the sounds of the women. The smoky hut seemed to be of another world, and he could barely remember who he was.

"What do you see?" Konukoni asked.

"I'm riding a white horse into battle. But the horse is on top of the water. I see the enemy; they're not men but dogs and wolves. The enemy is charging. I pull my sword out, but it's strange, not like a sword I've seen before. The dogs are attacking all around me. I cut them down without mercy. I then draw my pistol and shoot more of them. They begin to disappear."

Again James faded out. After some time, he woke. Tonkiwatu again handed him mushrooms and the strange drink. He again heard the women chanting outside.

"What do you see?" Konukoni asked.

"I'm, somewhere... it's strange, and I've not seen anything like it. The houses are all made of match sticks. The people speak different languages. But they're all sad. They're crying. I don't know why. Now they're all coming to me. They're asking me something, but I don't understand them. I don't know what to do. Now, I'm climbing a hill. There's a large house made of matchsticks. It's... it's, empty and this seems strange to me. I don't know why, but it's very strange that no one is there."

The images evaporated in his mind, and James faded out again.

It seemed he had been in this state for years. His mind often wandered from past battles to events he thought must be in the future. He saw a small hut in the woods and he and Sachisomi were married. Then he saw a village and felt as all the people were his neighbors. From here his mind raced back to a bloody battlefield, and he was fighting for his life. Sweat ran down his forehead, and he thought he might die there in the cramped hut.

James slowly opened his eyes to see Sachisomi holding his head in her lap. She smiled down at him, and he thought perhaps he was dreaming. She spoke to him, and James understood enough to know she was telling him the ritual was over. He smiled and faded back out.

It took James a week to recover from the exhaustive trial. During the ritual, he'd spent several days in the strange trance-like state and spoke of many things to Chief Konukoni and his adoptive father, Tonkiwatu. From these visions, the two perceived numerous things about James and the future. They revealed little of this to him though and he, in turn, was more concerned with the marriage and harsh winter moving in.

The wedding took place as the cool Autumn days were ending. The two moved into the small cabin, and the tribe settled in for the cold months that were approaching.

As the days passed by, James increasingly learned the Aqukolo language, and he slowly became Kalakone, husband of Sachisomi. As the winter pressed in on the small tribe, he began to forget about James Taft. The bitter battles and memories started to fade in the light of Sachisomi's love. He affectionately began to call her "Sachi" and she, in turn, began to call him "Kalie."

Four months after his marriage to Sachisomi, James stood with Chief Konukoni. The snow was melting, and the two observed the village as it appeared to be waking from a long winter sleep.

"We should move as soon as possible. Tonkiwatu said the new land could be reached before next winter if we don't delay."

James nodded to his father-in-laws' assessment and then replied. "Sachisomi and the other women have a good supply of dried meat and fish for the journey. We should have enough to last a month, perhaps longer if we can catch some game along the way."

"Excellent, we'll ready the tribe and move as soon as the weather permits." Konukoni then patted James on the back, and they moved towards the village to make preparations.

Soon the tribe was on the move again. James scouted the trail in front of the main group. He made every attempt possible to avoid other native tribes. The Shaman Tonkiwatu often spoke of getting closer to their destination as spring brought warmer temperatures.

Day after day James left behind the man he was and the battles he had fought. Every smile from Sachi brought warmth to his battered heart. As the group came closer to the land they had been searching for, James began to feel whole again.

Finally, in mid-summer, James could smell the salt on the breeze. Two days later he led the weary tribe from the Woodlands to the Pacific coast. Everyone's spirit rose; a small celebration took place with the sea in view.

"I would like for you to locate a good area for us, Kalakone. I'll stay here with our people. Take several men and scout out a good location to settle in." Chief Konukoni then smiled slightly to his son-in-law.

"I'll get everything ready, and we'll go tomorrow. I'll find a good place for our people." James replied and then went to Sachi. She was cooking a fish over an open fire.

"This will be very nice, Kalie. There's fish in the sea and game in the woods. We'll be happy here."

James sat and smiled at his wife. "Yes, father wants me to go locate a good place to settle. I'll leave tomorrow."

Sachi's expression immediately changed to one of concern. "How long will you be gone?"

"It depends upon how long it takes to find a good place to live. We must be sure we're not settling on another tribe's hunting and fishing grounds. I think a week, maybe two. Once we find a place, we'll scout the area to be sure it's uninhabited."

Sachi nodded, but still appeared unhappy about her husband leaving.

The following morning James packed supplies and picked several young men to travel with him. By mid-day, he and his small group were heading North along the coast.

For three days the men searched for a place to call home. Early on the fourth day, they arrived at a potential settlement area. James stood gazing out over the land. The sea had carved out a small inlet, around two miles wide and three miles long. The water was calm in this area and protected from the ocean by a long stretch of land.

For the remainder of the day, James traveled along the water and into the woodlands. There were hills around the area, but also a stretch of land not far from the water that would be ideal for huts. The hills would protect the community on one side, and it was also far enough from the sea to be relatively protected from storms and such.

The two men that traveled with James had not uttered a word all day. They only moved about with their leader and looked at the things he looked at. Finally as dusk began to settle in the area, one of the young men spoke.

"What do you think, Kalakone?"

James glanced at the young man; he then looked back over the area as if to be certain. Finally, he replied, "I believe we've found our new home."

The two men smiled at each other. The next morning they started back to retrieve the others.

Once the tribe had moved to the location James found for them; they immediately began work. Huts and cabins were built, and much effort went into preparing for winter.

James began making he and Sachi's log cabin while also assisting the others. His hair by now had grown long and he had completely adopted the ways of the Aqukolo.

Rain often hindered the work, but the community endeavored with a renewed spirit of hope. As James labored on the finishing touches of the cabin, Sachi watched him.

"I hope we can have children soon, Kalie."

James turned from his task of putting clay into a wall. He looked at his wife with a bit of surprise.

88

"Is that what you want, Sachi?"

She nodded and smiled. "Yes, and I hope to give you a son. But I want three or four children, at least."

James wiped his hands on a rag and moved over to her. He sat on the makeshift bed that he was also in the process of building for them.

"Well, I've never really thought about being a father." He held her hand and gazed out into the room.

"You'll be an excellent father, Kalie." She smiled, and James felt his heart warm.

"We should do our part to help the tribe survive. We should have many children." She said.

James studied her face. "Well, we can try to make a baby every night, starting tonight. What do you think of that plan?"

Sachi smiled coyly. "I like your plan."

They embraced and had to put forth some effort not to start with the plan right then.

The warm summer slowly gave way to cooler autumn days. As the weather changed, James and several other men began work on a small fishing hut by the ocean inlet. The hut would allow those who fished and searched for food along the beach area to have a place to stay warm and clean the various fish.

With the food obtained from the sea, combined with hunting and farming, the tribe would have sufficient resources year round.

Winter came with a blast from the North. Sachi and James spent the cold nights inside their cabin trying to make a baby. But month after month the two would be disappointed.

During the days, James often hunted in the woodlands around the village. His father-in-law spoke with pride every time James brought fresh meat in for the community.

The seasons began to blur with the incredible love of Sachi and his new life in the tribe. Spring came, and the two doubled their efforts to produce a child.

"Perhaps there's something wrong with me Kalie. My womb may be barren. You can choose to have another wife if you wish. It's not uncommon for men in our tribe to have two wives. At least, I heard it has happened in the past. I know there are several young women available. They may be able to produce a child for you. I would understand."

Sachi appeared on the verge of tears as once again her menstrual cycle had arrived and once again the two were deeply disappointed.

James moved over to his distraught wife. He hugged her.

"I would never do that, Sachi. I love you and only you. If it's just you and me forever, then that's alright. I'll be happy as long as I have you."

Now Sachi began to weep. She embraced her husband.

"It would be alright with me Kalie, but the tribe needs children. I'm so afraid that I'll disappoint my father and everyone else."

She wiped the tears from her eyes and continued. "Everything has been good. We have love and this new home. Why can't we have a child?"

James kissed her on the head. "Don't worry my love. When the time is right, we'll have a child."

Later that day James went to his father-in law's house. Inside the small, smoke-filled cabin, James also found his adoptive father Tonkiwatu sitting with the chief.

"Please have a seat, Kalie." His father-in-law motioned to a crude chair.

The three sat and discussed general topics for a while, but eventually, James brought the subject up he had come to talk about.

"My Fathers, I am troubled that Sachi and I have not been able to produce a child. Perhaps there is something wrong with me. Sachi is also disturbed about this as we feel an obligation to help the tribe recover."

The chief and Tonkiwatu glanced at each other. They both considered this for a few seconds and then the chief spoke.

"Kalie, I want you to begin your training as a Shaman. You've made my daughter happy, and you shouldn't worry about children right now. Your adoptive father, Tonkiwatu and I have discussed the situation. We feel you should start your training very soon."

James was a bit surprised by this. He tried to think of an answer but wasn't prepared to discuss this topic.

"Alright, if it's what you wish father. But what about Sachi and me, is there anything you can tell us? Is there anything you know to help us?"

Now Tonkiwatu spoke. "Kalie, I had a vision not long after we arrived at this place. I have told our chief, but I cannot tell anyone else right now. It's a vision of the future, and I feel you need to begin your training soon. In my vision, there were many people that looked to you for guidance. You were very troubled and in darkness."

He stood and moved over to the fireplace. As a small blaze crackled, he continued. "There will come a time when your father-in-law and I are not here to help you, Kalie. A time will come that you must climb a mountain and find the path for others. We've talked about this, and we want to do what we can now, to help you make the right decisions in the future."

James thought one or both must sense that they were growing old and may pass away before preparing him as the future chief of the tribe. He nodded his head and replied in a soft voice.

"I'm ready to start my training anytime, Father."

Tonkiwatu turned and smiled. "Son, there are things we can't talk about right now. You have a long and challenging path ahead of you. I've seen this. We want you to be ready for the future."

Again James felt they spoke of him leading the tribe after Chief Konukoni had passed away. He again nodded in agreement. "I understand, Father. We can start the training whenever you're ready."

Tonkiwatu came over and patted James on the shoulder, "Good, we'll start tomorrow."

James began his formal training as a tribal Shaman the following day. Tonkiwatu showed him many herbs and plants that would help heal wounds and intestinal maladies.

Sachi calmed some with this move. James told her of his thoughts that the tribe elders were concerned for the entire community and they should work towards the elder's objectives and not just their own as man and wife.

As the summer days came and passed James became tanned by the sun, and his hair was almost the length of the other people in the tribe. Sachi noticed this one evening as he came in from training with Tonkiwatu.

"Kalie," she walked over to him. He wore the garments of an Aqukolo Shaman. His hair was long and tied back, feathers of the Seahawk dangled from the leather hair tie. His skin was tanned, and his face shaved.

James looked at his wife curiously. "Yes, what is it Sachi?"

She moved around him. "I just noticed something. I can't remember what you looked like when we first met. In my dream, however, you were a white man. Isn't that odd?"

James smiled slyly. "Me, a white man, my dear Sachi, what sort of dream was that?" He then took her in his arms as she laughed.

"It was a strange dream, my love. I remember it well; you wore white man's clothes and spoke white man's language. But then you bought me these beads, which I'll never take off, and I fell in love with you."

James began to kiss Sachi's neck, "Well, other than me buying you those beads, which never leave your neck, and you falling in love with me, it was just a dream from long ago. I'm your husband, Kalakone and I think we should try to make a little Aqukolo baby." He then began moving her towards the bed. She laughed as they fell onto it and started making love.

Winter again closed in on the village. James learned many things concerning ceremonies and interpreting dreams. He heard of the spirit world and the place of animals and man in this world. Tonkiwatu told him the story of the Great Spirit that created and watched over everything.

James loved to hunt and fish when not learning the ways of an Aqukolo Shaman. He enjoyed the hut they had built beside the ocean inlet. He and his father-in-law often spent days catching and cleaning seafood, then hanging the bounty out to dry. It was during one of these cold winter days that the Aqukolo chief spoke strange words to James.

"Kalie, I need to tell you something." The chief was cleaning a fish inside the hut. A small fireplace put enough heat out to keep the inside above freezing, but it was still cold. James looked at his father-in-law.

"What is it, Father?"

A pause of silence held the room. The small crackling fire and James' knife cutting into the fish were the only sounds as the chief thought about his words.

"Tonkiwatu has foreseen something. It was after we came to this place."

He continued to clean the fish. James also cut the ones he had washed and put them in a basket.

"The Aqukolo will fly from this land and become a spirit of the air. Our people will not remain attached to this earth as we had thought and hoped."

James grimaced, "What do you mean?"

Chief Konukoni looked at his son-in-law and smiled slightly. "It's the natural order of things, Kalie. I feel this may be why you and Sachi have not been able to have a child."

James stopped his work. "But what does that mean, Father? How can that be?"

"I don't know, Son. But if the vision is true, then the Aqukolo will not recover and become a proud tribe again. I know it's what we have worked and hoped for. But the Great Spirit may have other plans for the Aqukolo. You must keep a strong heart, Kalie. Some of us will fly from this world and others must climb a high mountain."

James stared at his father-in-law. He spoke with respect, but confusion. "So, are you saying there will be no more children born to our people? I don't understand."

His father-in-law also stopped cleaning the fish. "I don't understand either, Kalie. But I want you to know that you've done what I had hoped for. You have made Sachi very happy. Our tribe has always had only a small hope. If Tonkiwatu's vision is true, something will change our hopes of reviving the tribe. We don't know what that thing will be, but as my Son, I felt you should know about the vision. It may be wrong. I hope it's wrong. But it is a vision that has significance, and we must look at that."

James turned back to his fish; he stared at it. "It must be wrong, Father. We must recover. We have everything we need here. Even if Sachi and I can't have a child, there are still enough others for us to recover. We've got to keep trying. I won't accept it. I'm finally content and have a real path in my life. I can't give up based on a vision."

Chief Konukoni nodded as he slowly returned to cleaning the fish. "I don't expect you to, Kalie. I want this to be something we look back on years from now and laugh about. But, your adoptive father is strong with the spirit world. You must be aware of this vision."

James also returned to his task of cutting up the cleaned fish. He spoke after a few seconds of work. "I understand, Father. And, whatever the destiny of the tribe is, so will be my destiny."

His father-in-law again stopped cleaning the fish. He turned to James. "Son, we cannot claim our destiny. We can only live the best way possible and do the best we can with what comes our way. Please, remember these words."

James considered this and nodded. "I will."

As winter once again slowly gave way to spring, the discussion faded in James' mind. His soul was at peace, and the village was thriving. He had almost forgotten his life before becoming an Aqukolo. He was not even sure what year it was and cared very little about such things.

Then, sometime around what he thought was possibly early May, the news from Sachi lifted his spirits even more.

"Are you sure?" James stood hovering over his wife as she prepared some vegetables for cooking.

"No, I'm not sure, Kalie. Like I told you, it's around ten days late and that has never happened. My monthly woman's cycle is always on time. But it's not for certain."

"But it's very likely, right? I mean, if it's always on time and now it's late, then it's very likely." James began to pace back and forth now.

"We've got to get everything ready as it'll be cold when the baby is born. We've got to get ready."

Sachi smiled. "We should wait a while longer before we tell Father. I don't want him to get disappointed if I'm just late. You know that does happen with women."

James stopped and looked at Sachi. "Yes, we don't want him to be disappointed." He then knelt down in front of her and sat the bowl of vegetables beside her so he could embrace her.

"This is wonderful! If you are pregnant, then Father will be so happy."

Sachi smiled and took him in her arms. "Yes, I can barely wait to tell him. Perhaps in a few more days, we can tell him."

Almost a week later, they told Sachi's father and Tonkiwatu. A new excitement stirred around the village as summer moved in. James was happier than he could ever remember being.

Chapter Eight: Thunder of Distant Guns

A month after telling Sachi's father of her pregnancy, on a warm summer morning, James took his rifle from two pegs that held it over the small fireplace.

"How long will you be gone Kalie, Father wants us to have a late meal with him. I think he's going to have Telatota over as well."

"Really," James replied as he inspected the rifle. "I should be back this afternoon. I would like to get a young deer so we can smoke some meat. I saw traces of some on the Northern hills."

He then took some ammunition from a small leather bag and began loading the rifle.

"Do you think Telatota and Father will marry?" James asked.

Sachi smiled slyly. "I don't know, but it seems possible. I think he's waited until I was happy before he would consider his own happiness. She is a lovely woman, though, and I think she's had her eye on him for a long time."

"Hmmm, well I hope he can have some happiness. He's worked so hard to get the tribe here. He deserves to be happy." James then kissed Sachi and started out the door. He stopped and then went back. Leaning down he kissed her stomach. Sachi laughed and then rubbing her tummy said, "Bye, Father."

James hiked into the woods and before mid-day was in the Northern hills. He silently moved about as he hunted for a small deer.

Around noon or a little after, James heard a rumbling in the distance; out towards the ocean. He looked up into the sky, but there were no clouds to be seen. For a second he wondered about this but then thought there must be a storm out over the sea somewhere.

James continued to hunt. He scanned the ground for hoof prints. Almost an hour passed. Then, much closer but again towards the sea, a loud boom was heard. Startled by the closeness of this noise, James turned towards it. That was an odd sound for thunder he thought. It sounded more like; a sudden fear clenched his body as he realized what the sound he heard was--cannon fire.

Without a second thought, James took off running towards the village. Brush and tree branches scratched his body as he maneuvered through the woodlands.

He came to a place where he could see out over the inlet and ocean. He tried to catch his breath as he could barely comprehend what he was viewing. In the inlet was a ship. Smoke was billowing from the vessel, and it had visible battle damage.

Out in the ocean was a much larger ship. Having a basic knowledge of warships, James identified this one as an ironclad frigate. It had the smoke stack of a steam driven engine but also tall masts for sails. It seemed the large ironclad sat too low in the water and could not follow the smaller ship into the inlet.

A short distance from the smaller burning ship, James could see several boats rowing towards the fishing hut.

James again took off running towards his village, almost falling several times as his legs began to feel stressed.

The small boats that had disembarked from the burning ship reached the bank of the inlet, and from the fishing hut, they followed a worn trail straight to the village.

The small Aqukolo community was caught almost entirely off guard when around thirty heavily armed men entered.

"Kill them all if you have to. Find the food, weapons, and horses. Hurry, before the Frenchman arrives." With these orders from a large and rough dressed captain, his men immediately began shooting down the men, women, and children.

As the shots rang out, Chief Konukoni came out of his hut; he ran to Sachi and James' hut. Sachi opened the door as her father approached. "Get out, run to the woods!"

As he said this to her, a bullet slammed into his back. His face grimaced in pain, and he fell in front of her.

Sachi screamed out, "Father, Father!" She knelt to him as chaos reigned in the small village. Women screamed, and men attempted to fight the invaders, but almost all were shot without mercy. Very few made it to the woodlands and safety.

Sachi held her dead Father for several seconds. She was in shock, and her mind struggled to understand what was happening. Then she realized he had wanted her to escape. She stood, but before she could get out the door, a large white man was standing in front of her. His appearance was weathered and unkempt. He wore a faded white shirt with a green vest and held a rifle straight to her face. She thought he would shoot her. But the man instead pushed her into the cabin. She fell to the floor.

Meanwhile, James could hear the shots being fired, and his heart beat faster as he struggled to reach the village. He stumbled and fell several times as his legs were giving out, but he stood again and continued forward.

In the Aqukolo community, the massacre continued. Sachi stood and tried to get out the door, but the large man pushed her onto the bed. She fought him. He grabbed her throat and squeezed. She struggled fiercely, but he squeezed harder. Slowly the air in her lungs lost its life giving power. Her arms gradually fell limp to the bed.

Her killer let go of Sachi and examined her as a few more shots rang out in the village behind him.

Noticing the strands of beads around her neck, the man pulled them off of her and placed them around his neck. He then rubbed her breasts and began pulling her buckskin dress up.

The roughly dressed captain came to the door. Looking in, he yelled out, "We don't have time for that, Randle! Just get any food or weapons and let's go, before the Frenchman gets here!"

Randle glanced back at the captain and then at Sachi's dead body. Seeming reluctant to quit his morbid activity, he shouted back. "Are you even sure the Frenchman is coming? The Valiant couldn't come into the inlet. They may not even come ashore."

The captain had started to walk away, but stuck his head back into the doorway, "I'm not fer sure of anything, but if'n you want to wait around, then maybe you can slow him down some for us if he should show up!"

Randle huffed about this. His face twisted as he considered it. He rubbed Sachi's breast once again. Then he moved away from her and began searching the cabin. Soon he had a handful of food items and met up with the others outside. They hastily left the village and headed inland.

Several minutes later James staggered into the devastated village. His eyes strained at the bodies lying around; he then ran to his cabin.

"No, no, no...." He glanced at his father-in-law and then went inside to find Sachi dead on their bed.

"Noooo... no, no, no..." Tears filled his eyes as he lifted her lifeless body into his arms. He rocked her and wept as his heart and soul crumbled inside.

For a while, he was lost in the depths of darkness. But then, slowly, anger began to rage in him. Fire as had never erupted in the deepest recesses of his being, lit up his insides completely. As he held his dead wife in his arms, James knew what he would do. He would die today, but he would make them pay first. He would take down as many as he could before his pain was ended.

After laying Sachi on the bed and covering her up, he reached far under the bed. Hidden in a leather bag, he pulled out his revolvers. He loaded them and strapped them on. It had been a long time since he'd felt the weight of the pistols. He took his knife and rifle, then went to find the murderers.

The men from the ship were easy to follow as they left obvious tracks. As the wrath inside him boiled, James trotted along the trail, much like an animal hunting its prey.

He first came to a fat man that was falling behind. He had a large bag over his shoulder and was struggling to navigate the rough terrain.

James crept silently up behind him and with one quick movement sliced the man's throat. The fat man fell, and as he lay dying on the ground, James looked ahead for the others.

The attackers were moving towards a hilly area that James knew well. He came to where he could see the end of the group. He raised his rifle up and shot a man that was climbing an outcrop of rocks. The man tumbled down the jagged boulders and was dead before hitting bottom.

The other men took cover. The roughly dressed captain yelled out, "Chauveau, listen, we can work something out! Let's hold a truce and sort through this without a lot of killing."

James could see the man searching the woodlands for him as he spoke. He lifted the rifle up and took aim. Just as he fired, the captain moved, but the bullet winged his shoulder.

"Ahgggg..." The captain held his wound and moved behind some cover. "Alright Chauveau, if that's the way you want it!"

Soon James saw men cautiously moving around both sides of him. He shot at one but missed due to a large rock. As nine of them crept back in different directions to envelop James, he noticed the larger group traveling forward again.

Moving back a bit, James waited and soon had a sure shot. Another of the murderers fell dead from his rifle. But now the remainders fired in his direction, and several bullets came close to hitting him. He ran back a short distance to draw them farther from the main group. As he moved from cover to cover, they fired again, and the air sang with hot lead.

He crouched and watched both sides while the two smaller groups crept closer into position. Glancing back, he saw a defensive position. There was an open area around it, and he could make one last stand.

He again moved back, and again, shots were fired at him. He jumped over several rocks and settled in.

"It looks like an injun!" One of the men yelled out to the others.

"Don't take any chances. I heard the Frenchman has all sorts with him. This may be one of his injuns." Another yelled back. Then he continued as if he were the leader.

"Randle, you and the Scott move around the back, we'll cover you."

James watched as several men attempted to move around to his left. As they were scurrying through the brush, James raised his rifle and picked another one off.

"Damn it; he got the Scott!" Randle shouted.

The leader moaned in disappointment.

Silence held the area for several seconds.

"Did you hear me, Leveran?" Randle yelled out again as he crouched behind a large rock.

"Stay there, Randle, we'll move around."

James glanced out over the rocks and realized to his right was a low area that he couldn't cover. Now, six or seven men could be heard crawling behind this secure area.

"Don't let him move, Randle!" Leveran shouted from behind the covered area.

Immediately a shot rang out, and bits of rock sprayed all over James. He ducked down a little more.

"He ain't going anywhere," Randle shouted back.

James now realized he was trapped. He sat his rifle down and pulled his two pistols out. They could come one at a time or all at once. Either way, they would suffer before killing him.

Soon, there was talking behind the area that James faced. He felt certain they were planning to charge him. He leaned back on the rocks, cocked his pistols and prepared himself.

He waited only a few seconds as men came up over the jutting boulders. James fired one shot after another. One man went down and then two, three. But as they came they fired their guns and James was hit, once in the right shoulder area. His right arm lost control. He fired again with his left hand, and another man fell. Again, he was hit, in the leg and a bullet grazed his left arm. He attempted to fire again, but his aim was off, and missed. Another bullet hit his left side. He slid down into the hollow of the rocks. He fired again and missed. He pulled the trigger once more, but the pistol only clicked.

After the few brief seconds of hell, all became silent, and the men that remained slowly came from their hiding spots. Leveran was a large man with a bushy black beard. The men walked up and carefully examined James as he lay bloodied and broken in the hollow of the rocks.

"It's just one damn injun!!" Leveran exclaimed.

Then a man came from behind; it was Randle. When James saw the man, he immediately noticed Sachi's beads around his neck.

"I'll kill you! I'll kill you!!" He shouted in Aqukolo. He tried to raise the pistol in his right hand but couldn't.

"What did he say?" Leveran asked the man on his right.

"How should I know, I don't speak injun! But he doesn't seem to like Randle one bit." The man replied.

"Well, I don't care for injuns either. But I do like them Colt's he's got. I think I'll take those." As Randle spoke, the other two also took notice of James' two revolvers.

As soon as Randle began to reach down and take one of the pistols, Leveran shouted, "Stop! You two get on up there with the others, I'll finish this one off and catch up."

Randle sneered at Leveran, "You're just wantin his revolver's is all!"

Leveran sneered back, "Rank has its privileges... Randle, now do as I said and go catch up with the others."

With some reluctance, the other two men recovered the weapons from their fallen comrades and then made their way back in the direction the main group had gone in.

When these two were out of the area, Leveran examined James.

"What the hell is an injun doin with two Colt revolvers?" He studied James curiously for a few more seconds.

100

"Well, it don't matter none, their mine now." Leveran then raised his rifle to finish him off.

Anger rushed through James that the man named Randle had gotten away. But he was glad his pain and suffering would end. He looked up at Leveran to face his death with courage.

Suddenly, it appeared as if Leveran's chest exploded. Blood sprayed all over the place. Leveran's face went blank and his arms dropped; the rifle fell to the ground. He looked down in shock at the hole in his chest, then fell backward dead. At this instant, James heard the shot, far off in the distance and behind where Leveran had stood.

He looked around for what could have caused this. James had seen enough men killed in battle to know a high caliber bullet had gone through Leveran's back and came out the front of his chest. But it was quite unexpected and startling.

Silence hovered over the area. His wounds were inflicting much pain as he continued to stare in the direction of the gunshot. He'd thought death would bring an end to his misery, but now, it seemed he would die slowly and painfully.

The one thing that distracted him from his agony was a curiosity about who fired the shot that killed Leveran. Perhaps Randle would pay for his crimes after all. He watched intently in front of him as the moments ticked by.

Then, after what felt to be hours, but was likely around ten minutes, something moved in the brush. James watched with amazement at the sight that developed in front of him.

An Asian man crept from the vegetation, he held a repeating rifle and wore light green clothes that were similar to a uniform but appeared Asian in design.

About twenty feet to this man's right, another Asian man stepped from the woods; he was also dressed in the odd clothing. Then several more crept out from the trees. These men had rifles strapped over their shoulders and were carrying a rectangular wooden box. The box had two handles on each end and was colorfully painted. There were also odd inscriptions on the sides.

Cautiously, several more men stepped into the area. There were two white men, and one black man, but most were Asian. These men held their rifles in a ready position and scanned the small battleground with interest.

Then, a large Asian man stepped from the woods. In his hands was a long rifle with a scope attached to the top. James had once seen this type of rifle during the war but had never witnessed one in action. They could fire at such a distance that the bullet would hit before the sound was heard.

The assortment of odd soldiers stood in ready positions amongst the men that James had killed. The large Asian man with the long rifle came over to James and looked down at him. But none of the men said anything.

A few seconds later, and as if things could get no stranger, a tall white man stepped from the woods. He wore a silk coat over gentleman's clothing. He gazed over the battle area with interest and pulled a slim cigar from an ornate case. He then placed the case back inside his coat pocket.

A man immediately stepped up to him with a lit match. The white man held his cigar up to the match and pulled a few draws from it until he was expelling smoke.

He then walked slowly up towards James. The man was around forty years old or in his late thirties perhaps. He had long, dark hair that was tied back, along with a stylish mustache and thin goatee. He also wore tinted glasses, in an effort, it seemed to shade his eyes.

The man casually stepped up to where James lay. He looked down at him and blew a stream of smoke out. He lifted his right hand into the air and immediately one of his men unfolded a canvas stool and placed it on the ground.

The man sat down and again briefly studied James before speaking.

"Parlez-vous Français?"

James stared at the man. He thought the man spoke French to him, but he didn't understand.

After a brief pause, the man spoke again.

"Vozmozhno, vy govorite Russkiy?"

James nodded his head with a puzzled expression.

The man then looked closely at the revolvers that were still in James' bloodied hands.

"English?" He asked with a strong French accent.

"Yes," James replied in a withering voice.

"Ahh, I should have known. You're holding two; fine American made revolvers. I really should have guessed English first. It's difficult to know in this area." The man then pulled another draw from the cigar and expelled the smoke.

James had found himself so puzzled by this odd man that he was somewhat distracted from the excruciating pain. His breath was labored, and he could barely focus, but simply watching this man seemed to keep his mind off the agony.

"And what, may I ask is your name?"

"Kalakone," James replied with some effort.

"Uhmm, well, what is your English name?" The man asked and then examined his cigar closely.

"What makes you think I have another name?"   ·

The Frenchman examined James for a few seconds. He took another draw from his cigar, expelled the smoke, and then replied.

"Well, I am pursuing a charlatan by the name of Benjamin Pearce. He's a pirate, a blackbirder, and murderer, amongst other things. I see at least six of his men lying around here dead; seven if we count the one with his throat cut a ways back. And then, we find you, with a couple of US Army revolvers. Now, I would guess that you have not only an English name but also some military experience."

James grimaced as the pain was almost unbearable. "James Taft." He replied, and then moved a little to help alleviate some of the discomfort in his right shoulder, "9th Pennsylvania cavalry."

"Ahh, yes, the 9th Pennsylvania, now I understand." The man again glanced at his cigar, as if it were a time piece.

"Well, James Taft. My name is Quenton Chauveau. I'm the commander of the Valiant. We intercepted two ships as they left Vancouver, the Carthage and the Sumatra. The Sumatra is captained by one 'Billy Hays' and the Carthage was captained by Billy's partner, Benjamin Pearce. Both men are wanted by a certain Asian leader, among others. These men have been kidnapping his people as well as other Asian peoples and selling them as slave labor. Our mission is to put an end to their activities, by whatever means necessary.

"Unfortunately, the Sumatra slipped away during the night as the two ships separated. But we pursued the Carthage until maneuvering for a broadside and damaging her. She slipped into the small inlet back there to evade the Valiant. I was very saddened to see what the Carthage crew did to your village, and... well, I'm very sorry for what happened to your people."

James coughed as the pain again surged in his body. "Please, kill all of them. They murdered my people."

"Yes, we'll take care of them. Don't worry about that." Quenton then pulled another draw from his cigar.

James glanced around at the few men with Quenton.

"He has twenty or more men with him. Are these all the men you have?"

Quenton glanced back at the men, then replied. "Well, he may have more than twenty men, but, I have ten Marines. So, we'll be alright."

As Quenton said this, James looked behind him and noticed one of the Marines picking his nose. He realized James was looking at him and quickly turned away.

James continued. "There's a man named Randle. He's wearing a white shirt with a green vest. He murdered my wife and unborn child. Please make sure you get him."

When James said this, Quenton's face expressed deep compassion. He again studied James and then looked carefully at his wounds.

"I'll tell you what, Mr. Taft. I'll have a man stay here and patch you up some. He can stop the bleeding and such. I'll send another man back to the Valiant to retrieve our ship's doctor.

"Now, if you'll stay alive, I'll bring this man back here and allow you to decide his fate. I only ask one thing. You should deliver justice, not vengeance."

James looked at Quenton. He thought he might die at any moment, but then again, he may perhaps live long enough. He wanted to see this man punished and if Quenton really could bring him back, James knew the fate he would deal with Randle.

"Alright, I'll try. I may be able to make it if you don't take long."

Quenton smiled. "You can make it if you decide to, Mr. Taft. I've seen men live that I would have never thought could. Just stay alive Mr. Taft, we'll not be long."

Once again Quenton glanced at his cigar. He then reached down and put it out on a rock. Immediately one of his men came and took it. Quenton then said something to him in what sounded like an Asian language. The man spoke to several others. One came over and went to work on James to stop the bleeding. The other one took off at a jog towards the ocean and the Valiant.

Quenton and his remaining men then left the area in the same slow walk they had entered with. As they went, James wondered if he would live long enough to see them return.

The evening slowly came, and the ship's doctor arrived as it was growing dark. He was a man of forty-something. His hair was black with tints of gray. The doctor wore a suit jacket and shirt with what looked to be army breeches and a pair of black, high-top boots.

"Hello, Jolli said the commander needs me to keep you alive."

He expressed a distinctive British accent as the Asian man named Jolli led him to James.

"My name is Robert Jefferies or Doc Jefferies as most call me." He then proceeded to examine James.

"Well, ahh yes, I see the commander has presented me with a bit of a challenge. First, we'll get these wounds cleaned and properly bandaged."

Doc Jefferies proceeded to get James more comfortable. He then cleaned the wounds with a solution that burned and caused James to yell out in pain.

After James had regained his senses from the burning medicine, he spoke with the doctor.

"You don't need to go to all this trouble Doctor. Just keep me alive until Mr. Chauveau returns. That's all you need to do; I just need to live until he returns."

"Mr. Who," The doctor expressed confusion. "Oh, you mean the commander. I've seldom heard him called 'Mr. Chauveau', sorry. Well, you see, the commander gave Jolli instructions, and he gave those instructions to me. They were to keep you alive. I received no time limit on how long to do that, so I'm simply working to keep you alive, period."

James nodded painfully as the doctor tended his wounds. Doc Jefferies then gave James a dose of something that dulled the pain.

As the darkness settled in, Jolli built a campfire, and the doctor fed James beef jerky that he cut into small pieces and added water to.

The night proceeded long and painful as James struggled to find rest and comfort from his injuries, but resolved within himself to hold on. Finally, daylight came.

"Your commander said he would bring the man that killed my wife back here alive. Can he do that?" James sat up against a large rock as the doctor drank some coffee.

Doc Jefferies' face winced slightly when James asked this.

"Oh, is that what this is all about? I saw what happened to your people. I'm very sorry. But if the commander said he would bring your wife's murderer back here alive then he'll do just that, you can rest assured he will do as he says Mr. Taft."

James relaxed a little and again looked in the direction the commander had left in.

Before reaching mid-day, James noticed the commander with his men walking from the woodlands and back towards the small campsite. In the middle of the procession was the man named Randle. His hands were bound behind him, and two long branches were tied around his neck. This kept him from doing anything other than walking as the two men holding the ends of the branches lead him where he needed to go.

"Doctor Jefferies, how is your patient?" The commander asked and went straight to the campfire and the coffee pot. Jolli immediately brought him a cup, and he poured some of the black liquid into it.

"He's surely alive Sir. That was your instructions from Jolli, to keep him alive, as you see, he's still that."

The commander took a drink of coffee as he glanced over to where James lay.

"Well, Mr. Taft, you'll be glad to know we've dealt with Benjamin Pearce and his crew. We also brought the man you spoke of." He nodded to Randle.

The commander then moved a little closer to Randle. "You've killed this man's wife. So, in a few moments, we will allow him to choose your fate as judgment for your crimes. You can consider this between now and then."

Randle's face expressed fear. "What makes you think I killed his wife? This is unreasonable!"

James then spoke up. "Please, take those beads from his neck. They were my wife's. Bring them to me."

Randle now seemed to recall the beads he wore. His eyes widened and expressed that he had indeed been caught.

106

The commander gave some orders to his men, and they quickly untied the branches and brought James the strands of beads. He carefully but painfully put them around his neck.

Now the small group of men gathered around as several held the ropes that secured Randle. The commander stepped into the center of the group and talked to his men. He spoke in the Asian language, and James didn't understand what he said.

"Yesterday this man murdered Mr. Taft's wife and unborn child. We have dealt with the charlatan Pearce and brought this man back to face justice. Are we all in agreement that Mr. Taft's sentence on this criminal will be considered final?"

Everyone nodded in agreement. The commander moved over to where James lay and asked in English. "What is your sentence upon this man, Mr. Taft?"

James wasted no time. "The sentence is death."

"And how will that be carried out?" The commander asked.

"Bring me my revolver. I'll do it myself."

One of James revolvers was loaded and brought to him as Randle became very agitated concerning his now obvious demise.

The men held the ropes to where Randle faced James. He cocked his revolver and shot once. A loud bang and the sickening sound of lead hitting flesh was heard. Randle doubled over as the hole in his stomach brought the immediate pain.

"Agghhh," he sank to his knees.

James sat the revolver down.

"What.... ain't you going to finish it?" Randle said. The men holding his ropes let slack in them.

"It's finished," James said.

"You got to finish it. You... aghh... can't just leave me to die like this..." Randle's face tightened as the pain increased.

"I want you to have time to think about the lives you destroyed in my village. This is the justice you receive."

The commander's eyebrows rose slightly as he looked back down to James.

"Thank you," James said to the commander. "I'm indebted to you. Please bury me with my people, beside my wife and unborn child. She's in the log cabin on the West end of the village."

James sank back down now, feeling ready for death to take him.

The commander, however, examined James again. He stroked his goatee several times and then reached into his coat pocket and pulled out one of his slim cigars. Immediately one of his men came to him with a match. He didn't light the cigar, however. After several long seconds of thought, he replied.

"We'll bury your wife. But you can't die just yet, Mr. Taft." The commander then held his cigar to the fire and after pulling a draw, expelled the smoke while examining James.

"What?" James looked up. "What are you talking about?"

"Well, as you said yourself, you're indebted to me. You can't very well pay that debt if you're dead. So, you must live Mr. Taft, and then once you've settled up with me, if you wish to die, that's your business."

The commander then gave some orders in the Asian language to his men. They immediately took the long branches used for Randle and soon had a makeshift stretcher put together and to James astonishment, began loading him onto it.

The commander had already started walking away, and the group began following behind, leaving Randle to die alone slowly.

The rough trip back to the sea was painful and arduous. Eventually, they were moving through his village where James saw that men from the Valiant had already buried the dead and were finishing up as the group proceeded through.

Down to the small fishing hut, he was carried. Then they all loaded into several long boats and were rowed out towards the mouth of the inlet.

As they passed by the still smoldering Carthage, James could see some of the commander's men aboard. They yelled something out to the commander, and he answered them in the same Asian language.

James was confused and shocked by this turn of events. As the salty breeze drifted over him and the rowers moved the craft towards the Valiant, he could barely grasp the situation. He had planned on surrendering to death once Randle had been dealt with. Now he was being swept off to an ironclad frigate and placed in the service of an odd commander that he knew little about.

Again, the pain racked his body as the men hoisted his stretcher up to the massive ship. Then across the deck and down into the bowels of the vessel, he was carried. Finally, the men moved him past the giant cannons of the gun deck and into a small room. They placed him on a bed, and Doc Jefferies tended him for a few moments.

"Does Mr. Chauveau believe that I'll live through the night? I'm not going to make it Doc, you and I both know that."

Doctor Jefferies looked at him with an odd expression. "Mr. Taft, if the commander believes you will live long enough to pay your debt to him, then I do as well. You should get those thoughts of dying out of your mind. It's my job to help you stay alive. So, you just rest and recover, that way we'll both be alright."

James' face twisted as he attempted to understand this turn of events.

"I just said I was indebted to him, meaning I was grateful." James grimaced as the Doctor again applied the burning medicine.

"Well, perhaps you should have chosen your words more carefully Mr. Taft. The commander seems to have taken them seriously."

Finally, after this, the doctor left him alone. James gradually drifted into what would be a long, blurred state of being.

Time almost stood still as men came and went, some tending to him and others apparently working around him as the room he was in appeared to be used for storage as well.

Once, he awoke to see the doctor and the commander standing over him, talking in a language he thought might be French. His mind was foggy, though, and he couldn't think straight.

Again, he would wake up with the terrible burning sensation of the medicine. The doctor and an assistant would roll him over and apply the medicine and new bandages. His bed pan would be changed, and then he would be turned back to rest.

James woke up one morning to the sound of cannons firing. He could barely comprehend that the ship was engaged in a battle. He looked out the open door to the gun deck. There he saw the commander walking about casually, smoking a cigar, as the cannons fired and men moved about to reload them. James then faded back out.

Another time he woke to find Nancy sitting beside his bed and staring at him. He couldn't remember her name but just remembered the face.

"What.... what are you doing here?" James struggled to remember who she was. He reached out to her, and she faded away as if she were mist.

How many days passed by James wasn't sure. His mind began to clear slowly, and one morning he sat in bed and finally recalled who he was. As the Asian man carefully spooned food into his mouth, James began to remember the events that had brought him to the place he was at now.

A deep sense of loss fell over him, and though he knew his body was slowly recovering, James felt dead inside.

Chapter Nine: Sandrilan

A week after James was able to sit up and feed his self, the Valiant docked. He heard bells ringing, but still, couldn't get up and walk.

After an hour or so by himself, several of the crew came and helped him into a chair that had handles and could be carried by two men. They moved James up on deck to a humid tropical heat. It was the first time he saw the main island that he later found to be named Sandrilan.

The ship was nestled in a natural harbor. Hills that gradually sloped up surrounded the small port, and all along these hills were houses and buildings. Many were in the process of being built, and everywhere he could see signs of a growing and developing community.

Towards the top of what James identified as a road winding up through these houses and buildings, he noticed a large wooden structure that had a distinctive Asian design and it too was in an obvious state of construction.

The men carried James along the road. Many people were outside of their houses or establishments. It seemed some of these were family members of the crew serving on the Valiant, as James saw several men in uniforms with them.

Slowly they moved up the winding road until reaching a dwelling with a sign indicating it to be a doctor's office. Once inside, James saw Doc Jefferies and an Asian woman talking and laughing together. The doctor then noticed the men bringing James in.

"Oh, it's Mr. Taft. Hello! I'm sorry, we almost forgot about you. There's always excitement here on Sandrilan after the Valiant returns."

Doctor Jefferies then motioned to the men, "Please sit him over there."

After placing the chair down, the two men bowed slightly and then left the building. Doc Jefferies pulled a wicker type chair over by James and sat.

"You'll be staying here in my office for a while Mr. Taft. We don't have any beds available in our newly built clinic, but I have a spare room in the back, and we'll have a bed placed in it for you."

Doc Jefferies studied James for a few seconds. "You're mending fairly well. I don't think infection has set in anywhere, though it was a struggle for a while."

James said nothing and simply stared out at the floor.

"That's my wife over there." Doc Jefferies motioned for the Asian woman to come over. She walked across the room and stood beside her husband.

"Meili, this is James Taft. He's had a rough go of it. He'll be staying here at the office while recovering."

Meili bowed slightly, and James nodded, but again gave no reply.

"I also have an assistant by the name of Oshai. He's from India and is quite reliable. I'll introduce you to him later. Don't worry Mr. Taft; we'll have you back on your feet soon."

James remained silent. The words made little sense to him. Why would he need to stand and walk? His life was over. He had no real concern about getting onto his feet again. It was this 'Commander Chauveau' that had brought him here. He was the one that wanted to keep James alive. If not for the commander wanting his re-payment, James would already be resting beside his beloved Sachi.

After a few seconds of waiting in vain for James to reply, Doc Jefferies nodded slightly and stood up. "I'll have Meili bring you something to eat shortly."

As the day moved into evening, James watched men come and go. They carried pieces of what he imagined to be his bed and other assorted small furniture items. They worked quickly and then moved him into the room.

Once James was helped into his bed, one of the men took a few pillows and propped him. He then opened the window made of bamboo. The man spoke in an Asian language and pointed up the hill to the large structure.

James leaned over and looked out the window to the building. The man smiled and nodded, then again said something that James didn't understand, bowed and left.

After twenty minutes or so James fell asleep. He awoke some time later to the sounds of music. Leaning over to look out the window he realized the large structure on the hill was lit up with lamps and lanterns. Music and laughter rang out, and he thought every resident of the community must be inside the building celebrating something.

For a while, he listened to the music and many voices filled with joy. He wanted to close the window. He didn't feel happy or joyful. James slowly maneuvered himself lower in the bed and with some effort moved one of the pillows around and laid it over his head to muffle the celebratory noises. Finally, he went back to sleep.

For several weeks, James stayed in his room recovering. Several men, including the doctor's assistant Oshai, helped James and brought him his meals. Then one day the doctor had James moved out to a veranda. They sat him in a reclining wicker chair that faced the large structure on the hill.

"There you are, Mr. Taft. You need some fresh air, and I think you may be pleased with the view of the palace there. At least, I've found it to be rather pleasant on days such as this."

Doctor Jefferies then smiled and left. Soon Meili brought out a tall glass of fruit juice. She smiled and nodded up to the palace as she said something in the Asian language that he didn't understand.

James sat quietly by himself after this. He took a drink of the juice, and it was quite good. A humid breeze moved through and cooled things a bit.

After around thirty minutes, there was movement upon a large open area by what he would come to know as the Palace. James took notice and realized some women were moving about on the flat area.

Music began to play, and the women began to dance. James could see they were dressed in what appeared to be Asian dance costumes. He'd seen pictures of these type of dancers while in the army. Some of his fellow soldiers proudly displayed photographs of what was dubbed 'belly dancers' or exotic oriental dancers. They were always dressed in much less clothing than American women wore. Even the dance hall girls were dressed modestly compared to some of the women in the photographs.

For a short time, James watched as the women appeared to be practicing their dances. Then he stopped watching and simply stared at the wooden floor of the veranda. He felt no desire to be entertained.

Oshai came out to where James sat. "Do you need anything, Mr. Taft?" He asked with his strong Indian accent.

"No, I'm alright, thank you."

Just as Oshai was about to leave, James asked, "who are the women up there?"

Oshai glanced up towards the women dancing about. "Ahh, those are the Palace butterflies. They are beautiful, aren't they? Their dances are so splendid. I don't think Sandrilan could be the same without them."

Oshai turned to James after saying this. He was smiling, but as he noticed James wasn't, the smile fell from his face.

"I'm sorry, sir, I realize you haven't had an opportunity to attend a Palace celebration yet. Don't worry; you'll get to see them dance at the next one." Oshai then smiled again and left.

Doctor Jefferies continued to insist on James getting back onto his feet. He had Oshai help him to the great frustration of James; they developed a routine for him. Every day Oshai brought James to the veranda where he would use a cane and move up and down it at least twice. Then there were the arm exercises and breathing exercises.

Although James went along with the tasks, he felt they were futile. He thought he should talk with the commander to find out just what it was James owed him, and how long until he could do something to repay that debt.

Before James ever had an opportunity to speak with the commander, the Valiant shipped out early one morning. He wondered why Doc Jefferies had not mentioned the departure to him, but then considered that he seldom spoke to the doctor or anyone else for that matter.

With the Valiant gone, Oshai and occasionally Meili were the only people James initially saw much of. Oshai continued to lead him out to the veranda and sit him where he could see the Palace butterflies. James would stand up and hobble around once Oshai had left since pleasure and beauty had lost their luster for him.

Although he was recovering and used his cane less and less, continuing to live seemed insignificant to him.

From his position on the veranda of the doctor's office, James often watched the activity around Sandrilan. Construction occurred every day, and he was greeted each morning by the sounds of hammers and saws, among the other related noises that accompanied a booming town.

In the port below, James noticed small cargo boats moving in and out with loads of timber and other items used for the building process. These were large boats and a few raft type craft, but they

114

weren't ships and certainly would not be strong enough in the open ocean.

When Oshai brought his lunch one day, James asked about the boats.

"Oh, they're bringing wood and materials from other islands around Sandrilan. There are twelve islands altogether. The Kingdom of Sandrilan was founded by our ruler, King Chauveau, six years ago. These islands are too small to be of importance for large countries. The natural port is also much too tiny for any other kingdom to desire. But it's just right for the Valiant and our needs."

James thought about this. It was very strange to hear Oshai call the commander a "King."

"I thought Quenton Chauveau was simply the leader of the Valiant."

When James said this, Oshai chuckled.

"Oh my, no, no, he may rather be called 'Commander' than King. But he is the founder and King of Sandrilan. All of this you see is because of our marvelous benefactor and ruler."

James' face twisted slightly, "I see, he certainly has set himself up nicely."

The days crept by and James began to walk around without his cane. Being free to move on his own two feet, he began taking strolls around the island community. Going up and down the winding road and steps of Sandrilan strengthened his muscles and lungs. And though unaccustomed to the tropical climate, he did gradually become more adjusted to it.

Eventually, as James began to walk farther and more normally, he reached the gates of the magnificent Palace. Inside the compound, he viewed a multitude of workers, busily expanding the elaborate structure.

Being built in a mountain setting, the Palace required many 'stilts' or long beams to support different sections of the structure. As James stood outside watching the work, several groups of men came quickly up the road pulling two-wheeled carts that were loaded with long pieces of wood, or at times the bamboo poles used for support.

Occasionally a man and cart would pass through the gate with some clay that appeared to be placed on the outside of the structure.

After five weeks of walking around Sandrilan, and sitting to watch the work on the palace, James was beginning to think the

Valiant may never return. Then, as he was eating his mid-day meal out on the veranda, bells began to sound in the harbor. They were for certain the bells of a ship. They sounded with three quick rings, a short pause and then three quick rings. This repeated several times.

A few seconds after the ship signaled with the bells, James was astounded by many large bells, all around Sandrilan replying the same three rings, pause and three rings.

The bells of the island were deep in tone and seemed to be of a style other than American or European. James imagined they must have originated from Asia.

He did vaguely recall hearing these bells when first arriving on the Valiant, but he was in the ship's bowels and not entirely aware of anything. Now, being in the middle of them, he was quite surprised and impressed with the jubilant welcome the warship received.

James went to the rail and positioned himself where he could view the ship. People gathered all around as the vessel docked and the gangway moved to it. He could clearly see at least twelve Palace butterflies at the front of the group.

Soon, Commander Chauveau walked across the gateway and music erupted. He was followed by several ranking men and then the regular crewmen.

As soon as the commander walked onto the dock, the Palace butterflies began tossing what appeared to be leaves or possibly flower petals in front of his path.

Men with cymbals and chimes played their instruments and followed him as he moved towards the Palace. James grunted at this, though he watched until the commander was halfway to the Palace before he turned away.

Looking back to the ship, James noticed several people moving onboard and soon they were escorting around twenty-five, poorly dressed civilians from the lower decks and off the Valiant. It was an odd sight, and James wondered about it.

A short time later, Doctor Jefferies arrived at the office and immediately embraced Meili. She giggled and expressed joy that her husband was home. James could see them inside from his spot out on the veranda. He heard them chattering back and forth in what was possibly Meili's native language.

Doc Jefferies then stepped out onto the veranda, and soon Oshai joined them.

"Mr. Taft, how are you? You appear much better than when I departed."

"Yes, I'm doing better, thanks."

"You see, he is walking without a cane now, Doctor," Oshai said enthusiastically.

"Well, we'll need to find you some nice clothes then. You'll certainly want to attend the celebration. I'm fairly sure I have a suit that will fit you." Doc Jefferies then stepped back and looked James over as if ascertaining his suit size.

"I don't believe that I'll be attending the celebration. I don't feel like celebrating." James replied.

"Nonsense, Mr. Taft. I understand your sentiments, but it will be good for you. You've healed well, and now you should be around people. Besides, it'll be an opportunity for you to see the Palace. It's becoming something wonderful, and we're all very excited about it."

James considered this. "I would like to talk with the commander soon."

"Yes, certainly, and I must say, the commander asked me about you on several occasions while we were away. I think he would like to talk with you soon too."

"Alright, I guess I can go then. If you have a suit, I can borrow."

"Yes, yes, we'll find something I assure you, Mr. Taft. You will be quite impressed with our little event, I'm sure. Sandrilan may be a new country, but we're proud and blessed with many talented people."

The doctor then leaned over and whispered, "The butterflies are fantastic, you'll fall in love with them." He then excused himself and went to search for a suit.

The following evening, after getting cleaned up and dressed in his borrowed suit, James left the office and met up with Doctor Jefferies, Oshai, and Meili. A procession of Sandrilinians moved up the winding road to the palace. Lamps were lit all along the way, and the palace itself was bright with lanterns and different lamps.

As they moved through the gates, the sound of music and laughter could be heard. The smell of roasted meats and other foods drifted fragrantly through the air, and the mood was festive.

Through two large wooden doors, everyone moved. A vast, open area presented itself and along the walls were many seats and pillows for sitting on the smooth wooden floor. At the front was a stage and here James spotted the commander dressed in elaborate silk robes, reclining on large pillows. He was smoking from a long flexible tube that was attached to a round ceramic pot with legs and a bowl to put the substance for smoking in.

All around the commander were women that James had now come to identify as the 'Palace Butterflies.' They were dressed in beautiful but somewhat revealing outfits. Most were Asian or Indian, but he spotted several that were European in appearance. They reclined around the commander as if they were his pets and seemed content in doing so.

The group found seats and soon the show began. First, there came jugglers and acrobats; then musicians and magicians. It was all remarkable and fantastic just as the doctor had said. One act followed another. Then the food was brought out, and everyone ate and ate. James watched the commander, however, rather than socialize as everyone else was doing.

After eating a little, James walked over towards the commander. As he approached, he saw the commander whispering in one of the butterflies' ears and then she laughed with delight.

When James came within twenty feet in front of the stage, guards appeared from seemingly nowhere. They stood in front of James holding swords pointed at his heart.

"I just needed to talk with the commander," James said as he held his hands up to indicate he had no weapons.

The commander noticed the situation. "Oh, Mr. Taft, please come here."

Stepping aside, the guards allowed him to pass. James walked cautiously to the front of the stage area that was only a few feet off the floor.

"I see you've recovered well. That's marvelous." As the commander said this, several butterflies moved closer to him.

James wondered if the women were moving close to him for protection or in a show of protecting the commander. It was an odd display, but he quickly recalled his initial directive.

"Yes, Mr. Chauveau. I want to talk to you about the 'debt' I owe and when I can begin to settle with you."

"Oh, that... Yes, well Mr. Taft, this is no time to discuss boring 'business' details. We never do such things during our little celebrations."

He pulled another draw from the odd smoking device as he appeared to be considering the situation. He then replied as the butterflies watched James curiously.

"I'll tell you what. I'll come and visit you tomorrow at Doctor Jefferies' office. Will that be satisfactory?"

"Yes, that will be alright." James started to turn.

"You are staying to see the butterflies' dance, aren't you?"

James had already decided to leave, but when the commander asked, he quickly changed his mind, so as not to offend anyone.

"Yes, I suppose that I will." He replied.

"Excellent, they'll be up next. You will be impressed, I'm certain." The commander then smiled and expelled another stream of smoke.

James nodded and went back to his seat with the others.

The food tables were moved away, and the lights were dimmed. A hush of anticipation fell over the gathering.

Music began slowly, and the butterflies seemed to almost float out to the center of the floor. James didn't want to watch the dance, but it demanded everyone's attention. It was a beautiful display, and the dancers moved effortlessly in the grand setting.

James, however, would not allow himself to enjoy the show. He watched and was indeed impressed, but he felt guilt with any shred of pleasure. He shouldn't be here; he should have died that day. He felt as if he'd somehow let Sachi down by surviving and being here at a celebration. He was glad when it was over.

The following morning James walked into the main room of the office and was surprised to see Meili and Oshai working feverishly. They were cleaning and moving furniture about.

"Good morning Mr. Taft. The king will be arriving soon; you may wish to change clothes before he arrives." Oshai spoke with a nervous tone and quickly returned to his tasks.

James was again frustrated by the pomp and fuss. The commander was just a man, and James was not certain yet what he thought about this man.

Slowly he turned and went back to his small room. He again put the borrowed suit on and returned to the main area. Meili was now making some coffee, so James poured himself a cup when she'd finished it. He then sat down in a corner wicker chair.

A few moments later, James heard chimes outside the door. He sipped his coffee and watched as the others in the room quickly moved to the doorway. Oshai opened the door, and after stepping back he and the others bowed slightly.

Flower petals came floating inside the entryway, and then several Palace butterflies came in, tossing more all about the room. They then proceeded to find a spot by the wall and sat down in a very delicate and feminine fashion.

The commander entered, wearing his tinted glasses and using a cane. He wore another elaborately crafted silk jacket with tails, along with gentleman's pants and shirt.

Behind The commander was a petite Asian woman who was around thirty years old and she too was stunning.

Then, a beautiful sight entered the room, surprising James. She was like no other woman he had ever seen. She appeared to be Asian, but her face was painted white, and her lips were painted bright red. She wore an elaborate silk outfit, and her hands were tucked into the sleeves as she held them close to her stomach. Her hair was made up magnificently and decorated with dainty and colorful trinkets.

Behind this woman came the musicians and several guards. Soon all were sitting, and servants came from the back room to begin serving coffee. The group began talking in what James perceived as the language of Sandrilan and which he didn't understand. So, he simply watched and drank his coffee.

"Yes, it was a splendid show last night. The entertainers always impress me."

The commander spoke in a language that was used around the Pacific for trading purposes. Though not an official language; it had become the default language of Sandrilan and most now spoke it, at least enough to communicate.

The commander continued as he glanced over to James. "So, how is your patient Doctor? He seems to have healed well."

The doctor glanced over at James, and though he knew they must be talking about him, James understood nothing they said.

"Yes, he has healed and is doing well in the physical sense. But I'm afraid his spirit is still struggling."

James now noticed the woman with the white face glance at him. Her eyes expressed concern and compassion. She quickly looked away after their eyes met.

120

"Well, you see that I've brought Madame Zhou and she requested that Sno accompanies us. I felt this might be a situation in which a woman could tell us something more."

The commander looked at the small Asian woman and smiled. "Madame Zhou, this is the man I spoke to you about last night, the one that approached the sitting area. I would like your thoughts."

Madame Zhou glanced at James. She then discreetly studied him while sipping her coffee. After a moment, she replied.

"I would like to see what happens when a light is shined. Then I can tell you my thoughts." She turned to the woman with the painted face. "Sno, would you please perform a special dance for us?"

Sno bowed her head.

The commander smiled slyly and then turned to James.

"Mr. Taft, we will discuss our business soon. First, however, Sno has agreed to perform a special dance for us. She is a Japanese Geisha. I highly doubt that you've ever seen anything like this. The Japanese are closed to the rest of the world. We are very, very fortunate to have this remarkable Geisha here with us."

Sno stood and moved to the center of the room. She moved into a stiff pose with her face looking up to the ceiling. A musician in the corner began to play a stringed instrument, and she began to move in an unusual way. James watched with interest. He'd not seen anything like it before. She was indeed a beautiful young woman of around twenty-one or twenty-two maybe. And he had certainly never witnessed anything such as this dance.

Before her performance ended though, James had lost interest and was thinking of how long it would take before he could talk with the commander. His head sank, and he stared at the floor.

As Sno sat back down after her dance, the commander again turned to Madame Zhou. "Well, what do you think?"

After some additional thought, Madame Zhou replied. "This man is not dead, but he is not alive either. He's like a machine. He has pushed feelings out of his life. Beauty is only a brief smile for him. I've seen few men return from such a place."

The commander nodded subtly and replied. "But, some have..."

She turned quickly to face the commander. "Certainly, but very few do. I've witnessed strong men wither and die from such a thing. Few have the ability to overcome such darkness."

The commander sipped his coffee as he considered her words. He then spoke.

"This man has the experience needed to be a good Marine. Perhaps there is some hope for such a man, although I've never seen a person that could lose interest in one of Sno's dances."

When the commander said this, Sno turned to James. She gave no expression but examined him for a long moment.

"Alright Mr. Taft, we can speak of our business now." After the commander had said this in English, James sat back up in his chair.

"Thank you," James replied.

"So, you were with the 9th Pennsylvania Cavalry, and you fought during the war of the states in America. How many years were you with this unit?" The commander asked with his strong French accent.

"About, four and a half years."

The commander considered James reply and then continued.

"Then you've seen plenty of action. It's either a remarkable bit of soldiering or luck that enabled you to survive such a horrible war; perhaps a little of both."

The commander then retrieved a cigar from his case, and Oshai immediately lit a match for him. After pulling a draw of smoke from the cigar, he continued.

"I don't have any cavalry, but as you saw, I do have a small contingent of Marines." He rubbed his goatee in thought and then went on. "What was your rank with the 9th Pennsylvania?"

"I was a staff sergeant." James replied.

The commander rolled his cigar in his fingers and stared at it for a few seconds.

"Here's what I'll do, Mr. Taft. I'll bestow the rank of corporal on you and give you a position with my Marines. I'll not place any men under you however until you prove yourself. I'll consider your debt paid after two years of service."

"Two years?" James sat up straighter.

The commander glanced over at him and then replied in a calm voice. "Well, that is, if you should live that long."

James sat back a little. This had an appealing sound to it.

"So, just who do you fight? I mean, other than men such as Benjamin Pearce."

The commander pulled another draw from his cigar as the others sat watching the discussion with interest.

"Oh, the Valiant is in almost constant action, Mr. Taft. We have an ongoing conflict with South Sea Pirates and Serbian warlords; not to mention a host of other criminals. There's always a line of work for us. And it's always dirty, dangerous work."

James considered this as the commander watched him with interest.

"So, you're bounty hunters?"

The commander smiled with obvious amusement. He laughed a little, and the others laughed with him. "Bounty hunters, well, I've never actually thought of it that way."

He turned to the doctor, still smiling. "Have you ever considered it in that manner, Doctor?"

"No Sir, I've never thought of it in that way." Doc Jefferies also replied with a smile.

"Well, Mr. Taft, that is perhaps one way to look at it. To keep things simple however, we'll just say that it is, in a remote sort of way, 'bounty hunting.' Now, what is your response?"

James felt he was being taken advantage of with the two years of service. But if the Valiant saw extensive action then he would likely not see the end of the two years anyway.

"Alright, that'll be fine, two years service, or until killed in action."

The commander smiled in a sly manner, which left James even more concerned.

"Yes indeed, Corporal Taft, two years, or until killed in action. Welcome aboard the crew of the Valiant. I'm sure you'll find service on her like no other you've experienced."

The commander then stood up. With this move, everyone went into action. The musicians stood, and the butterflies began tossing flower petals before his feet as the commander turned. Oshai went to the door; opened it, then bowed. The chimes and small bells began to ring, and soon the commander was out the doorway with his entourage following behind.

Chapter Ten: The Soldier Returns

The morning following the commander's visit, a large Asian man came to the doctor's office. A closer examination revealed this to be the man that carried the long, sharp shooting rifle, which killed Leveran.

"Mr. Taft... or, I mean Corporal Taft, this is Kenji. He will be taking you to your new quarters aboard the Valiant."

When the doctor said this, James stood up. He was a bit surprised by the rapid change in housing, as well as now being called "Corporal." But it mattered little as he had only a few items of clothing donated by the doctor and no other plans in gaining additional worldly goods.

"Alright, thank you Doctor for everything you've done." James then turned to Kenji. "I only have a few things; I'll get them and be right with you."

Calm and stern-faced, Kenji nodded.

A few minutes later, James was following Kenji down the winding road to the small harbor. A strange feeling came over him as he walked the gangplank onto the warship.

Though he'd spent time on this vessel, it was vague and dark memories that came to mind. Now, in the sunlight and being clear minded, he marveled at the battle-scarred frigate.

In the lower decks, James was assigned a bunk, a small footlocker and an odd marine hat that seemed to have both Asian and European influences in the design. After this, a small Asian man came up to him and began measuring his body with bits of string. Then he left, and Kenji motioned for James to follow again.

They moved through the bowels of the ship until coming to a small area that was used for dining. Behind a counter was the kitchen. It was hot and humid inside; James thought he would rather eat out on the deck if there were a choice.

Kenji continued to point out various areas of the ship, and soon they were back at his little bunk, sandwiched between four others.

There were few men on the ship. Kenji left James after showing him around but never uttering a word. James suspected he spoke no English and since pointing at the various rooms and locations on the ship worked well, he also never attempted further communication with the large Asian man.

For the rest of the day, James wandered around the Valiant. A small bell rang out at noon, and he followed one of the men aboard to the dining room. There he was given a plate of food and ate quietly as three other men sat and ate while speaking in the Asian language to each other.

As the day moved into evening, men came back onboard. Many had been drinking too much. Most were from Asia, but a few were from India, along with several Russians and one black man named Samson.

All the men spoke in the Asian language James now recognized as the common language. As more men streamed into the bunk area, they took notice of James. He watched them closely as a number gathered around him and chattered to each other. Finally, Samson stepped closer and spoke in broken English, with a strong African accent.

"You are de Indian man that was near dead?" As Samson asked this, several Asian men apparently talked about James amongst themselves.

"Yes, I almost died. I remember seeing you with the commander." James replied.

Samson turned and spoke with the others; more chattering back and forth occurred.

"We think you was dead by now. You hard to kill, Indian man!" Samson smiled, and James also smiled a bit.

"I suppose. Doc Jefferies did a lot to keep me alive."

Samson laughed out loud with a booming voice. "We all owes Doc Jeffries much. He sew me up many a time." Samson pointed at several large scars on his arms.

The large black man stepped forward. "My name is Samson. What is your name Indian man?"

James thought about his tribal name. But he could not bear hearing it every day. To listen to the name Kalakone would bring the memories back, again and again.

"My name is James."

Samson shook his hand. "James, that is a good Indian name. Like Samson is good Africa name."

The African man then turned to his comrades, and after more chattering in the Asian language, the men returned to their business. Some played cards and others went to bed.

For a while, James watched the men and listened to the conversations. He tried to understand what they were saying, but soon lost interest and laid down in his bunk. As lanterns glowed long into the night, James finally rolled over and fell asleep.

The next morning, he awoke with the ringing of the small ship's bell. He concluded it must mean the morning meal was available.

Walking into the dining area, which he would soon learn was called the 'galley,' James found a line of men. Once he'd received his meal, he followed some of them to the top deck. The breeze cooled everyone off, and it seemed most also preferred to eat their meals in the fresher air.

After this, almost all of the sailors and Marines left the ship. As in any military, they went somewhere else to spend their time off.

James was only sure about Samson and a few other's actual duties. Samson, Kenji, and Jolli, he decided, must be Marines.

For a week, the same routine transpired. Some men stayed on the ship, but most went into town and acted as military men do. They would begin to stumble back to the ship after dark and continue coming onboard all through the night.

James had no desire to follow them. But on several nights, he did sit on the deck and listen to the excitement echoing around the hills of the town. He determined there were a number of entertainment establishments scattered about and could hear lively music from these various areas.

The following week everything changed. Monday morning was ushered in by Kenji walking through the deck shouting "appu, appu!"

Very quickly the men moved to dress in their uniforms. James had received his uniforms from the tailor a few days earlier but had resisted putting the unique clothing on. Now he reluctantly pulled a set out of the trunk and dressed.

Quickly breakfast was eaten before duties were assigned.

James was herded into a small group along with Samson. They walked from the Valiant to an area that housed tools. Each was given a shovel, and soon they were laboring along the roads clearing debris from drainage channels. Samson began to sing a song and all day the men worked.

126

The following day James was assigned to another group. This group was making repairs on the Valiant. Day after day he would either be working on the ship or the island. Then when Saturday arrived the men would be off duty and once again they would go into town. For three weeks, this routine continued.

On a Sunday evening, James noticed men sharpening knives and talking with serious tones. He felt certain something was about to change.

The next morning after the men ate breakfast they loaded onto some of the island boats used for moving materials from one island to the other.

The men rowed quickly out of the small harbor and were soon headed towards one of the many smaller islands dotting the area.

After a half hour of rowing, they landed in a small lagoon and were soon ashore. Following along, James found himself outside a bamboo hut. He was given an old musket that appeared to be non-firing due to age and neglect. The other men took their equally out of date muskets without complaint. Then each man was given a battered and rusty sword with sheath.

James watched curiously but followed suit as the Marines strapped the old swords on.

"Come along Indian man. We will earn our monies now." Samson then chuckled as he buckled his sword belt and slung the old musket over his shoulder.

Soon the group was trotting through the tropical vegetation with Kenji in the lead. As they moved farther along, the pace quickened. James found himself struggling for air.

Dodging obstacles and jumping over fallen trees, the men finished their jaunt at a full run and at what appeared to be the opposite side of the island.

James labored to breathe, as did a few others. Samson seemed little affected by the exercise and laughed aloud after sucking in some of the tropical breezes.

With only a short break, the group was off again. They walked swiftly along the beach in a marching fashion. The wet sand caused each step to be more difficult than the previous. Finally, after almost an hour of this strenuous effort, they came back around to the hut they'd started from.

The group replaced the out of date equipment and were back in the boats. James was given oar duty. Beside him, Samson hummed a tune as they rowed back towards Sandrilan.

Entering the small harbor, James noticed a large cargo vessel sitting next to the Valiant. Men were busily unloading something from this vessel onto the Valiant.

"Our beloved Valiant is taking coal. We leave soon, Indian man. You see, the sailors earn their monies now too." Again, Samson chuckled after saying this.

Once he and the other Marines were back onboard the Valiant, things began to move fast. First, they assisted in loading food, fresh water, and coal. Then the supply ship, which flew the flag of the Dutch East Indies, left the small port.

When everything had been prepared, the commander came down from the Palace with all the usual pomp and ceremony. The butterflies walked in front of him tossing flower petals. Behind him, two men carried the odd rectangular box that James had seen the first day he met the commander. And behind them was Madame Zhou with the rest of the entourage that always accompany the man.

After The commander was aboard, the ship was assisted from the dock and then moved out to the open seas.

James watched as the small cluster of islands gradually drifted from sight. He ate an evening meal and then began to experience the terrible condition known as sea sickness.

For several days, James struggled with sea sickness. Doc Jefferies did what he could, but told him only time would solve the problem.

James finally began to feel better after a week. And just as he did so, the Valiant went into action.

The ship's bell rang in a rapid, crisp alarm. Men off duty and resting in their bunks jumped out and moved towards the higher decks.

James moved from the quarter's deck up to the gun deck. The sailors were busily loading the large cannons. Before he'd stepped onto the stairway leading to the upper deck, five of the Valiant's large port side guns fired. The shots rocked the ship and left James' ears ringing.

After recovering from the shocking noise, he continued to the upper deck. Smoke from the large guns drifted by him. He spotted the ship being fired upon, and immediately another round of cannon fire belched out from the gun deck beneath him.

He located his fellow Marines lined up and receiving rifles from the armory officer. As he went to get in line, cannon shot began landing close to the Valiant. He looked again at the enemy vessel in the distance and saw smoke floating all around it from the ship's guns.

Samson moved past him with a repeating rifle and ammunition. He smiled at James.

"We gets to kill some pirates, Indian man. Or maybe they kills us." He laughed out loud and continued. "These China men, they hate de Valiant. But de Valiant, she always wins in the fight."

James smiled as Samson began loading his rifle and then walked towards the railing of the ship.

Again, the Valiant's guns fired. James felt his heart beating faster. He knew the feeling well. It was the feeling he always got before going into battle. He was excited and a little frightened at the same time.

James received his rifle and a box of ammunition. The rifles were in excellent condition. He began loading the gun as the ships closed in.

Twenty-two Marines lined the port side of the ship. They crouched down behind the armored railing. James glanced towards the wheelhouse. Commander Chauveau stood gazing towards the enemy ship. He appeared rather odd to James as the sun glistened like liquid on his silk coat.

Again, the Valiant fired a salvo at the pirate ship. This time several cannon balls connected violently with the wooden hull. Shards of wood flew into the air.

The ship was of Asian design, and it seemed was attempting to keep its distance from the Valiant, but remain close enough for its cannons to be in range.

The pirates fired a salvo from its guns. One shot hit close by, causing a large spray of water but no actual damage.

Having been hit themselves, the pirates now turned with the wind and began to move away. Kenji, in turn, was given orders by the commander, and the Valiant began pursuit.

For over an hour the Marines sat watching as the chase ensued. Finally, the men on deck were dismissed when the damaged enemy ship was barely visible on the horizon.

"No fight today, Indian man! These pirates they know times to run, eh?" Samson slapped James on the back and laughed. James nodded as he unloaded the rifle and prepared to turn it back into the armory.

"So, are we hunting these pirates down for a bounty?"

Samson had begun unloading his rifle as well when James asked this. He appeared to consider the question or perhaps had a little difficulty translating the English. After a few seconds, he replied in his jovial African accent.

"We are in a war with de pirates, Indian man. You don't know about de war?"

James nodded, "No, I suppose I don't know."

As they turned their rifles in and walked back to the bunk room, Samson explained.

"The Valiant she fight many bad peoples. But the stories I hear is that de commander he have another little ship before the Valiant. These China pirates, they try to take this little ship, and most of them die in the fight. One of them pirates that die, he was first son of big pirate boss.

"De commander, he does not know this, though. A few pirates, they surrender, so he puts them in small boats and give them some foods and water. These men ask to take their captain's body with them. The dead captain is the big pirate boss son. So, the commander he lets them do this, not knowing about that. They take the body, and then they look close at the flag of Sandrilan on de commander's boat.

"The commander, after he lets those surrendered pirates go, he takes their ship and sells it in America!"

Samson laughed loudly, seeming delighted by the commanders' actions.

"So, when the pirate boss finds out about his son dying, he is very, very angry and make war on any ship that flies the flag of Sandrilan. This pirate boss sends many ships to kill the Valiant. We fights these China pirates many times. They always lose though."

Samson laughed again and sat down with three other men as they prepared to play cards. He began talking in the common language that they communicated with, and James moved over to his bunk.

For another week the Valiant sailed unopposed. James cleaned the ship with his fellow Marines and became more accustomed to life on the sea. He also began learning the language everyone spoke. Samson helped him and told him about the language being used throughout the Pacific for trading purposes.

After almost a month at sea, James awoke to find the Valiant anchored in a small natural harbor. After the morning meal, the men lined up to be issued rifles and other equipment.

When James came to the armory person, he refused to issue James his equipment. He waved his hand and motioned for James to move aside. This made James angry.

As the other Marines were preparing to board the smaller boats and go ashore, James walked to the wheel house. The commander and Kenji were talking together as James moved up with an air of frustration.

"Why am I not being issued equipment?"

The commander and Kenji turned to him with surprise. Kenji then spoke to the commander in the Asian language that James had not yet learned.

"Sir, please allow me to execute this man now. I assure you, I'll clean up the blood."

The commander studied James for a few seconds. He then glanced at Kenji, as if trying to decide. Finally, he exhaled with some exasperation and replied.

"No, not at this time, let me speak with him."

The commander then turned to James and spoke in English.

"Corporal, this mission is very... shall we say 'delicate' and dangerous. We must march many miles and fight at night. Then we must return with the same speed. I feel you've recovered remarkably well, but I would rather you stay aboard the Valiant for this mission."

The commander's words did little to ease James' anger. He grimaced, nodded and marched back to the sleeping quarters. Sitting among the empty bunks, he could hear the boats being lowered.

After throwing his cap on the floor in anger, and then walking over and picking it back up, James returned to the top deck. He watched as the Marines landed on the shore, then hid the boats and moved inland.

Time slowed as he waited for the others to return. The Asian sailors stood at watch on deck day and night. James paced back and forth, from the lower decks to the upper deck. He examined the large sixty pounder cannons on the gun deck as several of the gun crew cleaned and polished them.

After three days, James heard some movement and excited conversation from the crew. He slid out of his bunk and quickly walked topside.

He could barely believe the sight he beheld. All three boats were rowing towards the Valiant. But rather than just the contingent of Marines in them, the boats were also filled with people. As the small craft came slowly closer, he identified men, women and children, all packed into the boats.

The sailors on deck were now chattering up a storm, and some were laughing at the sight. They gathered around the side of the ship and carefully assisted the people aboard.

It seemed they were from India, as a few spoke strongly accented English to the commander. There were twenty-eight men, women, and children altogether. They had some baggage, but most appeared to have only the clothes they wore.

Samson came aboard and laughed when he saw James.

"You miss a grand fight Indian man! We win again!" After saying this, the large African Marine began unloading his rifle.

"Yeah, I would have liked to got in on it," James replied as he watched the new passengers mill about on deck, seeming lost.

"Who are they?" James asked.

"Oh, them are Reffusez."

"Reffusez… What's that?"

Samson glanced up from his task. "Reffusez, you know, they are de war lost."

James thought for a few seconds. "You mean, refugees?"

Samson laughed aloud. "Yes indeed! I could not recall de word. Yes, they are poor, lost souls of de war. The commander, he help them. Too bad we have so little room."

James nodded. "Yes, I suppose so."

That evening Kenji came to the sleeping quarters of the Marines. Everyone stood up as the tall Asian man came in. He began

132

talking to James. Samson realized James didn't understand and began translating as best he could.

"Kenji say, 'You show the King respect, or he will pull your eyeballs out of head, and then kill you.'"

James was surprised and stared at Kenji. After a few seconds of thought, James replied, and Samson translated.

"Where I come from, we don't have Kings."

Kenji considered James' words as well. He then replied and again Samson translated.

"Mr. Kenji say, 'You are also very far from that place.'"

James stood silent for a few seconds. Before he could respond Kenji had turned and left the room.

Samson eased up closer to James.

"You be careful, Indian man. Kenji will not allow you to be no respect for Commander. No other man on Valiant will either. You should be happy, de Commander, he save you life."

James looked at Samson, then replied in a low voice, "I didn't ask to be saved."

For the next few weeks, the Valiant felt more like a wagon train than a fighting vessel. Children scurried about from the top deck all the way to the men's quarters. Clothes were hung all around to dry, and the smell of unfamiliar spices drifted through the ship.

Two weeks after the mission, the Valiant docked at a port in the Dutch East Indies. The commander gathered the refugees together and informed all that they could either disembark here or travel to Sandrilan and become citizens there.

After a discussion, two families disembarked, but the remainder chose to stay with the Valiant.

James was able to go ashore with Samson and a few other men. The odd sights and sounds were intriguing, and he temporarily forgot the sadness inside his soul. After taking on coal and provisions, the Valiant again ventured out onto the open seas.

Several weeks after leaving the East Indies port, James heard the familiar ringing of the ship's bell; three rapid rings, a short pause and then three rapid rings. He climbed out of his bunk, still half asleep. As he walked towards the upper deck, he could hear the large bells of Sandrilan sounding out a joyful reply.

The Valiant steamed slowly into the small natural harbor. James and his fellow Marines moved to the top deck and stood to watch the people of Sandrilan on shore. As always it seemed, the palace butterflies arrived and waited to throw their fragrant flower petals before The commander as he disembarked.

"The King, he is a fortunate man. There is no butterfly on that dock which is not beautiful." Samson smiled and nodded as he almost whispered this to James.

James now experienced the Valiant's return from the ship rather than the shore. As The commander walked across the gangway, the butterflies began tossing the flower petals in front of him. Then the chimes and cymbals started to ring out.

The entire event was quite impressive. But James refused to be swept away at the moment. As the others laughed and hugged family and friends on shore, James slipped out of the crowd.

Later, he found himself at Doctor Jefferies office. He sat out on the veranda and watched the people of Sandrilan below. Then he turned and glanced up towards the palace. He could hear music and laughter. This caused him to frown; he again wished he could have been a part of the mission. Perhaps he wouldn't be here now and wouldn't have to endure the music, laughter, and feast that were sure to come.

"Corporal Taft. Do you have something to wear for the celebration tonight? I can loan you the suit again, if not."

Doctor Jefferies came out to the veranda with Meili happily hanging onto him. Both smiled with delight.

"No, I don't have anything to wear. But I don't think I'll attend tonight. It's not mandatory, is it?"

The smile slipped from the Doctor's face. "Well, I don't suppose it's mandatory, but everyone attends. It's a tradition on Sandrilan. You really should go, Corporal. I think it will help you. Perhaps not in the physical sense but, well, otherwise I feel it would do you good."

James looked at Doc Jefferies, who expressed concern. Meili still had a smile on her face, indicating she understood little of what they had spoken about. James looked back down towards the wooden floor.

"No, I really don't feel like going. I'll be alright, thank you."

Later that night, James laid in his bunk on board the Valiant. Even from this distance, he could hear the music of the celebration far up on the hillside. He rolled to his side and finally fell asleep.

134

The following day a small Asian quartermaster came aboard and paid all of the men. James held his two gold and three silver coins. They were heavy in his hand. He hadn't received pay since his days on the Oregon Trail. He was at a loss for what to do.

"Indian man, you go with me this night. I know where there are womenz almost beautiful as de butterflies. They will like Indian man, and me to bring them, Indian man." Samson then laughed with his booming voice. He slapped James on the back, and the coins almost leaped from his hand.

"Uhm, thanks, Samson. I believe I'll just stay on board the ship tonight. But I appreciate the offer all the same."

The days passed slowly while the ship was docked. Other than during their guard duties, and to sleep, the Marines and sailors spent their days in the growing town of Sandrilan.

Eventually James did go with Samson during one of their off days. He bought a few books that he thought might help him learn the language. These were written and printed in the Dutch East Indies and also in the trading language spoken on the Valiant and in Sandrilan.

He also went to Doc Jefferies' office and began playing chess with the physician. This took his mind off other things, and though the Doctor attempted conversation, James said little. He found that refraining from speaking kept his past closed up, where it was easier for him to deal with. He simply replied to the doctor in short sentences and avoided any lengthy discussions.

It was during one of these chess games on the veranda that James first learned about Sir William Barrett. It was a humid day as usual. A slight breeze moved about just enough to give some reprieve from the tropical climate. With the sudden ringing of bells, James and the doctor both were aroused from their focus on the game.

The Doctor stood and moved over to the rail. James also stood and moved beside the Doctor. There, they could see a small ship easing into the harbor. It wasn't a warship and was only around half the size of the Valiant.

"Ahh, our good friend Sir William Barrett; the Valiant will soon be back in action." The doctor then stepped back to the table and sat down to finish the game.

"Sir... William Barrett? Isn't that the title of a Knight?" James could not hold back his curiosity.

"Yes, it is indeed, Corporal." The Doctor then moved one of his pawns.

James tried to focus on the game but found himself more interested in the arrival of this 'Knight.'

"So, why do you say we'll be back in action soon?" James then moved his pawn to block the Doctors' move.

"Well, we always are after the arrival of Sir Barrett."

Now James began to realize that Doctor Jefferies was giving him the same conversation tactics as he had been giving.

Doctor Jefferies moved his rook. He glanced up at James and smiled slyly.

"I suppose you would like more information about Sir Barrett?"

James moved another pawn, "If it's not too much trouble."

Again, the Doctor smiled. Then he began to explain as he continued to study the chess board.

"Sir Barrett brings the commander tasks from time to time. There are hundreds of political and military situations occurring every day, all around the world. Large countries may not wish to handle particular problems directly. So, the Valiant has become a tool of choice for many, shall we say, 'undesirable issues that need to be resolved indirectly.'"

James considered this. "You mean such as tracking down the Carthage and its captain, Benjamin Pearce?"

The doctor glanced up at James. He smiled and then moved the rook once again.

"Precisely. Benjamin Pearce was a criminal. He preyed on islanders in the South Pacific. He kidnapped them or deceived them into thinking they would work and earn a lot of money. Either way, he simply sold them as slave labor.

"What Benjamin Pearce banked on was that large countries would not get involved with the relatively minor issue. He thought that the Chiefs and small governments of these islands had no navy of its own to pursue him. He felt he was safe in his criminal activities, but, woefully neglected to consider the Valiant. Nor, it seems that even though these islands had no navy, they did have enough money to hire the Valiant."

James moved a pawn to block the Doctors' rook.

136

"So, the Valiant is the bounty hunter, and Sir Barrett supplies the information concerning bounties available."

Doc Jefferies looked at James. His mouth twisted slightly as he considered this. Finally, he replied.

"Sir Barrett often brings information as to what tasks are available. The commander then chooses which tasks the Valiant will pursue. I don't feel that 'bounty hunter' is a fair description of what the Valiant does. But, to each their own, I suppose."

James took a drink, sat his glass down and replied.

"Well, call it what you wish Doc, but in the United States we don't try to sugarcoat such things."

A quiet came over the veranda as James studied the chess board. He then continued in his assessment.

"So, we're all paid to hunt down bad people... It's not a profession I would have considered getting into, but I suppose it's better than being the one with the bounty on your head."

James then glanced back to the harbor below. The small ship had docked beside the Valiant, and some people were disembarking. A few moments later the group was walking the winding path up to the palace.

That night there was another celebration. James lay in his bunk as the music could again be heard deep in the bowels of the Valiant. James and only a few other personnel were on the ship, and these had the unfortunate task of guard duty, or they too would have been at the Palace.

Several days later Sir Barrett was escorted to his small craft by the commander and his entourage. James watched from the deck of the Valiant as the two men shook hands. A short time later the small vessel was assisted by boats back to the open seas.

The following day James and the other Marines once again rowed out to the small island. This time they took their rifles and some ammunition. After running around the small piece of land, they had a round of target practice. Then they rowed back to the main island before lunch time.

Back aboard ship, the men checked their gear.

"I wonders where it is we going to now." Samson expressed his usual jolly tone as he seemed to be speaking his mind rather than asking anyone in particular.

"I loves this ship, an I loves that we never knows where the Valiant may go, till we gets there."

As Samson said this, James re-holstered his pistol. Slowly, and almost one piece at a time, he received a Colt Army revolver, holster, mess kit and knife; then a week later he received his kit pack and various other items.

"Well, maybe I'll get in on the mission this time," James replied as Samson also packed his gear.

"Oh, you will get some fighting for sure Indian man. The commander, he like us marines to stay sharp. You will get plenty of fighting soon." Samson then laughed as if he had told a joke.

The next morning James stepped up on deck to find they were far out to sea. He no longer felt the sea sickness, and as the salty breeze caressed his face, he felt excited to be on the move again.

The Marines stayed busy with chores around the ship and when not on watch or cleaning, they would play cards and gamble what little pay they'd not spent on Sandrilan.

James, however, stayed to himself for the most part. He did begin to understand the language better, and as the warship moved farther out to sea, he spoke words to Samson that he'd learned. This caused the jovial black man to laugh and encourage James to speak more.

For the most part, the Valiant used its sails. Samson mentioned on one occasion that the commander always conserved the coal whenever possible. "The steam engine, she is used as the Valiant's edge. When you see's much smoke come from the stack, then you knows we are sure in for a fight!" Then Samson slapped James on the back. It seemed the large South African man was always ready for a scrap.

A week later, the Valiant dropped anchor in sight of a hilly, tropical land mass.

James stood on the deck staring at the trees and forest in the distance. As the evening light grew dim, Samson walked up beside him. "I know this place, we will fight Te Kuotie again."

"Te Kuotie?" James asked.

"Yes, Te Kuotie. He is very fierce war Chief. He attack many peoples and take prisoners. Big fight we have ahead. But, first, we must fight forest to get to Te Kuotie. Very difficult travel, but we always win de fight... so far."

138

Samson laughed again, but it was a nervous laugh this time. As the large black man walked away, James again studied the distant land.

The following morning after breakfast, Kenji called the Marines together on deck. He stood by the wheelhouse and spoke in the Asian language that James was still trying to learn. He could only understand a few of the words; he struggled to catch bits and pieces.

As Kenji spoke and made gestures with his hands, the commander strolled casually back and forth behind the large Asian man. After around fifteen minutes of talking to the Marines, Kenji turned to the commander, who then stepped up and said a few words, nodded his head and stepped back. Kenji then appeared to dismiss the men, and they moved to the armory to retrieve their rifles and ammunition.

Samson moved up beside James. The African man expressed a fondness for him, or he may have just liked speaking English, James wasn't for certain. Either way, he was glad about it as Samson had become his best source for information.

"Oh, we in for big fight! Te Kuotie, he has surrounded a village that he say too friendly with the colonials. Much suffering these people have had. We must find it and free the peoples before Te Koutie kill them all. This will be a big fight. The commander, he surely will bring the special box this time."

As they stepped up closer to the armory person, James asked, "Special box? What is that, the wooden box with the Asian writing on it?"

Samson laughed, again with a nervous tone. "Yes surely, Indian man. We will surely need the special box this time. You can see why we carry the special box this time; we in the big fight ahead."

Samson took his rifle and several boxes of ammunition. James stepped up to retrieve his gear. Again, the Asian armory person waved his hand.

"What? No, I'm going on this mission!" James became flush with anger.

"Tidak, tidak..." The man said, waving his hand.

James gritted his teeth and wanted to shout at him, but he knew it would do no good. He turned and made his way straight to the commander's quarters. He knocked twice and opened the door. The commander was standing behind his desk holding a slim cigar as if smelling it.

"Commander, why am I not being issued a rifle and ammunition?"

The commander glanced at James and grimaced as if the intrusion was an irritation. He took a deep breath and exhaled slowly.

"Please, sit down Mr. Taft." The commander then sat down behind his desk, and James rather reluctantly sat down in a chair facing the desk.

"Mr. Taft, you'll not be going on this mission. Nor, for that matter any mission, until you begin to act more like a soldier. Your half-cocked eagerness to get into action concerns me. I'll not endanger my men to indulge what appears to be your... desire for self-destruction."

James sat back a little when the commander revealed this awareness of James innermost thoughts. The commander continued.

"Do you have any idea who we are about to engage in battle with?"

James replied rather meekly.... "Te Kuotie."

"Yes, Te Kuotie, a tribal warlord, and a ferocious fighter. He has established his own religion, and his many followers are quite willing to die for him. But, before we engage this group of fighters, we must first cross dangerous and treacherous lands. Now, if you thought as a soldier should, you would understand that by not speaking the common language very well and having little knowledge of our current enemy, you would be a liability rather than an asset on this mission."

The commander paused; he leaned back in his chair. James glanced at him. The commander then continued with his strong French accent.

"Unless, that is, you planned on being killed quickly. In which case Mr. Taft, I would have no chance of obtaining the two years of service from you that we agreed upon."

The men looked at each other for several long seconds. James felt deflated and uncomfortable. He realized the commander was correct. He'd not been thinking like a soldier at all.

The commander seemed to sense James' thoughts. His tone softened some.

140

"When you learn the language better and show me you're able to recall your training and skills as a soldier, then you can go on the missions, Mr. Taft."

James nodded his head. He stood up sluggishly. He then did something he'd not done for years; he came to attention and saluted the commander. This caused a brief smile to cross the Frenchman's face. The commander quickly and casually returned a salute.

Once outside the commander's quarters, James walked aimlessly along the deck as the other marines prepared to load onto boats.

"You not going Indian man?" Samson asked as he adjusted the shoulder straps on his kit pack.

"No, not this time, maybe next time." James still felt empty from his meeting with the commander.

"Yes, maybe next time. These warriors of Te Koutie, they have lost minds. They kill without mercies. You should be ready before fighting them."

James nodded, with little enthusiasm. Samson moved over with the other Marines.

As James stood watching, two Asian men walked past him carrying the strange wooden box he had seen the first day he met the commander. He examined it with interest as it was lowered into one of the boats. The other Marines appeared quite pleased to see it and spoke with smiles and laughter upon its arrival.

Soon The commander and Marines were loaded, and six landing boats were rowing away from the Valiant. James watched them until they disappeared inland. He then went to his bunk and lay down. He reconsidered his talk with the commander. It was true that he had been languishing in despair all these months. Only now did he feel strong enough to stand back up. He decided at this time that he would give the commander his two years. If nothing else, it would be a good distraction from the dark past behind him.

Time slowed to an almost standstill as the sailors and James waited. Day after day he would gaze out to the distant shore. The rain came often and caused the air to be heavy and damp; still, no sign of the marines could be seen.

Ten days after their departure, James woke in the middle of the night to the sound of a baby crying. Climbing out of the bunk he was surprised by the sight of women, children and men clamoring down the steps to the bunk area.

As he made his way through the scantily dressed natives, he came upon Samson, struggling to get to his bunk. The large African appeared weak and exhausted.

"We had grand fight Indian man. Many refusez..." Samson then collapsed into his bed.

James moved to the upper deck. From the starlight and several small lanterns, he could see more refugees climbing to the ship. He spotted the commander assisting the natives. He also appeared exhausted.

"Sir, is there anything I can do to help?"

The commander glanced at James. He thought for a few seconds and replied wearily, "There are more refugees ashore Corporal. We have only a little time before Te Kuotie's men find them. Can you help with the rowing to retrieve them? The men are exhausted. If you and the sailors are not able to bring these people back in time, they'll be slaughtered."

"Yes, Sir, we'll get them onboard."

As soon as the last refuge was safely aboard, James and the sailors took the boats quickly towards the shore. Small fires had been lit on the beach to direct them to the waiting natives. James rowed hard, and as they came closer to the land, he could hear the sound of women and children weeping from fear, causing him to put even more effort into his task.

Once the boats slid onto the sandy shore, James and the sailors jumped out. They began helping the group of natives and a few Marines guarding them aboard. As they did this, torches could be seen in the forest and headed towards the beach.

"Hurry, hurry..." James told a young woman holding a baby. He helped them into the boat as shouts were heard from the woodlands. Te Koutie's warriors were closing in. Frantically the sailors pushed the packed boats back into the water. There was barely enough room for James to climb in.

As the boats moved farther out to sea, a mass of warriors came to the beach. Arrows and projectiles began to hit the boats and a few unfortunate natives. Women screamed, and babies cried as the Marines fired several shots at the enemy on shore. James rowed with a renewed strength, ignoring the fire and pain in his muscles.

As they came up to the Valiant, Te Koutie's warriors remained on the beach, shouting and waving their torches in anger. James climbed aboard and met the commander on deck.

"That's all of them Sir." He said while still trying to catch his breath.

The commander appeared thoughtful as Kenji walked up to them.

"So, Corporal, you're saying the only people left on that beach are hostiles...?"

James nodded, "Yes Sir, we've retrieved the remainder of our men and all the refugees from the beach."

The commander turned to Kenji and said, "Memberi mereka rasa Valiant's meriam."

Kenji smiled slightly and bowed to the commander. He then shouted out something to the sailors and they, in turn, began shouting and gesturing for the natives to get down.

Kenji meanwhile jogged off and down towards the gun deck. A few seconds later the sailors were motioning to the natives to hold their ears. The commander turned to James and smiled slyly. At this instant, James realized what was about to happen. Suddenly the guns of the Valiant fired a full broadside, and the deck shuddered under his feet.

The mass of cannon shot roared onto the shore, decimating the hostile warriors. The natives onboard and those still in the boats screamed in terror from the loud guns. Then, slowly, as they regained their senses and realized what had happened, an expression of joy rang out.

James watched the commander as he gazed over the refugees. He turned to James with a smile of satisfaction on his face.

"Well played, Sir," was all James could say.

The commander appeared pleased with this remark. He nodded and said, "And that was a fine piece of soldiering as well, Corporal. Please double your efforts to learn the language of Sandrilan. I would like you on our next mission, if possible."

James smiled and saluted. "Yes Sir, I'll do that, Sir."

The voyage back to Sandrilan was extremely unusual as barely clothed natives moved about the ship with obvious sea sickness. Children appeared to weather the trip better and played their usual games. The crew and James endeavored to help the refugees as much as possible, and all were glad to slip into the small harbor of Sandrilan finally. The bells rang out and welcomed the weary traveler's home.

Again, the Palace butterflies tossed the flower petals before the commander as music and cymbals played. Once the commander had moved up towards the palace and the crew was all off, the refugees began to disembark.

As if assigned to do so, there were men and women from Sandrilan helping the natives as they left the ship. It appeared that some people among the community spoke the language of the refugees and as they helped them, they uttered rapid sentences back and forth.

James felt glad these people were rescued. He also felt like attending the celebration, which he knew would take place. It was an odd sensation to feel like celebrating again. Yet, he'd finally come to a place where he could be happy for the work he had done.

The next morning James stood in formation on the deck of the Valiant. The quartermaster moved down the line until he reached James. He spoke a few words as he glanced at a worn leather accounting book. He handed James four gold coins and four silver coins, then moved to the next man.

James glanced down at the pay. Hmm, he thought; must have got a raise...

After receiving his pay, James went with Samson to buy new clothes. He had never really noticed how fantastic Sandrilan was until now. The buildings lined winding walkways and small roads throughout the hills of the tropical island. There were many varieties of structures, and this coincided with the mixture of people and cultures.

Samson took James to a quaint little tailor shop. It sat perched on one of the many hills of Sandrilan. The tailor began to measure James when something very odd began to happen. From the palace area, bells began to ring out. Then, from the high area of Sandrilan bells joined in until there was a symphony of ringing around the tropical city. James had heard this odd bell ringing before but had paid little attention to it. Today he would see the effects first hand.

As the bells began to sound out, the tailor stopped measuring. He then chattered something in the language of Sandrilan and immediately began to usher the two out.

While they walked towards the door, James asked Samson, "What's going on?"

"The King, he climbs to top of Sandrilan. He needs to think, and all must be quiet. Sandrilan will stand still until the King returns."

"What?" James asked as the tailor shut the door behind them and locked it.

Samson pointed to the highest hill behind the palace. It was the pinnacle of Sandrilan.

"That is special place where de commander goes to think. He must look to the future of Sandrilan. We must be still and wait for him to come down."

James could barely believe this.

"So, the commander goes up there for some 'quiet time, 'and everything stops?"

"Yes," Samson replied with a smile. "We can wait here or go to de ship. It may be a while before he comes down."

James shook his head in amazement. "The commander is just a man, Samson. I find it difficult to believe everyone just... holds their collective breath while he sits up there and 'thinks.'"

Samson obviously disliked this, "He's not just a man, he's your King and Commander. You show more respect Indian man. He save your life."

James glanced at the large African man and expressed no fear. "Yes, but I never asked him to save my life."

The two strolled around Sandrilan for about an hour and a half. Every shop and the business establishments were closed tight. People sat on benches and moved about, they did so in an extremely peaceful manner, as if not to disturb someone that was sleeping.

Finally, bells rang softly from the palace, and a cascade of bells joined in all around Sandrilan. This time the bells were ringing in a subtle manner, almost as if to gently wake the island from slumber.

"Now we go back and finish your clothes," Samson said and began walking towards the tailor shop.

The skilled Asian tailor quickly returned to work, and by late afternoon he had completed a nice silk jacket and pants.

As daylight turned to dusk, James cleaned up and dressed for the celebration. He then joined a procession of Sandrilinians moving towards the Palace. The people all smiled, laughed and expressed great joy while walking the small winding roads up to the royal complex.

Upon approaching the structure, James was impressed with the amount of work that had been accomplished since his last visit. Now, a large covered pavilion area could be seen as he passed through the gates.

Lanterns, lamps, and torches lit up the grounds and added to the excited atmosphere. The covered pavilion allowed ample room for the hundreds of people that began to settle in for the occasion.

James found a place to sit among some of his fellow Marines, including Samson. He glanced to the front and could see the commander sitting on his elevated stage. As seemed his custom, the commander was dressed in elaborately styled, silk clothing. He smoked from the odd bowl with tubes. Samson told him it was called a 'Hookah.'

As the commander smoked and drank, the butterflies moved close to him. They seemed delighted at the prospect of a simple glance from their king. To the commander's right side and off the platform that he and the butterflies sat on, James could see Madame Zhou, Sno, and several other women. Sno was dressed in her beautiful Japanese Geisha attire and sat daintily watching the crowd. There were several other women of Asian appearance beside Sno, and these were also dressed in costumes which were much more elaborate than the butterflies' outfits.

Soon a gong sounded and the celebration began.

First, drums sounded and sticks were hit together causing a clicking sound. Men ran out and into the center of the performance area. They twirled torches that were lit on both ends, while others juggled regular torches about, throwing them into the air and catching them. The women and children gasped and laughed with joy at the sight of these fire performers.

Next came the butterflies, some of which had obviously slipped away from the commander during the first performance.

Everyone became quiet as the music began. The group of around twenty dancers floated out to the performance area. They all moved together in precision and what looked to be a mix of several Asian influences combined. It was a spectacular show, and James enjoyed watching the graceful and delicate moves by the beautiful dancers.

Once their dance was over, they appeared to float away and soon acrobats ran and flipped into the open area. Again, the crowd gasped and shouted with approval of these talented performers.

Eventually the lights were dimmed and a strange but beautiful music began to play. Sno stepped gracefully out into the performance area. She began to dance and move in an elegant and extraordinary fashion.

As James watched with interest, Samson leaned over and whispered, "This woman is magic for a man's heart, yes?"

James nodded but refused to let her magic affect him. He couldn't bring himself to feel emotional in the respect Samson spoke of. He was impressed with Sno but doubted that he could ever again feel the things the other men felt while watching her great dance.

Next came more dances and performances of many different and exciting types. Then a grand feast was served, and finally, the celebration ended around midnight.

James walked wearily back down to the Valiant and gladly fell into his bunk for a restful sleep.

As he had told the commander he would do, James doubled his efforts to learn the common language spoken among Sandrilans. Samson helped him and often laughed at James' mistakes. But it was a hearty laughter, and James found himself also chuckling with his new friend.

After a few weeks, the Valiant returned to the sea. The Marines went on several missions and always seemed to arrive back at the ship with refuges that wished to escape the troubled areas.

James would stand in line to retrieve his rifle and ammunition before each mission, but would be turned away each time. However, now James would simply nod his head politely and step out of line.

Every mission, the mysterious 'special box' would be placed into the boat that the commander resided in.

On several occasions, James asked Samson what the box held. The large African would laugh and say, "De box, she hold de gates of hell; someday you will see them open, Indian man."

Sometime later James asked again. Samson now appeared quite entertained by James' curiosity. "In de box is a... typhoon, to let go on our enemies..." He laughed again and walked away. James decided it would be pointless to ask him again.

The days, weeks and months began to pass by routinely. When not at sea, James would occupy his time reading, or on occasion, he would venture to the 'entertainment' areas of Sandrilan with Samson and some of the other Marines.

He would have a few drinks and watch as the women would entertain the Marines with erotic dances and other feminine skills. Often one of the ladies would try to escort James to a room in the back so she could entertain him in a more personal way. James would smile and at times simply give the woman some money. He could not bear such a thing; it hadn't been a year since the loss of his beloved Sachi.

James also visited Doc Jefferies and enjoyed a challenging game of chess, when the Doctor could spare the time. Doc Jefferies was now training Jollie to be a doctor, and this consumed much of his day when not attending to the sick or injured.

By this time, the small clinic had developed into a hospital and needed a full-time doctor. Jollie would take over as the ship's doctor, and Doc Jefferies would remain at Sandrilan to care for the growing population.

On one occasion, however, around nine months after James had entered service on the Valiant, he and the Doctor sat on the veranda playing a game of chess. As the Doctor moved his bishop to take one of James' pawns, a question came to James' mind and erupted from his mouth.

"So, Doctor... What exactly does the 'special box' contain?"

Doc Jefferies face became strained when James asked this. He appeared slightly startled. He sat the pawn down beside the chess board and replied with a nervous voice, "Just what special box are your referring to, Corporal?"

James could tell this was an effort by the Doc to stall. He studied the chess board briefly and then asked, "Is there more than one 'special box', Doctor?"

Doc Jefferies now expressed obvious frustration. "I would rather not discuss this right now, Corporal."

James moved one of his pawns. He thought for a few seconds and continued. "Are you... frightened by the box, Doctor?"

Doc Jefferies looked at James again. His face twisted slightly. He sat back just a little. "Yes, Corporal, I'm quite frightened by what that box represents. You're a soldier; you're in the business of death;

perhaps you can speak of such things casually. I'm a doctor, however; my business is to preserve life. I have no words to describe what that box is about. Now, if you'll excuse me I have things to attend to."

Doc stood and walked away. James sat and considered his words before he returned to the Valiant and took a nap.

The next day, after his usual duties, James walked around Sandrilan. He noticed several of the natives that had been saved from Te Kuotie's warriors. He also saw they wore more clothing than when first arriving on the Valiant. This prompted a smile.

He continued and stopped at several shops. He liked practicing his language skills and now communicated fairly well with the shop keepers.

At times, he would watch as small cargo ships would arrive and depart from the harbor. These brought trade goods and various materials needed by the kingdom. James learned that the vessels were often ships owned by the kingdom of Sandrilan. Only a few 'special' Dutch East Indies ships and Sir Barrett's vessel were allowed into the harbor otherwise.

Throughout the hills of the main island, well hidden by the tropical vegetation, were heavy cannon emplacements. Samson pointed a few of them out to James on one occasion and mentioned that the south sea pirates would certainly attack Sandrilan if they ever discovered the location. This was why the commander only allowed specific cargo ships to carry goods in and out.

Chapter Eleven: Sip Song Chau Campaign

The following week the Valiant left Sandrilan and headed for Singapore. After a lengthy journey, they arrived at the busy Asian port. The men were not allowed to disembark on this occasion and could only view the bustling port city from the Valiant.

On the second day, the Marines and sailors were ordered into their dress uniforms to receive special guests onboard.

James stood at attention with the other marines as an elaborately dressed Asian man, and his entourage boarded the Valiant. Behind this group and to James surprise, came Sir William Barrett and what appeared to be several Asian assistants.

The commander and Kenji met the men and shook hands. The group then went to a meeting room below the main deck. The Marines and sailors were dismissed after this. James and the Marines eagerly retreated to the bunk deck and took off the fancy dress uniforms.

The next few days were spent loading provisions and coal. The last items loaded were some large crates. Upon opening these wooden boxes, the men were happily surprised to see new Winchester rifles and ammunition. These were state of the art repeating rifles. The Marines handled and examined the new weapons with excitement before being ordered to turn them into the armory.

The following morning the Valiant slipped out of the busy port and steered northeast.

Samson seemed concerned as he and James stood out on the top deck. He relayed his apprehension in the language of Sandrilan that James now understood very well and spoke fairly well.

"I wonder about this mission. We've never done these things before. I think this will be a very different mission."

James nodded but made no comment. He had yet to go ashore and fight with his fellow Marines. He struggled with frustration about this. But, as a soldier, he knew it was a decision the Commander must make, not him.

A week later, the Valiant quietly moved into a small natural harbor. James could see this was a tropical region and some Asian sailing craft were tied up to the crude docking facilities.

The people came from the 'house' boats and the small town to stare at the massive warship sitting in their midst. For several hours there was a crowd around the docks, all jockeying to get a better look at the visitors. Finally, a small contingent of soldiers arrived and dispersed the crowd. The people moved back from the docks but continued to linger in the distance and marvel at the Valiant.

Again, a small group of Asian men came aboard. James and several other Marines expressed gladness that they were not ordered into their dress uniforms as at Singapore.

After an hour in the commander's quarters, the group left one man on the ship while the others disembarked. The man they left appeared to be an officer and James realized he also spoke the language which was spoken on Sandrilan.

The following morning, after breakfast, the commander called the Marines and sailors of the Valiant together on deck. Standing by the wheelhouse, he began to speak.

"Gentlemen, this is Captain Chatri of the federation army of Sip Song Chau." The commander pointed to the soldier that had remained on board the previous day.

Captain Chatri bowed slightly, and the commander continued.

"We are currently docked in a small, isolated harbor in Southern Tonkin, which is currently a French protectorate."

The commander paused, scanned out over his men and continued.

"The country of Sip Song Chau is a neighbor of Tonkin and has been invaded by gangs of murder's and thugs known as 'Yellow Flags.' These are remnants of military groups fleeing the Siamese army. They've entered the small home country of Captain Chatri, and the results have been savagery and brutality upon his people.

"The Sip Song Chau Federation does not wish to pursue French assistance as this would likely open the door for French annexation. Their own army is also ill-equipped to handle this type of situation. They need an outside force to come in and put the bandits and murders are on their heels; if only long enough for them to get their own army into an offensive situation."

He paused and looked over his men. The tropical heat beat down as the sun rose higher in the sky. The Commander then continued.

"We've been commissioned for a six-week mission. We'll travel inland by river, and once we reach Sip Song Chau, we'll travel with Captain Chatri and his regiment to hunt down the Yellow Flags.

"Sir Barrett has researched this campaign well for us, and I assure you, we will be saving many innocent lives." He paused again and then ended his talk with, "We'll also be paid very, very well."

The men erupted into cheers upon hearing this and the commander, as well as Kenji, couldn't help but smile.

James, however, couldn't bring himself to cheer. He suspected that once again he would be lingering onboard the Valiant. He felt it would be a miserable and long six weeks as he waited for his fellow soldiers to return.

The day wore on as Captain Chatri moved a contingent of guards around the Valiant. James heard the captain and commander discussing the situation. Kenji would remain with the Valiant. Soldiers of Sip Song Chau would protect the ship, but if there were any excessive threats, the ship would leave and move to another anchorage location farther South. Here it would wait for the men and bring them on board once they returned.

The next morning the Marines were ordered to receive their new firearms and ammo. James had packed his kit bag as usual and stood in line to retrieve his Winchester rifle and ammunition. He was already prepared for the small Asian man to turn him away. To his delight, however, the man handed him the rifle and a large supply of ammunition. James felt his entire being shudder slightly as he struggled to hold onto the ammo and move from the line. Finally, he would get back into action. It was satisfying and yet a bit frightening at the same time.

Events began to occur rapidly after receiving their firearms. The group of twenty-five marines moved from the Valiant to the shore and from there marched single file along paths used by the native people. After some time, they arrived at a river and found seven long boats with another small contingent of Captain Chatri's men waiting.

The men loaded into the boats and the special box was loaded in with the commander. Off they went again, swiftly up the waterway. Chatri's men rowed with expertise and efficiency.

Around noon, the boats pulled into an area that looked to have been prepared as a resting point for the group. Several Asian men had a fire going and began cooking a meal immediately after the boats pulled ashore. The Marines ate, and as they briefly rested, the hosts came around with pungent oil. Captain Chatri told the men to rub the oil on their exposed skin as it would deter the mosquitoes. After this was done the Marines loaded into the boats and were again moving with a sense of purpose up the dark river.

As dusk settled across the tropical land, the boats slipped into another rest area. They ate and slept. Early the next morning the trip continued with little time wasted.

James watched the passing scenery with interest as they moved swiftly up the river. Bamboo huts with grass roofs blended into the deep forests and lush vegetation. The rain came down often and at times in torrential quantities. More than once, James and his fellow Marines found themselves frantically scooping water from the boat as Chatri's men continued to row non-stop.

The group moved in this manner for six days. Then, early on the seventh day, they came to a small army outpost. The soldiers were dressed in the same manner as Captain Chatri and his men. James had a feeling they must finally be in Sip Song Chau territory.

After a meal and short rest, the group moved onto a roadway. The Marines were slightly shocked to find themselves amongst elephants. Captain Chatri's so-called 'regiment' consisted of around one hundred and fifty men, ten elephants that carried provisions and a few elaborately dressed officers.

As James examined the Sip Song Chau soldiers, he realized very few had an actual firearm. Of the few that did, these were old, outdated muskets and flintlocks.

The group began to move steadily along ancient roadways. James wondered when they would encounter the enemy, but he didn't wonder for long. Two days out from the Sip Song Chau army outpost the group came under attack.

The commander and Captain Chatri discussed the situation as sporadic musket fire was heard two hundred yards to the front. Soon they appeared to have made a decision. The captain moved towards his men, and the commander came back to James and the waiting Marines.

"Alright men, the enemy are attacking our front. They're unaware that a squad of highly skilled and heavily armed Marines is nearby. Captain Chatri is moving the elephants to our flanks right now." The commander pointed to the open fields. The elephants were seen moving to each side of these areas.

The commander continued. "The captain will have his men charge the enemy and then fall back. The hope is that they will pursue. I'll place you in positions to ensure we have an advantageous crossfire, once the enemy is in that area there." The commander pointed out a large open field. "And, after Chatri's men have passed, I'll give the order to open fire, and you take down as many as possible."

He then became quite serious. "Have no mercy on these savages, men. They're murdering thugs and will not have any on you if you're captured."

James was given a position behind a leafy bush. Samson was to his right. The large African man turned to James and smiled as he cocked his Winchester. James smiled back and cocked his rifle as well. The distant but familiar feeling of an approaching battle subtly came over him. He wiped some of the oily sweat from his brow and focused on the front.

The sounds of war grew closer. Men shouted, and muskets fired. Soon Chatri's men were seen moving back in a barely organized retreat. When they reached the open area, they began to run. The scruffy looking Yellow Flag soldiers then came into view.

Twenty or more had muskets. They would fire and then stop to reload. Most had spears or some other crude handheld weapon. With the retreat of Chatri's men, the Yellow Flags became obviously emboldened. They shouted and gave chase, but seemed reluctant to get too far from their men with muskets.

James almost felt pity for the Yellow Flag men that were rushing towards their death. They were full of a victorious feeling at this instant. He'd felt it before; he knew it well, as well as he knew the feeling of being pursued by an unrelenting enemy.

He raised his Winchester and aimed at one of the strangely dressed warriors. He picked one that had a musket, these would be the most dangerous. The man had loaded his weapon and was

154

placing a cap on the firing mechanism. He also had a smile on his face. Little did he know a bullet was about to remove that smile. James felt his stomach turn as he realized he would soon end the man's life.

The last of Chatri's soldiers passed by the Marines; the commander yelled out "Fire!" James pulled the trigger just as the man was about to shoot at one of Chatri's retreating men. He never knew what hit him.

A blaze of bullets slammed into the Yellow Flags' lines, and before they could react, twenty had fallen. As they turned to run, twenty more fell. James cocked his rifle and fired shot after shot. Each time, his aim was true, and an enemy fell. It was a slaughter as James had not seen since the bloody battlefields of the Civil War.

Few of the Yellow Flags reached the opposite end of the field and of the few that did, many were wounded. This small firefight would mark the beginning of four weeks in almost constant battle.

The group was unrelenting in their pursuit of the enemy, and with this new advantage, Chatri's men fought much harder. The Marines were used as a specialized weapon. They would at times charge or possibly hide and ambush. And, they were always distributed amongst Chatri's men, to appear as Sip Song Chau soldiers.

Regardless of the battle situations, the Yellow Flags were undoubtedly in a chaotic retreat. They'd become disorganized and frightened. That is until the Marines finally cornered one of the high ranking, Yellow Flag leaders. It was on this hot and humid day that James would find out what was in the special box. And it would be a day he would never forget.

"What? Please calm down, I don't understand you. You must talk with Captain Chatri." The commander motioned with his arms as he said this to the elderly Asian woman. She was obviously upset, and James watched the scene with interest.

"Corporal, please see if you can find Captain Chatri, I can't understand a thing this woman is saying."

"Yes Sir," James gave the commander a quick salute and moved back towards the last place he had seen the captain.

A few minutes later James quickly returned to the commander with Captain Chatri following.

"Oh, good, there you are, Captain. This woman has been chattering to me about something, but you're the only one that can translate."

The captain nodded to the commander and then began talking to the woman, who it seemed had continued to speak almost non-stop and with an apparent fear in her voice.

After some discussion with the woman, Captain Chatri turned to the commander.

"She says the Yellow Flag soldiers came through her village a short time before we arrived. They have many guns and one cannon. The leader told his men to take hostages and food. They went to an old stone temple on a hill. The leader told the town's people not to say anything to us, or they would kill the hostages. But this woman has said they took her granddaughter. She is young and beautiful. She feels the Yellow Flags will rape and kill her no matter what if we don't hurry to save her. This is why she is telling us this. The other people of the village have locked themselves in their homes, they are all frightened."

The commander appeared in thought concerning this new information.

Captain Chatri then said, "This may be the leader we've been pursuing. I'll have some of my men go take a look. Perhaps we've finally cornered the devil."

The commander turned to James, "Corporal, get a few men together and go with Chatri's men. Find out all you can about the stone temple these Yellow Flags are holed up in."

James gave another quick salute. 'Yes, Sir," He then went to find Samson and another marine to take along. Soon the three were following four of Chatri's men and the elderly woman.

They moved quietly through the village and then up a rough pathway to the edge of an old brick and mortar wall. The woman spoke to Chatri's men in a hushed voice. She pointed to the entryway a few feet down the wall and then scurried away, back towards her village.

The Marines stood by the wall as Chatri's men began to investigate. Two men walked to the front of the entryway, and before they took a step in, both were shot down.

James saw Samson's face twist slightly at the sight of Chatri's men dead on the ground. The large man said in a low voice. "Death comes quickly for these poor soldiers. They have so little training."

Chatri's other two men ran away quickly. James motioned for Samson and the other marine, who was a small Asian man, to move closer to the entrance.

When they were near the gateway, which was around ten feet across, James whispered, "I'll take a shot, and you go to the other side Samson. Then you take a shot, and I'll get a look as they take cover. After a minute or so, I'll take another shot so you can get a glance. We'll do this a few times and should be able to get a better idea of the situation than those men." He then nodded at the two dead soldiers on the ground.

James cocked his rifle and waited a few seconds as Samson readied himself. The large black man nodded, and James quickly moved around the corner of the gateway far enough to fire two quick shots. As soon as the second shot was fired, Samson sprinted across, looking up towards the entrance as he went.

In the few seconds that he glanced at the entry, he noticed the walls ran all the way to a wooden doorway of a two-story structure. He looked up at the wall he now leaned against and noticed it was at least eight feet high.

Samson motioned that he was ready and raised his Winchester. The African soldier then moved around the edge and quickly fired two shots. After the second shot, James took a brief look at the entrance. He saw a large open window above the wooden doors and as he looked at this, a man rose up and fired a rifle. James had begun to move away when he saw the man rise up and was able to get back behind the wall just as the bullet hit. The impact of the shell caused a spray of rock and sand, which peppered James and the Asian Marine close by.

After a few seconds, James nodded and again cocked his rifle. Samson signaled he was ready and James took two shots in the area he had seen the man raise from. Samson took a look and then fired a shot from his rifle as he jogged back to James.

"What do you think?" James asked.

"Well, tough to attack, especially with the cannon."

"A cannon…" James' eyes widened.

"Yes, a cannon, you didn't see it?" Samson replied as he quickly took in another breath of the humid air.

"No, I didn't see it."

"It's a small one, but it was at the bottom of the window and pointed at the entrance."

"Wonderful," James replied in English but continued in the common language of Sandrilan. "Let's go around and see if there's an easier approach."

The three moved cautiously along the wall and towards the back. Before they ever reached the rear of the temple, the three men could see a steep edge. Easing up to it, James looked down at a long drop.

"That's a hundred feet at least. Let's try the other side."

Around the building, they went. Again, they darted quickly past the gateway and around the other side of the wall. Once again, they found a cliff.

"I certainly see why they picked this place. We can't get to the back. If we go over the wall, they'll simply pick us off one at a time. The front entrance is also well fortified." James spoke as if thinking out loud, but Samson and the other marine nodded in agreement.

"Alright, let's go back." James then took off at a jog towards the commander, with the other two following close behind.

They arrived to find the upset grandmother once again pleading to the commander and Captain Chatri. When James walked up, the man almost appeared relieved to break away from the conversation with the woman.

"Corporal, I'm glad you're back. The woman feels there are at least twenty civilians being held in the temple, along with her granddaughter. What did you find out?"

"I'm afraid the temple is impregnable. They've picked an excellent spot for an extended stand. I don't see any way to make a successful breach. They're apparently prepared for a siege."

When James said this, the commander stiffened up a bit, and his face twisted slightly. He almost appeared speechless, but after a few seconds, he replied.

"Impregnable... is that what you said, Corporal?"

James answered quickly, "Impregnable Sir, it means..."

"Yes, Corporal, I know what it means. May I ask if that is your final assessment of the fortification?"

James studied the commander briefly. He stood looking at James with an expression of disbelief.

"Well, yes Sir. There is a lengthy entrance with a high wall on both sides. They also have one small cannon."

James turned and found a stick; he then smoothed out an area in the dirt to draw in.

The commander, however, paid no attention to James as he sketched the layout of the stone fortification. Instead, he casually removed his jacket.

Immediately, one of the Asian Marines came and took the silk coat. He then motioned to several soldiers about twenty yards back. These were the men that carried the special box. They quickly took hold of the handles and moved up to where the commander stood.

As James gave a lengthy and detailed explanation as to why the stone temple was impregnable, the three Marines went to work with the precision of a clock.

Once the special box was open, some items were brought out in a manner suggesting the men had done this many times before.

One man put a leather coat on the commander. This item had several holsters sewn onto it and was tailor made to fit him. Another man placed leather chaps on their leader. These were also made to be strapped up and fit in the manner of tailor crafted leather pants.

After the commander had these items put on, a leather belt with a pistol holster on each hip area was strapped on to him. Then the holsters were quickly tied to his legs so they would be secure.

The two other Marines had loaded his pistols by this time, and they were handed to him. He placed two larger revolvers in his hip holsters and two smaller revolvers in the holsters that were attached to the leather jacket, allowing the pistols to fit on each side and under his arms. Finally, the commander was handed a loaded Winchester rifle.

In a matter of two minutes, the commander was fully dressed for battle. As he quickly examined the rifle, one of the Marines pulled six sticks of dynamite from the box. The commander glanced at them, nodded and held up two fingers. The Marine then put four sticks back into the box.

James meanwhile finished his assessment and turned back to the commander saying, "As I said Sir, impregna..."

As the corporal became speechless at the sight of the commander, another Marine handed his battle-ready leader one of his slim cigars. The commander glanced at it, smelled it and said, "Come along, Corporal. Let's take a look at this, 'impregnable' fortress."

Samson, who had been watching the commander being prepared for battle, rather than giving James' assessment any attention, smiled and took off at a jog, leading the way to the stone temple.

Before James had time to comprehend what had happened during the previous two minutes, the commander had also taken off at a quick pace behind Samson. The other Marines began to fall in behind him, and James suddenly needed to run to keep up with his leader.

At this time, James oddly felt as if he were outside of himself. A strange sensation began to overtake him. He had an idea that the commander wished to attack the stone fortification. He felt this would indeed be suicide. And yet here he was, following this man in an apparent death run, through the village, up to a hill and towards a frightening encounter.

The group reached the edge of the wall. The two dead men lay sprawled out on the ground in a manner to display the eminent threat.

James moved up to the commander, who glanced around the corner of the entrance. As he quickly moved back, a bullet hit the edge of the wall and again caused a spray of fragments around the area.

The commander then took the two sticks of dynamite, that had now been tied together, he pulled his knife out and cut the fuses down to a few inches. He replaced the knife and held his cigar to a lit match that another Marine was holding up to him.

James' mind was grappling with confusion. He turned to Samson, who had a wide smile on his face. Then, the large Marine spoke to James in English. "Woe to the wicked," he said, with satisfaction in his voice.

James felt a fear growing inside him as the events were happening faster than he could adjust to. And, to make matters worse, the commander held his cigar to the dynamite fuses and lit them. He turned to James and said, "Follow me, Corporal." Then, he glanced at the short, burning fuses and added, "But, cover your ears first."

James stepped back, still startled at the immediate plan that he had no control over. He put his hands up to his ears just as the commander tossed the two sticks around the corner and towards the doorway of the stone temple.

The sudden explosion rocked the area and caused dust, smoke, and debris to go everywhere. A few seconds later the commander disappeared into the cloud, and immediately two quick shots rang out from his Winchester.

James fumbled clumsily to cock his rifle. He staggered nervously into the smoky chaos. The Yellow Flag soldiers began to yell out as he tried to spot the commander. Another shot from the Winchester gave him a direction to move. His heart raced and the air he pulled into his lungs felt thick. He held his rifle in a ready position, though he could see almost nothing.

Approaching the large temple doors that had been destroyed by the blast, James almost tripped over a dead Yellow Flag soldier. He lay staring up at the sky with a bullet hole in his forehead. James moved around the dead man and cautiously stepped into the structure, just as several more shots from the commander's Winchester was heard.

With the dust settling some, James examined his surroundings. He realized there was a balcony area running along a second story and all around the inside of the structure. He saw movement and became aware of the enemy shouting and sneaking from one area to another. They seemed to have their attention on the commander, though James still hadn't spotted his leader. He moved closer to a wall and under the balcony area.

James began to maneuver himself along the side of the building, searching for the enemy through the dust and smoke. Then something caused him to trip and fall.

His arm hit the floor, inflicting some pain. He glanced back and realized he had stumbled over another dead soldier.

As soon as he noticed the dead man at his feet, an odd, round object came from the balcony area across from him. Shocked, he realized it to be a crude grenade as it hit the floor and rolled straight up to his face. James felt the heat from the burning fuse as his mind grappled with what to do.

Unexpectedly and from seemingly nowhere, the commander stepped up to James. He looked down at him and smiled as he picked up the grenade. He then casually tossed it back across the room and up to the balcony area from whence it had originally been thrown. The Yellow Flags shouted in terror just before the small bomb exploded and extinguished their screams.

James' mind again struggled with the ferocity of the enclosed environment as more smoke and debris from the grenade filled the building. He looked back to where the commander had stood, only to find his leader had disappeared once again.

More shots from the commander's Winchester brought James to his feet and moved him towards the area of fighting.

As he stepped cautiously towards a doorway, another shot rang out from the Winchester. Shouts that sounded as if the Yellow Flags were cursing the commander came from all directions. James strained to see through the haze as he turned into the doorway and found stairs. Laying on the first flight of steps was another Yellow Flag soldier with a bullet hole in his head. James stepped over him and moved towards a corner leading to the second flight.

Two more shots rang out from the other side of the stairway. A noise that James knew to be bodies landing on the stairs could be heard.

James raised his rifle again and stepped cautiously around the corner. Two Yellow Flags lay on the stairs, their blood flowing down the wooden walkway. Leaning against the wall was the commander's rifle, but there was no sign of him.

James stepped up and around the two dead men. As he could see the balcony floor in front of him, another grenade rolled past. More voices were heard from his left where the grenade had originated from. James ducked a little, but then saw the same grenade roll back in the direction it had come from. The Yellow Fags that initially rolled the bomb shouted in terror, but it was too late, the grenade exploded; again smoke, dust, and debris choked the air.

James stood up from the crouching position he'd taken when the grenade had rolled back. He stepped up to the balcony floor and peeked around the corner on his right. He finally spotted the commander, and for the next few moments, James found he could do nothing other than watch the spectacular events play out before his eyes.

The commander had his back to the wall and an army revolver in his left hand. In his right, he had one of the smaller pistols that were often called a "pocket revolver."

162

A Yellow flag soldier came from behind an open door, and the commander shot him. Another came and was shot down immediately. The commander continued to casually smoke his cigar and side step along the wall.

The Yellow Flags then shouted to each other, as if deciding to charge him. In the next few seconds, five men came from different areas of the upper floor. Several stepped out of hiding on the lower floor and attempted to shoot the commander above. In rapid succession, the commander fired one shot after another while continuing to move in the side step fashion; each shot hitting its mark.

James wanted to do something, but he was frozen in fascination and awe. He'd never seen anything like this and couldn't make his feet move or take his eyes from the scene playing out.

The Yellow Flags yelled out. The commander was now on the balcony at the far end of the building, opposite of the front entrance. Seeming to sense they were facing only one man, the Yellow Flags advanced with all they had left. The commander fired two shots from his army revolver, holstered it while firing the smaller revolver and pulled another pistol without missing a shot. He fired round after round as if it were as natural to him as breathing.

James thought the actions were more of a machine than a man. His leader knew when each pistol had fired its final shot and automatically pulled the next one out. He used the smaller pistols for close range and the army revolvers for the farther targets.

Smoke filled the air, and James' ears rang from the loud battle sounds. After nine or ten more Yellow Flags fell to the commanders' revolvers, all became quiet.

The commander moved cautiously around the balcony. James watched him now from almost directly across the building. One more enemy came out of a room, only to be shot down immediately by the commander, who then went quickly into the same room and fired another shot, indicating the leader of the group had also been eliminated.

James now took the last few steps onto the balcony and gazed through the smoke at the multitude of dead Yellow Flags lying around. He also spotted some them on the floor level below.

As he made his way towards the door which the commander had gone into, Samson and the other marines could be seen below, cautiously entering the now quiet structure.

James stepped over more dead men, and as he approached the room of the Yellow Flag leader, the commander stepped out with a bottle in his hands. He was nonchalantly examining the label, but then looked up at James.

"Corporal, do you know anything about Chinese wine?"

James was almost speechless, but managed to utter, "No Sir, I don't."

"Well, there's an entire crate of this in the room there with these fellow's leader. Seems he was keeping it all to himself. I believe it's rice wine or something of the sort. I think we should get a few bottles before Chatri's men find it."

James nodded meekly and said, "Yes, Sir," as the commander made his way back to the balcony towards the stairs.

James glanced down at the rifle in his hands and realized he'd not fired a single shot during the firefight. He turned and also made his way back down the stairs. He told Samson about the wine, and his friend went to retrieve some of it for the commander before it disappeared.

From a back door, Marines came in escorting the hostages. They quickly told the commander the captives were found locked in a storage building behind the main temple. The men, women, and children were obviously shaken, yet glad to be free. The woman that had led them to the temple stood at the front gateway and reacted with joy upon seeing her granddaughter amongst them.

James then followed the commander back to camp. Within a few minutes, the men had his fighting gear removed and placed back in the special box. The commander then took a cup of the rice wine that was being handed to him. He smelled it as another Marine helped him put his silk jacket back on. He shifted the drink from one hand to the other, then took a sip from the cup.

From a distance, James struggled to understand what had just occurred. It was as if... taking over a well-fortified enemy position, single-handed, was nothing out of the ordinary for this man.

James turned away and rubbed the side his head as he recalled what he had seen. In all the battles he'd survived, never had he witnessed something such as this.

That night James continued to go over the events in his mind. How could a man fight that way? He recalled the bravest warriors he had known during the war, and none of these men had the ability to walk into a strongly fortified building and take down thirty or more soldiers in a few short minutes. Much less, have the composure to sit and drink a cup of wine afterward.

The following morning the group prepared to leave. They would now be traveling towards the river to make their way back to the Valiant. Within a few hours, the Marines were on the move again.

After three days of almost constant marching, they arrived at the river. As the Marines camped, Chatri traveled to a nearby military post to retrieve boats as well as the remaining payment for the Marines' service.

Soon the captain returned, gave the payment to the commander and the Marines took to the river once again. By this time, all, including James were exhausted. It had now been over five weeks of fighting and moving through often very rugged terrain.

The group repeated their routine back towards the Valiant. They traveled the waterway by day and stopped at prepared locations for the night.

At one of the stops, a soldier of Sip Song Chau managed to communicate enough to relay a message from Captain Chatri. The Yellow Flags were in full retreat he said, and would soon be expelled from the country. James and the other Marines gave a modest cheer upon hearing this news.

After nine days of travel on the river and another short march, the group arrived back at the Valiant. The sailors shouted with joy upon seeing their comrades wearily making their way towards the ship.

Once he had cleaned up and eaten a cooked meal, James considered the mission. In the slightly over six-week period, they had traveled many hundreds of miles. The Marines had successfully engaged the enemy almost daily for a month. They then returned to the Valiant, two days late, but without having lost a single man. James realized he had a new-found respect for the commander. He'd never seen or been a part of warfare undertaken with such skill and efficiency.

Chapter Twelve: Valiant

A few weeks later, the usual and welcoming bells of Sandrilan sounded out. James and Samson stood on deck with the other marines as the warship was assisted into the small harbor by several large row boats.

"It's good to be home," Samson said and then took in a deep breath as if absorbing every aspect of the island.

James thought about this and replied, "Yes, it is."

He'd never imagined that he would consider this place home. But it had become a place of refuge for him. And this he thought was what a home should be.

As always, the butterflies waited on the dock. The commander disembarked first, and then Kenji and several other non-commissioned officers followed behind. A number of Sandrilan residents followed this group up to the palace. Finally, the crew and marines left the ship, with many families and friends waiting to welcome them home.

The following night, James attended the celebration. He again noticed some the natives saved from Te Kuotie's Warriors a few months before. They were laughing and appeared to now be at home in Sandrilan. James felt satisfaction about this. Finally, his life seemed to make sense. As he watched the dancers and those around him, James felt he belonged to something good. He didn't know much more about this new home and life. But he felt he had a positive purpose, and this was something.

The next morning, after receiving a considerably large amount of pay, James walked to Doctor Jefferies office.

"Do you have time for a game Doc?"

Doctor Jefferies glanced up at James. "Uhm, I suppose I do, Corporal. I rather expected some work from the Valiant, considering the length of the mission. But everyone returned fairly healthy and with all limbs intact. So, yes, I do have time."

As the two played a game on the veranda, James finally said what he had really come to say.

"I now know what's in the special box, Doctor."

Doc Jefferies glanced up from the chessboard. He studied James briefly before replying.

"I suspected as much, Corporal. It was only a matter of time before you witnessed what the commander is capable of."

James moved his bishop. "I've been in more battles than I can count, Doc. I've seen many brave men fight and die, some of them from my bullet or blade. But, I've never seen such a thing as that. It was like...." James grimaced as if searching for the correct words.

Doc Jefferies replied, "As if the commander took the Angel of Death in his arms, danced the waltz; then slipped away from her grasp before she realized he was gone?"

James looked at the Doctor with an impressed expression. "Uhm yes, that sums it up very well, Doctor."

"Hmm, well, since you asked about it some time back, I've tried to think of the words to describe what the special box represents. That's the best I could come up with."

Both men studied the board again. The doctor moved his pawn to block James. A breeze moved across the veranda.

"I would really like to know where a man learns to fight like that, Doctor."

Doc Jefferies glanced up at James, then back to the chess board. He said nothing for a few moments. James waited patiently.

Meili brought two drinks out to the men. Doc Jefferies asked her to bring "the bottle from under his desk," and she went quickly back towards the office. Still, James waited for a reply.

Soon Meili came back with a bottle and two small glasses. The contents of the bottle had a hazy amber color and appeared to be something with alcohol in it; though it had no label.

"Would you have a drink with me, Corporal?" The doctor opened the bottle and began pouring his glass full.

"Will I need one?" James asked.

"You may. At the very least it should help us both; myself with the telling, and you the hearing of this tale."

"In that case, I'll have the drink," James replied and moved the small glass over to him.

Doc Jefferies poured James' glass full. He then took a sip of his own. He leaned back in his chair and seemed to be recalling something. Finally, he began.

"I first met Quenton Chauveau in Sydney Australia. The year was 1867. I had traveled to Australia to open a practice and eventually buy myself a ranch. I had a fair amount of money saved and felt success was merely around the corner.

"Unfortunately, I knew nothing about women. I met a beautiful Australian Lass. I fell head over heels in love with her. In the short period of seven months, this woman was able to obtain all of my money and left me a broken man. To this day, I don't know where she disappeared to. And, it really no longer matters.

"I became unable to work regularly after that. I started drinking and lost all of my dignity as a doctor and a man. As had become a routine day for me, I sat in a waterfront tavern, fairly well inebriated and full of self-pity... It's unfortunate, but true, that darkness must at times be complete, before we notice the subtle glimmer of hope.

"That's the state I was in when the commander approached me. He'd been searching for a ship's doctor. He wasn't having much luck when someone told him about me.

"I explained to him that I was no longer a doctor. He said, 'Sir if you were trained as a doctor then it's something you are until you're dead.' So, I asked him if he hadn't noticed I was busy killing myself with alcohol.

"The commander considered this for a few seconds and replied, 'We see a lot of action on the Valiant, now wouldn't you rather be killed in a grand fight against bloodthirsty pirates than to die slowly and alone in a dark tavern?'

"It was the first flash of inspiration I had received for some time. I realized this man was right. I told him that I indeed would rather for such a thing. But I asked how he felt that I could be trusted, considering the state I was in at the time.

"The commander replied, 'Doctor, I have no one to care for my wounded now, even a drunken physician would be better than what the Valiant has at present.'

"So, I hired on as the ship's doctor. And as time passed, the commander and I became good friends. He had in fact saved my life that day, though it took a while for me to realize it. It was not long before I saw what he was capable of. I was stunned by his mastery over death. He was like a one-man army. His moves were always precise and deadly in battle.

168

"The Valiant was very busy for several years after I signed on. We were and still are at war with the pirates. I wondered about this but never asked. Then one day while things were calm, the commander and I were playing a game of chess, just as you and I are doing now. I asked him about his past and to my surprise, he told me the story."

At this point, the Doctor stopped. He looked at James as if trying to find a place to start. He took another drink and then continued.

"The commander joined the French Foreign Legion in the year 1848. He served in many battles, from the Crimea to Italy and Mexico. But, I believe his skills were refined and sharpened to a razor's edge in Mexico.

"In 1863 the commander, who was a Master Sergeant, along with 63 other Legionaries, were escorting a wagon train of supplies in Mexico. They were trying to reach a besieged city by the name of Puebla. On the way there, they were attacked by 3,000 Mexican soldiers."

The doctor took in a deep breath and then exhaled slowly. He took another sip of his drink. James also took the opportunity to do the same. Then the doctor continued.

"The small group moved quickly to a village by the name of Hacienda de la Trinidad and made a stand there. The Legionaries fought bravely. Again, and again, they repulsed the attacks, but every time, more Legionaries fell.

"Finally, there were only seven left. The commander and six other survivors decided to charge the enemy rather than surrender. They had no more ammunition, so they fixed their bayonets, and the seven soldiers ran out and attacked the thousands of Mexicans.

"Three were immediately shot dead, but the Mexican general was so stirred by the Legionaries bravery that he ordered his men to cease fire. The commander along with the other four was wounded but alive and was taken as prisoners.

"Later, after the four men recovered, they were allowed to escort the body of their fallen captain back to Paris.

"The four men were received as heroes in France. And as hero's they were given retirement from the Legion, as it's not good to have a county's heroes die soon.

"The commander had some savings, so he bought a small sailing vessel. He learned to sail, and after a year back in France, he decided to travel around the world.

"Few would dare to do such a thing, but even fewer still would attempt such a journey alone. But this is what the commander did. In early 1865, he loaded his small craft with provisions and set sail.

"It was during his travels that he came across Sandrilan. He immediately fell in love with the small, isolated islands and stayed here for several weeks. The commander named the islands and noted their location in his journals. He then put together the purple and white flag of Sandrilan and began flying it on his small vessel.

"It was also during this time that he first encountered the pirates of Zheng Qui. Several weeks after leaving these islands, the commanders' boat was pursued by an Asian Junk with eight guns.

"The commander realized this wasn't a good situation and attempted to outrun the pirates. But the winds were not in his favor and eventually the larger ship with more sail caught up to him.

"The Pirates tied his craft to theirs and boarded his sloop with guns and swords drawn. They immediately began ransacking the small craft. From what I understand of the tale, the commander waited in his cabin. As the pirates entered he silently killed one after another with his sword. The bodies began to pile up. More came in search of the others, and they too met their death. It was growing dark at this time, and the commander slipped off of his boat and slid into the water, then moved around and onto the pirate's ship. As they called down to his boat in search of their comrades, he attacked from behind.

"When he had disposed of those on the deck, he made his way through the lower parts of the ship. He killed the captain and almost all of the crew without firing a single shot. Then he found a number of captives in the bowels of the ship. These were being guarded by some men that immediately surrendered to him.

"The captives, as it turned out, were Madame Zhou and a number of Korean sailors. He placed the remaining pirates that had surrendered on a small boat, along with the body of their captain, as well as some food and water, then he left them to fate.

"As he was able to communicate with Madame Zhou, he found out that she was the concubine of a high ranking Korean officer. They were in transit when the pirates took over the ship. They'd killed most of the sailors but were holding her and a few of the high ranking men for ransom.

"The commander asked Madame Zhou if she wished for him to return her to the Korean officer. She said it would be a useless thing as once she had been in the custody of the pirates, her master would feel she was tainted and would not allow her to return. She had resigned herself to being raped and killed once the ransom payment was refused. The sailors also believed it would be futile to return to Korea. They would be considered traitors for allowing the officer's concubine to be captured and would surely be put to death. All asked to stay with the commander.

"The commander considered what he should do at this point. With the Korean sailors in his service, he had enough men to sail the Pirates' Junk. And, as he searched the ship he found a small fortune that the pirates had accumulated.

"After some thought on the matter, it seems he was struck by inspiration. He put the flag of Sandrilan on the pirate's ship and set sail for California."

As the sun began to set on the horizon, Meili brought two plates of food out. The men sat the chess board aside and began to eat. As they ate, the doctor continued his story.

"Sometime later, the Asian Junk slipped into the San Francisco harbor with his smaller craft in tow. He rented a docking spot as a ship of the Kingdom of Sandrilan. The commander then went to work straight away. He hired a translator to help him communicate with Madame Zhou and the other sailors. He told them about Sandrilan and that he wanted to find a suitable ship to fight the pirates, as well as anyone that was harming innocent people. He said the fortune the pirates had stolen would be turned to good and would help end their threat on the seas. Madame Zhou and the Korean sailors were excited about this and jubilant to have a place to live, even if it would need to be built first.

"The commander then began searching for a ship. He found the Valiant in a small, insignificant port, South of San Francisco. He checked around and was informed of her story.

"The local officials told the commander that in 1863, the Confederate government had commissioned a Russian shipyard to build an ironclad warship. At that time, the rebels were doing well in the war. The Southern states used Treasury gold to pay half and would pay the other half when the ship was handed over to the Confederate Navy.

"The Russians would deliver the ship to a secret area south of the California border in the spring of 1865. The shipyard went to work, and the war continued.

"By the time the Valiant, which would have been called the CSS Mississippi, was headed towards the delivery point, the Confederates were on the verge of collapse.

"The Union found out about the ship and intercepted it before it reached its destination. Since the Confederates had used US treasury gold to order the ship, the US government claimed ownership; however, the documentation was not clear on the matter, possibly this was on purpose, but it left the situation indecisive. At this point, the Russian government intervened on behalf of the ship builder and asked the United States for a clear case. Otherwise, it perceived the situation as the US simply 'stealing' the ship.

"So, the vessel was moved to an obscure area until the matter could be resolved. The Russian ship company kept a skeleton crew on board and provided their food and other necessities, while the US government for its part, restricted the ship to leave.

"The war ended shortly after this. The ship became an insignificant problem and languished alone in its docked status. The Russian shipyard petitioned the US government to release it, and the US Government continued to claim it as being partially purchased with US treasury funds, of which it wanted repayment.

"The commander began a methodical and strategic approach to this situation. He still had connections in France due to being a national hero. He contacted the French Ambassador and soon had a few letters of 'slight' reconnection by the French government as the King of Sandrilan. He then began speaking with the Russian ship company officials as well as the US officials that were in charge of the case.

"After four months of diplomatic maneuvering, the commander was able to purchase the remaining half of the amount owed on the ironclad from the Russians. He had also made an agreement with the US to pay storage fees for the ship. These fees amounted to the price the Confederates had used to order the ship. So, both sides were happy and the problem was solved to the satisfaction of each.

172

"The commander now owned an ironclad frigate. He immediately renamed it the 'Valiant' and began work to return it to service readiness. Within another month, he had the ship loaded with provisions. He sold the Pirate Junk and his small sailing craft as well and was soon headed back to sea with his Korean crew and a few other select sailors he had acquired in California.

"It was not long after this that the commander was in Sidney and recruited me as the ship's doctor. And, it was during the first few years of service that our war with Zheng Qui's pirates was the most violent.

"The pirates that the commander had put into the small boats did, in fact, find their way back to their group and leader. They had asked to take their captains' body with them, and the commander had allowed this, perhaps due to his own experience. Though he didn't completely understand why they had asked to do so, as it turned out, the pirate captain whom the commander had killed was the first-born son of Zheng Qui, the leader of one of the largest pirate groups in the South Seas.

"Although Zheng Qui didn't know who had defeated and killed his son, he did know what the flag looked like as the men bringing his son's body back described the purple and white flag of Sandrilan. Zheng Qui immediately put a large bounty out for any ship flying this type of flag."

The sun had by now drifted below the horizon. Meili brought several oil lamps out to provide some light. She then offered her husband and James a cigar and both accepted. After the doctor had lit his cigar, he continued with the tale that James had become extremely interested in.

"I wasn't on the Valiant long before we were attacked by the pirates. Our crew was loyal and hard-working, but not accustomed to ships such as the Valiant. They knew how to sail, and were growing more familiar with the warship every day. But in those early times, we were boarded on several occasions as the crew just didn't know how to manage her big guns. Nor did they know how to effectively use the steam engines.

"It was when we were first boarded by the pirates that I saw the commander in action. He had several revolvers in his belt and had strapped on a saber. I stood in awe as he shot or struck down at least twenty pirates. The crew of the Valiant rallied around him and when it was over we had a slightly damaged but salvageable pirate ship. Upon further investigation, we found a dozen women below the decks. They were in a desperate situation and had obviously been abused by the pirates.

"With the captured ship in tow, we made our way back to Sandrilan. The women stayed on the captured ship, and everyone else stayed on the Valiant.

"This was when a great effort was put into the construction of Sandrilan. There had been some primitive structures put together, but now a renewed effort was made to accommodate Madame Zhou and these unfortunate ladies. Madame Zhou immediately took these women under her wing and began to care for them.

"After several months of work, we had many buildings and living quarters constructed. I can't adequately express the feelings we had during these early days. It was exciting and wonderful, as well as a bit frightening. We were in the process of building a new life and a new settlement. Everyone worked hard as this was a second chance for them.

"As the women were able to communicate with us, they told about a village on the coast of Southern China, which had been overrun by the pirates. Some of the women were taken from this village and gave fair descriptions of where it was and what it looked like. The commander decided to investigate.

"We set sail for the area, with a determination to help these people. I don't believe the commander actually had a clear plan, other than to meet the pirates in battle and bring them to a just end. We all felt this way after witnessing what they had done to the unfortunate women.

"As we sailed along the coast, in search of this village, the Valiant was attacked by three Junks that were harbored in a small port. They came quickly out of their anchorage, and we suddenly found ourselves in a pitched battle. It was chaotic for an hour or more as the men struggled with their new duties and ship. But the Valiant withstood the attack, and with several lucky shots from our much larger guns, she had the advantage.

"Two of the attacking ships were damaged and sat dead in the water as we maneuvered to engage the last ship. As we turned to give the enemy a broadside, the ship moved to flee. The commander personally assisted the novice gun crew and with three out of eight shots hitting their target, the ship sank quickly.

"We then turned to the two remaining ships, only to find the crews had abandoned their vessels and were almost on land. The commander ordered every available man to grab a weapon. Then, he and around eighteen men boarded landing boats and rowed quickly to the village.

"Though I remained on the ship, it was said the commander took down many of the enemies and with him leading the men, they soon destroyed most of the pirates.

"A few were injured, and the commander interrogated them. As it turned out, this was not the village they had intended to assist. Yet, it was revealed by the injured pirates that the commander and any ship which flew the flag of Sandrilan were to be immediately attacked by ships of Zheng Qui. They revealed to the commander that someone had killed the pirate leader's son and, that the person who did this was flying the same flag that the Valiant flew.

"Realizing now what was going on, the commander told the injured men that he had killed Zheng Qui's son in the act of self-defense. He told them to inform Zheng Qui that he and the Valiant would destroy any of the pirate leader's ships and men that came after them. And that they should also tell their leader that he planned to someday take down Zheng Qui himself.

"When I first heard of this, I felt the commander was too boastful. But, over time I realized that these pirates only understood force. For the commander to say anything else, would seem as weak. The statement he made was meant to alarm and possibly anger Zheng Qui. He was telling the pirate leader that his evil ways had started this conflict, but the commander planned to finish it.

"At this time, many of the people of the village came to us seeking escape. The commander knew well that these people would be tortured and killed in reprisals of the pirate's defeat. He told them to gather their things, and they could go to Sandrilan. He sent men to repair the larger of the two damaged pirate ships.

"Soon the Valiant was loaded with refugees. In tow was the damaged pirate ship, also loaded with people from the village.

"When we reached Sandrilan, the people went to work building homes and businesses. The cannon from the pirate ship was placed in strategic areas to add protection to Sandrilan.

"The commander then began to put a solid plan into place. He started training the men to fight. He assigned some to specific duties and set up a civil administrative system. A small governing force was also established. I also took on an assistant, her name was Meili, and she would eventually become my wife. She would be an on-duty nurse for the small clinic that we planned to build.

"The commander also knew he needed small arms for his newly formed Marine unit. After things were organized in Sandrilan, the Valiant set sail for Singapore. It was there that the commander would be reunited with a friend from the Crimean war.

"He began seeking firearms once the Valiant reached Singapore. The docked warship had not gone unnoticed, though. The British were not familiar with any place by the name of 'Sandrilan.' And though the Valiant paid for anchorage in a private owned area of the port, the British still wanted to know more about this mysterious armored frigate.

"It was not long before they sent an ambassador to visit the ship. With some armed guards around him, Sir William Barrett stood on the dock and requested a meeting with the Valiant's Captain.

"The commander came out from his cabin, and immediately the two reacted with surprise and delight. As it turned out, they had met and to some degree fought together during the Crimean conflict.

"Sir Barrett not only gave approval for the commander to dock in Singapore, but he also expressed a desire to help him in his fight with the pirates. He said the British and Americans were growing weary of the pirates preying on merchant ships. Both nations were slowly moving to engage and eliminate the sea criminals, but it was taking longer than he or the shipping merchants of Singapore were hoping for.

"With Sir Barrett's help, the commander found and purchased new repeating rifles and Colt revolvers. He also acquired ammunition and cannon shot for the Valiant.

"Sir Barrett soon concluded that the Valiant and Sandrilan, being something of a wild card, could do things that other governments couldn't do. Being a member of the Singapore consulate, he had privy to information and situations that average people didn't have. As time passed, he has become something of an agent for the Valiant.

176

"When small countries or territories came to Singapore seeking aid from the British government, Sir Barrett was always aware of this. Very often, the British, Americans or other large countries, would not be in a position to help without disturbing the delicate balance of power in the Pacific.

"So, in certain situations, after the victims of some suppressive force had pleaded their case and failed to receive assistance, Sir Barrett would approach them and offer an alternative. And, very often, these people were happy to pay what would be a small amount in comparison to what might come with a larger country's involvement.

"For example, the king of Sip Song Chau could have asked the French for help in fighting the Yellow Flags. However, for a large country such as France, this would also mean an invitation for being taken over and colonized. The price paid to have the highly effective and heavily armed marines of Sandrilan come in and give his country a quick advantage, was much less than it would have cost to have a country such as France or Germany's help.

"Also, the large financial payments received for such services, have made Sandrilan a rich and successful country. We are a defender of the weak and innocent, as well as a refugee for those that wish or need to escape the evils of this world. In fact, many that find their way here have called this place a paradise."

The sun had long set by this time. Most of the oil lanterns in Sandrilan had also been extinguished. James took another sip of his warm drink that tasted like some type of rum. He considered the tale as Doc Jefferies also took a drink and studied the corporal.

Finally, James commented. "A place where the ability to wage war is the thing that's most needed..."

Doc Jefferies appeared puzzled. "I'm not sure what you mean by that, Corporal."

James smiled and replied. "Years ago, I met a woman in Independence Missouri. She said something that I've never forgotten. She said, 'I would find peace when I found a place where the thing that burdened my heart was the thing that was needed the most.' It seems that I'm destined to be a soldier, no matter whether it's what I want or not. It also seems that being a soldier for Sandrilan is a good thing. The commander has helped many people and if I'm destined to fight, then I want to fight on the side of good. Perhaps I've finally found the place that I can have peace."

Doc Jefferies downed the last of his drink as the small oil lanterns flickered a dim light.

"I hope so, Corporal. You've helped many people already. I suggest you consider this as you do the fighting you seem destined to do. I don't know what it's like to kill a man, I've never done such a thing. But it seems there are some that must do so to protect others that have little ability to defend themselves. In the service of Sandrilan, you will always be doing just that. Perhaps that will be sufficient to give you peace."

James nodded, "Thank you Doc. I believe your story has helped me. I do feel better about where I am and what I'm doing."

Doc Jefferies smiled and nodded as well. James stood up and said good-night. He then made his way in the moonlight back to the Valiant.

As the days passed by, James realized that he had indeed found some peace in his heart. While walking through Sandrilan, he again noticed people that he had helped rescue. They were now doing jobs around their new community. Many were smiling and appeared content in their new homes. He felt good to be a part of this, and in a flash of inspiration, he wished to do even more. As the idea solidified in his mind, he slowly began making his way towards the palace.

Before reaching his destination, the now familiar bells sounded out their low and vibrant notices that the commander was going to his special place. The shops began closing their doors, and a hush came over the island as he continued up the winding road.

James arrived at the palace gates and found several guards on duty.

"I wish to speak with the Commander."

One of the guards motioned for James to follow him. They moved around the back of the complex. James had never been to this area of the island. They walked along a small pathway, through thick foliage.

After a short stroll, the two arrived at some stairs that were built up a hill. James followed the guard up what turned out to be four short flights. Then they came to an open area. Here, James saw the palace butterflies sitting in front of more stairs that led up to the top of the hill overlooking Sandrilan. This would be the highest point around all of the twelve islands.

The guard turned to James. "The King is at his special place. You may wait for him here."

James nodded, and the guard turned and left.

As he examined the area, the palace butterflies studied him curiously. They all sat daintily on the ground with their baskets of flower petals in hand. Madame Zhou sat closest to the stairs with the commander's silk jacket draped over her arm. She also glanced at James with interest but said nothing.

The feeling of being in a church came over him as he sat down. There was a hushed silence, and after a few minutes the butterflies again turned their attention to the top of the stairs in anticipation of the commander's return.

The musicians and cymbal players sat at the edges of the open area. Though James' arrival had also distracted them, they soon turned away from him and began watching for the commander as well.

The humid air was sweet with the smell of tropical plants. Exotic birds bristled and sang in the trees. A sweat bead rolled down the side of James face. Still everyone watched towards the top of the hill.

After thirty minutes of waiting, James grew weary of watching for the commander. He examined the ground and followed the movement of an unfamiliar bug for several moments as it made its way past him.

Suddenly, everyone jumped up, and several cymbals sounded their crisp chime. James looked up to see the commander making his way down the steps.

The butterflies formed lines along both sides of the stairs; their hands in the baskets, waiting to toss the petals before their king's feet. Madame Zhou stood on the right side with a smile and the commanders' jacket ready.

As the commander came closer, James stood. The musicians began to play the now familiar tones and beats that indicated the commander was moving. From these initial cymbals and chimes, the bells of the palace could be heard sounding out the message of the commander's return from his special place. Then from the Palace,

James heard the larger bells of Sandrilan as they echoed in response to the Palace bells.

The butterflies began tossing the petals onto the ground as the commander moved from the last step and his foot touched the earth. Madame Zhou held his silk jacket so he could slide his arms into it. A man came to him with a glass of wine, which the commander took as he moved towards the path leading back to Sandrilan.

He stopped in front of James, "Corporal, what a pleasant surprise. Is there something you needed?"

"Yes," James replied, "Well, actually I just wanted to talk with you, Sir, if you weren't too busy."

The commander appeared to give this some thought as his entourage patiently waited for him. "I'm not too busy, but let's talk at the palace. Madame Zhou tells me the butterflies have something special planned, you can join us, and we can talk during our meal."

The commander then began walking again and the procession moved towards the palace with James following behind.

The group arrived at the royal complex and entered the large open area. The grounds seemed strangely vacant to James as he had only been here during the celebrations. Now, only a few gardeners and caretakers milled about as the procession made its way into the shade of the pavilion.

In the corner of this covered area, Sno sat with her attendants. She played a large stringed instrument, and the music floated delicately through the air.

James, the commander and some butterflies sat down on the large platform. Several men carried a hookah and sat it down beside their King. This was followed by a stream of servants bringing numerous dishes of food and drink.

As James and the commander began to eat, music erupted and ten butterflies floated out to the area in front of the platform. They danced about in their exotic silk outfits, and James noticed the commander watching with a keen interest as he ate.

After the meal, the commander smoked the hookah as more performances were presented for his entertainment.

Finally, the commander turned to James. As he expelled a stream of smoke, he asked, "So, what is it you wished to talk about, Corporal?" He then turned his attention back to more beautiful dancers as they twirled about in front of him.

James winced slightly as he considered what to say. He would have preferred a more private setting, but he decided to ask what he had come to, regardless of the distractions.

"Well, Sir, I wondered if it was possible, to be trained to fight as you do... Sir."

The commander turned to James with an odd but thoughtful expression. After a few seconds, he lifted his hands into the air and clapped twice. The music stopped immediately, as did the dancers. The butterflies on the stage, as well as everyone else, quickly moved from the area of the pavilion, as if to escape something dangerous. Within a few short seconds, the entire room was vacant, other than the commander and James. Silence prevailed as the commander continued to stare at him.

After expelling another stream of smoke the commander spoke with a serious tone.

"First, Corporal, it's my opinion that no man should fight as another. Each man should fight according to his own experiences and abilities. Beyond that however, I would say the more important question is, 'Why would you wish for such a thing?'"

James gazed around the empty pavilion. It had seemed a simple thing when he started up the hill towards the Palace. Now he struggled with the question of why he desired to kill and destroy life on such a grand scale. He turned back to the commander.

"It seems to me, Sir, that you are helping people that can't fight for themselves. If I am to fight, then I wish to fight for such a thing. And if I am fighting for such a thing, I wish to be the best at it that I can be."

The commander pulled another draw from the hookah as he continued to study James. The seconds ticked by long and silent as he seemed deep in thought. Finally, he expelled the smoke and replied, "I feel you are partially correct, Corporal. And for that reason, it may be possible for you to have additional training. If, however, you are to receive this training, it will be the most difficult thing you have ever done, I assure you of this. So, you should consider it well while you have the time to do so. I'll ask you once again before such training is embarked upon."

Again, silence permeated the air around the two men. Then the commander continued.

"You've been an asset to our group, Corporal. In fact, I wish to tell you that I consider your debt to me paid in full, as of today. You may remain here at Sandrilan and continue in the capacity you're in now, or you may leave if you wish. We often take on coal in Singapore, and from there you can obtain passage to the United States, if you desire such a thing."

James considered this and replied, "Thank you, Sir. I believe I'll stay, though. I've found a purpose here, and that's something I need in my life."

The commander nodded as he pulled another draw from the hookah. "In that case, I'm promoting you to Sergeant. You've proved yourself in battle, and I feel you're capable of leading. I'll get back with you about the training. And, if you should go through with the training that I have in mind, and survive, there will be another promotion for you."

After saying this, the commander watched James for a few more seconds and then asked, "Was there anything else, Sergeant?"

James replied, "No, Sir."

The commander raised his hands and again clapped twice. Immediately the dancers, butterflies, and musicians moved back into the pavilion area as if they had been waiting in the wings. The performance was then restarted, almost exactly where it had left off.

Chapter Thirteen: No Turning Back

As the days and weeks went by, James considered the commander's words. The notion of 'not surviving' the training was unsettling, and yet if he were to gain a level of fighting skill even close to what the commander possessed, he would, in fact, have an advantage that most soldiers were not even aware existed.

Images of the commander's mastery in battle continued to replay in his mind. Eventually, he decided it was what he must do, regardless of the dangers. If fate had determined him to be a soldier, then he would move to be the best one that he could be.

A month passed by, and then two. The Valiant and her crew embarked on several missions and returned home to Sandrilan, but still no word from the commander concerning the training.

After three months had passed by, James felt he must have forgotten their talk. He'd never told James the training was for certain. Perhaps it had not worked out, and the commander had only neglected to tell him this.

Then, Jollie came to the ship one day in search of James.

"Sergeant, the doctor needs to see you right away." The small Asian man bowed slightly and then turned and left the crew's quarters.

James dressed and after a quick breakfast made his way up the winding road to Doc Jefferies' office. Once he'd stepped inside, the doctor stood from his desk.

"Sergeant Taft, please come in. I need to do an examination on you right away. The commander sent word this morning; it seems this needs to be addressed before the Valiant leaves tomorrow."

James remained in front of the doorway, not sure of what to think about this new information.

"Examination...did he say why? And, I haven't heard anything about us leaving tomorrow."

"Of course, you haven't, Sergeant. Has the commander ever informed you, or for that matter me, of his plans? No, and we don't ask, do we? Which is why I don't know what the examination is about, nor did I ask."

The doctor motioned to James as he moved towards the small room in the back. "Come along Sergeant, let's get this over with."

A few moments later Doc Jefferies was peering into James' mouth.

"So, you don't know anything either, Sergeant?"

"Ahhuuh, mho."

The doctor looked curiously at James. "Oh, you can close up now. Your teeth are in good shape by the way. You were saying?"

"I suspect it may concern some training I spoke to the commander about a few months back. Other than that, I don't know anything."

Doc Jefferies had the appearance of considering this. He picked up a stethoscope and put the listening tubes in his ears.

"That would explain the physical examination I suppose. What type of training will you be receiving?"

"I'm not certain what the training would be or where I would get it. From what the commander said, though, it'll be tough."

The doctor looked at James as he listened to his heart. He then stepped back and pulled the tubes from his ears. He studied James briefly.

"Well, Sergeant you're in excellent physical condition as far as I can tell. But I wonder why the commander would send you to such training. You've been through a lot and faired as well as anyone could expect. Do you know why he would put you through this 'training'?"

"I asked him about it. I requested it, Doctor."

Doc Jefferies sat his stethoscope on a small table. "I see... Sergeant, I don't wish to alarm you, but, if the commander says this training will be involved, then you should be prepared for an intense struggle. The commander understands well what 'difficult' means. He would not say such a thing unless it is such. I would be ready for nothing less than severe. If you are certain, you wish to go through with it that is."

James expelled a breath through his nose and glanced down at the floor. "I'm sure, Doc. I've thought about it for some time now. I feel better when we're helping people. I think this has been what I've needed. When I see people around Sandrilan that we've assisted in some way, I have peace. I want to do the best I can in the service of

Sandrilan. If I get this training, then I feel I'll be able to do my job at the greatest level possible."

Doc Jefferies nodded. "It's good to have a purpose, Sergeant. It sounds like you have one, and a good one at that. I'll send word to the commander that you're as fit as can be expected." The doctor paused and appeared a little concerned. He then continued. "Good luck, Sergeant. I'm confident you can be successful in the endeavor."

"Thank you, Doc. That means a lot to me."

The next morning the Valiant's bell rang out. Soon the warship was moving out to open seas. Before mid-day, the commander called James to his quarters.

"Please, sit down Sergeant. Would you like a drink?"

James sat down in front of the small desk and asked, "Will I need one, sir?"

The commander chuckled as he poured himself a glass of wine.

"I don't suppose you'll need one, but we may be here awhile, so if you want one just ask and I'll gladly pour you one."

James nodded, "Yes Sir, I'll do that."

The commander continued, "You may already have an idea as to why you're here. It has to do with the training we spoke of some time back. And, the reason you're here now is for me to explain the nature of this training and to be certain you wish to proceed. The destination for which this training will take place is rather far, so you should be confident of your wishes before we embark on the journey."

James again nodded and then replied. "Yes Sir, I understand. I also think that I'll have the drink you mentioned."

The commander smiled and poured James a glass of wine. Once James had taken a sip, the commander began with a puzzling statement.

"Sno is a beautiful creature, don't you think, Sergeant?"

James again sipped his wine rather nervously, then replied. "Yes Sir, I would agree with you on that."

The commander continued. "She's like a flower that has been tossed upon the wind and landed gracefully in our home of Sandrilan. Have you ever wondered how Sno came to Sandrilan?"

James realized this had never crossed his mind. "I guess not Sir. But now that you mention it, I am curious."

"Sno is a Geisha, as you know. They are beautiful and talented women, trained in the art of entertaining Japanese men of nobility or social standing. Sno and Kenji were in the service of Shogun Tokugawa Toshinobu. Do you know anything about the Japanese Shogun?"

"No Sir, I don't," James replied.

"The shoguns of Japan are something like nobility, perhaps similar to a prince or duke in Europe. They have vast stretches of land and people which they govern over. Shoguns answer only to the Emperor.

"In 1867, a war broke out in Japan. It was an internal war, and the fighting had a lot to do with Japan becoming modernized and attempting to be like the Europeans and Americans. Many wished to stay purely 'Japanese' as they had done for centuries. But the country was opening up to the world, and this war was the last resistance to that situation.

"The Samurai warriors of Japan are highly trained fighters. They are certainly among the best educated in the world and are the shoguns' 'Knights,' if you will. They are fierce and relentless in battle.

"During this war, the Samurai fought on both sides, in accordance to their masters' loyalty.

"Shogun Toshinobu was, unfortunately for him, not on the winning side. In 1869, he went into exile and moved to Tukushima, an island South of Japan. Toshinobu's large household, with its many wives, children, concubines, and servants, had all dispersed into the lands and found refuge. Slowly, over several months, the Shogun retrieved his people by ships and brought them to his island location.

"I knew nothing of these events until late 1869 when the Valiant came upon two ships in battle. For many reasons I'll not go into now, the Valiant had by this time, become a priority target for the notorious pirate leader, Zheng Qui; before the British and Americans had gained the upper hand on such pirates. We were engaged in battle quite often with this enemy, and I immediately recognized one of the ships as a Zheng Qui vessel.

"The Valiant went into action against the pirates, who turned from the badly damaged ship they had been attacking and began firing upon us."

186

The commander finished his glass of wine and lit up a cigar. He examined it as he expelled the smoke and rolled it in his fingers. He then continued.

"The large guns of the Valiant quickly decimated the pirate's ship, and it sank with all hands onboard. We moved up beside the sinking vessel that the pirates had been attacking and quickly began transferring the survivors onto the Valiant. The last of the crew came onboard as their ship was slipping into the sea under their feet.

"This was the first time I met Kenji and Sno. We had a few Korean sailors on board the Valiant and were able to interpret what Kenji said to us.

"Kenji's commanding officers were killed when a shot from the Pirates' ship hit the steering house. Although he was a lower ranking, non-commissioned officer, he found himself in charge of the vessel.

"He went on to explain that the ship was in the process of transporting the possessions of Shogun Toshinobu to his home on Tukushima island. The cargo included household furnishings and other miscellaneous items. But also among the possessions of the shogun was one of his favorite Geisha and her attendants."

The commander glanced at James after saying this. He seemed to be interested in the sergeant's reaction. James sipped his wine but otherwise made no outward expression. The commander continued.

"Sno began her training at the tender age of twelve. She has been taught over many years to entertain men with the natural charms of a woman, rather than sex. She is, in my opinion, one of the most beautiful and wonderful creatures that have walked this cruel world. And yet, she is entirely dedicated to her position as a Geisha.

"After initially seeing this remarkable young woman, it was a bit unbelievable when Kenji told me his master, Toshinobu, would no longer allow Sno into his household. Kenji went on to explain that his master would, however, be glad to know what happened and would likely reward me if I could bring him to Tukushima island so that he could explain the situation to the Shogun.

"I agreed, and the Valiant made it's way to the Shogun's home. Once we reached the island, there were many messages sent back and forth before we could step foot from the Valiant's deck. Even after this, only Kenji, myself and one interpreter were allowed to meet with the Shogun.

"We were taken inland and waited several hours in the shade of cherry trees before we were finally able to proceed to the shogun's palace. Once we arrived, Kenji explained to his master what had happened. He then offered to be executed or take his own life to pay for losing the shogun's ship and disgracing Sno.

"After several long moments of thought, Shogun Toshinobu asked that everyone leave so that he may speak with me. Only my interpreter and a few of Toshinobu's closest aides were allowed to stay."

James had become quite interested in the commander's tale by now. The ship rolled slightly with the sea, and a rhythmic creaking of the floorboards under his feet were the only other sounds. The commander poured himself another glass of wine and offered James another glass. After James extended his glass and received more wine, the commander took a sip of his drink and continued.

"Toshinobu explained to me that, Sno was very dear to him. But, he could not allow her back into his household. Although the Pirates may not have touched her, being in proximity to them meant she was forever tainted. Though he may not consider it such, the other women of the Palace would ostracize her and be very cruel. They would assume the Pirates had raped her and would treat her badly.

"Kenji knew this and realized that being the highest officer to have survived the attack, meant he would need to take responsibility for the disgraceful situation. Although Kenji was not a Samurai and wasn't subject to the bushido code, he had offered to give his life as recompense, and the shogun was impressed by this.

"At this time, I offered sanctuary for Sno, Kenji, and the surviving crew members. I told Toshinobu they would be welcomed at Sandrilan and treated well. Toshinobu expressed gratitude but said Kenji would not rest with the burden of losing the ship. He said Sno and the others should go to Sandrilan, but Kenji would likely end up killing himself to atone for the loss of his master's ship.

"I considered this for a moment and then proposed something to the shogun. Since the Valiant was in constant battle with the same pirates that sank the shogun's ship and caused such mischief, I suggested that the shogun order Kenji to service on the Valiant. He should fight the Pirates to atone for the loss of Toshinubo's ship. In this way, Kenji could regain his honor and be an asset for the Valiant and Sandrilan. The shogun expressed agreement with this and said it would be completed.

"Before bringing Kenji and the others back, Toshinobu asked what payment I would like for this great favor. I told him it was not something I could accept payment for as it was, in fact, an honor to do such a thing. Again, the shogun expressed satisfaction with my answer. After some thought, he told me that if I should ever need a favor, ask it of him and he would do what he could to provide it. This way it would be one honorable favor for another honorable favor, and the deeds would not be tainted by the stench of money. I agreed."

The commander extinguished his cigar in a small clay tray. He again studied James, as if he wondered the Sergeant's thoughts. He took a breath in and continued.

"That favor has never been redeemed, Sergeant. But I believe it may be soon. You are a soldier that has done most of your work on horseback. You are an exceptional warrior, but you need training for close quarter fighting. The Japanese have long perfected this type of instruction, and the result is the Samurai warrior. These fighters are sharpened to perfection and in all manners of battle, especially close quarter fighting."

James could not help but perk up when the commander said this. The commander, in turn, took notice of it before continuing.

"The problem I see is this. The shogun may or may not take you in and allow his Samurai masters to teach you. But, even if he does allow this, you will be at a considerable disadvantage. The training will be quite difficult, and to complete it successfully in a few short years would be an enormous feat even for a Japanese soldier. But you, Sergeant, will need to learn the language quickly, while subjected to the harshness of the Samurai master. You may not survive. But if you do and are successful, then I feel your fighting skills would be equal to my own. Not like my skills, but of a high level, in the sense that fighting skills have such levels."

Again, a calm came over the small cabin area. The floorboards creaked, and the ship rolled gently from one side to the other as James considered this. He finished off the last of his wine and sat the glass on the desk. Finally, he replied.

"Years ago, I was close to a woman in Independence Missouri. She was a saloon girl and had seen the worst of men and life. I think

I may have loved her. I don't know for certain, but I remember something she told me. She said, 'That I should find a place where the thing that burdened my heart was the thing that was needed the most.' If I could do this, then I would find peace. For many years, I thought that no such place existed. But here with the Valiant, and Sandrilan, I have found that place. I have found peace, and I'm no longer tormented as a soldier. I'll follow the same path that led me here, Sir. I'll take the training if the shogun allows it and if I should not survive it, then so be it. The fate that Sandrilan deals me is the one I'll accept."

The commander said nothing, but he nodded his head slowly and with a sense of agreement. Once again, the cabin became void of noise, other than the Valiant's subtle nuances. Then The commander stood up, as did James.

"That is a respectable answer, Sergeant. And, the Japanese regard honor as one of the highest attributes that a soldier can possess. I'll ask Kenji to work with you and assist you in learning the Japanese language, while we are en-route to Tukushima."

The commander paused and then ended their meeting with, "If anyone can complete this training successfully, Sergeant, I believe you can."

"Thank you, Sir," James replied and after a quick salute left the small cabin.

Chapter Fourteen: In the Service of the Shogun

The Valiant sailed northwest for three weeks. Kenji seemed a little reluctant to work with James at first, but after learning the reason warmed up to the task and was able to teach James some basic words in the Japanese language.

The weather grew cooler as they ventured farther North. It was an odd sensation for James as he'd not felt the bite of winter since leaving America. He often stood on the deck and gazed out over the gray horizon, considering the unknown path in front of him. He thought of what the commander had told him.

As the Valiant approached the island of Tukushima, James spoke with Kenji.

"I need you to teach me a phrase in Japanese."

Kenji appeared curious. "What do you wish to learn?"

James thought for a second and then replied, "Teach me how to say, 'If I fail, it will forever stain your honor.'"

Kenji thought about this. Then, a subtle smile broke over his face. "I think that one phrase could save your life, Sergeant. I'll teach it to you, and I suspect you may need it someday."

The two found a quiet place for Kenji to go over this with James, who repeated it over and over until it was branded into his mind.

Finally, as a light drizzle fell upon the deck, the Valiant moved into a small natural harbor of Tukushima. After a few hours, row boats came out, and Japanese men in fancy silk dress clothes boarded the warship. Kenji spoke with the messengers, and they soon left.

"We'll now wait for Toshinobu's invitation," the commander said to James. "It may take hours or days before he'll see us. . . If he'll see us at all. I'm inclined to believe he will, but when he's ready.

"The negotiations for your training may be very delicate. You should follow Kenji's lead while in the presence of the Shogun. Also, try to speak as little as possible. For Toshinobu, the thought of repaying a favor by training a Westerner in the arts of a Samurai may be the equivalent of mixing fire and ice."

"Yes Sir," James replied.

The ship and crew waited two days for a reply from Toshinobu. Finally, in the evening of the second day, a small craft came out to the Valiant. The messenger brought word that Toshinobu would receive them the following morning.

"Put your best suit on tomorrow, Sergeant, you'll be meeting Japanese royalty." The commander then smiled slightly and moved towards his cabin.

The following morning James stood on the deck waiting for the others. He felt excited, and a bit frightened as well. It was the same feeling he had right before going into battle.

Soon Kenji ventured onto the deck. He was dressed in an elaborate Japanese outfit. It was well-crafted and made of silk. James was astonished to see him in such attire, but the real surprise came when the commander stepped out onto the deck.

James' eyes widened, and it was apparent as the commander noticed this. He was dressed in what could only be described as a cross between Asian and European royalty. His coat was silk; had tails and was an Asian fashion. Under the bright coat was one of the finest western style vest and shirt that James had ever seen. The collar of the crisp white shirt had a fluffy cravat that was tucked into the vest, as well as pleated cuffs. The commander's hair was oiled, and his goatee had been braided and also oiled.

As the commander came closer to James, he spoke in a soft voice that only James could hear.

"This... dressing up all fancy and fringed; it's the thing I like least about being the King of Sandrilan. I've never adjusted to it, Sergeant."

James smiled, and this caused the commander to smile as well.

The small party, consisting of James, the commander, Kenji and two aides, all boarded Toshinobu's craft and were taken to land.

Onshore, a host of neatly dressed men met them. On the small road behind these greeters were some wheeled carts, to be pulled by a man. Later, James would learn these were called rickshaws.

The Japanese men greeted the party from the Valiant and soon all were being transported along what fairly well amounted to a dirt trail.

After around twenty minutes of travel, the group arrived at the gates of a vast complex. Grandiose and impressive Japanese architecture stood several stories high behind the walls. As the gates slowly opened, James became even more delighted by the Shogun's Palace.

192

Swiftly moving towards the massive, main building, the procession passed carefully tended gardens and trees decorating the exterior of the complex. Beautiful women in splendid silk outfits stood on balconies and watched the visitors with interest.

Soon, the group arrived at the steps of the palace. Large marble dragons adorned the sides of each portion of the ascending path. Colorful tile mosaics enhanced the short walls that framed the walkway up to the main structure. After several levels of steps, James found himself in front of two sizable and elaborately decorated doors.

Several guards dressed in Japanese armor and holding long spears opened the entrance. Exotic and unusual smells greeted James as the now accessible Palace presented itself.

Inside, the group moved through finely decorated, marble pillars until reaching a large open area. At the end and upon a stage, similar to the one the commander sat upon in the palace of Sandrilan yet much higher, sat Shogun Toshinobu. They were escorted past many shorter tables with food items laid out in preparation for a feast.

Upon reaching the front of the stage, the men bowed, and James noticed who he presumed to be the shogun in his forties. His hair placed into a high ponytail with a long hanging goatee and mustache. His hair was black, and the man had a distinct appearance of wisdom and experience.

His silk garment lay around him loosely but also as if placed in this fashion purposely by attendants. He sat up straight and gazed down upon his guests. He had a stern expression and for almost a minute, only stared at the men. Finally, he spoke, and Kenji interpreted his words for the commander and James.

"The King of Sandrilan would kindly send word before his next visit. I have found it necessary to assemble a hasty reception for the king, in a short two days time. I hope the preparations are adequate."

The commander bowed slightly and replied. "I am sure the preparations will be more than adequate, Lord Toshinobu. I am honored and humbled that my friend, would take such time and effort to ensure my visit is a welcomed one. I only pray that I can provide a reception equal to this one, should Lord Toshinobu visit our fair land of Sandrilan."

Once Kenji had translated this, Toshinobu turned his head slightly and lowered it in a half nod, seeming to indicate the commander's words to be acceptable. He then replied.

"I believe the King of Sandrilan has come for the purpose of business as well as a visit. Perhaps our talk of business can wait until after the meal, which has been carefully prepared by a hundred servants."

The commander replied in a humble voice.

"That is a wise choice, Lord Toshinobu. Business should not be discussed on an empty stomach."

Toshinobu again smiled slightly and then clapped his hands together. Immediately servants came from doors and entryways. Several escorted James and the others to their seats. The commander was the only one allowed on the stage and at the same level as Toshinobu. James, Kenji and the assistants from the Valiant were seated on a side stage area that was lower than the two leaders.

As the servants began to present the meal, James realized this palace must have been the original inspiration for the palace of Sandrilan. There were many similarities, yet the palace and staff of Sandrilan were from many different Asian areas. This however, was a purely Japanese palace.

While they ate the meal, a variety of entertainers performed for the guests. Among these, many beautiful Japanese women danced or sang in graceful and delicate expressions of their preferred art form.

Finally, after several hours of food and entertainment, the host ordered all to leave other than a few of his guards and the party from the Valiant.

The commander asked the assistant from the Valiant for a cigar and then offered Toshinobu one. The shogun accepted the gift, and after both men had lit their cigars and took a few draws from them, Toshinobu opened the discussion.

"It is good to think you have traveled so far simply to indulge in my hospitality, but I know there are other reasons for your visit. Before we get into that, I must ask the king, how is Seno?"

The commander expelled a long stream of smoke as Kenji translated this to him. Then he replied.

"You are a wise man, Lord Toshinobu. Yes, there is another reason for my visit. Before I talk about these things, I will tell you of Sno."

194

He paused, as if considering the beautiful Geisha, then continued.

"Sno has been given full access to the Palace of Sandrilan, which is also her home. She sings and dances as no other woman could. Her beauty and grace are unmatched, and her presence blesses the palace. She is content I am sure, though I know she misses her first Master. I would venture to say she is even happy at Sandrilan. We have done all we can and will continue to do what we can do, to ensure Sno's happiness."

After Kenji had translated this, the shogun smiled and expelled a long stream of the cigar smoke. He then stared off into the room for several long seconds, as if also recalling Sno's beauty or one of her songs. He then appeared to pull himself back from a splendid dream and refocused his attention on the guests.

"Thank you for the care of Seno. Now, what is the business you've come for? I'm ready to hear this."

The commander readjusted himself and proceeded. "Lord Toshinobu, you've told me that should I need something; ask it of you, and you would do your best to supply it. I have a need now that I feel only a man of your standing can supply."

The commander pulled another draw from his cigar. He expelled the smoke and took a drink of his Japanese wine. Toshinobu watched him with interest as the commander swallowed the wine and continued.

"This is a young Sergeant of mine." The commander motioned to James. "He is an exceptional soldier and has served Sandrilan faithfully. Before he came into the service of Sandrilan, he was trained, on the back of a horse, in the United States Army and fought as a Cavalryman in the war between the States.

"I believe he has much potential as a soldier, and yet, I have little need for an extraordinary horse soldier. I need soldiers that can fight in close quarters. Therefore, I wish to have him trained by your best Samurai master. I will pay for his training if need be. I will also pay for his room and board. It is the training I'm in need of, and your fine bushido tradition would bring this soldier to the level I need him to be at."

Toshinobu sat back a little upon hearing this. His faced expressed a stern frown, almost as if he had eaten something bitter. He extinguished the remnants of the cigar. He readjusted himself and was in clear thought about the matter.

195

After a moment of consideration, the shogun replied in a low voice. "It is not a common thing for a Westerner to be trained in the arts of our Samurai. You are aware of this I'm sure. You must certainly realize that night is falling on the bushido tradition. War is now waged with machines and guns. There is little room left in the world for the Samurai. Do you need such a thing?"

The commander replied quickly as if prepared for any possible response from the shogun.

"I respectfully mention to your Lordship that it is somewhat expensive to navigate a warship across the Pacific. If I were not certain that this is precisely what myself and Sandrilan needed, I would not have ventured this far into it. As for night falling upon the Samurai tradition, even the night holds shining stars to be admired by all. Perhaps this would be an opportunity for your bushi master to reveal one last star."

Toshinobu again expressed the slight smile that indicated he liked or at least respected the commander's response. The smile quickly faded, and he said. "I must consider this appeal. You may stay here as my guests; my staff will ensure that you are comfortable."

The shogun then clapped his hands and immediately attendants came to his call. James and the group from the Valiant were escorted out of the palace and directed to individual rooms.

The group then began a patient wait as Toshinobu pondered the request. Two days after the reception, James sat in a garden area. He was dressed in a silk robe that the attendants had given him to wear while cleaning his uniform. The commander came upon him and also wore an elaborate Japanese robe.

"The Japanese have a wonderful sense of style and beauty, would you agree, Sergeant?"

James gazed around the garden, and up at several beautiful women standing on small balconies; apparently trying hard not to stare at the interesting Westerners below.

"Indeed they do, Sir."

The commander produced two of his slim cigars from a hidden pocket, or perhaps he had carried them in his hand. He offered one to James, and after taking it, James nodded his head in a thankful gesture.

As the two men examined their cigars, a small Japanese servant came from an unseen location, carrying a lit stick in his hand. He held the stick up, and the two men lit their cigars from it.

The commander puffed his cigar as he watched the small attendant retreat into obscurity.

"I believe Lord Toshinobu may have better service than I do at Sandrilan. But, I suspect his servants work for less and could be beaten if they do anything wrong. I could never have a man beaten. I feel people respond to kindness much better than fear."

He then took another draw from the cigar. After expelling the smoke, he continued in a soft voice.

"If Toshinobu allows this training, you'll be on your own, Sergeant. The training will take some time, perhaps five years. I'll try to get it shortened, but it will likely be some years, regardless. You should also know that the Japanese can be quite ruthless, and they don't have a very high regard for what they call 'westerners.' You'll need to summon a strength and resolve as you've likely never gathered before. There's still time to say no. After the deal is agreed upon, there will only be two ways out; success or death."

James expelled a long breath that had smoke mixed with it. He again glanced up at a beautiful young Japanese woman. She held a fan up to her face and giggled softly when she noticed James admiring her. He, in turn, looked around at the garden. The weather was cool, and the air was brisk. Finally, he replied.

"After the war, I was lost. I never believed that I would survive it, so I never thought about what I would do afterward. For several years, I wandered around aimlessly. When I settled down with the Aqukolo tribe, I thought I had found my future."

James' gaze lowered to the ground as the memory of his lost love brought anguish. He pulled in a breath of the cold air and continued.

"I don't know that I have a destination anymore. But I feel that I have a purpose. That's better than nothing. This training, if I get it, will give me one destination and one thing to focus on, if only for a few years. If I succeed, then it will help me in my purpose. If I fail, there will be no more concerns about anything."

The commander examined his cigar for a few seconds. He rolled it in his fingers and then tapped it to knock off the ashes. After taking a draw from it, he replied in the same soft voice.

"Well said, Sergeant. And I assure you that you have a very important purpose with the Valiant and Sandrilan. I will be expecting you to get through this and to be ready to continue in that purpose."

James glanced up at the commander, who smiled slightly and then patted him on the shoulder before walking away. James finished his cigar and admired the scenery a bit longer. He then went back to his room to prepare for the evening meal.

The following morning the group received their cleaned uniforms and were informed that the shogun would receive them at the midday meal.

The group once again made their way into the palace of Toshinobu. As before, they ate and were entertained. Finally, the shogun was ready to talk and had almost everyone leave.

"I have given the King's request much thought. Although I would like to provide this thing and repay the favor, I'm afraid this decision must fall upon the person who can provide such a thing. If my senior Samurai master agrees to train this man, it will accomplish both our desires. My favor will be repaid, and your Sergeant will be trained.

"However, should he refuse, I'm afraid the favor will remain unpaid, until such a day that I can supply the need. Will the King consider this a fair resolution?"

The commander nodded slightly and replied, "This will be acceptable, Lord Toshinobu. And thank you for your attention in this matter, regardless of the outcome."

The shogun also nodded and said something to a nearby servant, who then left the room.

Soon a distinguished and fierce looking warrior entered. He was in his mid to late forties. His black hair was tied back in a high ponytail, similar to Toshinobu's. He did not have facial hair however to soften his stern expression.

"Master Ichiro, I've called you here in the hope that you can settle an issue for us. This is the King of Sandrilan." Toshinobu motioned towards the commander. "I owe the King a favor, and I would like to repay that favor. However, for this debt to be repaid, it will require your services. Since the King's request is not something I can supply without your assistance, I will allow you to make the

198

decision as to whether this favor is paid now, or at some later date and with some other request that I can perhaps supply myself."

Ichiro bowed low to Toshinobu. "Please, tell me what I can do for you, Master."

"The King needs a man trained in the arts of bushido. If you can do this, it will repay my favor to him."

Ichiro turned to Kenji, "This is the man?"

Kenji rather quickly shook his head and pointed to James. Ichiro's face immediately soured again and twisted slightly. A low growl was expelled under his breath as he studied James. After a few more seconds of thought, Ichiro replied.

"A westerner would not survive such training. It would be a slow and painful death. If the King of Sandrilan wishes for this man to die, I can remove his head now, and it would be quick and merciful."

Kenji translated this, and the commander smiled slightly. He then said, "This man is a brave warrior, but he is trained to carry out warfare on horseback. I need him trained for battle in close quarters. I am confident of his ability to survive the training. What I find myself being unsure of now, is the ability of the trainer that I have traveled far to find."

As the commander finished, Kenji's face tensed with fear. He lowered his voice and spoke to the commander. James was close enough to hear the muted conversation.

"Sir, if I translate that to Master Ichiro, we may need to fight our way out of here. I did not bring a weapon."

The commander thought of Kenji's words for a few brief seconds and replied in a soft voice.

"Not to worry, Mr. Kenji, I brought one," he tapped his cane lightly and continued. "And, I'm sure we can find a few more around here somewhere; please proceed."

Kenji swallowed and cleared his voice. He then relayed the commander's words.

Master Ichiro appeared to swell up. His face became flush. Toshinobu raised his eyebrows while watching Ichiro, as if the Samurai master might explode.

It was evident Ichiro could barely contain himself. The commander expressed no concern. Finally, Ichiro spoke with a strained voice.

"You should have no concern about the ability of the trainer. Perhaps this man could survive. But it would take far too long. He would be of little use to you by the time he completed the training."

The commander wasted no time in replying. "It's good that I need not worry about the abilities of the trainer, Master Ichiro because I'll need him back in two years time."

Kenji expressed fright once again. His head lowered a little, and he spoke to the commander in a meek voice, "Sir, please, this is a Samurai Master we are talking to."

The commander retrieved a cigar from his coat, and a servant lit it. He pulled a draw from it and said to Kenji in a quiet voice as well, "Very true, Mr. Kenji, we should be ready for a fight." He then turned to James. "Sergeant, be ready for battle, we may need to fight in the next few seconds."

James nodded slightly and replied meekly, "Yes, Sir."

"Alright, we're ready Mr. Kenji, proceed."

With a pale face and a weak voice, Kenji relayed the commander's words. Ichiro's face again became strained. A frown stretched across his mouth, and a low growl heard once more. He turned to Toshinobu as if hoping his master would grant him the right to kill the visitors. Toshinobu simply stared at him with an expression of interest.

Ichiro slowly turned back to the commander, "That is not possible. Perhaps five years, if he is the warrior you say he is."

The commander replied, and Kenji translated. "Three years if you are the trainer your Lord feels you are."

Ichiro sat back a little, "Four years if he should live that long."

The commander again replied quickly. "We'll cut it in the middle then, three and one-half years."

Kenji translated this and Ichiro's face continued to grow red.

The commander then stood up, turned to Toshinobu and bowed. "Thank you Lord Toshinobu; I'm sure Sergeant Taft will excel in Master Ichiro's capable hands. Please keep track of your expenses, and I'll be glad to cover the cost when we return for him."

Toshinobu listened to Kenji relay this, but he was also closely watching Ichiro, who was now quite beside himself. Without a word, the Samurai master stood up, bowed to Toshinobu and stormed out of the room.

The shogun turned to the commander and replied, "Don't be concerned about the expenses. If your man lives through this, I'll be glad to supply all of his needs."

They all bowed to the shogun and left the palace.

The following morning, James and the commander sat in a garden after breakfast. As they were talking, Ichiro and several samurais came up to them.

"Well, it seems that it's time to say good-bye, Sergeant."

James stood up and nodded, "Yes, Sir."

One of the samurais shouted out in Japanese, "You are now in the service of Lord Toshinobu; under the instruction of Master Ichiro. You will not speak unless your master allows it."

James didn't understand what the man said. He turned to the commander, "I'll see you in three and a half years then?"

In a flash, one of the samurais threw James onto the ground. He held him with one arm behind his back and pushed James' face into the earth.

"You do not speak unless your master gives you permission!" The samurai shouted down to James.

The commander winced at the sight of James on the ground. "Yes, certainly, Sergeant, I will return for you."

With one side of his face in the dirt, James spoke, but thru obvious pain, "Alright, Sir, three and a half years..."

"I'll pull your arm off if you speak again!!" The samurai pulled back on James' arm, causing him to cry out in agony.

The commander gave James a quick salute, and with an expression of compassion left.

James was immediately stripped of his uniform. He was given rags to wear, and after a day of no food or drink, along with being constantly shouted at, he was given a room that he was barely able to lay in. A thin woven mat with no pillow was his bed. He lay shivering all night as the cold penetrated his body.

In the morning, an attendant brought a small bowl of rice. James barely had time to eat before being ushered out and into an open area. The two samurai from the previous day forced James to stand in this area until noon. If James tried to sit, they came and hit his legs with bamboo rods.

Finally, they moved him briskly outside the palace walls. The remainder of the day he was instructed to pull weeds from around the exterior of the complex. He was given two bathroom breaks, and if he attempted to speak, the men would again strike him with the bamboo rods.

That night, he was returned to his room and given another small bowl of rice.

For at least two weeks, this routine continued. James never saw Ichiro during this time, only the two samurais that escorted him back and forth to perform some menial duties outside the palace walls.

James began to lose track of the days. After three weeks or so, he was led to a stream. In a deep area were several oxen and it was there that he was instructed to bathe. He gladly did so as he had begun to stink horribly. He also quickly washed the rags he wore. That night he slept better than he had in days.

After what seemed a month or so, James was deteriorating into a desperate condition. He had lost weight and often felt he would pass out during his hours of standing in the large open area. He was always glad to move to the tasks of pulling weeds or cleaning up after the oxen; he could kneel or at times, even sit.

As this routine dragged on, James came to believe that Ichiro intended to kill him in this manner. This would be the way that he would free himself from the task of training James. He would do this until James died and when the commander returned for him, Ichiro would inform him that James was not strong enough.

Then, one day, perhaps two months after the ordeal began, Ichiro came to the open area as James stood. It was still an hour or so until noon. Ichiro walked around James. He had an expression of disgust as he examined him.

The other two samurais also strolled behind their master. James knew he would be punished, but he could no longer hold back.

"Are you going to train me, or just kill me?"

One of the samurais immediately kicked James in the stomach. "You do not speak!"

On his knees now and bending over in pain, James replied, "This is how you repay your lords' debts?"

The samurai now kicked James in the face; he fell back onto the ground and blood began to run from his nose.

Ichiro said nothing, but walked over and stared down at James. Finally, he spoke.

"Your master should have never brought you here to die this way. Why would he think you could complete such a thing and in such a time?"

James understood none of this. But he had little doubt that Ichiro would allow him to perish under these conditions. As Ichiro turned to walk away, James shouted in Japanese the one phrase he knew.

"If I fail, it will forever stain your honor!"

Immediately one of the samurais began beating James in the face.

"You do not speak; you keep your filthy mouth closed!"

James tried to cover his face, but the blows were coming hard and fast.

Then, Ichiro shouted, "Tomari!"

The samurai quit hitting James, but his face had already been battered. He had no strength left to sit or stand. The sun was hot, and the dusty air was difficult to pull into his lungs. He heard Ichiro talking to the other men, but couldn't understand what they said.

A few minutes later, the men picked him up by his arms and drug him to his tiny room. A small bowl of rice was delivered, and James tried to eat with his bloodied mouth. His body in pain and completely exhausted, he finally slept.

Chapter Fifteen: Training, with a Dash of Natsu

Early the following morning, the door to James' room opened. Sunlight streamed in, and James held his hand up to block some of it. His battered eyes were swollen. He strained to see.

One of the Samurai stood holding the door open. Another stood on the other side.

In from the morning light walked a beautiful young Japanese woman. Her hair was in a great bun on the top of her head. Many delicate ornaments dangled from the bun. She wore a colorful silk dress and carried a small tray with a bowl of rice and one large boiled egg.

James maneuvered so that the young girl could enter the tiny room. She knelt down and smiled. James tilted his head and struggled to open his swollen eyes wider. He could barely believe the sight he beheld.

"Gohan," she said with a soft, sweet tone and pointed at the rice.

"What?" James asked. His voice was coarse from a lack of water.

"Gohan," she said again and pointed at the rice.

James noticed her face grimace slightly as she looked at him. He realized his condition must be dreadful and had little doubt that he smelled from the lack of a bath.

The Japanese woman then smiled again with an obvious effort, and her face expressed compassion. James looked at the rice.

"Gohan...?" He asked.

She nodded, "Gohan." The woman then took two sticks in her hand and picked up a small amount of the sticky rice.

James labored to breathe as his ribs still ached, but he pointed to the sticks.

"Hashi," the woman said.

"Ha...shi.," James replied. The woman nodded again.

As James tried to eat the rice with the sticks, rather than his dirty hands, the woman left and soon returned with a large cup of water. This was clean water, not the murky and muddy tasting water he had become accustomed to.

After eating, James lay in the small room. He expected the two samurais to retrieve him and force him to stand for several hours. This didn't happen.

Around noon, the woman was brought to him again. She had a meal and some water. This time there was meat with the meal. It was chicken, or perhaps duck, either way, the taste was wonderful as James had not had meat since dining with the shogun.

He wasn't sure how long he had been here. His face had a full beard, though, and his hair needed to be cleaned and combed.

Once again, the woman taught him several Japanese words. She also pointed to herself and said, "Natsu."

James repeated the name as he ate. She nodded and said it again, "Natsu."

"James," he said as he pointed to himself.

"Gems," she said and then giggled.

James smiled and replied, "that's close enough. It sounds very nice when you say it."

Again, Natsu giggled.

The third day, Natsu led James to a room with a large heated bathtub. She motioned for him to get in. James expressed discomfort with her in the room.

"I'm uh, not used to bathing with someone around, particularly a woman."

Natsu laughed. Though she didn't understand the words, she seemed to notice his reluctance.

"Furo!" She said and pointed to the bath.

James hesitated.

"Furo, furo!!" She said and this time waved her hand in front of her face, to show him he smelled very bad.

"Yes, yes, alright, I'm going." He turned his back to her and began to take the filthy rags off.

Slipping into the hot bath felt like heaven. He let out a moan as the water comforted his sore muscles. Natsu giggled again.

As he soaked in hot water, Natsu came close and began to trim his beard, while holding a pan underneath to catch the whiskers. Once it was short enough, she began to shave him. He looked at her, and she said something softly, but he didn't understand.

Once he had bathed, Natsu gave him a thin towel. He draped it around his waist, and she motioned for him to lay down.

As he lay on the floor, she began to rub warm oil on him, but she stopped.

James looked up to see what she was doing and realized she was staring at his upper body. She then began to touch his many scars, one by one. He had forgotten about these. Some were from the war; others were from his fight with Sachi's killers.

As Natsu touched each one, she said something softly, as if naming each mark. Finally, she looked at James' face. A tear almost erupted from her eye, but it never escaped. She smiled and seemed to shrug off the emotions. Then, she returned to her task of oiling his body.

After this, Natsu brought him a silk robe and led him to a large room with a much nicer sleeping mat as well as other furniture. He also found clothes that were not as nice as the samurai's, but much nicer than the rags he had been wearing.

It was only now that he fully accepted his words to Ichiro had made a difference. It became apparent that Ichiro realized not putting forth any effort to train James would be an automatic failure on his part. Whereas trying to teach him and then, James failing, would not be such for the samurai master.

As he lay down, James realized it would be up to him from this point on. He must summon the great resolve that his commander had spoken of and complete this training. He then slept soundly for the first time in a long time.

Natsu continued to bring his meals every day as he recovered from the harsh treatment. She tutored him in Japanese and James focused his energies on learning the language quickly.

After two weeks and when James was back in good health, Ichiro came to visit. He spoke, and James listened intently. He understood a few words, but the one that had the most meaning was 'tomorrow.'

When Ichiro had finished speaking, James bowed and said "tomorrow," in Japanese.

This appeared to impress Ichiro, and he bowed very slightly and said "tomorrow" again, and then left.

The following morning James prepared himself for what he hoped would be the beginning of his education as a bushi warrior. Not long after this, the two samurais came and escorted him to an open field.

Here, would be the start of an intense course of training. All aspects of martial arts, sword, spear, armor, and bow and arrow tactics were introduced and exercised on a daily basis. Hour after hour, James practiced and studied. In the evenings, Natsu tutored him in Japanese, and as he learned more and was able to communicate with her, the lessons became more interesting and exciting for both.

"What are you to me?" James asked Natsu in Japanese. It had been around six months from the time she had begun to assist him. He felt he could finally ask her.

Natsu looked at him shyly. "I am your helper," she replied.

"How many... ways are you supposed to help?" James asked, struggling for several words.

Natsu turned away from him and straightened a small marble statue on a table as if it were in the wrong place. After a few more seconds, she replied.

"I am to assist you in any way you need." She spoke with a soft voice but continued to adjust the statue.

She then turned and looked into his eyes. His heart beat stronger which caused him to turn away from her. It was too frightening for him to think of such things.

As James became more proficient in Japanese and was able to communicate better, he excelled in his training. Natsu became a close companion when not being instructed by Ichiro. It seemed she wanted to be more, but James could not bear to feel for her the way she was beginning to feel for him.

The following winter, and what James thought to be around a year after he had arrived, he was summoned to see the shogun. He put his best clothing on and Natsu fussed to make everything perfect.

"Why does he wish to see you, Gems?" She moved around him like a bee, straightening this and that.

"I don't know; perhaps he'll have my head removed." He then chuckled lightly.

Tears immediately welled up in Natsu's eyes. "Please don't say such a thing, Gems." She sat down facing the wall, her hand up to her face.

"I'm sorry Natsu. I was just making fun." He sat down beside her.

After she had wiped her eyes several times, Natsu spoke.

"I'm not a pure woman, Gems, but I am a woman, and I have woman feelings." She turned to him. He reached up and removed a tear from her face.

"Natsu, you know I'll not be here forever. I have another master that will come and retrieve me some day."

She turned away from him, but asked softly, "Have you ever loved a woman, Gems?"

He thought about this and knew he must be honest with her; she deserved that.

"Yes, I've loved one that I'm sure of, perhaps more than one." A sad expression came upon him as he recalled Sachi.

Natsu turned to face him. "What happened to her, Gems, the one you loved?"

After a few seconds of reflection, he replied, "She was murdered, along with our unborn child." He then moved away from her as the memories overwhelmed him.

Natsu crawled over to him. "I'm so sorry, Gems."

She stroked his hair as if primping the high pony tail he now wore as a samurai in training.

"So, that is when love left your heart?"

James turned and gazed into her eyes. He'd never considered such a thing. He then moved his gaze back to the floor as he wondered about her question.

"Perhaps it is. I'm a soldier, Natsu. I've tried to leave that life, but it's continued to find me. I've accepted that my work lay on the battlefields. And, that love and battlefields don't mix well."

Natsu moved in front of him. "Love can find its way back into a heart, Gems. I know it can, there are stories of such a thing. It can return, I promise you." She moved closer to James. He knew she wanted him to kiss her, but he moved her away and stood.

"Maybe it can for some. But, I don't believe that I could survive something like that again." He glanced down to her. "I need to go."

The commander and Kenji were with him the last time he had walked up the steps to the shogun's palace. As the doors were opened, he again sensed the spices and fragrances that he'd smelled at that time.

As he moved through the decorated columns towards the shogun, he noticed there were no entertainers, nor assistants, other than a few guards close to the shogun. Ichiro stood at the foot of the stage, he closely watched James approach, as did Toshinobu.

Upon reaching the foot of the stage, James bowed long and low to the shogun, who in turn nodded, ever so slightly.

"Master Ichiro informs me that you have excelled in your training, even with the 'assistance' or perhaps 'distraction' of a young Japanese teacher by the name of Natsu; of which I've somehow only become aware of today." Toshinobu then turned to Ichiro with a slightly irritated look.

Ichiro appeared to be embarrassed but quickly recovered as Toshinobu continued.

"Since you've done well in all areas of training, I have Master Ichiro's word that no further disruption will come to your schedule. And, Natsu will remain as your assistant, as long as your development in bushi training does not suffer."

James again bowed to the shogun, realizing that Natsu had been given to him initially as a distraction more than anything else. Now, the shogun was rewarding James for not falling into the trap of becoming distracted and was allowing her to continue assisting him.

"As for the reason, you are here today." Toshinobu readjusted himself and went on. "It has come time for you to receive the tools of a samurai. You have trained with bamboo sticks long enough. We should commission the making of your swords."

James glanced at Master Ichiro, who almost smiled, though it faded very quickly.

"Our sword maker has been with my family since he was born. He learned the art from his father who learned from his and so on. This family of sword makers has created many, many samurai swords. And yet, they have never been asked to craft swords for a westerner.

"These weapons will be a part of you. The sword maker must meet with you before he begins. He needs to know you, and therefore he can make swords that have the personal characteristics of their master.

"Because of this, Master Ichiro and I feel you should have the name of a samurai. Even though you are not yet one, you seem destined to become one. This name will allow the sword maker to create for a samurai warrior, rather than a westerner that is training to be a samurai.

"It is something you should not take lightly. We expect great things from you. Please do not disappoint us."

James again bowed with respect and replied, "I'll not let those who have placed their trust in me down, my Lord."

Once again Toshinobu bowed his head very slightly. He then continued.

"I have given this much thought, and the name I have decided on is 'Michio Toshino.' The first part refers to a man that is on a long journey. The second I give as part of the favor I owe the King of Sandrilan. It will always connect you to the Toshinobu household.

"I feel this is an appropriate name. Master Ichiro has agreed. From this day forward, you will be known by this household and all those connected to Japan, as Michio Toshino. You may go now. Master Ichiro will take you to the sword maker within a few days."

Later, when James returned to his room and told Natsu, she became very excited and fell into his arms.

"Oh, finally, I can call you Master! I've wanted to do so for many months now."

James moved her from his grasp and stepped back.

"But I have a long way to go before I'm bushi. It's just a name so that the sword maker can be commissioned."

"It doesn't matter; you have the name, you are my Master." She moved back to him and looked into his eyes.

For several long seconds, they searched each other's, soul.

"I don't know that I can give you what you want, Natsu." He said, still gazing into her eyes.

After a few seconds, Natsu replied, "Then give me what you can, for as long as you can. That is all I will ask of you."

Several days later, Ichiro took James to the sword maker. It was a surprise for the small senior man. But, since James was introduced by the samurai name of Michio Toshino, the man bowed and began to study James. He asked questions about his past battles, as well as questions about his character and demeanor. Then he said he had enough information and would begin right away on the swords.

It was also during this time that James began to train in the fine arts. As Master Ichiro explained it, a samurai must understand and appreciate the beauty of the natural world around him. James painted pictures for Natsu. He also wrote poetry that she made a fuss over, though James doubted it was as good as she thought it to be.

210

Though his appreciation for the natural beauty around him grew, he was well aware that Master Ichiro did not instruct him to love anyone or anything. Love was not in any of his classes. And though he grew very close to Natsu, he restrained from the feelings she obviously felt for him.

Several months after visiting the swordsmith, James was presented two beautiful and deadly Japanese samurai swords. One was short and the other quite long. He immediately felt a bond with these two instruments of death.

He often practiced with his swords rather than bamboo rods. Though he was not allowed to wear both of them at one time yet, just possessing the weapons made him feel more like an actual samurai. He immersed himself further into the world of bushido.

Chapter Sixteen: Battle of Flaming Arrows

As the days and months passed by, the samurai in training would take turns traveling by horseback around the island. It was a security measure, as well as to let the islanders know who was in charge and that Toshinobu would protect them if need be. James enjoyed these journeys as they reminded him of his days in the cavalry.

Through traveling about in this way, he became familiar with the island that had become his temporary home. By this time, he dressed as a samurai as well as wearing his hair in the Japanese warrior fashion. Still, the islanders noticed he was not a native Japanese man. Most became quite fond of the "Western Samurai," and loved to get a slight smile from him, or even a nod as he passed by.

Around three years into his training, an alarm moved through the palace grounds and outlying villages. A slight panic crept about as the word spread and eventually found its way to James' room.

A rapid tap on the door caused him to break away from Natsu. He pulled a robe on and slid open the oriental entryway. It was a young samurai in training, he almost shouted with nervous excitement.

"Master Michio, we have been called to the inner palace grounds. The island is under attack. You are to put on your armor and weapons, then meet there with your fellow students right away. Master Ichiro will direct your actions."

The young trainee then bowed quickly and took off to spread his message to another samurai.

James began to get ready, but Natsu took hold of his leg as she began to weep.

"My love, please, my love."

James reached down and took hold of her; he pulled her up.

"My dear Natsu, I've asked you to not fall in love. It would be better if you don't."

He gazed into her tear-filled eyes, then hugged her.

"I've got to go. Don't worry; I'll be alright."

She continued to weep as he started for the door. Though he didn't hear it, as he slid the door closed, Natsu spoke in a soft voice, "It's much too late for that."

James retrieved his armor. Common foot soldiers along with samurai and those being trained as samurai all moved about with a sense of urgency.

Under normal conditions, an assistant would have helped him with the armor, but now he struggled to put it on without help. As he moved towards the central grounds, samurai on horseback moved swiftly by and towards the gates.

Master Ichiro was speaking to some students as James approached.

"We feel it's one of Lord Toshinobu's rivals, Takeda Sadaaki. He has long disputed lands that belonged to our Lord. Now that he has been chased from the homeland, we suspect he is attempting a takeover of this island."

Ichiro paced back and forth as he spoke. More soldiers moved behind them with a fast pace, on their way to the developing battle. Ichiro continued.

"Their ships have landed hundreds of warriors to the Northeast. We will move out in a few minutes and run the invaders back into the sea."

As James was still attempting to secure his armor, the group walked to the stables. Here, he found the assistants that would have typically helped with his armor; they busily prepared the mounts and helped the group into their saddles. With little time for thought, the warriors galloped out of the building behind their master.

As they came closer to the fighting, smoke and gunfire greeted them. Ichiro reined his horse in as they slowed and moved over a slope to witness a massive battle unfolding on a flat plane before them. Many ships could be seen anchored on the edge of a cove. The smaller landing craft was moving back and forth as they loaded and then unloaded fighters.

James had viewed many battles, but none such as this. He moved up beside Master Ichiro as they all examined the carnage. One thing immediately struck him as odd. He stared at the layout as his horse moved nervously under him.

With only a few moments to study the situation, Ichiro spoke. "We have no time to spare. If they break through, we'll not be able to hold them. They will indeed reach the palace. We must advance and do what we can."

James moved his mount even closer and spoke as Ichiro searched for what might be the best place to make a charge.

"Master, may I respectfully say, they've left their flank exposed."

Ichiro turned to him, and James bowed slightly to express respect. Ichiro glanced to the large cliff that James had pointed to. It ran along the beach for about a mile, and the enemy seemed to be using it to protect their left flank.

"Michio, you're mistaken. That cliff runs along the beach, we can't get forces in that way, and the tops are too rugged to move artillery onto them. That's why they're not worried. The cliffs are their protection."

"Yes Master, but we can get archers up there."

Ichiro studied the area. "Perhaps we could get some up there, but the distance is too far to hit the enemy and do much damage. What are you thinking, Michio?"

James replied quickly, "Not the men Master, but the boats bringing the men. If we send at least forty of our best archers, with fire arrows, they can set the landing boats on fire. The men in front will see that their escape craft are being burned and this will frighten them. Then, we charge and split the forces; this will cause confusion and panic."

Ichiro studied James with a strained but thoughtful face. He turned back to the battle.

"The ships will surely use their cannon against our archers."

James looked at the ships. "Yes Master, they will. But they have their cannon pointed to the beach area. They're prepared to defend the landing boats from an attack inland. They're not prepared to fire against the cliffs. I know ships and naval warfare, it will take thirty to forty-five minutes to adjust the ships towards the cliffs. By that time, we can gain the advantage."

Ichiro studied the cliffs and the ships. He turned to James.

"I like it, Michio. We're samurai, why should we try to defend when we can attack. I'll arrange the archers on the cliff. As soon as you see the enemy becoming frightened, lead the men in and split their ranks. Hopefully, this will give our foot soldiers the edge they need."

He then turned to the other students, "Follow Michio when he attacks. Destroy the enemy and kill as many invaders as you can.

You are samurai; you will win this battle! The enemy will regret the day they set foot on our Lord's land."

Master Ichiro then spurred his horse and galloped away.

James and the other men watched from a distance as the battle slowly moved towards them. The enemy was advancing, and it was apparent they could break through soon.

Then, James noticed around fifty riders moving swiftly along the top of the cliff area. Soon they were in place, and a slight bit of smoke floated into the air as their arrows were lit. Within minutes of this, the beautiful sight of flaming projectiles landing onto the boats could be seen. Chaos slowly took over the beach as some men tried to put the flames out and were themselves stuck with the burning arrows.

On the battlefield, the enemy began to notice the smoke rise. Little by little the realization took hold that their means of returning to the ships was being attacked.

James pulled out his sword and held it ready. He spotted the area that he wanted to charge into and could hear the men behind him also unsheathing their swords. He turned to them.

"Follow me, my brothers! Today, we're the violent wind that cuts down its enemy!"

He could see a new confidence come over their faces. He had been in this situation many times before. He felt the familiar fear, mixed with excitement. They were ready. He turned his mount and spurred it towards the battle. The horses' hooves thundered upon the ground.

As they came closer, the foot soldiers moved to give way, but a few were trampled by the charging samurai. James placed the horses' reins in his mouth, pulled his other sword and placed them in a ready position.

The enemy became panicked as the rapid advance slammed violently into them. James immediately began removing heads as he trampled through the mass of men. A wide swath of dead and dying soon lay behind the charging warriors.

As they arrived at the enemy's flank and turned, James could see half of Takeda's forces attempting to hold, while the other half moved back towards the beach. The foot soldiers of Toshinobu now rallied with the samurai's charge and were advancing again.

Behind the retreating enemy, James noticed a small group of Takeda samurai. The leader was shouting to the soldiers and turning them back to the battle. James yelled out, "Follow me!" He placed the reins in his mouth and spurred his horse towards the samurai. Arrows and bullets sang by his ears. He lowered his head and once again began to remove the heads of enemy soldiers.

James and the men with him arrived at the samurai and began circling them. There were still enemy foot soldiers fighting all around them, but a panic was slowly moving through their lines. Now, with James and his men holding the group of samurai at bay, the foot soldiers in this area again lost their nerve, and Toshinobu's forces moved them steadily towards the beach and their burning boats.

At this time, cannon fire from the ships began to randomly rain down on everyone to avoid the developing route by Toshinobu's forces. A few of the ships had also turned enough to fire upon the cliffs, but were still relatively ineffective. The archers continued to rain flaming arrows down, despite the cannon shots from Takeda's ships.

With the samurai surrounded and chaos erupting all around them, one of the enemies stepped out and shouted, "Your leader should face me here and now if he has honor!"

James glanced around as his mount moved nervously under him. He noticed several of the other students looking at him. He knew that Ichiro had placed him in the lead position. He reined in his horse and jumped down.

The other samurai stepped back slightly, still holding up their swords, and James' men quickly formed a lose circle. The samurai James faced was obviously the ranking man as his armor was of a higher quality than any of the others there, including James and his fellow students.

As the leader came closer to James, his face twisted, "You! You're a Westerner!"

James raised his long sword into a fighting position, then replied, "And you, are trespassing!"

The samurai leader became infuriated at this and charged with a violent ferocity. The two swords clashed together time and time again. Within a few moments of battle, James knew well he was outmatched. He struggled to defend himself. His enemy also knew who the better swordsman was. A cannon shot landed nearby as the sword duel unfolded.

James' mind raced for a solution as his energy swiftly drained away, and his muscles became weary. In a flash, it came, perhaps out of desperation, but it came quickly. He was a westerner, and he had always used his sword with one hand and his revolver in the other. The samurai used two hands on their long sword. He had a brilliant idea, though questionable concerning its nature.

As his enemy struck again and again to overpower him, James watched for the right blow. It didn't take long; the fight was fast paced. The samurai struck down from the right. James used his left hand to block the blow with his long sword. With his right hand, he pulled the short sword out, stabbing it forcefully through the creases of armor and into the samurai's mid-section.

An immediate grimace came over the Samurai's' face. His arms lost power and slowly fell to his side. He looked down at the sword in his lower chest. He looked back at James, who pulled his weapon out of the dying warrior. It seemed to be the only thing holding him up. He dropped down to his knees and then fell face first onto the hard ground.

The enemy samurai became shocked with this development, and the students with James immediately attacked them. Now the chaos all around came back to his senses. James climbed onto his horse and continued to kill as many of the retreating enemies as he could.

From behind them, the sounds of cannon were soon heard. James looked back and noticed a few of Toshinobu's large guns coming into action. With this event, he moved the men back towards their lines to gain distance from the enemies' cannon fire. After moving back some, they turned and watched as the enemy struggled to return to their ships.

It became a slaughter as Toshinobu's soldiers killed them on the shore. Very few made it back to the ships, which soon left as Toshinobu's artillery pressed towards the beaches and began firing upon them.

The battle was over before darkness fell. James, as well as most of the other warriors, camped not far from the battlefield as they were exhausted.

The following morning, Master Ichiro came to the campsite. They had not seen him since the previous morning when he had left to move the archers up to the cliff. He had a long Katana sword and shorter sword in his hands.

Everyone stood up as their master approached. James realized the swords he held were those of the samurai he'd killed the day before.

Ichiro appeared slightly irritated as he gazed around the group. Finally, after studying the men for several seconds, he spoke.

"Someone killed one of Takeda's Samurai yesterday. Though many of his samurais were killed, this one was killed in a sword duel. I've been told it was one of the students that charged into the enemy from the eastern slopes. So, I know it's one of you. Who killed this samurai?"

James stepped forward and bowed low. He then said, "It was I, Master."

Ichiro straightened, and his gaze became even more serious.

"Michio, I have already ascertained that it was you. I wondered if you would dare take credit for killing this man."

Slowly, Ichiro began walking around the small campfire that was still smoldering. He moved in front of James as he continued.

"This particular samurai was Ikeda Ieyasu, a well-known warrior. I often thought that I might someday face him in a duel. I have no doubts that Ikeda was the better swordsman. Can you explain yourself, Michio?"

James considered the question and then replied, "It is true, Master, Ikeda was the better swordsman. But I was the better tactician." James then bowed very low, to show respect and not appear to be boastful in front of his master.

As James held the bow, he heard a slight grunting sound from Master Ichiro. He didn't want to rise to see what was happening, so he held the bow, but raised his eyes enough to see Ichiro.

The samurai master appeared to be stifling a laugh. He again grunted slightly, and James noticed a subtle smile trying to erupt onto his face. Ichiro turned and looked off into the air as James recovered from his bow.

After staring off into space for a few seconds and regaining his composure, Master Ichiro turned back to James. All the other students also appeared very interested in their masters' response.

218

"Michio, that is, indeed the answer I would expect from a samurai. Your training will continue, but as of yesterday, you are a Samurai! Congratulations!"

Master Ichiro handed the two swords to James and then went back to his horse and left. The other students appeared to expel a sigh of relief as they advanced to congratulate James.

The warriors remained close to the battlegrounds and on alert for another day. When it seemed certain that Takeda's forces would not return, the samurai and soldiers began returning to the palace.

As James rode to the gates, he was met by a woman he knew to be Natsu's friend.

"Master Michio, please come quickly. Natsu is very ill."

James jumped down from his mount and after handing the reins to a servant followed behind the woman, who moved with urgency towards Natsu's quarters.

In the dimly lit room, he found Natsu lying on a mat. He knelt down and stroked her hair. She opened her eyes wearily. When she saw him, she began to cry and put her arms around his neck. He kissed her forehead.

Later, after he had fed her some broth, she fell asleep. He stepped out of the room, and Natsu's friend spoke to him.

"She searched the dead and wounded as they arrived. She would not sleep or eat. For two days, I stayed with her and tried to make her rest, but she continued to search and ask about you. No one knew anything for sure. Some said you were alive and others said a samurai had killed you. Yesterday she collapsed, and we brought her here. I then waited at the gate for you. I think if you had not come back, she would have died."

James nodded, "Can you stay with her until I get a bath. I'll take care of her after that. You can then get some rest."

The woman bowed and slipped back into the room. James bathed quickly and came back to care for Natsu. As she slept, he thought much about their relationship. Finally, he put out the small oil lamp and also slept.

Natsu began to recover, but neither she nor James spoke much. A week later she sat in the garden area. James stood close and examined the buds on a tree. Natsu spoke softly to him.

"I'm sorry my Master. I'm sorry that you must care for me... as if I were an infant. I'm a weak woman, I know. I'm very sorry."

James turned and looked at her. A tear rolled down her oval face. He reached over and gently wiped it with his thumb. She looked up and smiled.

After a few seconds of thought, James replied.

"You're not weak... you're delicate. Like a beautiful flower that gently sways in the breeze. You absorb the warm sunlight and thrive in a subtle rain."

He turned and again examined the tiny buds on the low tree branch. He reached up and lifted the bud so he could get a closer look. Then he continued.

"I, however, am a sharpened blade. My purpose is to cut and kill." He paused and looked out into the air as if trying to find something. Natsu watched him closely. He went on.

"A delicate flower can be injured easily if it's too close to a hardened blade. It's not the flowers' fault. The flower is meant to be beautiful and graceful. The blade is meant to be cold and destructive. The blade won't be injured by the flower. But the flower can be destroyed by the blade, simply by dwelling too close to it."

Natsu lowered her head as several more tears rolled down her cheeks. When she spoke, James knew she was weeping, though he didn't turn to her.

"Perhaps, I could become strong. Perhaps in time, I could be strong enough."

Now James turned to her. His face held compassion as she looked to him. He then walked several feet away from her. He took in a deep breath of air and began to speak again as if talking to the gentle breeze.

"When we sail from Sandrilan, we never know where we're going, or how long we'll be at sea. It may be six weeks or three months. We never know, and we never ask. But we always know there will be battles to fight."

He turned and walked back to the tree that Natsu sat beside. He continued.

"When the Valiant returns to Sandrilan, it rings bells as a signal to the people, the wives, and mothers, the daughters and lovers. The bells signal that all is well. Or, they signal that there are dying or wounded on board."

He looked down to her. She lowered her head so he wouldn't see her cry. James caressed her hair with his hand.

"I would ask no woman to be that strong. I don't think that I could be that strong; to go for months, not knowing if you were well or not."

Natsu nodded her head slightly but didn't look up at him.

After this, they saw less of each other. On a few occasions, they each found the other, as if a force within could no longer be restrained. Both knew however, it was only a fleeting shadow of things that could never be.

James continued to train and glean every fragment of information he could from Master Ichiro. He sensed the time to leave growing close but had stopped worrying about time or anything other than his training. Then, one day, as he was painting a picture of a black bird that often sat outside his window, an assistant came to deliver a message.

"Master Michio." The small man bowed low outside of James' doorway. He then continued. "Please forgive this intrusion. Lord Toshinobu and Master Ichiro request your presence in the main palace room, at mid-day."

The man rose and glanced at James.

"Thank you. Please tell Lord Toshinobu and Master Ichiro I'll be there."

The man bowed again after James said this and then left quickly.

James put his paints away and prepared his nicest clothes. He sensed the meaning of the meeting. Inside, a part of him wanted to stay. He had become something that he could have never imagined. A samurai was considered almost royalty and the samurai in him wished to remain where he would be treated as such.

A few moments before the sun hit its mid-day zenith, James approached the palace doors. The guards opened them wide and bowed low as he went in.

His intuition was justified as he came closer to Lord Toshinobu. On one side of the stage, stood the commander and Kenji. On the other stood Ichiro and to his surprise, Natsu dressed beautifully. James went to the front of Lord Toshinobu and bowed low and long.

Toshinobu nodded to James as he rose up from his bow. Then the shogun spoke.

"Master Michio, your previous master has come to collect you. You are, however, welcome to stay here if you wish. As a samurai, I insist that you chose your destiny."

Lord Toshinobu turned to the commander and spoke. Kenji translated.

"King of Sandrilan, I present to you, Master Michio Toshino. As you were aware of, this man is truly a warrior. He has excelled in all training. He fought against the forces of my enemy, Lord Takeda Sadaaki. In this battle, Master Michio fought bravely, with honor and defeated Ikeda Ieyasu, one of Takeda's most feared samurai."

Lord Toshinobu paused, and James noticed the commander's eyebrows raise slightly, his mouth turned down a bit, and he glanced at James with an expression of being impressed.

The shogun continued. "Being a samurai, I will not order Master Michio to go anywhere. It will be his choice, and we will accept this decision."

After Kenji had translated, Lord Toshinobu turned to James.

"Master Michio, it is your choice, you have earned that."

James looked the room over as all watched him with anticipation for an answer. As a samurai would always do, he chose his actions carefully and his words before they were released from his mouth. After a few seconds, he looked at the shogun and responded in fluent Japanese.

"I am grateful for all Lord Toshinobu and Master Ichiro have done for me. I am grateful to all that I have been privileged and honored to know here. I am proud to have helped defend Lord Toshinobu's land and honor. I have found a home here and hope to always have a home here. But my destiny is intertwined with the Valiant and Sandrilan. I will return with the King."

James glanced at Natsu after saying this. Her eyes closed and did not open again while he watched her. Lord Toshinobu sat back slightly, but otherwise simply nodded to James. He then spoke to all as Kenji had finished translating James' words.

"Master Michio has chosen, and I am sure it is the correct decision for him and the King of Sandrilan." He looked at James, "Be not concerned; you will always have a room in my house, Samurai Michio. You have also earned that."

He then turned to Ichiro, "Please relate to the King of Sandrilan the training Michio has received. If it is satisfactory, then I will consider my favor, to be paid."

Master Ichiro lifted a sheet of paper and began reading a long list of training and achievements attributed to the Samurai Michio Toshino.

Natsu did not open her eyes until Ichiro had uttered the last words from the list. She then looked at James and lowered her head to gaze at the floor.

"Is this sufficient to repay the favor?" Toshinobu asked the commander.

"That is sufficient, Lord Toshinobu. And rest assured, I will protect and care for Sno as long as I have a breath of air in my body. I am grateful for your generous repayment."

The commander bowed, and Toshinobu nodded.

"Master Michio, I now release you back into the service of the King of Sandrilan."

James bowed to Lord Toshinobu, and the meeting was dismissed.

Once his things were packed, and James had bid all good-bye, other than Natsu, whom he could not find, they each got into a rickshaw.

Just before departing towards the Valiant, James heard someone call out. Natsu came quickly to the small rickshaw.

"Good-bye, my darling Samurai. I will never forget you." She then took his hand, kissed the back of it and pressed it to her face.

James replied softly, "and I will never forget you, my dear Natsu."

As a tear fell onto James' hand, she replied.

"Please take care and remember that love can always find a way back to your heart, if you let it," She then turned and rushed back into the gates.

The rickshaw man glanced back to James. He nodded for the man to proceed and soon all were moving towards the Valiant.

Chapter Seventeen: A Samurai for Sandrilan

The large warship was a welcome site to James as they approached the harbor. He continued to stare at her as the small boats moved them closer.

He could see new scars and repaired areas on her hull. There were numerous indications the Valiant had seen many battles during his absence.

As he stepped upon her deck, he could smell the familiar scents of wood, salt water, and gunpowder.

"Are sure you don't wish to take the woman, Lieutenant?"

James looked at the commander with a bit of wonder, "Lieutenant?"

"Yes, Lieutenant... you've been promoted. I've also procured some gunnery books during your absence. I would like for you to command the ship's gun deck. We have an excellent gun crew, but they could be better with an outstanding gunnery officer."

James thought for a few seconds and then replied, "Yes sir. Thank you, sir."

The commander nodded and said, "Now, about the woman, it's not too late to go back and retrieve her."

James replied softly as if he had just come out of a dream and was not quite awake yet.

"No, she's much too delicate for a life I would give her. It would kill her. She'll live and find love again here. She would wither and die on Sandrilan, waiting for the Valiant to return time and time again. I know this, and she knows it as well."

"I see," said the commander as he glanced down at the wooden deck. He then looked at James and asked, "Well, is there anything I can do, or get for you?"

James watched as crewmen worked to raise the Valiant's anchor. Then he asked, "Can you tell me what year it is? I seem to have lost track, and I'm not real certain how old I am."

The commander appeared a bit surprised by the question but quickly answered, "It's 1877."

James nodded but said nothing. He continued to watch the men. After a few seconds, the commander asked him.

"So, just how old are you, Lieutenant?"

"Thirty-seven, sir," James replied.

The commander smiled, "That's a good age. I wish I were thirty-seven." He patted James on the shoulder and continued. "We'll be leaving soon. Let me show you to your cabin. You're a commissioned officer now; you'll not be sleeping in the crew quarters any longer."

James followed the commander and was shown a small cabin that as far as he was aware of, had never been used before. He began putting his things up as the Valiant moved out to the open seas.

During the voyage to Sandrilan, James began to study the books. The Valiant sailed South, towards Singapore to take on coal.

A week into their return trip, James approached the commander as he stood near the wheel house.

"The heart of Zheng Qui territory, it seems odd we've not run into any of them yet."

The commander turned to James and after a second of thought replied.

"Well, Lieutenant, the British and Americans have become much more active lately in destroying pirates as soon as they come across them. It seems they've finally had a fill of their merchant ships being raided.

"Zheng Qui, however, is still a force to reckon with. We've had many tangles with his ships during the last three years and nine months that you've been in training. Though his fleet has dwindled and he can't operate anywhere near the capacity that he did five years ago, he seems determined to destroy the Valiant before he's tossed from the seas for good."

James took a deep breath and exhaled slowly. He nodded and then went back towards his cabin to study.

In the port of Singapore, the commander suggested James go to some of the many excellent tailors and have a wardrobe assembled.

"You need something that expresses your new... 'Personage,' Lieutenant." The commander looked James over and continued, "I would suggest something of an Asian and European mix perhaps. You'll certainly provide them an inspiration to draw from. These tailors will do exceptional work; they're artists if I know the least thing about art."

James looked down at his mix of Sandrilan uniform and Japanese Samurai blouse.

"I uhm, well I don't have any money with me, Sir."

The commander laughed, "Lieutenant, do you suppose you were not paid during your training? Go to the quartermaster and ask for your pay information. Then draw as much as you think you may need to get a new wardrobe. Lieutenant, I would like my 'only,' commissioned officer to look a bit more refined. Tell the tailors you want something of a naval uniform in appearance and you'll be reimbursed for the new wardrobe. How does that sound?"

James nodded and replied, "Yes, Sir."

When the quartermaster handed James a paper with the amount of pay available in his account, he could barely believe it. It was more money than he'd ever had, or seen in his life. He asked the quartermaster to confirm the amount, which the small Asian man immediately did.

James requested some of the pay, and soon Samson was escorting him to what he described as the 'very best' tailor in Singapore.

"I tell you what you need, Lieutenant. You need a woman to help you with your new clothes. This tailor, he has a beautiful wife and two beautiful daughters that work with him. I will ask that the women help create your clothes. You will see, they will make the best uniforms you could imagine."

As Samson told James this, the small two-wheeled rickshaw moved through the busy streets of Singapore. Soon they arrived at the tailor's business, and James was indeed impressed by the beauty of the women working there.

After Samson quickly explained to the tailor what he thought James needed, the women, as well as the tailor, began to study James carefully. They talked together in a language other than English and pointed at areas of his body. James felt a bit awkward, but soon the man was again chattering to Samson with strongly accented English.

Samson laughed in his booming voice and nodded to the man. The tailor and the women went into the back room.

"They say you will be the greatest challenge and the most interesting project they have ever had. They have never known a western bushi warrior before. And when I tell them you were an American horse soldier, they were all very impressed. I think the women like you. They tell this tailor that it must be their greatest work for a man such as you."

James nodded as the tailor returned from the back room and ran a string around his midsection.

"Well, thank, thank you, Samson. I do appreciate your help." James replied, struggling to talk as the tailor continued his work.

"It's my pleasure, Lieutenant. I come here to have clothes made, but mostly to see the women. If I were you, I would marry one of them. But they are not so impressed with me, I think."

Samson moved a bit so he could look into the back room where the women were busy searching through different materials for the new wardrobe.

After all the measurements had been taken, the tailor assured James the uniforms would be ready in two days. James and Samson then went around Singapore, eating and exploring the many small shops.

As the Valiant took on coal and provisions, Sir Barrett came to visit. James was instructed to put on his best uniform and dine with the commander, Sir Barrett and several of Singapore's top officials.

"Sir Barrett, this is Lieutenant Taft, I don't believe you've met him yet." As the commander introduced James, he shook hands with the visitors.

Everyone was seated around the largest table available on the Valiant, and the commander continued.

"Lieutenant Taft has just returned from almost four years of training as a Japanese samurai warrior." The commander turned to James. "You were in some battle while in training, is that correct, Lieutenant?"

The guests immediately became impressed and interested. James lifted his glass of wine for a drink and examined them quickly from the rim. He sat the glass down and replied to his commander.

"Yes, it's being called the battle of, 'Honoo no you na Yajirushi,' or roughly translated to mean 'flaming arrows.'"

"As food was placed on the table by well-dressed crewmen, Sir Barrett leaned forward and expressed intrigues with his thick British accent, "Please, do tell us about it, Lieutenant. But first, could you tell us how you managed to acquire such training? The Japanese are such a closed society, even today, after years of opening up to the world."

James glanced at the commander, who cleared his throat and answered Sir Barrett.

"I'm afraid there are secrets which Sandrilan holds dearly, Sir Barrett. As for the battle, though, I would also like to hear the story." He then turned back to James.

The group began to eat, and James relayed the battle to them, from start to finish. They asked questions, and he answered them. After the meal, the men continued to smoke cigars, talk and drink wine well into the evening. Finally, the guests left.

"Well done, Lieutenant," The commander said as James was leaving out the door.

Several days later, as the Valiant was preparing to leave port, James went to pick up his new uniforms. The women at the tailor's shop insisted he put one on, and then made quite a fuss about how dashing he looked in it.

As James came aboard the Valiant, the commander also commented.

"Well, that is much better, Lieutenant." He then turned his attention to the crew as men were securing the anchor. After another quick examination of the incredibly well-crafted uniform, which had distinct Asian and European influences, the commander glanced down at his own impressive but weathered uniform.

"The next time we're in Singapore, I would like for you to introduce me to your tailor, Lieutenant."

James smiled, and the commander smiled as well.

"Yes sir," James replied as the Valiant was slowly maneuvered from its docking position.

The Valiant sailed unopposed to Sandrilan. James was astonished as the warship slipped into the small natural harbor. What was a large town, now looked like a small city. Buildings nestled all around the hills and the palace itself sat majestically and much more impressive in appearance at the highest point.

As the ship was maneuvered towards the dock, the Valiant's bells rang out four times quickly and then there was a slight pause. Again, it quickly rang four times and paused. The large bells of Sandrilan then began to ring their reply. James had not heard this signal before and moved over to the commander.

"That's a new signal, sir."

The commander turned and looked at James with an expression of surprise.

"Yes, it is. Much has changed since you've been in training. Sandrilan has thrived and now holds perhaps twice the population that it had when you were here last."

James considered this and examined the commander with a bit of suspicion.

"Yes, sir, so, what is the new signal for, sir?"

The commander turned to James; he seemed reluctant to answer but finally replied.

"Well, Lieutenant, we uhm, well, we've planned a little coming home celebration for you. But, we weren't for certain that you would be coming home, so we created a new signal."

The commander appeared slightly embarrassed. James watched him curiously for a few seconds as he seldom saw the commander express such a thing.

"Yes, sir. Thank you for the celebration. I'm glad that I didn't disappoint everyone."

A smile broke over the commander's face.

"That's the spirit, Lieutenant, and while we're on the subject. As we depart the ship, please walk about ten paces behind me and join me at the palace for a while. The crew has been instructed to follow behind you. This is the new departing order; alright?"

James grimaced slightly. "Is that necessary, sir?"

"Rest assured that it is, Lieutenant. Pomp and ceremony are not the friends of a soldier, but they are a part of being one. There is a place and a reason for such things. Someday you'll understand how these customs apply to life in Sandrilan. Until then, trust me, they are necessary."

"Yes sir," James replied as the ship settled up against the dock.

Soon the musicians were playing their unique Asian rhythms as the commander stepped off the Valiant. The butterflies, which had increased in numbers by two-fold, at least, began to toss the flower petals in front of their King's feet.

As James stepped off the ship, around ten paces behind the commander, he took in a deep breath of the fragrant tropical air. "It's good to be home," he thought.

Several women with small children came up and handed him flowers. He bowed slightly and continued towards the palace.

The procession moved up the winding roads. Most of the crew drifted away at different areas, with their wives, or sweethearts. Some just went to their favorite tavern or brothel.

Once inside the palace, the commander took his usual seat on the stage area and several of what James thought must be the commander's 'favorite' butterflies, quickly settled in around him.

As James was ushered to an area at the right of the commander, but at a slightly lower level, he noticed Sno sitting not far from him. She was, as always, very beautiful and immediately caught his eye. She turned and also looked into his eyes. He had difficulty shifting his gaze away from her but did so after a few seconds.

A servant brought fresh fruits around, along with a Japanese wine that James now knew to be called 'sake.'

While James ate some of the fruits and drank the wine, several men came in and spoke to the commander about events and occurrences that took place while the Valiant was away.

It was all rather interesting as James had never known what happened after the commander reached the palace. He'd always stayed with the ship or went to visit Doc Jefferies.

After an hour of these meetings, the commander called Kenji up. He spoke with him for a few seconds, and Kenji came over to James.

Kenji bowed and then spoke. "Sir, the king has asked that I show you to your new quarters. Please follow me."

James finished the remainder of his drink. He stood and turned to the commander, bowed quickly. He then moved with a swift pace to catch up to Kenji.

Not far from Doc Jefferies' office, Kenji opened the door to a small two story house. James walked in to find it had apparently never been inhabited. There was still sawdust in the corners and the furniture, much of which was bamboo, had no signs of usage.

"Is there anything else I can do for you, sir?"

James had become astonished by the much nicer living accommodations and had forgotten about Kenji. He turned to the Japanese man that stood in the doorway.

"No, that will be all. Thank you, Mr. Kenji."

Kenji again bowed to James, as he must do now by his position as a samurai. James nodded slightly as Kenji backed out of the door and shut it.

James explored the small house and found it to be quite well constructed. The upstairs held two small rooms, one of which had a comfortable looking bed.

After retrieving his belongings and a few of the books from the Valiant, James cleaned up and slept well in his new quarters.

The following day, he went to visit his friend Doc Jefferies.

"Hello there, Sergeant! Or, rather, Lieutenant I should say. It's so good to see you after these long years."

James shook the doctors' hand.

"It's wonderful to see you as well my friend."

Doc Jefferies ushered him to the veranda and asked Meili to bring some refreshments.

"My, how the time has passed by, you look well indeed Serg... oh my, I mean, Lieutenant. I was so glad to hear the four bells ringing."

Doc Jefferies put his hand to his mouth, seeming to realize he'd said too much.

"It's alright Doc, the commander explained the four bell signal."

The doctor appeared relieved. "Oh, very good, I was dreading the explanation I should have to conjure. Well, in all fairness, we weren't sure if you would survive. The Japanese are wonderful people, but they can be rather brutal as well. I'm sure you know that better than I do, though."

James smiled and nodded. He took one of the drinks that Meili sat on the table along with a box of cigars.

"No more brutal than any of us, Doc. Perhaps their brutality is simply, less disguised than in other cultures." James thought back into his memory. It had been something he'd avoided for many years. Now, he no longer felt the pain in his gut as he did before. After taking a drink, he continued.

"I've seen thousands of men cut into bloody pieces on the battlefields of America. They were slaughtered like cattle. Young men, old men, sometimes they were merely boys, dressed in uniforms to look like soldiers."

His face twisted as he remembered the body parts lying strewn about on the ground. Doc Jefferies watched James closely. He'd never heard these tales from James and found it intriguing. He picked up a cigar, lit it, and then waved the match to put it out.

James continued, "The sword of the samurai can remove a man's head with one clean stroke. If anything, it's less brutal than the musket balls that shatter body parts and leave holes in the middle of a man.

"At times, I still hear the dying men on the fields of Shiloh. They called out for help. But we all knew there was no help for them. We wanted to go out there and give them water, or a puff from a pipe. They didn't want to die alone. They didn't deserve to die alone. But what could we do? There were hundreds, perhaps thousands out there. Some were holding their guts in. Others had arms or legs shot off. Where would you start if you could go out and help? We just had to sit and listen to them, all night long. I wanted so much for the morning to come so that I didn't hear those dying men any longer."

James turned to the doctor. He then took another drink as Doc Jefferies expelled a long stream of smoke and replied.

"I consider myself fortunate; I am something of a military doctor, and yet I've never had to treat more than a few men at one time. That goes with being a ship's doctor I suppose. But I've often thought of how terrible it must be to hear those soldiers or to decide which one must die for another to be treated. I believe you're correct, Lieutenant. We can all be brutal. But we can also be kind. Someday, perhaps by the grace of God, we may learn to live peacefully. Until then, there will always be evil men. And, there will always be the need for men such as you, and the commander."

James took a cigar from the box. He examined it briefly and then lit it. The doctor continued.

"Well, perhaps a change of subject would do nicely. I possibly shouldn't be telling you this, but there is a certain, beautiful Japanese woman that has asked of you on several occasions over the time of your absence."

James knew it could only be Sno. He expelled a draw of smoke from the cigar.

"She is beautiful indeed. Too beautiful to be crying and heartbroken when a soldier doesn't return from battle. Love and the battlefield don't belong together, Doc. It's something I've learned the hard way."

Doc Jefferies considered the words. After a few seconds, he replied.

"Though it's only my opinion, Lieutenant, I feel there's no places that love doesn't belong, or isn't needed."

James thought about this, but the recollection of Natsu's tears caused him to dismiss it quickly.

The two men began a game of chess and talked until long into the night. James ended up staying in the spare room that he had initially recovered in after first arriving at Sandrilan.

The following evening there was a tremendous celebration at the palace. It was more extravagant than James had ever seen.

The highlight was the performances of Sno. James could not help but notice her dark almond-shaped eyes gazing ever so subtly at him as she danced. His senses were stirred by her beauty and grace, yet his heart refused to be moved by her charms.

At the end of the celebration, fireworks were set off, and cheers rang out across the island city. It was a wonderful time, and James felt bonded to this place more than ever before.

Over the next few days, James began to decorate his house. He also studied the books and began immersing himself in his career with the Valiant and Sandrilan.

The Valiant sailed a few weeks later, and soon James found himself in battle again. Everything had changed. He moved as if he were dancing rather than fighting. Men fell to his blade and revolver almost as if they were running to their demise, rather than James trying to kill them.

Weeks and months passed by; he grew more and more proficient as an officer and a soldier. After seven months of study, James was promoted from the Second Lieutenant to First Lieutenant and placed in charge of the cannon on the Valiant. His command of the guns immediately improved the warship's fighting ability.

Almost a year after James returned to Sandrilan, the Valiant intercepted one of Zheng Qui's ships.

"It's a six gun Junk sir," As Kenji lowered the spyglass and reported this, several shots from the enemy ship landed around thirty yards from the Valiant.

"Bring her three degrees starboard, Lieutenant." After giving James this order, the commander moved over to Kenji and took the spyglass.

James moved the large wheel to the specified point as the commander peered through the spyglass, and the Valiant moved to increase their distance from the ship.

As the commander studied the enemy vessel, several more puffs of smoke were seen. Soon, two more cannon balls hurled in towards the Valiant. One ball landed very close and the second hit the lower section of the Valiant's port side. A loud thud was heard as the cannon ball glanced off the iron plates of the ship. A salty spray of sea water came down onto the deck.

"Seems they have an impressive gunnery officer that's eager for a fight, would you care to take him on Lieutenant?" The commander yelled back as he wiped some of the salt water from his uniform.

"Yes sir, I would love to." James replied.

"Very good," said the commander, "Mr. Kenji, please take the helm."

Kenji stepped up to the wheel. James moved over to the commander and motioned for the spyglass. The commander handed it to him, and James studied the enemy ship for a few moments. He then handed the spyglass back to the commander.

"Bring her six degrees port, Mr Kenji."

Kenji nodded as James moved quickly down to the gun deck.

A few seconds later the pirate ship fired again, and two shots landed very close and at the back of the Valiant.

On the gun deck below, James had the men load six of the sixty-pound guns and two of the twenty-four-pound guns.

He watched out one of the open hatches as the Valiant began to cross the path of the pirate ship. At a precise moment, he stepped behind the guns and began having them fire one second apart. They roared with furry, and a thick smoke soon drifted across the gun level.

On the top deck, the commander raised his spyglass as the large guns caused the warship to tremble. The first two shots landed close, but in front of the vessel. The third, fourth and fifth shots landed square on the bow, mid and aft section of the ship, causing tremendous damage and a subsequent explosion. The final three shots landed behind the now burning vessel.

The commander examined the ship closely through his spyglass as James came back up onto the deck. Another large explosion ripped the enemy ship apart, and the commander moved his eye away from the glass.

"Is that satisfactory, Sir?" James asked as he stepped up beside his leader and looked out to the now sinking ship.

The commander looked at James with a bit of surprise. He then replied.

"Well actually, Lieutenant, I expected a bit more game. But, no need to dally around I supposes when proving who the better gunnery officer is. It is a game of life or death after all. So, yes, that is satisfactory."

James smiled, and the commander also smiled a little as he slid the spyglass together.

"Do you suppose Zheng Qui will ever give up sir?"

The commander considered the question. He took a deep breath and expelled it. Finally, he answered.

"Zheng Qui is a proud, though ruthless man it seems."

He paused for a few seconds and continued in a softer voice.

"Perhaps he knows he's through as a pirate, but continues to hold hope for revenge. He's still a wealthy man on land. I think he'll continue to raise the bounty on the Valiant as well as sending ships after us, for as long as he can... or is still alive."

The commander then looked at James and took on a brighter tone.

"But, I don't believe we need to worry much, as long as we have a gunnery officer of your caliber."

He patted James on the back and left towards his cabin.

As the months and then years passed by, the Valiant and its crew circumvented the globe several times. James and the Marines of Sandrilan fought in tropical jungles, on deserts and tundra.

Throughout the pacific, south seas and even beyond, the Valiant was becoming a legend. Many sailors heard tales of the old ironclad warship taking on four or five pirate ships at a time and being victorious. Others heard stories of the highly skilled marines that could turn the tide of war in small Asian countries. Most, however, thought these to be only sailors' 'tall' tales. Few believed the rumors but had no reservations about retelling the stories and often adding more details. In this manner, the myth and the legend of the Valiant slowly became intertwined.

As for the crew and Marines assigned to the Valiant, they knew little about this and wouldn't have concerned themselves with it even if they had known. Life on Sandrilan was fantastic, and all the men worked and fought hard while away on the missions. After which, they happily returned home to warm welcomes from all their family and friends.

While the Valiant was docked at Sandrilan, James enjoyed the celebrations, as well as painting, reading books and playing chess with the doctor.

James and Sno were noticeably attracted to each other, but neither would move past an invisible boundary between them.

The situation became almost unbearable after James requested the privilege of painting a portrait of Sno. She agreed and for eight months, on and off, when the Valiant was home, the two met for an hour at a time.

James seemed to absorb the beauty of the Geisha. And Sno posed with the grace and style of an ancient Grecian model. Her eyes sought out the painters' and gleamed with every slight glance from James.

Doctor Jefferies described the atmosphere of the lieutenant's studio as, "a barely bridled storm of energy and passion."

Though the commander, Doc Jefferies and Madame Zhou often talked about the seemingly star-crossed pair, James and Sno remained apart and apparently destined to never satisfy the deeply felt desire within.

The Valiant, however, remained busy and in high demand, with no lack of suitors for its services. And, with the success of the Valiant came the success of Sandrilan. By early 1880, the small island kingdom bristled with activity. As the Valiant came and left its home port, the much smaller craft could be seen moving about, to and from the other islands.

The large payments received for the Valiant's services most often came in gold or silver coins. The money worked its way through the many shops and skilled tradespeople and families of the kingdom. Some felt it would never end. James seemed unable to completely relax, however, as he knew very well that fate could often be cruel.

"Lieutenant," Doctor Jefferies called out as James walked down the winding road towards the Valiant.

"Hello, Doc," James replied and moved back up towards the doctor.

"Lieutenant, I wonder if you could do me a favor the next time you find yourself in Singapore."

"Sure, I'll do my best. What is it you need me to do?"

236

"Please step into the office, and I'll explain." The doctor walked back into the door, and James followed him inside.

"I want you to purchase a camera and all the needed supplies. I want to document life on Sandrilan, as well as the Valiant and, well, anything else of interest. I feel the Kingdom of Sandrilan should have some records of its history. Though tiny in comparison to other countries, Sandrilan is a wonderful place, and I've decided to be its historian."

James considered this briefly. "That's very good Doc, but I know nothing about cameras. Now, if you needed a good rifle or sword, then I'm your man."

The doctor chuckled at this and then raised his hand and nodded his head as if recalling his initial thought.

"Yes, well I do know some about photography, Lieutenant. I've also been studying some books that I've acquired over the years."

He then stepped over to a desk and pulled out a satchel and a coin bag. From the satchel, he retrieved some papers.

"Now, I've written down everything that I would like to have and might need. If you give this to the camera vendor, he should be able to fill the order. I've also instructed the salesman to add anything he may feel that I forgot or wasn't aware of. There's enough money here to cover additional chemicals and supplies as well as items I may have neglected to make a note of."

The doctor put the papers back into the satchel. He handed the bag of coins and the satchel to James and continued.

"There will be a lot to carry lieutenant so you should have some crewmen go along to assist you. Also, this is delicate equipment. Please take care to move it gingerly to the ship and then place it somewhere safe until you return to Sandrilan, alright?"

"Sure Doc, I can do that."

"Thank you, Lieutenant. And, I would like to get a photograph of you in your Japanese warrior attire. What is it called, 'Samurai' clothing?"

"Yes, that's correct Doc. And, I would be honored for you to take such a photograph. Actually, could you take two? I wouldn't mind having one for my house!"

The two men chuckled a little by James' request. James then left to help prepare the warship for its departure the following morning.

The Valiant sailed for several weeks to arrive at a secret area on the Northern Australian coast. James, Kenji and ten marines then rowed to the shore and were soon on a rugged march twenty miles inland.

After two days of careful, though constant travel, the men located their objective.

"It seems the information was useful. That looks like him, what do you think?" James lowered back down from the edge of a small slope. He then handed the spyglass to Kenji, who handed a large piece of paper to James and cautiously moved up to take a look.

James examined the wanted poster that Kenji had handed him.

Kenji carefully studied the layout as some men moved around several weathered shacks. He then located the man they were primarily interested in and followed him for several seconds, then slid slowly back down to where James sat.

"Yes Sir, that's him alright. But how can we take him alive? Are you certain the British government won't accept him dead?"

James shook his head and replied in a hushed voice.

"They want him alive. If we have to kill him, we may as well leave him out here to rot; he'll be worthless to us. He's one evil man from what I understand, and personally, I would just as soon take him back dead. But it seems he has the information they need to get out of him."

James took another look at the poster. A large printed '10,000-pound' reward hung over the top of the photograph. Under the man's picture was the name "Harold 'Blackie', Larson."

"So, how are we going to do this, sir? It looks like there are at least six men with him."

James thought of Kenji's question. He rubbed his chin and looked out at the sun as it was about to settle on the horizon.

"Each one of those men is worth five hundred pounds. If we storm the shacks, I'm sure Blackie will try to shoot it out."

Kenji listened with interest, and the other ten marines remained alerted as their leader made a plan.

"I think this is a one-man job."

Kenji looked at James, seeming a little startled. "What do you mean sir? And who's the 'one' man?"

James smiled and continued.

"I believe that I can slip into the camp and bring the six men out one at a time. It's the only way to avoid a shootout. I'll save

Blackie for last as he's the most dangerous. Also, if I need to kill one of them, we'll not lose as much. After I get them all back here to you, we'll slip in to retrieved Blackie. Just keep the others quiet, even if you need to kill them."

Kenji expressed some reservation, "Are you sure, sir?"

James thought for a few more seconds. "It's the only way I can see to catch Blackie alive. I'll wait until they're asleep. Hopefully, there will only be one guard. If we come up with a better plan in the meantime, we can follow it."

Kenji nodded, and the men settled down for a long wait.

Around midnight James again studied the shacks. There was a single, small campfire in the middle of the makeshift dwellings and one man with a rifle slung over his shoulder; walking around casually, as if he were more worried about falling asleep than being attacked.

Soon, James slipped away into the darkness. Kenji and the other marines all watched the area, fully prepared to charge in if need be.

Ten minutes later, James crept from the darkness and moved up quickly behind the man. He maneuvered a rope around the man's neck and pulled it tight.

"If you ever want to breathe again, you'll be quiet," James whispered to the man in English. The guard struggled some as James maneuvered him towards Kenji and the others, but as the air diminished in his lungs, he stopped fighting. Quickly, Kenji and several Marines moved to meet James and help subdue the prisoner. James pulled the rope away to allow him to breathe. With some blades pointed at him, the man gasped for air but otherwise remained quiet.

James moved back to the campsite. Kenji again watched closely.

Squatting down outside one of the shack doors, James held his revolver in one hand and his short sword in the other. Using the tip of the sword, he tapped on the door lightly. Again, and again, he tapped until he heard movement. Soon a man came out of the door to find out what the noise was. James stood as the man stepped out. He placed the revolver to the man's head and the sword to his heart.

"Make a noise, and you're dead," James told him in a hushed voice. The man, fortunately, complied and slowly raised his hands.

One by one James captured the criminals. Finally, the sun began to rise.

Blackie Larson rolled over and slowly woke from sleep. As he opened his eyes, the first thing he saw was James and a room full of Marines. James sat in a chair and held his longsword very close to Blackie's neck.

James then spoke in English. "Harold Blackie Larson, you're a wanted man. And we're going to take you to the people that want you."

Blackie cringed and with a thick cockney accent almost shouted, "You won't get me there alive!"

"Yes, we'll get you there alive." James replied, "You may have fewer fingers and toes, but we'll get you there alive. You see Blackie, the British government didn't say anything about getting you to them in one piece; they just want you alive. So, every time you try to escape, I'll remove a finger or a toe. And if one of my men get hurt, I may remove a hand or a foot. We've got an exceptional doctor on board our ship, and I'm sure he can patch up the stubs and keep you alive."

Blackie's face winced at the thought. He began to sit up, and James followed his neck with the blade.

"You can't do that." Blackie said nervously, "The British government doesn't allow that sort of treatment to prisoners."

"We'll you're probably right about that, Blackie. And that's most likely one of the reasons we're here. You see, we're not the British government. So, we can do as we like, until we hand you over to the British government."

Blackie now seemed to notice Samson, and that most of the other men were Asian. He expressed confusion and said with bewilderment, "you're, bounty hunters?"

James smiled and replied, "Bounty hunters, just... doesn't sound very nice, Blackie. We prefer to think of ourselves as... 'Soldiers of Justice'.... it sounds so much better, don't you think?"

The criminal expressed, even more, confusion. James reached down and picked up his pants from the floor. He tossed them on Blackie's lap and said, "Get dressed."

Several days later the Marines moved the prisoners onto the Valiant, and the ship set sail for Singapore.

Blackie and his men didn't test James, and a week later they were being turned over to Sir Barrett and the British government in Singapore.

240

The following day, as the Valiant's coal bunkers were being reloaded and provisions brought aboard, James took Kenji and five men to purchase the camera and supplies for Doctor Jefferies.

After two hours in the camera seller's shop, James and his men loaded up the large boxes and supplies, then boarded rickshaw's and instructed the drivers to take them to the harbor.

At the end of a long and somewhat bumpy ride, the rickshaw drivers stopped around three hundred yards from the harbor. James spoke to the man pulling the two-wheeled carriage.

"To the harbor, all the way to the harbor," James insisted.

The man bowed and replied in accented English, "So sorry, Sir. We can no go close to the harbor. It is law. We can go no close. Sorry." The man then bowed again.

James expelled a long breath of air. "Yes alright, I forgot, you can't go any closer." He then stepped out and picked up the camera supplies he had been carrying.

"Well, men. It seems we'll have to carry everything from here."

James paid the rickshaw drivers and took the lead towards the harbor.

Almost halfway to the ship, the group came to a long, narrow bridge. Several people could pass each other going the opposite directions, but they would need to move very close to the side for the other person to get by. James and his men were almost halfway across when seven sailors began to cross from the opposite direction.

James came close to these sailors as he and his men were around three quarters across.

The first sailor in the group was a large burly man with several tattoos on his forearms. James quickly identified their uniforms as being American.

The hefty American sailor in the lead blurted out, "Get out of the way you stinking chinks!"

James stopped and those following him stopped. He looked at the man with some obvious irritation but said nothing. With his hair in the high ponytail of a samurai and his oriental styled wardrobe, he realized the sailor had mistaken him for an Asian, along with his crewmates.

The lead sailor again spoke. "I said get off the bridge, chink! Don't you understand English?" The man then motioned with his hand for James and his men to back off the bridge for him.

The men behind the burly sailor began to move and examine James and his men. As they did this, the large sailor in front became even more agitated.

"I said, get the hell off the bridge, chinks! If you don't, I'll pound you all and throw you into the sea!" The sailor pointed down to the water, which was around fifteen feet below.

James glanced down at the water where the man pointed but still made no move.

"Are you too stupid to understand?"

As the large sailor said this, the others behind him began to laugh. The sailor at the very back, however, looked at James very carefully.

"I'll give you ten seconds to get off the bridge you stinking chinks. If you don't get off, you're going to get it."

When the lead sailor said this, James turned and handed the box of supplies to Kenji, who was directly behind him.

"Would you like some help, Lieutenant?" Kenji asked as James handed the box to him.

James glanced back at the sailors and replied, "I only count seven, why would you ask such a thing?"

Kenji smiled, "I was being polite, Master Michio." He then bowed slightly to his leader.

James nodded as if accepting the reason and the show of respect. "Well, thank you, and I will certainly ask for your assistance, should I need it."

The burly man could be heard laughing under his breath as he began to anticipate a fight.

Behind them, the sailor in the rear shouted, "Burt, I don't think we should bother these men. I think I know who the one in front is!"

Burt glanced back, "Shut yer pie hole, Price!" He then began to take off his uniform top.

"Get ready for a whipping, chink. And after I'm done with you, I'm gonna kick all your friends off the bridge as well."

"Burt, listen, I think these men are from the Valiant." Price yelled out.

James began to take his silk uniform jacket off. When Price said this, he glanced at Price and then turned back to Kenji, "Perhaps there are only six. The one at the rear may have more sense than the others."

Burt spoke to James in a gruff voice, "Stop talking chink to yer buddies and get ready to fight!"

Again, Price moved to the side and almost shouted, "I think that's Lieutenant Taft your talking to Burt!"

Burt laughed at Price's statement, "Stupid fool Price, that stuff is just sailor's talk. Don't you know anything?"

Price again moved to get a better look at James.

Once James had taken his jacket off, it revealed his short sword on his right side, and his Colt revolver on his left with the handle back, as always, so he could draw with his right hand.

"Well, well, lookie here, the chink is armed. No weapons China man, just fists alright?" Burt pointed at the arms and then moved his fists in a fighting fashion.

James looked down at the revolver and sword; he then pulled them out and handed them to Kenji.

"Burt, didn't you see that old ironclad in the harbor?" Price asked with concern.

One of the other sailors now shouted, "Shut yer mouth, Price, er I'll clobber you myself."

Then Burt replied, again with sarcasm.

"Yeah, I saw that old bucket of rust. They probably can't get it to stay afloat long enough to haul it out of the harbor and sink it. Now shut your mouth, Price. I'm about to teach this stinking chink a lesson."

With that statement, Burt moved towards James with his fists up in a fighting fashion. James stepped back as Burt swung. He grabbed Burt's left fist in mid-swing and twisted it and his arm around quickly. This caused the man to move towards the railing to keep his arm from being broken. As Burt almost fell over the rail, James struck him in the lower rib cage with several rapid blows. He then let the large sailor go and stepped back casually.

Burt fell to his knees in pain. "You damn chink!" He held his side and began to stand. "What the hell was that?"

After getting back to his feet, Burt came at James with his right this time. The lieutenant blocked the punch and immediately delivered a nose breaking hit to Burt's face. The large sailor stumbled back and almost knocked the six other sailors down. They managed to catch him and as they picked him up the group pushed him towards James.

James lowered a bit and caught the sailor in the midsection. With the momentum Burt had gained, James simply flipped him over his back and then across the bridge railing behind him. Burt fell screaming into the water as James stood up straight. He then glanced down to his shirt, as if inspecting it for dirt or blood from Burt's nose.

The sailors, other than Price, now began to charge James. One by one he beat them mercilessly. Several went flying over the bridge to accompany Burt. Very quickly the other three lay, bleeding and grunting with pain.

Price had remained where he was, but his face expressed shock, mixed with admiration.

James then casually turned to Kenji, who handed him his weapons. After these had been sheathed and holstered, Kenji handed the jacket to his Lieutenant. Finally, James took the box of camera supplies and sidestepped the injured sailors to get across the bridge.

"You are Lieutenant Taft, ain't you? And that's the Valiant out there ain't it?" Price asked as soon as James came close. The group stopped, and James examined Price with curiosity.

"How is it that you know my name, sailor?" James asked.

"I knew it! I knew it! I knew that old ironclad was still in action. I knew it must be the Valiant." Price became quite excited. James, however, appeared somewhat irritated.

"Just what do you know about me, and the Valiant for that matter?"

Price seemed surprised. "Well, Sir, you and your ship, well, are legends... or myths, most sailors think. Our ship's doctor told me about you. He's been here to Singapore before, and he saw the Valiant. He told me you were for real, but I never thought that I would get to see the Valiant or meet you, Sir. It's a real honor."

James grimaced a bit, seeming slightly embarrassed from the attention. He then began to move on across the bridge.

"Yes, well thank you, sailor Price. I'm not sure of what all you've heard, but I suspect not all of it is true." James stopped in mid-stride after saying this and seemed to realize what he'd just said.

"Well, perhaps much of it is true, but it concerns me some that stories about the Valiant and myself are circulating on ships. I happen to spend much of my time on a ship, and I'm fully aware of the type of stories that can be circulated."

James began to walk again but continued, "Please be careful about rumors, sailor Price. Now if you'll excuse us, we need to get back to the ship."

The group moved quickly towards the harbor and Price replied, "Yes, Sir. It is a real honor to meet you, Sir." Then he began helping his fellow sailors up.

Once onboard, James carefully packed the camera and supplies in his quarters for safe travel.

Chapter Eighteen: Nowhere to turn

The following day, the Valiant slipped out of the harbor, setting it usual course for Sandrilan.

A week out from Singapore and as the ship passed through island littered straights, the Valiant came upon something odd.

"Can you make anything out Lieutenant?"

"No sir, with all the smoke I can only determine that she's a steamer, an older one most likely. She appears to be at full speed, though. Perhaps the crew is fighting the fire and has neglected to inform the boiler room."

The commander stepped up beside James, who stood right outside of the Valiant's small wheelhouse. He put a spyglass up to his eye and again examined the smoking ship in the distance.

"Perhaps, or she may be trying to reach land. With so many small islands in these straights, the captain may know someplace to get help. He's possibly moving at full steam in the hope of reaching a landing area before the fire overtakes the vessel.

"Strange, though," the commander seemed puzzled.

"What's strange, Sir?" James asked and then also put a spyglass to his eye.

"The smoke, it looks too dark to be wood. It's an odd color. It looks to be an oil of some sort."

After a few seconds of examining the ship, James replied. "Could it be their cargo on fire?"

"I suppose it could be." The commander said. "I don't like it, though, a steamer on fire, moving through these islands at full speed. It's all rather odd. Stay behind her but at a distance. If she slows, we'll move close enough to offer assistance."

"Yes, Sir," James replied as the commander slid the spyglass together and moved towards his cabin.

The Valiant followed the ship for almost an hour. James had Kenji take the helm, and he moved to the bow to get a closer look. He put the spyglass to his eye and strained to see through the thick smoke.

As the ships maneuvered through two islands, James caught glimpses of activity onboard the mysterious ship. What he saw began to frighten him. He turned and shouted an order to any crewman in earshot.

"Get the commander, quickly!"

A sailor darted towards the commander's cabin. James turned back to the ship and again struggled to see through the smoke.

Soon the commander moved swiftly to James.

"What is it, Lieutenant?"

"Sir, I've been watching the activity, and I'm having doubts that the ship is actually on fire. I'm almost certain I saw men fanning flames in something that's creating the smoke."

As James said this, the Valiant continued between the two islands. The commander examined the ship through his spyglass. He then looked at where the Valiant was. He looked at one island and then the other. He held his hand up to check the wind.

James watched his commander's face grow suddenly stark. He backed up several feet and looked back towards the way they had come. He then spoke with a nervous voice.

"They're not on fire, Lieutenant. That ship is not in distress... it's the bait."

James looked back at the ship and then around as he suddenly noticed the things. The commander had been looking at.

"Shall we come to a full stop, sir?"

The commander looked towards the smoking ship.

"It's too late for that."

James looked back at the ship, as they moved from between the two islands, he could see two heavily gunned, Junk pirate ships appearing behind the smoke. One on each side of the path the Valiant must cross to move past the islands.

"It's a trap Lieutenant and a brilliant one at that. Zheng Qui must have hired a new strategist."

James examined the situation again as the commander darted back to the wheel house. James then moved quickly towards the wheelhouse also and overheard the commander shouting an order into the pipe that led to the boiler room.

"Full steam! I need full steam as soon as you can get it!"

From the pipe, James heard a coal man reply, "Yes, Sir."

The commander then shouted Kenji, "Ready for battle, Mr. Kenji!"

Kenji replied, "Yes, Sir." He then stepped to the side of the wheelhouse and began ringing a small bell rapidly.

"They'll tear us apart, Sir, it will take far too long to get the steam up!" James spoke as he followed behind his leader.

The commander raced about with an urgency that James had never seen before.

"It's our only option Lieutenant! We can't turn and if we stop they'll close in and kill us while we're trying to back away. The two Junks are sail powered, and the wind is in their favor. They've brought us here for the specific purpose of destroying the Valiant, and they may well do it!

"Ready all your guns Lieutenant! I'll get the Marines armed and in place."

"Yes, sir," James replied and started towards the gun deck.

"Lieutenant," the commander yelled back.

James stopped and turned back. The commander moved to him as if wanting to say something that only he could hear.

"Lieutenant, we must get through this gauntlet. We cannot stop or slow down, no matter what, fire at will, as soon as you have a shot. They'll be hitting us before you have that opportunity though and we'll be an easy target. Regardless, we cannot stop, no matter what. That's an order."

James looked into the commander's face. He didn't quite understand the need for a direct order, but he quickly replied, "Yes sir," then darted towards the gun deck.

"Ready all guns!" He shouted as he ran down the steps. The gunners had already begun to do so, and James began assisting the men in bringing additional powder charges to positions behind the large guns.

Smoke began rolling out of the Valiant's single stack, but it was obvious she wasn't picking up speed fast enough.

The Marines loaded their Winchesters as they positioned themselves on each side of the ship. Puff's of smoke were seen from the enemy ships as they began to fire on the Valiant.

"Fire at will men, as soon as you're in range, try to keep the Gunners pinned down if you can, and get ready for hell boys, it'll be a hot one today!"

248

Just as the commander finished shouting this, cannon shots began landing on the deck and all around the Valiant. Several Marines were killed instantly, and bits of wood and debris flew all around.

On the gun deck, James had all twenty guns moved as far forward as he could get them. Still, he didn't have a shot. He again saw the enemy ships fire. He stepped back from a gun port just before a cannonball slammed into the iron plated hull of the Valiant. Debris flew inside the gun deck, and several men fell screaming as bits of wood hit them in the face.

"Steady men!" James shouted out as others helped the injured men from the area.

He again glanced out the portal, and still, the Valiant had no shot. James gritted his teeth. A few minutes more and they could fire on both ships.

On the top deck, men lay dead and wounded. The commander had cuts from flying debris but continued to move about and rally the men.

"A little closer and we can dish some back to them men, just bit closer! Show no quarter; they'll give us none!"

The commander stepped back towards the wheelhouse. Kenji stood at the helm steering the course. Below, James watched for the right second to fire.

The enemy ships fired again. Five shots from each ship came hurling towards the already damaged Valiant.

"Steady men!" James shouted again and then stepped back from the portal as he knew the ship was about to be hit again.

Several shots hit the iron hull, several more hit the masts and rigging. One hit the top edge of the deck, tearing the railing off and killing several more men.

As the shots were hitting, Kenji lowered down for cover but held the wheel. A large sail beam came crashing down. The ropes caught it and caused it to swing rather than fall onto the deck. It came across the top of the wheelhouse and smashed through the roof, nearly getting the wheel and Kenji both.

A yell was heard, and as Kenji was recovering from the shock of the crashing beam, he realized it was the commander.

Kenji moved back from the demolished wheelhouse to look for his leader, but he was gone.

The sound of the Winchesters began ringing out as the Marines fired on the enemy ships.

"Fire one, fire two, fire three," James shouted as they came into position to strike. The acrid smell of gunpowder filled the air.

All twenty guns rang out, one after another; it felt as if the entire ship would come apart. The large guns of the Valiant immediately inflicted heavy damage on the Junks but didn't destroy them as James had hoped. The gun crews worked feverishly to re-load.

Samson came running down to the smoke-filled lower deck.

"Lieutenant, Lieutenant, we've got to turn back! The commander, he's overboard!"

James turned to Samson, who had blood all over him. He couldn't tell if Samson was wounded or if it was the blood of another crew member.

"What?" James stepped back from the gun portal.

"The commander, he's overboard, we must get him!"

James turned back to the gun crews, which had now stopped working to listen to Samson.

"Keep loading, fire when ready!" He yelled out and then rushed topside.

Chaos greeted James as he came up from the bowels of the Valiant. Wreckage and body parts lay strewn across the smoking deck. The Marines continued to fire at the enemy and bullets from the pirate ships hit all around as the ironclad began to move between the two damaged Junks.

James struggled to make his way to the almost destroyed wheelhouse, also trying to avoid getting shot in the process. Under his feet, the cannon of the Valiant thundered out intermittently as each gun was loaded and fired.

"What happened? Where's the commander?"

Kenji looked up at James as he asked this. Another bullet landed close by, and James quickly knelt to gain some cover.

"He was struck by that beam, I think, Sir. I'm not sure what happened, I knelt, low like this, the beam came through the wheelhouse and almost took out the wheel. I know the commander was over there, the last I saw him. I heard him yell out or make a sound as if he were hit. When I looked, he was gone.

"Can we turn back and look for him?"

James examined the large beam and the area where it would have hit. More fire thundered under them from the gun deck as the Valiant moved past the two badly damaged pirate ships.

"No! Straight ahead Kenji, stay on course unless I tell you otherwise."

"But Sir," Kenji shouted over the noise of battle.

"That's an order, Mr. Kenji!"

As James shouted this, more bullets hit close by, and a cannon ball took out another part of the forward mast. More wreckage and debris fell around them.

James covered his head, as did Kenji and Samson. He then stood up and crouching began to move back to the gun deck. Before getting far, he saw something very disturbing. The steamship that had lured them into the trap had turned around and was now moving straight towards them.

He stepped back and took Kenji by the arm, then pulled him over a little to see the ship.

"Looks like he's going to ram us, Sir," the Japanese Marine said.

"That looks like his plan! Zheng Qui must have upped the bounty on us!" James shouted.

As they gained some distance from the two Junks, the battle calmed slightly. James quickly studied the situation. They were moving almost full steam towards the enemy vessel. He knew they couldn't slow down until getting clear of the enemy. They had taken too much damage to do anything other than run now. If they moved to one side or the other, the enemy ship would have a clear shot to the side of the Valiant and sink it for sure.

"When we're a hundred yards from him, take us sixty degrees port."

"Will we clear him, being that close?"

James glanced back. "I don't know, Kenji, but we'll soon find out."

He stood up and ran towards the gun deck.

"Hang on men; we're going to make a tight turn in a few minutes! James shouted as he made his way down to the gun deck.

Once below he shouted again.

"Load the starboard guns, quickly! Then lower them as far down as they'll go!"

One of the gun crew expressed confusion at this, "We'll be firing at the water, sir!"

"That's an order!" James shouted.

The men loaded the guns as fast as they could.

"Block the gun's wheels, hurry, were going be leaning hard to port in a few minutes, hang on and get ready to fire!"

The gun crew barely had time to follow James orders when Kenji turned the wheel hard. The Valiant leaned to the port side and as it did the guns on the starboard side leveled out.

As items slid across the gun deck and James held onto a beam, he saw the shot he had hope for. The pirates' ship slid by close and James shouted, "Fire all guns!"

The gun crews pulled the lanyards, and ten large cannons fired with fury.

Smoke prevented James from seeing anything after this. Several of the large guns jumped their tracks due to the angle they were fired from. As the Valiant leveled back off, James struggled to the upper deck.

The steamship was badly damaged, and smoke streamed from her deck and hull. In the distance, the other two ships also appeared to be in bad shape. The Valiant itself was in no condition to fight any longer. She had held together, but now she must make it to safety.

"Set course for Sandrilan, Kenji. We'll try to get some sails up to conserve coal. We've got to get out of this area. If we run across any more of Zheng Qui's ships, I don't think we'll survive."

Kenji grimaced. "What about the commander sir? We've got to go back for him."

James expelled a breath with sadness. "That's an order Kenji. Put us on a course for Sandrilan."

Kenji appeared hurt, but replied, "Yes, sir."

As the Valiant steamed from the battle area, a new battle to save the wounded began. Darkness overtook the ship, but deep in the bowels, screams rang out as Jollie made several amputations.

Those that were not wounded or only slightly wounded appeared to be in a daze. James had seen it many times in the past and had also found himself doing it; staring into nothingness with empty eyes.

The ferocity of the battle and losing the commander was difficult to comprehend. James finally lay on his bed and slept a few minutes. He then went to the wrecked wheelhouse and relieved Kenji, who appeared to be ready to fall over.

Chapter Nineteen: Where Dreams End

Only necessary words were uttered during the difficult journey back to Sandrilan. James weakly talked of the dead before they were slid into the sea; he almost felt as if he were breaking a rule or law. The words seemed to be out of place. He was glad when there were no more of his comrades to send into the darkness of the ocean. He didn't feel like speaking.

Makeshift repairs were made to the sails and masts. This allowed the Valiant to harness some wind and conserve coal. As they came closer to Sandrilan, James let the boilers cool. The battered warship slowly drifted into the small harbor.

The dreaded signal rang out, indicating there were wounded onboard. Soon, smaller boats were rushing to aid the Valiant. Some helped move it closer to the dock, and others came to examine the damage; expressing astonishment at the mighty warship's wrecked condition.

The butterflies and Madame Zhou came quickly from the palace. They watched closely as James came off the ship first. Their eyes searched in vain. They appeared confused. One of them came up to James.

"Where is our King... where is the King?"

James looked at her and shook his head. Tears immediately welled up in her eyes. From behind her, another butterfly began to cry out and then another, and another began to shriek and moan in agony. Madame Zhou stood behind them; her face strained in shock.

The woman facing James shook her head in disbelief.

"No, no, no, not the King, no..."

James moved away from her as more men stepped off the ship.

Doc Jefferies came down the road with his bag in hand.

"What's happened? Where is the commander, Lieutenant?"

"He... didn't make it, Doc. It was an ambush. Three heavily armed ships of Zheng Qui. He didn't make it."

The doctors face turned pale. He took James by the arms and held him, his eyes expressing horror. James could feel the doctor trembling.

"He...he what, no, that can't be. No, it can't be."

James pulled away from the doctor and walked towards his house. He felt exhausted. The cries behind him became almost unbearable. As he made his way up the road, the people of Sandrilan came to him.

"Where is the King?" They asked again and again. "Where is our King?"

James shook his head and moved on. He went to his house and laid on the bed. He stared at the bamboo roof. He could still hear the butterflies crying. He had slept very little in over a week and quickly fell asleep from sheer exhaustion.

When he woke, James wasn't certain how long he had slept. It seemed several days, though it may have just been due to his depleted state.

He cleaned up and went to Doc Jefferies first. The office area had several beds with wounded men in them. Out on the veranda were more beds with his wounded comrades. Of the twenty-five Marines, six were killed, ten were wounded; five badly, two of which required amputations.

The Valiant had also lost five sailors, with many others wounded.

James went to each bed and encouraged the men, as well as family members that accompanied them. It was a somber experience, and the atmosphere was very gloomy.

He was glad to finally get back outside. He then made his way to the Valiant.

Onboard the ship, James stepped around mast beams and rigging that had been hastily secured to ensure it would not be lost on the return trip. As he moved down to the gun deck, it appeared the battered vessel was deserted.

He stood examining the twenty large guns. Several had jumped out of their tracks due to the odd angle they were in when last fired. He felt almost ill as he considered the massive effort it would take to repair the guns.

James realized he'd not eaten for some time. He was about to leave the gun deck when he heard a noise in the powder room.

Slowly, he moved towards the room and opened the door. Kenji sat on the floor, holding a bottle of sake. As he turned and looked at James, it became clear that he was very intoxicated.

Kenji sneered at his Lieutenant and then stood, wobbling in the process.

"We should have gone back for him!"

James stepped back a little as Kenji moved towards him with his finger pointed.

"We shouldn't have left him! He would never leave one of us! We should have gone back!" Kenji was shouting now.

"Kenji, it was his order to keep going, no matter what. He gave that order as we went into action. I was following the commander's order."

Again, Kenji sneered at James. He took another drink from the bottle and wiped his mouth on his sleeve. He wobbled a little and suddenly began to cry.

"He wouldn't have left us! We shouldn't have left him out there to die. We shouldn't have."

James got Kenji sat back down. He stayed with him for a while and then went to the galley to get something to eat. Again, there was no one there and after eating he searched the ship and found that Kenji was the only person onboard.

On his way to the palace, James passed several women in front of their house. They were dressed in black and sat crying and moaning. They would raise and hold their hands into the air and then lower their faces to the ground again.

Other people moved about as if in a daze. No shops were open that he could see. No sounds were heard other than crying and mourning. He continued to the palace.

As he walked into the elaborate complex, cries were again heard from various rooms throughout the main structure. The celebration area was strangely vacant. The oil lamps that always burned had gone out, and a dark, dreary feeling immediately came over James.

He stood alone several minutes looking over the large pavilion that had held so many happy celebrations. He wondered if there would ever be another one.

Madame Zhou quietly came in and sat at her usual spot on the stage area, then watched James. When he turned and noticed her, James walked over and sat across from her. She said nothing and they studied each other for a few seconds.

James finally spoke, "I guess you and the butterflies are free now."

The beautiful Asian woman expelled a quick, short laugh that sounded like a grunt. She almost sneered at James but then regained something of a blank expression. He was a bit confused about this but waited patiently for a reply as the distant cries of the butterflies filled the air.

Finally, Madame Zhou spoke.

"You have seen much, Lieutenant, but you understand little." She paused briefly, as if to gather her thoughts, and then continued.

"The butterflies were free while the King was alive, but now they feel the cold shackles of slavery closing around their necks once again.

"All of the butterflies and me as well, are products of powerful men's desires and lust to own and control everything around them.

"I suspect all of us were also chosen at a young age because of beauty. We were trained to do only one thing...to please our masters. We danced and sang; we excited these men's eyes and senses. It was always because we must do so, and we must pretend that our only wish is to please the men that held our chains. It is the only thing we know how to do. We have no skills to grow food or make clothes.

"The king knew this well. And as he rescued almost everyone that is here at Sandrilan, he also rescued us from our desperate situations. I, like many of the butterflies, would have been long dead if not for the king.

"When he brought us here to Sandrilan, he knew what would happen if he sent us into the general population. He knew well we would end up selling our bodies for food and necessities. He told us one by one that we were free. He told us we could live in the palace and do as we wished. 'Your beauty alone will make things much more wonderful here in the palace; there are no tasks required of you unless you wish to do something. You're free,' he said.

"Though some left to sell their bodies for money, most all stayed. We wanted to do something in return for the king, to let him know how happy we were. So, we began to dance for him. It is the butterflies that chose to dance for the king, he has never asked or told us to do so. And the butterflies chose to throw flower petals before his path; he would never have requested such a thing.

"No Lieutenant, we are not free now. Our freedom died with the king. We're now bound by the fears of what may come for women such as us. Our protector is gone, and few men have the strength to let things of beauty remain free. We know well that most men with power wish to capture and cage beautiful things. They want to possess them and put their brands upon them so that all will know who owns them.

"Once again, we are bound by our fears and the fate that men choose for us."

James was astonished by this. She was correct, though, and the truth was crystal clear. How did he miss this? He had always thought the commander had kept the butterflies as his trophies and playthings. He'd never considered anything else. And yet the misconception burned in his mind now. He remembered the joy on the faces of the butterflies. They had always danced with happiness and not as a task or duty.

He lowered his head and felt ashamed. He stood and left the palace. Slowly he walked back down the winding roads. As he came close to his house, it started to rain. He went inside and sat in one of his wicker chairs. The feeling of being lost began to take hold. If he was wrong about the butterflies, how many other things was he wrong about?

James stayed inside for the remainder of the day. He could think of nothing to do. He was empty and void of a direction to go. He slept restlessly through the night.

The following morning, he once again visited the wounded. He smiled and tried to cheer them. But he could see the fear in their faces. He had been in battles many times with these men. They were among the bravest he had ever known. Now they were afraid; not of death, but of the unknown.

He left the wounded men and went to the Valiant. Again, his heart sank as his beloved ship came into view. She was like an ill friend, who needed medicine, yet no one knew what medicine to give her, or where to find it.

As he stepped aboard the ship, he saw Samson sitting on a large mast beam that had been knocked down during the battle. James walked over and sat next to him. Samson stared up at Sandrilan and took little notice of him.

James remained quiet and looked up at the island city. After a few moments of silence, Samson began to speak.

"When we are asleep, and we dream, we never know when the dream will end until we wake. I now think the same is true in life, Lieutenant. I think we live in a dream until one day we wake and realize the dream has ended."

James looked at his friend. He thought about what he said and after a few seconds asked him, "Do you think the dream is over, Samson?"

Samson glanced at James, then looked out over the ship's railing, as if in thought.

"A child is brave and proud while he walks with his father. He looks up at his father and feels the man is invincible. The child has no concern of where he is going or what he is doing, as long as he is with his father. When the child's father is suddenly gone, the child looks around and realizes that he doesn't know where he is. He then sees that he is much smaller than he had thought. The world he knew begins to come apart and what he finds around him is much more frightening.

"I think Sandrilan is full of children. We didn't realize we were children because our father was with us. Now the father is gone, and we are frightened. We don't know what to do, and our world is falling apart. Sandrilan is falling apart, Lieutenant. I see now that the king was the only thing holding us all together. Without him, we are lost, children."

James sat with Samson a while longer until he eventually left to find something to eat. After which he walked around Sandrilan. The shops were still closed, and very few people moved about. He passed by one of the taverns and saw many of the crew inside. They were intoxicated and obviously depressed. He continued without entering.

Eventually, he found himself back at Doc Jefferies office. The doctor was less busy than he had been the previous two days. When he saw James, he appeared to give Oshai some instructions and then walked over to him.

"You look exhausted, Lieutenant. Would you care to have a drink with me on the veranda?"

James nodded that he would. The doctor retrieved a bottle and several glasses. The two then walked out past the wounded that were under an overhanging roof. Once they were in the open area, they sat at a table.

Doc Jefferies poured two glasses half full of bourbon whiskey.

"I save this for very good times or very bad times. Either way, it seems to help some."

James took a drink, and the doctor did as well. The area they sat in was where he had sat when first seeing the butterflies. He gazed up to the palace as if hoping they would magically appear.

"I wonder if we'll ever see them dance again." Doc Jefferies said, seeming to know what James was thinking.

James gave no reply but looked back down to the table. He tapped a finger on his glass and then took another large drink, almost finishing the amber colored liquid.

The doctor took the bottle and poured a little more in James' glass. He then said something that immediately gained James' full attention.

"Lieutenant, there's something that I haven't told you about the commander."

The doctor then stared out over the veranda, seeming to recall memories. After taking a deep breath, he spoke again.

"Some years back we sat here, almost in this exact spot, and I told you how the commander had gained his fighting abilities. But there was more to the story than what I told you."

He took a drink, then sat his glass down and continued.

"Before the commander joined the Foreign Legion, he was married and had a small son. He could never bring himself to tell me exactly how they died; he could only say they were murdered. Afterward, he stated that he wasn't able to function as before. He had been successful and a highly paid professional in France. After he lost his wife and son, he could no longer work. He became extremely depressed and contemplated suicide.

"Yet, he'd always considered suicide as being a coward's way out. He decided to join the military. This way, he could die in battle. The French Foreign Legion seemed to hold the best chance for this as it was the most active and had the highest percentage of deaths in battle.

"He was trained and very soon afterward his unit was sent to the Crimean conflict. He decided that running into an enemy bayonet or bullet would be the same as suicide, so he would fight as he had been trained and felt sure death would come soon.

"But death didn't come soon. He fought battle after battle. As time went by he became a seasoned soldier. He told me, at that time, he came to regard his life as being in competition with death. It was a challenge, to fight and deprive death of his soul for as long as possible. It was this sort of, game if you will, that kept the commander going. He felt he would die at any time, but the simple challenge of surviving one more day, gave him a goal each time he woke in the morning.

"He was, subsequently, highly decorated for his actions in the Crimean war, not only by his mother country France, but the British also awarded him with several honors. It was in this manner that he met Sir Barrett.

"Finally, after years of fighting and numerous wars, the commander thought his luck had run dry in Mexico. Though not afraid of death, he had, at this point recovered some from his loss and the Legion had become the vessel that had helped him heal.

"As his comrades fell one after another in Mexico, he prepared himself for what must have seemed certain death. With the seven surviving legionaries, they fixed their bayonets and charged out to meet their demise. The Mexican general became so impressed however by the act of bravery, that he called a cease fire before they were all killed.

"Once again, the commander had cheated death. He was received as a hero in France. The Legion retired the surviving legionaries, and the commander considered what to do.

"As you already know, he eventually chose to sail around the world. I think this may have been another effort to either continue the healing or die in the attempt. It would have been suicide for most men to try such a thing alone. But, we are talking about the commander.

"Eventually, he found this group of islands and stayed here for a while. He named the group of islands after his beloved wife, Sandri. He climbed to the highest point and looked out over the area.

"He said it was there that inspiration came to him. He didn't tell me what the inspiration was, but from this time on, he was a changed man. And from this time forward, things changed for him. He became the man we all knew and loved. I believe he truly became the King of Sandrilan at that moment."

The doctor stopped and looked at James, who appeared deep in thought.

"I've never told anyone else this story. But there's a reason I tell you today, Lieutenant. I've come to believe the commander saw some of himself in you. Your lives have similarities, and it seems to me, he may have intended for you to take his place, should anything happen to him.

"The day we found you half dead after your wife had been killed, I don't think he wanted you to repay anything or any debt. He may have felt that it was the only thing that would keep you alive. If you were like him, you would survive, if only to repay a debt. And it seems to have worked. You did survive wounds that most men would not have."

James took another drink and again almost finish the contents of the glass. He cleared his throat and replied.

"I've also thought that's what he intended, Doc. And now that you've told me this, I have even fewer doubts about it."

James paused and gazed out over Sandrilan, then continued.

"When I first saw the commander fight, during the Sip Song Chou mission, it was as nothing I'd ever seen. He moved with precision and grace that defied all logic or reason. It was as if his very nature had been intertwined with the ability to fight.

"I thought that, if I could fight that way, and for a good purpose; to help others, then my life would mean something. And with his help, I've been able to do that.

"If I'd been asked a month ago, I would have thought that I could take his place if anything happened to him. But now that he's gone, I see that he ruled Sandrilan with the same skill and grace that he possessed in battle.

"I'm a soldier, Doc. I would venture to say I'm an exceptional soldier. But I know nothing about being a ruler, or a father. I've not been trained to be a protector. Perhaps he was trying to teach me, and I didn't know about it. But, I've either overlooked something or never received it.

"It's as if, I am once again looking at his movements and once again his abilities far exceed anything I could ever hope to achieve without years of training, much less today or even tomorrow.

"How can I take the place of such a man, Doc? I've only hoped to meet his expectations, and yet, I have no clue of how to do that now."

The doctor appeared to understand James. He nodded and expelled a breath of air as he considered this. After another drink, he spoke.

"I'm afraid I have no magic solution for you Lieutenant. But I can perhaps give you a clue. I believe every great man leaves a legacy. Sometimes we must be years away from the passing of the man to view his legacy from a distance. And at times it's from a distance that we realize the greatness of the legacy.

"The commander put his very essence into Sandrilan. It seems to be a tribute to his dearly loved wife, Sandri. If there is an answer for you, I feel it is here somewhere. This is the commander's legacy, and I am certain he left us with enough to survive if we search for it."

James thanked the doctor and went to his house. He lay in bed for several hours considering the conversation.

The morning brought another overcast day. James sat staring at the wall for a while, trying to decide what to do. He dressed and began walking to the palace.

Once again, a dark and vacant pavilion presented itself. He didn't hear any of the butterflies crying. He walked over and sat on the edge of the stage. Leaning over, he placed his arms on his legs and stared at the floor.

After a few seconds of silent thought, he rose and rubbed the sweat from his hands. Then he noticed something. In a dark corner of the pavilion, he saw the special box. It had been on the ship, and he'd not ordered anyone to retrieve it.

As he stood and walked towards it, he saw something draped over the top. It first appeared to be a bundle of cloth.

Coming closer, he realized it was a woman. She was sitting on the floor, while her head lay on her crossed arms, which were resting on the wooden container.

James carefully sat and watched the woman that at first appeared to be asleep.

She then raised her head, and James saw it was Madame Zhou. Her eyes were wet and swollen from crying. She looked at James and then pulled some hair from her face. She wiped her eyes with her hand.

"I'm sorry, I didn't mean to disturb you," James said softly.

She nodded and pulled a part of her dress up to better dry her eyes.

"It's alright, Lieutenant."

After clearing her eyes, she continued. "I had several of the palace guards bring this from the Valiant. I thought that I would feel better if it was where it belonged. But it simply made me miss him all the more."

James examined the box. He looked at the inscription on the side. It appeared to be Chinese. He knew it wasn't Japanese.

"Do you happen to know what the inscription means?" He asked.

Madame Zhou sat up a bit more and appeared to be glad for any distraction from her mourning.

"I only know that in English, it translates to mean, 'Woe to the wicked.' The doctor knows more about it than I do, but he told many of us the story years ago while the Valiant was doing some exercises around the islands."

James considered this.

"I've heard that before. Samson said it right before the commander..." He stopped and expelled a breath as if recalling a dark memory. He then continued.

"Well, he said that right before the commander single handed took over a fortress that I had determined to be 'impregnable.'"

Madame Zhou laughed a little as James chuckled.

"Could you tell me the story of the box?" He asked.

She again pulled some hair from her face.

"The doctor would be better at telling the story since he was there. I would just tell you the story as he told me." She replied.

James thought of asking the doctor about it. But he sensed that talking at this moment was helping both him and Madame Zhou to feel better.

"That would be fine Madame Zhou. I would like to hear it from you if you don't mind telling it."

As she considered this, James noticed several butterflies step cautiously into the pavilion area. They looked around, and when they saw James and Madame Zhou, they stepped up to the stage area and sat, as if waiting for the commander to arrive.

Madame Zhou watched the butterflies briefly before she began the story.

"It was when Sandrilan was still very young. There were only around thirty men, women and children on the island. The palace was merely a small house, but it was being built. The king had requested work on a variety of projects, and though there were few here, there were jobs available, and he paid very well for the work being done.

"The Valiant at that time was almost alone in its war against Zheng Qui and other pirates of the area. This was long before the English and Americans began to fight them.

"During one very fierce battle against three or four ships, I don't remember for certain, because the Valiant was always outnumbered in those days. Anyway, during a very difficult battle with Zheng Qui's men, the Valiant rescued some captives from one of the pirate ships, just before it sank.

"The commander delivered these captives back to their homes, or as close as he could get them. He even gave several of them money to purchase fares back to their homes.

"One of the captives was the first born son of a wealthy Chinese merchant from Hong Kong. The Pirates had likely planned on asking a ransom for him. The father had not heard what had become of his son but only that the ship he traveled on had been taken by pirates.

"When the king brought him home, the father asked what reward the king demanded. The reply given was that he and the men from the Valiant demanded no reward. The reward was seeing a son reunited with his father.

"The Chinese merchant considered this for several moments. He then said something such as this to the king, 'There are many wicked men; men that do unspeakable evils, without the slightest bit of remorse. He knew the character of these men because he's had to defend against them his whole life. Men such as the king, however, were few in this world. He didn't know much about such men because they were seldom around when needed. So, he could only ask a question that now burned in his mind.'

"The merchant said, 'I am certain the wicked men will come for the king. They always want to destroy such men. There will be many, and as time goes by, more and more will come to kill the king and his men. The Valiant will always be outnumbered by these evil doers. What then? What happens when there are hundreds of wicked men advancing to kill the Valiant?'

"The king thought about the question and simply replied, 'Woe to the wicked, Sir.'

"The Chinese merchant was astonished by the reply. He then asked the king if he would accept a gift since he had not asked for a reward. The King said he would be honored to receive a gift. So, the man requested they stay the night, as it would not be ready until the morning.

"The merchant ordered his craftsmen to work all night and prepare the special box. He was so impressed with the king's reply that he had it put on each side of the gift.

"The following morning the merchant presented it to the king. He told him that such a brave statement should not be forgotten and that he hoped it would always be true. The merchant then opened the box to reveal some finely crafted silk robes for the king.

"The king thanked the merchant and accepted the box and robes. Later, however, when the king had returned to Sandrilan and pulled out the robes, he found two hundred silver coins in the bottom."

Madame Zhou paused. James glanced over at the butterflies and saw that two more had entered the pavilion and joined the others on the stage area. Madame Zhou continued.

"I don't remember when the box was first taken on the Valiant. But the men would always bring it here after the ship returned. It always returned here with him; to not have it here now seemed wrong."

Silence took over the large room. For several long moments, James considered the tale she told. Then, rather unexpectedly and almost in a whisper, Madame Zhou said, "Sandrilan is dying, Lieutenant."

James glanced at her but said nothing. He turned back to gaze at the almost empty room. She continued in a soft voice so that only James could hear.

"She's very ill. Her heart is no longer with her. She's dying. What can save her, Lieutenant?"

James looked over at the butterflies. Several lay on the stage area as if hoping it may bring rest. He thought of her question, then replied in the same soft tone.

"I think the commander hoped I would take his place if something should happen to him. But how can anyone take the place of such a man? I can order soldiers into battle, but I can't order a city to recover. I can't replace its heart and soul. I want to do something to save her, but what?"

After a brief silence, Madame Zhou said, "It seems an impossible thing, Lieutenant, perhaps the same as taking over an 'impregnable' fortress. And yet, if you do not find a way, Sandrilan will surely die. I have heard there are already many planning to leave on the next supply ship."

James hung his head and remembered Samson's words. "And the dream ends, " he said softly.

"Yes, for most the dream ends."

James glanced at her. She looked over at the butterflies on the stage and continued, "But for those that must trust their fate to men, perhaps a nightmare begins."

Madame Zhou laid her head back on the box. James gazed over at the butterflies for a few moments and then stood up and went back to his house. Again, he lay in his bed, staring at the bamboo roof above. Finally, he slept.

The following morning James went to the Valiant. Several men were in the lower decks, they were drunk and somewhat disorderly, but James left without them becoming aware that he had spotted them.

Sandrilan was still withdrawn and quiet. Very few shops were open as he walked the winding road up to the palace. Again, he was greeted by a dark and dreary pavilion. Before, he'd never thought about who kept the lamps burning. But now there seemed to be no one that could bring themselves to revive the lights in the celebration area.

He again sat on the edge of the stage, but this time facing the large veranda that hung over a long drop. It seemed so long ago that he stood out there and talked with the commander on several occasions.

266

As these memories came to mind, James noticed four butterflies drifting into the pavilion. They daintily sat down in the corners of the open area and began watching him from the shadows. A few minutes later, several more came in and also sat to watch him.

Time slipped by slowly and silently. He struggled with the problem that seemed to have no answer. Finally, he stood and walked out to the veranda. He sat in one of the chairs and looked out over Sandrilan. The Valiant sat far below in the harbor. She too appeared to be ailing and in a desperate state. All of the Sandrilan seemed to be gazing up at him, in search of an answer. It was a burden as he had never felt or wanted. He'd never desired to be a king, nor thought of what was needed to be one.

A swishing sound, accompanied by the unmistakable clicking of small wooden shoes on the floor was heard approaching behind him. He knew who it was and turned eagerly to see Sno moving towards the veranda. He was glad to see her and happy to break away from the problems that tormented his mind.

She bowed low and gracefully in front of him.

"May I accompany you, Master Michio?"

Her voice was delicate and sweet as if laced with honey. She was beautiful and appeared to glow in the daylight.

"Please do." James replied.

She sat close to his feet and smoothed her kimono so that there were no unsightly wrinkles. She then looked up at him and smiled.

James smiled back and examined her closely. Her presence alone made him feel better.

"Thank you for accompanying me, Sno." He looked back out to Sandrilan and again tried to find an answer.

"I know that you are troubled, as we all are. Perhaps we can talk. It helps at times to talk."

James considered her words. "I'm not very good at talking. It seems I've only been good at being a soldier. Now, what's needed is a talker, a diplomat, a father. I have no experience with these things. Everything has changed, and I'm not at all ready for it."

Sno turned her head and again smiled at James. She spoke, and it sounded like music to him.

"In that case, may I talk for us both, Master Michio?"

"Please do," James replied.

Sno continued in her delicate tone.

"I was bonded to an Okiya when I was twelve years old. When I was still a Maiko, early in my training, our geisha house was hired for a celebration. By then, I was fourteen years old. During this celebration, Lord Toshinobu saw me, and for some reason, of which I don't know, he began to sponsor my training the following day.

"When I became aware of this, I was very frightened. A shogun was sponsoring my training, and as yet, I had never even met him.

"Lord Toshinobu later requested that each month I perform a special dance for him. So, every month I worked very hard to make the dance perfect for this generous man.

"As time went by, I became confused as to how I should think of him. I asked my onee-san, 'How do I think of this man? Should I consider him as my owner, or lover, or perhaps as my father?' I will never forget what she told me. She said, 'As a geisha, you must think of him in all of these ways. You must be obedient to him as if he were your owner. You must be appealing to him as if he were your lover. And you must be innocent and respectful to him as if he were your father.'

"I considered this thing she had told me. I said to her, 'This is a very difficult thing, how can I do all these?' She then said, 'It is indeed a very difficult thing. But if it were an easy thing to do, then every woman would be a geisha.'"

Sno stopped and looked up at James with a slight smile and a gleam in her eye.

James understood the point she was making. He knew that special responsibilities demanded many different skills. But, it still wasn't the answer he needed. Again, silence prevailed.

Sno then asked, "If the King were here now, what would you ask him, or say to him?"

For several seconds James thought of her question. Then he replied, "I suppose that I would thank him for saving my life. I've realized that I never did thank him for that."

Sno appeared saddened. Her head lowered slightly, and she said, "Nor did I. I believe there are many that never thanked him. We were only thinking of ourselves, while he was thinking of us."

Unexpectedly, a revelation came to James. It was in a flash; he stood as he tried to grasp it.

"That's it," he said, as he moved over to the rail.

"That's it, that's the answer."

Sno watched him curiously. James stared out over Sandrilan.

A rain drop landed on Sno, then another. She stood. "Master Michio, it will rain. Please come in."

James didn't hear her. Nor did he notice the rain. He had the answer within his grasp. It had to do with what Sno had said. He struggled for the solution.

Sno walked quickly into the pavilion area. There stood Madame Zhou and at least ten butterflies. They had all been watching from the doorway.

"That's it... we've all been trying to heal ourselves. But he was always striving to heal us...." James spoke to himself as there was no longer anyone other than himself on the veranda.

The rain began to pour down. James remained where he stood, leaning over the rail, deep in thought.

Sno went to the stage and picked up a rug to cover herself before she dashed towards the door. Madame Zhou grabbed her as she attempted to go out to James.

"No," Madame Zhou said as she held onto Sno.

Sno began to cry, "We must get him in, please..."

Still, Madame Zhou held her.

James was somewhere else in thought; the rain dripped down from his face. He went over the solution again and again. He had only been thinking of himself. He had never thanked the commander because he was only thinking of himself. They had all been thinking of themselves. But a true king always thinks of his people.

Without control, he began to weep. He suddenly wept for the commander, and for Sachi, her father Konukoni and his adoptive father Tonkiwatu, all of the Aqukolo people.

He wept for Natsu and Nancy, his mother and his family, whom he may never see again. He wept for all the people that he had lost in his life. Then he wept for Sandrilan. He now knew the answer, it was in front of him, as clear as it could ever be.

All this time, he had been trying desperately to heal himself. He had been doing everything to heal himself so that he could live again. But he wasn't living; he was only surviving. As the tears merged with the rain, James fully realized the difference between himself and the commander. James loved to help people; it was the medicine he needed to sooth his soul. But the commander loved the people he helped. He had found the solution to healing his troubled soul. The commander helped others to heal, and in so doing he also healed himself.

It was something that could not be trained into someone. It was something that came from the heart, not the mind. Finally, James' heart opened again, and the emotions surged inside him.

For almost an hour James stood in the rain. Sno sat by the door and wept with him, and for him, though he was unaware of it. All of the butterflies watched him anxiously as the rain slowly subsided and then stopped.

Chapter Twenty: The Wait of a Kingdom

As the sun began to break out of the clouds, James felt as if the burdens of a world had been lifted from him. He knew what had been absent and it came back into his life completely and unexpectedly. He had truly lost the ability to love, just as Natsu had said. He was afraid of almost nothing, but he had been afraid to love for so long. This was the difference. He could command, but he could not lead Sandrilan without the ability to love her.

His heart beat faster as he turned and moved slowly towards the door. Sno sat up and wiped the moisture from her eyes. Madame Zhou and all of the butterflies moved from the doorway to allow James to enter. They all sensed the change and examined him closely.

As he came into the pavilion area, he looked at Madame Zhou and said, "I have the answer."

"What must we do?" She asked.

James spoke as they gathered around and listened with interest.

"Years ago, my adoptive father had a vision. He said that one day I must climb a mountain and find the direction for my people. I thought he was talking about our tribe. But now I realize he was talking about Sandrilan. I believe that day has finally arrived. I must climb the mountain to find the direction for our people."

He moved out of the palace and towards the path that lead to the commander's special place, the highest spot in Sandrilan.

Madame Zhou sent one of the butterflies to find the bell ringers. She then began to instruct the others, and they all started to move with a purpose.

Halfway up to the top, James heard the bells ringing. It was the signal that all should stop as the king was en-route to the special place.

As the bells rang out, everyone in Sandrilan stopped what they were doing. It was unexpected to hear the signal, and they began to look towards the palace.

James continued to climb the stairs until he reached the top of the hill. There he found a flat area; in this space was a rough lean-to, built of bamboo with palm leaves for the roof.

As he examined the structure, he saw a crudely built chair under the lean-to. Beside the chair was a wooden chest with a thick leather covering.

James sat and looked around. From this spot, he could see all of Sandrilan, as well as the Valiant in the harbor below. From the left and right, he could see out over the vast ocean. He saw the many smaller islands that appeared as children huddling around the larger parent island.

He examined the chest and then lifted the top up. The hinges creaked from seldom usage. Inside was a variety of items. A tin of tobacco with matches, a long stem pipe, a box of the slim cigars that the commander smoked and several bottles of rum. He moved a few other miscellaneous items around and found three small glasses and a towel.

After wiping one of the glasses off, he poured it full of the rum. He then sat it down and lit one of the cigars. As he leaned back in the chair, smoked the cigar and sipped the rum, his mind began to relax. He drifted in thought, and it seemed his reasoning became very clear and much brighter than it had ever been.

He could hear the commander telling him that no man should fight as another. So, he felt that no man should rule as another either. He didn't want to replace the commander, and there was no way that he could do so if he wanted to.

Then he considered the commander's words concerning the 'pomp and ceremony.' He expelled a long stream of smoke and realized the commander was correct again. These things had little place in a soldiers' life. But for the people of Sandrilan, they were the traditions that connected and bound all aspects of the island community. These were the things that made everyone a part of the Valiant and its mission. It was what he hadn't noticed until now. The success or failure of the Valiant was shared by all, and everyone was a part of the family.

As he finished the cigar and rum, he began to see what had to be done.

After much time in thought, James slowly descended the steps and noticed the butterflies sitting in the area that they always waited for the commander. The musicians also sat waiting. As he came closer, a young man left quickly to give the signal to the bell ringer. Soon the palace bell could be heard signaling the king had returned from the special place. Then, a cascade of bells responded throughout Sandrilan.

As James took the last steps down, Madame Zhou gave a hand signal. The butterflies stood and began to throw the petals in front of his path. The musicians began to play their bells and chimes.

He had not desired it, but now knew it was what must be. A body cannot live without a heart.

He moved down towards the palace and found all of the people of Sandrilan lining the road. He moved past them as more and more bells began to ring. Soon, the people were also tossing flowers in front of him, and small bells and chimes were brought out to add to the music.

Finally, he came to the Valiant. He stepped onto the boarding plank and turned to face the people. He looked them over, and the music subsided and stopped.

He began to speak in a loud voice so all could hear.

"People of Sandrilan, we've lost our beloved King and Commander. We've been in the darkness and have been searching for a way to go on without him. I have searched for a way to take his place. But I now know; he cannot be replaced. I won't attempt to replace such a great man. But, I will lead Sandrilan. I will continue to move his dream forward. He did not rescue and bring us all together, only to fall apart now. This was his dream, and it has become our dream. The dream will live, and he will live with it, and we will honor him by keeping Sandrilan alive!"

A shout of joy erupted immediately after he said this. It was as if Sandrilan had been gasping for air, and now, suddenly she received the life-giving breath into her lungs.

James returned to the palace and began organizing a series of events. He asked Madame Zhou and the butterflies to prepare a memorial dance for the commander. He then gathered the cooks, and they were instructed to prepare a large meal. It would be of plain and ordinary foods, no sweets and few spices.

Two days later all were asked to attend the service. It was a solemn occasion, and many wept. The butterflies were dressed in dark outfits. They performed a slow and melancholy dance as the musicians played in a subdued manner.

This was the medicine needed. It brought everyone together to mourn their loss as a community. And, it allowed Sandrilan to let go of their beloved king.

A few days after this, James ordered the crew and marines onto the deck of the Valiant. He then explained that repairs on the ship would begin immediately. Though they didn't have the facilities to make complete or permanent repairs, they would get the Valiant in order and together enough to sail to Singapore, where she would be completely restored and refitted.

A cheer went up after the men heard this. They went to work with a renewed sense of purpose.

Life slowly returned to semi-normalcy as the days and weeks went by. James moved into a spare room of the palace but would not sit on the stage where the commander always sat. Instead, he had the special box placed there, and he continued to sit in his normal spot.

Madame Zhou asked, "What should be done with the commanders' things?" James opened the door to a room he had never seen.

He looked in at the dark area. It was spacious, grandly decorated and seemed strangely quiet.

"Will you be moving into this room, Sir?" Madame Zhou asked as James studied the commander's room.

"No, it's to stay as it is. No one is to disturb the commanders' room." He closed the door without going inside.

The following day he went to inspect the Valiant. The repairs were going well, and as he stood on the deck, Samson approached. James turned and smiled, then Samson smiled as well.

"The Valiant, she is feeling much better, Sir," the large African man said. He then continued, "The commander will like what we've done so far."

James had turned away from the Marine, but when Samson said this, he turned back and looked at him with a puzzled expression.

After a few seconds, James asked him, "Do you believe the commander is still alive, Samson?"

A thoughtful expression came across his face, then he replied, "No, I don't believe he is still alive... but I no longer believe he is dead."

James nodded a little and Samson smiled, then left to continue his task.

After two and a half months, James felt he could do something that had been on his mind for a while now. Sandrilan had grown strong again and the island city bustled with activity once more.

James asked Doctor Jefferies if he could use the office, or more precisely, the veranda. When James explained the reason, the doctor insisted that he do so. He then almost demanded that Oshai and Meili help James.

Two days later, in the twilight of the evening, Sno arrived at the doctor's office. She had been told that Master Michio requested her presence. She had put on her best clothes and had her hair made up beautifully.

Meili led her to the veranda. There stood James beside a table, wearing his best Japanese samurai clothing. His hair was also put up in a high samurai ponytail. Lamps lit the veranda and gave the atmosphere a very sublime effect.

Sno couldn't help but giggle with joy when she saw this. James smiled and pulled a chair out for her. She walked gracefully over to it and sat down.

James took a seat across from her and Oshai brought something to drink for the two. James gazed into Sno's eyes and saw that they gleamed with happiness.

Soon they were talking together in Japanese. The meal was brought to them. They continued to eat and glance into the other's eyes. Afterward, they lingered in conversation and laughter.

"My name is actually not Sno," she said as James took a drink.

"I know, it's Seno," James replied with a sly smile.

"Well, no it's Sen," she said with a slight blush.

"Really," He asked, seeming a bit confused.

"Yes, well you see, after my training and when I became a full geisha, I was moved to Lord Toshinobu's palace. He told me that there was already a geisha at the complex by the name of Sen. So, he would call me Seno.

"When the king saved us from the pirates, he asked my name. I told him 'Seno,' but he pronounced it Sno, and asked if it were right. I was so frightened and felt embarrassed to correct him, so I said 'yes' it was correct. And from that moment on, I've become Sno."

Both chuckled a little with the confession. It was the evening James had hoped for, and Sno had always wished for.

After this date, the two began to see each other regularly.

He knew with her every smile that his heart had healed. The light of love refreshed his weary soul daily.

Around three and a half months after the loss of the commander, James was woken in the pre-dawn hour by screams.

He struggled out of bed half awake and quickly grabbed a revolver.

The palace was barely lit by the sun that was slowly breaking over the horizon.

In the hall leading to the commander's room were several butterflies in their sleeping clothes. More soon came out and as James came closer, the hall began to fill with the women, all seeking to identify the trouble. They huddled together as the two that had screamed wept almost without control.

James moved past them and noticed the door to the commander's room was open. He glanced back to the butterflies and realized they were too upset to talk. He inched closer to the room.

Inside, someone was causing a lot of noise. He came to the doorway and pointed his revolver in.

There was someone in the room, rummaging through the commander's things. It was a man and James could hear the man talking in a low voice as if speaking to himself.

James moved back a little, and as he saw Madame Zhou approaching with a lamp, he motioned for her to give it to him.

He then moved back to the doorway with the lamp in one hand and his revolver in the other. As he entered the room, the lamp lit it up. The man appeared to be dressed in rags. His hair was long and unkempt.

The man turned, and James immediately cocked his revolver, with the sight of a rough looking, bearded stranger.

The apparent intruder's eyes widened when he saw James pointing the revolver at him.

"Oh, Lieutenant, you'll not need that pistol, it's only me."

James almost fainted as he suddenly realized this to be the commander. His heart wavered a bit as his leader turned back to continue searching for something.

Then, the commander appeared to find what he was in search of. He said, "Ahh," and turning again, held up a pair of scissors.

James continued to stand in disbelief as the commander went to a small mirror and began cutting the beard from his face. Then James said with a wavering voice, "Sir, we thought you were dead!"

The commander never turned from his mirror but replied, "Not dead, Lieutenant, but in desperate need of a bath and shave. Unfortunately, the butterflies don't seem to recognize me, or perhaps they think I'm a ghost. Either way, it seems I'll need to shave before I can obtain a bath."

He turned his head slightly to get a better view in the mirror as he cut the whiskers, then continued without ever looking at James

"Fortunately, the island I landed on had a source of fresh water. The pirates often stopped by to refill their water containers. I suspect this is how they knew about the location, to begin with. They were familiar with the islands and knew it would be a good location for a trap."

The commander then searched for something to place the whiskers in and after locating a plate, he placed the cut whiskers on it and then continued his trimming efforts.

James now realized he was still holding the revolver pointed at the commander. He un-cocked it and sat it on a table beside him.

The commander went on.

"My problem was staying alive and un-noticed until I could commandeer a vessel small enough to sail by myself. That day came a few weeks ago. It's a small, 'sloop' type boat; I tied it up down there next to the Valiant. Not a bad handling little craft, though it would have been easier to manage with two additional men."

He then placed more of the cut whiskers on the plate and moved in a manner to see better in the dim light, then once again began to cut the bushy beard.

James was still barely able to grasp the situation. He replied in a weak voice.

"Sir, we thought you were dead..."

The commander turned and glanced at James. It was only at this instant and possibly due to the expression on James' face that the commander stopped his activity long enough to consider what those on Sandrilan must have endured during his absence. He turned around completely, and an expression of compassion came over him. His hands lowered, and he became focused on James.

"Yes, well... I'm sorry about that Lieutenant. It was unexpected and unavoidable. You did the right thing by following my orders. If you had slowed or stopped it would have cost many more lives and perhaps the Valiant as well."

James realized he must say something before any other words were spoken.

"Sir, I must tell you something, and I believe that I speak for many, if not everyone on Sandrilan. Thank you for saving my life. When we thought you were dead, I realized that I'd never thanked you for that."

The commander swallowed and seemed to feel a little awkward. But after a few seconds, he replied humbly, "You're very welcome, Lieutenant. And, I'm glad to hear it."

Silence overtook the room for several seconds as neither man knew what to say next. Finally, the commander spoke to ease the stress they both felt.

"Well, I see you've held everything together, just as I had hoped. I believe with some decent food and perhaps some pampering from the butterflies, I'll be back in order within a few weeks."

Both men smiled, and the commander went on.

"I also noticed the Valiant has been patched up fairly well. She should be able to make it to Singapore. We'll have her completely refitted and repaired. She deserves that.

"Then we'll... well, ahh, what do you suggest comes after that, Lieutenant?"

James considered the question. He'd made no plans after having the Valiant refitted. But he had learned the real purpose of men such as himself, and the commander; as well as the purpose of the Valiant and all who sailed on her. He replied to his king and commander.

"After that…woe to the wicked, Sir,"

The commander expressed a little surprise, but then a smile broke over his face, followed by a laugh. He stepped closer to James and put his hand out to shake.

As James reached out to shake his hand, the commander replied, "Woe to the wicked indeed, my friend."

The End

The Seattle Star Newspaper October 17, 1902

The Legendary Valiant

By Price Nelson

Some of the Star readers may know that, before becoming a journalist, I was a sailor with the US Navy's Pacific fleet. For nine years, I sailed the seas and loved almost every minute of it. If not for an unfortunate accident, I would have likely remained in the Navy.

A few of the readers may have read some of the articles I've written over the years concerning a mysterious ship named the 'Valiant.'

Most of us living on the West coast have heard some talk of the Valiant's home port, often called 'Sandrala, or Shangrala.' It's even been more closely called, 'Sandrila' by a few.

While in the Navy, I heard many stories of this, practically mythical ship, along with incredible tales concerning her battles against the South Sea Pirates and almost every other conceivable enemy under the sun.

Initially, I believed little of it. One of the first stories I heard concerned a Marine detachment riding elephants in some distant Asian country. The story went on to claim that a mere thirty-five marines from the Valiant turned the tide of war in that country and returned to the ship without losing a man. 'Impossible,' I thought.

As the years went by I heard more tales. Some concerned a 'Lieutenant Taft,' of which little was known other than him being a white man that had been trained in the art of warfare by the Japanese military and had even fought battles in the service of a Japanese warlord.

Most of the sailors considered these stories to simply be 'sailors tales' and either embellished upon them or scoffed at them. But, our ship's doctor informed me that he had in fact seen the Valiant on one occasion, anchored in the port of Singapore.

I was skeptical, to say the least. Yet, a year later we entered the port of Singapore, and I was astonished to see an ironclad warship that fit the description of the Valiant.

As it later turned out; while on leave, seven men from our ship, me being one of them, met Lieutenant Taft on a narrow bridge. Initially, I wasn't for certain it was him, and my fellow sailors expressed no concern about the matter when I tried to tell them.

One particularly large sailor by the name of Burt was very insulting and insisted on fighting the lieutenant in order to have the bridge to himself.

After being forced to defend himself and within a few short minutes, Lieutenant Taft, single-handed, dispatched six stout Navy sailors. He appeared not to be winded in the slightest as he and his companions then walked around those same, now injured men that had insulted and underestimated him.

I was only able to speak briefly with this legendary warrior, but due to this meeting, I have for years sought out information and stories concerning the man; his ship, the Valiant and later her sister ship the Reliant, as well as what I then knew as 'Sandrala.'

After leaving the Navy, I was able to talk with sailors that had returned from duty in the Pacific. I heard fantastic tales of the Valiant, the Reliant and of a king that was, almost unbelievably, equal to or even a greater warrior than Lieutenant Taft.

I collected these stories as best that I could, never knowing how much was fact and how much was fiction. Then, around twelve years ago, the stories began to dry up.

About eight years ago I only found sailors that relayed stories I had already heard. As little as five years ago I had trouble finding a sailor that had heard of the Valiant.

Six months ago, I talked with sailors that were coming ashore after many months at sea. Only a few of the older ones had any knowledge whatsoever of the legendary Valiant or Lieutenant Taft.

I continued contacting leads that I had acquired over the years and recently, almost by chance was able to not only meet with someone that knew the lieutenant but had sailed on the Valiant and experienced many of the events I'd only heard of in stories.

Two weeks ago, I followed a bit of vague information and waited at the docks for a man that I had only been given a name and description of. Soon I spotted an elderly man moving down the boarding bridge and fitting the description.

I approached the man and asked, "Doctor Jefferies?"

"Yes," he replied in an accent that was British and sort of something else.

"I would very much like to talk with you about the Valiant and Lieutenant Taft if you have a little time," I asked.

The doctor appeared distraught at first. He then explained that he could only talk a short while as he should catch a train soon. So, we went to a restaurant close by, and I ordered us something to eat.

For slightly less than an hour, the doctor told me things I could never have dreamed of, nor fit into a short article such as this one. He had a satchel filled with photographs of the Valiant, the Reliant and what he told me was named 'Sandrilan,' then explained that it was a group of islands rather than one. When I asked where the islands were located, he said that would be a secret which he would take to the grave.

As I looked through the photographs, I attempted to ask as many questions as possible. The doctor, however, would only answer some of them. He would often say, "Out of respect for the two kings, I cannot answer that."

What I did find, amounted to there being the first king of Sandrilan. After the death of this king, Lieutenant Taft became the successor and King of Sandrilan. It also seems that after the death of Lieutenant Taft, or perhaps before his death, the inhabitants of Sandrilan were resettled, somewhere.

I then mentioned what I had heard from some of the sailors, that Sandrilan was around South America somewhere, thinking the doctor might give a bit more information. But he did not budge.

The doctor did mention that during the relatively short existence of the Kingdom of Sandrilan, it became very wealthy. Upon resettlement, the doctor said that each family or citizen of Sandrilan received a sizable amount of money to buy or build a new home with.

Lieutenant Taft eventually rose to the rank of 'Commander,' leading the also amazing, though slightly less famous warship, the Reliant.

Another bit of intriguing information was of Commander Taft being married to a Japanese woman by the name of 'Snow,' and the two having four children.

The first king, whom the doctor simply called, 'The Commander,' had, he said, married twenty-seven women and fathered more children than the good doctor could recall.

At that time, I asked where the two legendary warships were now, and he again said that was a secret which would be taken to the grave.

As the doctor was preparing to leave, I questioned where Lieutenant Taft had been buried.

The doctor hesitated briefly, but then replied just before departing to catch his train.

"Commander Taft was buried as requested, precisely ten paces behind his king and commander, who is also buried at the highest point in Sandrilan. Though they both requested simple graves, I had a stone placed at the site. The stone was engraved to read, 'Here rest two of the bravest and most noble men that the world has ever known.' I simply could not bring myself to leave their graves unmarked, and that is the truth of the matter, Sir."

The doctor then hurried away.

In that short time, however, I had a genuine glimpse into a world that few will ever know of, and in twenty more years, the world may, perhaps, have forgotten completely.

From all the information I gathered, and the brief meeting with Doctor Jefferies, I can only conclude that which the good doctor himself did in his years of personally knowing and working with these men. Although they were legendary, they were not myths. They were mysterious, but not reclusive. And though these men fought what most would consider being impossible odds, they were ultimately victorious.

In the doctor's own words, they must have surely been, "Two of the bravest and most noble men the world has ever known."

*

Thank you for reading Ever the Wayward Sky. We hope you enjoyed it. Please check out all of Oliver Phipps' books online. For your convenience we've listed a few Oliver Phipps books you may also be interested in.

Twelve Minutes till Midnight

A man catches a ride on a dusty Louisiana road only to find he's traveling with notorious outlaws Bonnie and Clyde.

The suspense is nonstop as confrontation settles in between a man determined to stand on truth and an outlaw determined to dislocate him from it.

If your life is subject to living a lie rather than holding to the truth, which would you do?

"Twelve Minutes till Midnight will take you on an unforgettable ride."

Ghosts of Company K: Based on a true story

Tag along with young Bud Fisher during his daily adventures in this ghostly tale based on actual events. It's 1971 and Bud and his family move into an old house in Northern Arkansas. Bud soon discovers they live not far from a very interesting cave as well as a historic Civil War battle site. As odd things start to happen, Bud tries to solve the mysteries. But soon the entire family experiences a haunting situation.

If you enjoy ghost tales based on true events then you'll enjoy Ghosts of Company K. This heartwarming story brings the reader into the life and experiences of a young boy growing up in the early 1970s. Seen through innocent and unsuspecting eyes, Ghosts of Company K reveals a haunting tale from the often unseen perspective of a young boy.

Where the Strangers Live

When a passenger plane disappears over the Indian Ocean in autumn 2013, a massive search gets underway.

A deep trolling, unmanned pod picks up faint readings and soon the deep sea submersible Oceana and her three crew members are four miles below the ocean surface in search of the black box from flight N340.

Nothing could have prepared the submersible crew for what they discover and what happens afterwards. Ancient evils and other world creatures challenge the survival of the Oceana's crew. Secrets of the past are revealed, but death hangs in the balance for Sophie, Troy and Eliot in this deep-sea Science Fiction thriller.

A Tempest Soul

Seventeen year old Gina Falcone has been alone for much of her life. Her father passed away while she was young. Her un-affectionate mother eventually leaves her to care for herself when she is only thirteen.

Though her epic journey begins by an almost deadly mistake, Gina will find many of her hearts desires in the most unlikely of places. The loss of everything is the catalyst that brings her to an unimagined level of accomplishment in her life.

Yet Gina soon realizes it is the same events that brought her success that may also bring everything crashing down around her. The new life she has built soon beckons for something she left behind. Now the new woman must find a way to dance through a life she could have never dreamed of.

Diver Creed Station

Wars, disease and a massive collapse of civilization have ravaged the human race of a hundred years in the future. Finally, in the late twenty-second century, mankind slowly begins to struggle back from the edge of extinction.

When a huge "virtual life" facility is restored from a hibernation type of storage and slowly brought back online, a new hope materializes.

Fragments of humanity begin to move into the remnants of Denver and the Virtua-Gauge facilities, which offer seven days of virtual leisure for seven days work in this new and growing social structure.

Most inhabitants of this new lifestyle begin to hate the real world and work for the seven-day period inside the virtual pods. It's the variety of luxury role play inside the virtual zone that supply's the incentive needed to work hard for seven days in the real world.

In this new social structure, a man can work for seven days in a food dispersal unit and earn seven days as a twenty-first century software billionaire in the virtual zone. As time goes by and more of the virtual pods are brought back online life appears to be getting better.

Rizette and her husband Oray are young technicians that settle into their still new marriage as the virtual facilities expand and thrive.

Oray has recently attained the level of a Class A Diver and enjoys his job. The Divers are skilled technicians that perform critical repairs to the complex system, from inside the virtual zone.

His title of Diver originates from often working in the secure "lower levels" of the system. These lower level areas are the dividing space between the real world and the world of the virtual zone. When the facility was built, the original designers intentionally placed this buffer zone in the system to avoid threats from non-living virtual personnel.

As Oray becomes more experienced in his elite technical position as a Diver, he is approached by his virtual assistant and forced to make a difficult decision. Oray's decision triggers events that soon pull him and his wife Rizette into a deadly quest for survival.

The stage becomes a massive and complex maze of virtual world sequences as escape or entrapment hang on precious threads of information.

System ghosts from the distant past intermingle with mysterious factions that have thrown Oray and Rizette into a cyberspace trap with little hope for survival.

Bane of the Innocent

"There's no reason for them to shoot us; we ain't anyone" - Sammy, Bane of the Innocent.

Two young boys become unlikely companions during the fall of Atlanta. Sammy and Ben somehow find themselves, and each other, in the rapidly changing and chaotic environment of the war-torn Georgia City.

As the siege ends and the fall begins in late August and early September of 1864 the Confederate troops begin to move out and Union forces cautiously move into the city. Ben and Sammy simply struggle to survive, but in the process they develop a friendship that will prove more important than either one could imagine.

Tears of Abandon

Several college friends start planning a two week kayak trip down an Alaskan river in late summer of 1992. Soon there are five young people headed to Alaska for a river expedition.

As the trip unfolds and the group gets farther into the wilderness a strange whispering sound attracts their attention. The wonderful vacation begins to take a turn for the worse when they follow the sounds and find something long lost and quite unexpected.

The House on Cooper Lane: Based on a true story

It's 1984 and all Bud Fisher wants to do is find a place to live in Madison Louisiana. With his dog Badger, they come across a beautiful old mansion that was converted into apartments.

Something should have felt odd when he found out nobody lived in any of the apartments. To make matters worse, the owner is reluctant to let him rent one. Eventually he negotiates an apartment in the historic old house, but soon finds out that he's not quite as alone as he thought. What ghostly secret has the owner failed to share?

It's up to Bud to unravel the mysteries of the upstairs apartments, but is he really ready to find out the truth?

The Bitter Harvest

The year is 1825, and a small Native American village has lost many of its people and bravest warriors to a pack of Lofa; huge beasts humanoid in shape but covered with coarse hair. The creatures are taller than any normal man, and fiercer than even the wildest animal.

Rather than leave the land of their ancestors, the tribe chooses to stay and fight the beasts. But they're losing the war, and perhaps more critically, they're almost without hope.

The small community grasps for anything to help them survive. There is a warrior on the frontier known as Orenda. He's already legendary across the west for his bravery and honor.

Onsi, a young villager, sets out on a journey to find the warrior.

Orenda will be forced to choose between almost certain death, not just for himself, but also his warrior wife Nazshoni and her brother Kanuna, or a dishonorable refusal that would mean annihilation for the entire village.

The crucial decision is only the beginning, and Orenda will soon face the greatest test of his life; the challenge that could turn out to be too much even for a warrior of legend.

*

50929036R00164

Made in the USA
San Bernardino, CA
08 July 2017